The Haunting of Dylan Klaypool

Whispers in Black Willow

JAMES ALAN ROSS

The Haunting of Dylan Klaypool: Whispers in Black Willow
By James Alan Ross
www.jamesalanross.com
Edited by Leslie Bauman
Cover layout by Katherine Gray www.kgray.ca

ISBN-13: 978-1983155581

To hear the truth,
she must listen to the silence.

Whispers in Black Willow

1

Willing herself to focus, she gently closed her tired, itchy eyes and concentrated. Dylan Klaypool's white earbuds fit snugly inside her ears which fought to curtail long strands of curly brown hair from tumbling in front of her narrow face. Still, one mischievous lock snuck from the top of her head and dropped to tickle her nose. With an angry puff of air from under her pouty bottom lip, Dylan briskly blew it away, but the undisciplined curl had already severed her attention.

It didn't take much to lure her attentiveness away from the three straight hours of total silence she was playing back on her digital recorder. Only the occasional sounds made by birds or bats randomly sprinkled through the otherwise tranquil sea of nothingness that had been washing over her ears.

Dylan exhaled her frustrations away, sank back into the hard, plastic seat connected by a bent metal rod to the wooden desktop, and watched seconds pass as the recording lagged on. She gripped the front of the desk with her sweaty palms, leaned back, and pulled her arms straight, staring at the miniature, black digital recorder.

As the quietness traveled from the small recording device over her delicate eardrums, her dry and scratchy eyes surveyed Room 234 for signs of life. Most of the students had their faces firmly attached to smartphones: posting and texting, spreading rumors, and making plans for the Varsity football game later that night (or more likely the party afterwards in a freshly cut hay field, with a large fire surrounded by rampant, underaged drinking). None of those things interested Dylan. Not even slightly.

Yawning, Black Willow High's newest student rubbed her sharp knuckles over a squinted eyelid and listened intently to more of nothing, like a phone call with no one on the other end or a CD with no songs. Spying through the window, she found that the boring hum of silence played the perfect soundtrack to the drably, gray skies serving as the backdrop to dozens of gangly, leafless trees that surrounded the school.

Dylan glanced up at her study hall teacher, Ms. Castle, who sat properly behind her shiny desk but whose thoughts looked to be somewhere else. Framed images of the teacher's twin toddlers posed by a hip, young photographer sat proudly facing out towards the uninterested students. The thin, tall, early-thirties teacher crossed her unseasonably tanned legs and laughed at the five-inch screen in her palm. Dylan swore she saw the divorced woman blush and wondered if the exchange happening through the teacher's personal device was appropriate for school hours. The way Ms. Castle carried herself, Dylan guessed not.

Dylan's brown eyes rolled in their deep sockets, as the eleventh-grader fought the urge to stand up, walk out, and never return. It had become difficult, pushing herself to achieve even average grades with all she was trying to accomplish outside of school. The real world had assigned Dylan other, more important things to worry about than math equations and forming a fluent sentence in French. Just passing and making it to graduation next year would've been sufficient enough for her.

Dylan was tired. Not just tired of her current life circumstances, which she truly was, but physically tired. She needed sleep. She ran the pad of her thumb over the tiny back-lit screen on the plastic digital recorder that she had retrieved from the rugged, abandoned house down the road early that morning. Her black sneakers still carried dust from the long gravel road between it and her grandma's house: the only two houses for miles on a rural, country road fittingly named Cemetery.

Closing both eyes, she laid her forehead on folded arms feeling the threads of her knitted sweater pressing into her skin. Her breathing slowed, each inhale stretched to full capacity, and the teenager could hear her heartbeat pulsating over the dull hissing that still funneled into her ears.

Buh-bump… Buh-bump… Buh-bump… "huh-huh-huh" *… Buh-bump…*

Suddenly, Dylan's sleepy shell shattered.

Between the beats of her heart, she had heard something. Quickly, she raised her head from the desk and hit REWIND on the device. She impatiently watched the seconds rewind from three hours, twelve minutes, and twenty-two seconds. Twenty-one, twenty, nineteen, eighteen, seventeen, sixteen. PLAY.

"...huh-huh-huh..."

Furling her eyebrows, she concentrated. Sitting alone in the abandoned house on Cemetery, the recorder had captured something. Something that did not belong.

REWIND. Twenty-two, twenty-one, twenty, nineteen, eighteen, seventeen, sixteen. PLAY.

"...huh-no-cents..."

Goose pimples covered Dylan's arms under the long, black sleeves of her sweater. Quickly, she sat up, straightened her spine like a wooden plank. REWIND. Twenty-two, twenty-one, twenty, nineteen, eighteen, seventeen, sixteen. PLAY.

"...huh-no-sense..."

There, on the recording made overnight in a house that no one lived in, were words. But, what were they saying? Dylan's thoughts ran a race with her pulse.

No sense? No cents? Know sense?

REWIND. Twenty-two, twenty-one, twenty, nineteen, eighteen, seventeen, sixteen. PLAY.

"...in no tents..."

The hair on the back of her thin neck stood tall; her hands trembled, as the whispering syllables became more apparent each time she played them. REWIND. PLAY.

"...in no tense..."

Past tense? Some tents?

REWIND. PLAY. REWIND. PLAY. REWIND. PLAY.

"...in no scent..."

Her bones, wrapped tightly with pale, stretched skin,

rattled together like primitive instruments playing a worship song to holy, unknown deities. REWIND. Twenty-two, twenty-one, twenty, nineteen, eighteen, seventeen, sixteen. PLAY.

"...*Innocent*..."

Dylan elevated six inches off her chair when a deafening bell reverberated off the four concrete walls that had held the stirring class hostage for the previous forty-five minutes. Rapidly, her classmates shuffled their belongings with eagerness to calm their rumbling stomachs downstairs in the cafeteria with pizza, chicken nuggets, and nachos.

Dylan, however, didn't budge. She sat frozen as solid as a block of ice floating in the Arctic Ocean. Placing her hand on her chest, the hopeful girl took several calming gasps into her heaving lungs, as eighteen other teenagers made their way past her out the door and raced to lunch.

Her left hand scribbled the tip of a ballpoint pen on a bright white, blue-lined sheet of paper. The black ink spelled I-N-N-O-C-E-N-T. A fiercely drawn exclamation point followed and a bold, deeply compressed line below it nearly tore through the page. The word repeated in her mind over and over and over...

"*Innocent.*"

"*Innocent.*"

"*Innocent.*"

Coincidentally, there had never been a word that meant more to Dylan Klaypool. Hearing it there, stamped into the white noise, it now meant more than ever.

2

Relieved to have made it through the house without being dragged into a pointless conversation about school, Dylan leaned her back against the door on the inside of her new bedroom. The plain, boring space felt like nothing more than a temporary, guest bedroom. The four walls, ceiling, and mangled carpet were just a chamber to her, nothing more.

She flippantly tossed her trusty backpack and nearly empty purse onto the unmade bed. The wadded-up, extra blankets her grandma had dug out of the closet for her when Dylan arrived laid at the foot and on the floor, like crumpled paper jammed inside a defective printer.

She dropped her jacket over top of the four boxes that had carried everything she owned from Illinois just two weeks ago. The boxes, once used to deliver food products to the supermarket she lived near in Evanston, laid in the corner, still half unpacked. The scene paralleled Dylan herself: a few scattered remnants of familiarity, but mostly just empty, unused space.

Plopping herself into the chair in front of the oak desk that sat against one wall, the anxious young woman plugged the tiny digital recording device into her laptop with a USB cable, and flipped open the folded computer. The faint reflection of her insipid face greeted her, bouncing off the laptop's blank, shiny screen. Her pastel skin found balance with the darker freckles laid out like constellations over a clear summer night. Promptly, she logged on – *DK2003*.

She gazed at the desk's faded varnish while the large file loaded into the audio editing software she planned on using to further investigate the sounds she had discovered while dozing off in study hall. The piece of furniture was surely an antique that could probably fetch a small fortune with the dealers back in Chicago. Perhaps, her grandmother had used it when she was a little girl or maybe Dylan's mother had. The speculating teen hoped not. The last thing she needed were demons attached to her mother swirling around her room at night watching her sleep.

A window popped up on the screen demanding to be acknowledged with a short, attention seeking bell announcing its arrival. Shaking off thoughts of her mom, Dylan clicked *OK,* and settled into her chair. Ignoring the first three-plus hours of the file, she fast forwarded to those precious few seconds where she had heard the voice.

The graphic line of the recording remained unchanged throughout its entirety. Unsurprisingly, the word she knew was there was not visually represented on the screen the way audio normally would be. A voice like the one she'd found, not even a whisper but just exhaled syllables, wouldn't show up on the screen the way spoken words would. This soft voice blended into the thin, blue wave of silence, lost inside the white noise.

She clicked the mouse and dragged the cursor over a few select seconds of the twelfth minute in hour three: sixteen, seventeen, eighteen.

Knock. Knock. Knock.

Candice's frail, wrinkled knuckles tapped feebly against the outside of Dylan's door. "Dylan, Dear? Are you hungry?" The old woman's voice matched the timid manner her knocking had displayed.

With her eyes glued to the screen, Dylan clicked the dropdown tab labeled *ENHANCE*.

"I'm... I'm okay," the girl said to her newly acquired roommate. Continuing to work, Dylan selected *DEHISSER* from the menu.

"What was that, Dear?" Candice said, knocking again. "Dylan, are you in there?"

"I'll be..." Dylan started again, her voice low and bashful. "I'm okay." She tried her best to speak loud enough for Candice to hear on the opposite side of the door.

"You're okay?"

"Yeah," Dylan repeated, her voice falling off.

"Okay, Dear. Can you come down and set the table for me in an hour or so? I'm sure you have plenty of homework to keep you busy until then."

"Sure," Dylan answered, paying little mind to what her grandma, Candice Smith, had said. The small, highlighted segment of sound wave had turned pink after the software completed the functions Dylan had selected. She clicked PLAY.

"...Innocent..."

Like a spider had crawled the length of her spine, she shivered. After clicking the *DENOISER* function, Dylan watched the software go back to work for a moment. Pressing PLAY again, she heard the soft word with even more clarity.

"...Innocent..."

The voice hauntingly seeped into her pores, spread like electricity through her veins. Her senses intensified. She clicked the *EQUALIZER*, turning the *HIGH* knob to the max and twisting the *LOW* to the extreme negative.

"...Innocent..."

It was as clear as if someone were standing next to her whispering directly into her ear.

In the next second, a million questions blossomed at once, scattering her thoughts.

The handful of evidence files she had saved in a folder on the desktop consisted of questionable audio and video clips from her prior investigations back home in Evanston, Illinois. Dylan believed at least one of those clips had an unexplained, disembodied voice of some sort recorded on it. Although nearly inaudible and not understandable, she was convinced that the clip contained a voice that was captured the night she had spent alone in the basement of a warehouse a few blocks from the house she shared with her mother and stepfather.

This new recording, however, was different and on another level entirely. This was a human voice or the voice of something that was once human. This was a word from the other side, a place she couldn't see with her eyes, couldn't touch with her hands. It was a word from beyond the grave.

Dylan grabbed her phone, opened the list of contacts, and touched the one saved as *Chicago Teen Crisis.* She energetically punched a message in with eagerly tapping thumbs. Hesitating, she debated herself on whether to send it, knowing the whisper she found wasn't enough on its own, but also believing that it could potentially lead to something that *would* be. She reread the unsent text a few times, half-heartedly trying to convince herself to delete it.

I might have something.

Finally, unable to resist, she pressed SEND. Seconds later, she received a stern reply.

Stop texting me until you do.

3

"Are you sure you wouldn't like me to drive you to the football game?" Candice asked Dylan, while sipping heated tap water from a ceramic coffee mug. The cup's oddly detailed design convinced Dylan it was purchased many decades ago. Most of her grandmother's belongings emitted the same vibe: vintage.

Looking up from her slow-cooked pot roast and whipped potatoes smothered with dark brown, creamy gravy, Dylan desperately tried to ignore the fact that she had declined Candice's offer to drive her to the game already on three prior occasions. "No, thank you."

"You'd probably see some of your friends there."

"I don't have any friends," Dylan blandly pointed out, unapologetically.

"It would be a great place to meet some *new* friends,"

Candice cheerfully countered.

"I don't need any friends."

Candice Smith, Dylan's maternal grandmother, scooped up her own plate from the table and stood up to rinse the smothered gravy and undesirable fatty remains of the roast into the sink. "Everyone needs friends."

"I don't *want* any friends," Dylan snapped, dropping her fork onto her plate causing a loud clang. The sudden outburst startled Dylan as much it had her unexpecting grandmother.

Candice stopped, abruptly, halfway to the sink, in the middle of the large, square kitchen. Dylan pretended to not notice her grandmother's reaction and just stared straight ahead at the flower-patterned wallpaper. The short-fused girl, sometimes lacking control enough to prevent lashing out, didn't mean to hurt the dainty woman's feelings.

Dylan knew Candice didn't deserve catching the brunt of her frustrations, but her suppressed emotions were a dangerous loaded pistol built with a hair trigger. Even the slightest nudge sometimes sent a round firing into whatever blameless bystander happened to be in the crossfire. Even little old ladies who had recently opened their home to her.

Candice let out a long, painful sigh before getting back on route to the stainless-steel tub with a circular garbage disposal in the center. After a mere step, her granddaughter began to mumble something from the table but stopped herself. Dylan swallowed the words. Instead of articulating herself further, she shriveled into an expressionless stare, gazing down at her unfinished dinner. She traced meaningless scribbles with one prong of her fork into the runny potato and gravy mixture before she couldn't uphold the pointless charade for a second longer.

Dylan erupted from her chair and sped to the stone counter, beating Candice to the sink. After a quick rinse under the running faucet, she placed her antique plate down against the steel basin. Rushing, she let it drop from her trembling hand before it was safely resting, causing a large chip from the edge of the dish to snap off, creating a fierce, loud crash.

Without stopping to even acknowledge the broken plate, Dylan hastily spun on her heel and stormed away. Embarrassed at her loud steps echoing through the kitchen, the flustered teen never looked back at Candice, leaving her to clean up the mess herself.

Scampering with long, fast steps, Dylan huffed out a forceful sigh, cramming a ball of emotion down her throat into her half-empty stomach. Daily, tears had picked vulnerable moments and made attempts to sneak from her poignant eyes since the time she was seven; a child caught in an unthinkable nightmare. This time, like nearly all the rest, she barred them from breaking the crest of the enormous barrier she had built between her shattered heart and the rest of the world.

Not bothering to close her bedroom door when she entered, Dylan wrangled her jacket on and squeezed a knit cap over her hair, past her ears. As she wrestled with her backpack, struggling to get it over her tense shoulders, all she imagined was Candice standing alone in the kitchen, buried in undeserved fault.

Finally snapping the clip in front of her chest, securing her bag of specialized equipment to her body, she turned and scurried through the house past a still stationary and confused Candice, out the front door leaving her with only a grumble.

"I'll be late."

The door slammed loudly when she closed it, leaving the atmosphere inside heavy and acidic. The kitchen windows shook, and the thick, chipping white paint on the door lost a few susceptible flakes from the impact. Dylan halted, just long enough to hold her palm to her perspiring forehead and pull in a deep breath of the brisk autumn air, cooling her panting lungs.

She considered turning back, apologizing but hadn't a clue what she'd say if she returned to face her anguished grandmother. Instead, she grabbed the thin, black gloves, one from each pocket of her jacket, and slid her already chilled fingers into them, shunning the tug of regret.

The tattered top step of the wooden porch creaked when her left sneaker pushed down on it, causing the two pumpkins Candice had brought home two days earlier to rock like basketballs in desperate need of air. Skipping the next two stairs, she dropped her right foot down, letting the soft dirt absorb her weight. The coarse tread under her shoes gripped the soil where trampling feet had caused the grass to quit growing long ago.

Dusk descended on the vast rural setting where she now took up residence: Black Willow Creek. With her steps scuffling the gravel that was Cemetery Road, Dylan looked at the cornstalks on her left and right and how they formed barricades that stood taller than her own height. The road she walked on coursed directly through the center of a cornfield that carried on for better than a mile in all directions. The dried, golden brown leaves of the crops stirred at even the slightest breeze, filling the scene with the eerie sound of peril and dismay. Dylan supposed that the noise created by a crazed maniac, a stalker, rushing out of the bronzed cornfield would play the same dreadful song of doom.

Along the road, at the precise midpoint between her grandma's house and her destination was the only respite from the rugged corn her eyes would get. On the left side of the gravel road, chopped from the cornfield, were a few acres of leaf-covered green grass, scattered with tall bare-limbed trees and rows of randomly shaped stones etched with writing. Words like *beloved, memory, born, died,* and *here lies* told short, direct stories on each of the gravestones. Carved into the perfectly planted rows of corn was the neatly polished, well-maintained Black Willow Creek Cemetery.

Finally succumbing to the October air, Dylan's pink nose surrendered a clear, runny liquid. She wiped it clean with her glove-covered fingers, sank both hands deep into her jacket pockets, and pulled her arms close to her body to keep her core heat from escaping.

Each step brought more of the pristine, tribute-filled property into her peripheral vision. As she passed, out of the corner of her eye, Dylan spied a mound of fresh soil piled high on top of the neatly manicured grass. Next to the hill of damp, black dirt was a green John Deere backhoe having one strong, lengthy arm for digging on the back end and a wide, deep bucket in front. Although the tractor was vacant, the passing girl knew the gravedigger was near, like he had been every time Dylan had ever walked by.

Keeping her face straight forward, Dylan glanced to spy the metal head of a shovel playing peek-a-boo over the edge of the grass. The gravedigger was down there, six feet below, raising the wooden-shafted digging tool to toss spades full of Earth up onto the growing heap.

Dylan picked up her pace, thankful the creepy, white-haired man that worked the cemetery grounds, either mowing grass, raking leaves, or the less appealing and current task of digging graves was hidden from view. The gravedigger regularly gave a docile grin and an awkward wave whenever Dylan passed. Harmless as it might have been, it never failed to fill her with uneasiness.

Hustling now, Dylan's half-mile journey ended when she reached the mouth of a bleak, dreary driveway. A mailbox, smashed in by bored, reckless teens long ago, stood guard at the border of the overgrown, unkempt yard. A large home, dismissed from former beauty, was nestled deep in the corner of the ragged looking lawn. Rows of corn, like armed soldiers, lined the back and sides of the house.

The endless, corncob army had safely ushered Dylan to the old, abandoned house on Cemetery Road. A tall, tangled tree with black bark, left naked after Autumn had snatched its leaves away, loomed above the roofline, peeking at Dylan from the back yard. It was the lone tree on the property.

The weathered wood siding of the building and its boarded-up windows outweighed the frayed *Welcome* mat with pretty flowers printed on it laying at the front door. Unusually, Dylan was never deterred by unsightly surroundings that would turn most in another direction. The leaning porch, broken shutters, and muddled overall appearance would read as clear as a glowing, neon *DO NOT ENTER* sign to anyone who approached.

But for Dylan, the house served as the place she felt most comfortable. And now after finding the message of *"innocent"* hidden on her recording, she finally, albeit here, felt her life was moving in the right direction.

4

"Ugh!"

Shoving with a sore shoulder, Dylan popped the rickety, jammed front door open. "Ouch," she grumbled, and heard a crackling in her neck, as she tipped her head from side to side.

Slowly, the derelict, old door freely swung into the dark caverns of the uninhabited house. Inside the rundown property, the air felt slightly cooler than the biting temperature outside. Dylan stepped through the entrance and, with two flat palms, pressed the solid, wood door back into its crooked frame until it was wedged again without a chance of coming loose.

"Well… here we go again," Dylan whispered. "I'm baa-ack." She chuckled slightly.

With her flashlight, Dylan could see not a speck of dust

had moved since she'd been there early that morning to retrieve the recording device she'd left behind Thursday night. She wandered through the expensive looking kitchen where the appliances sat in place. A few of the cupboard doors were open; one hung loosely, broken at the top hinge, where canned goods could be seen on the shelves exactly where they were put away.

Carelessly, Dylan flicked the light switch next to the refrigerator without even looking at it. In vain, she flipped it every time she entered the house. It was obvious there had been no electricity at the property since the people who lived here had vanished, seemingly into thin air.

Tonight, the phone still attached to the wall, the dust covered furniture, and countless other forgotten items held more meaning to Dylan than on her previous visits. The thought that someone who once sat on that sofa and chatted on that phone may now be reaching out to her - breaking through to speak - gave her hope. A hope she'd rarely had in her life.

Dylan strategically placed three flashlights throughout the living room, brightly lighting the lifeless space. Crouching, the snooping researcher slid her backpack off and unzipped the largest pocket. She lifted her eyes and curiously surveyed the living room - the room where she had left her digital recorder the previous night. Taking a sturdy, bright yellow device from deep in the bag, she spoke, loudly.

"My name is Dylan. I know I've told you that before, but... anyway... doesn't hurt to say it again." Pressing POWER on the electronic instrument, Dylan brought it out of slumber. The digital readout screen showed 42.6 degrees Fahrenheit underneath where the device's name was printed in a decorative, cursive font: Mel-meter.

Instantly, when she placed one hand close to the antennae at the top of the machine, green lights flashed and a screaming, high-pitched noise blared from its speaker. Dylan confidently arose from her crouched position.

"Do you see that? When I get close to this, it makes a noise. Can you do that? Can you make this light up?" The optimistic girl held her position, keeping still, waiting.

No lights, no noises.

Above the temperature readout was another, larger set of numbers that registered 0.00, showing that the device was currently finding zero activity in the electromagnetic field, or EMF. Taking gentle steps, Dylan moved around the room methodically.

"I heard you today... your voice. I heard you speak into the recorder I left here." She looked around, prayed for interaction. "All you need to do is come close to this. I'll know you're here." Gracefully, Dylan maneuvered her way around the coffee table to avoid bumping her shins, since bruises from before were still tender and mustard colored.

Still, no alarms, no signals.

Patience was part of it; Dylan understood that. But calming the excitement that came with knowing she had captured a voice wanting to be heard in that room already, was no easy task. Pulling her phone from the back pocket of her Levi's, she checked the time. 7:34 p.m.

No need to rush, she thought.

Dylan traveled from wall to wall, back and forth, keeping her breathing low and her heart from racing: listening. Spinning to move to the large picture window again, she stopped on a dime. Quickly twisting her neck, she gazed into the softly-lit corner behind her.

"Is that you?" she queried with a vibrant flutter in her chest. "Are you following me?" the nervous snoop asked with her voice cracking. Pausing, she gave the situation a moment to transpire. Dylan hadn't heard anything with her ears. She had *felt* something. Something that had uncontrollably changed her enthusiasm into apprehension.

She let her jacket slide off her body to the dusty floor and pulled up one sleeve of her sweater. Studying her arm, her eyes moved from her fragile wrist to her knobby elbow. The fine, light-brown hairs that covered her chalky skin stood tall. Gulping, she made the decision to confront whatever was causing her body to react so dramatically.

"I know you're here," she declared, her voice firm. "You can touch this device in my hand and show me you're with me in this room... *Please.*"

Looking at the temperature she saw 39.3 degrees. "Okay," she said with a smile. "Are you near me? Are you causing the temperature to go down?" Dylan gasped when it suddenly fell to 37.8 then 35.4.

"It's you. Isn't it? You're here, aren't you?" The young investigator struggled to keep her emotions in check, but soon realized her opportunity had already passed. After the brief burst of hair-raising action, the house returned to an obviously unconscious state.

Whatever she had felt, had quickly dissolved and no longer lingered near her. Stubbornly, the minutes collected like sand in the bottom of an hourglass.

Checking it again, her phone now showed seventeen minutes after eight o'clock.

No beeps, no flashes.

Unwilling to allow her hope to wane, Dylan continued trying to communicate. "Show me something. Please.

Touch the end of this rod. Make it light up." More minutes slipped away into the darkness that surrounded the flashlight beams.

"Come on," she whispered, fighting to ward off approaching disappointment. "Give me *something*." She gritted her teeth, took in a determined breath through her nostrils, and slowly let it escape through her mouth, as she watched the air from her lungs billow out in the chilly air.

Dylan made a fist at her side and spoke with confidence. "Please don't be afraid of me. Don't be afraid to let me know you're here. I'm just like you... More than it seems, I'm sure." Silently, the desperate girl begged for a response. "I know you don't know who I am. Or, or... or if you can trust me. But, believe me. I heard you. I believe you. I know you are innocent."

With a beaming smile and wide eyes, Dylan froze from disbelief. *Innocent* had been the magic word. Seconds after those three syllables rolled off her tongue, a magnificent moment ensued: a small, brilliant green light on the object in Dylan's hand seemed to light the entire house, like a flicker of lightning across the midnight sky. And the sweetest sound the shivering, exhausted girl had ever heard danced through the empty space and waltzed across her hopeful ears.

Blip.

5

Causing a thud that jolted her from a peaceful nap, Dylan's foot slipped off the metal leg of the desk in front of her. Her heel loudly slammed down on the industrial-grade carpet which provided little cushion.

Tossing her wavy blonde hair off her shoulder with an annoyed head turn, Carrie Holland huffed her displeasure at the creepy new girl sitting behind her.

"Sorry," mouthed Dylan with bashfully raised eyebrows. Her silent apology did nothing to cure the disgusted look smudged across the face of the recently crowned Homecoming Queen of Black Willow High. Properly ordained by last year's yearbook editors, the school's *Most Popular Girl* rolled her eyes and turned to face the front again, coldly leaving Dylan's apology behind, unaccepted.

Dylan folded her arms, squeezed her knees in under her desk, shrinking into a what she hoped was a tiny, unnoticeable ball. Her heavy eyes wandered to the windows on her right. The rain that had rudely spoiled her experiments at the old house on Cemetery all weekend long continued to fall, loudly and obnoxiously.

With her chair being in the back corner of the room, backs of heads were Dylan's scenery. It was obvious that many of her male classmates thought that because *they* couldn't see the hair on the backs of their heads that no one else could either. Ruffled locks of different colors and shades were left out of morning grooming routines, destined to remain crooked, matted, and flat.

The teacher, Mr. Amal, lecturing in French, had a habit of keeping his eyes on the smartboard and his back to the class. This disengaged tendency tempted even the best students to turn ill-behaved. Or to fall comatose.

Wiping a bit of drooling saliva from her lip with her sleeve, Dylan inadvertently looked Mitchell Wolf directly in the eyes. Shoulder length, jet black hair surrounded his wide, square face where his copper colored skin held his high cheekbones level with his smoky, brown eyes. Mitch sat a row over and a seat up. His desk was right next to Carrie's.

Promptly, Dylan averted her eyes, looked down at the open text book in front of her, then at Mr. Amal, then at the window, then back at Mitch. She didn't know *where* to look. She sat up straight, then slouched, then cowered like a reprimanded puppy.

Mitch glanced at Carrie before returning his mysterious grin back to Dylan. Slightly, he shook his head and made a signal with his hand. *Ignore her,* the motion implied.

Dylan raised her eyebrows and nodded, barely looking at Mitch before turning to stare at the back of Mr. Amal's head, as the teacher's voice slammed, muffled into the smartboard.

Dylan made certain not to accidentally bump Carrie's desk or to inadvertently look towards Mitch either. Those two small exchanges were already eventful enough to last Dylan the entire day... maybe even the whole week.

When class ended, Dylan swung her legs from under the desk and practically sprinted to the door. Usually lingering until she was the last kid to leave the room to avoid any possible interaction, she was the first one into the hallway.

Without even looking back, she could feel Mitch trying to say something to her. She figured shooting from her seat would save her the hassle of having to make conversation with the tall boy. Luckily, Dylan didn't believe that Mitch even knew her name, which meant he couldn't call it out, forcing her to acknowledge him. If she was far enough down the hallway, she'd be able to ignore him anyway, even if he did happen to shout her name.

Jostling her way through flowing rapids of the river of students, all hustling to their lockers to trade last period's materials for the next one's, Dylan navigated the waters like a small minnow through much larger, more noticeable fish. Most never even saw her, as Dylan worked tirelessly at being invisible.

Jerking on the latch for the third time, each yank firmer than the last, Dylan's locker finally burst open. She aggressively shook her left hand, wiggling off the stinging sensation caused when the sticky handle had finally activated.

She kneeled, unzipped her backpack, and pulled out her French textbook. The wide book barely fit into the dated, nearly antique locker, proven by the cuts and gouges scarring the book's cover. Still rattled by the awkward dealings with Carrie and Mitch, Dylan struggled to find her math book and folder. She put her hand against her forehead and closed her eyes. Two deep breaths, a short conversation demanding herself to relax, and she began to feel the anxiety disperse. Dr. Belmonte, as poor as the woman's judgment could be, would've been proud of her.

"Okay," she whispered. "Math folder is yellow. Math book is green." With her eyes closed, she visualized herself putting those items away the last time she'd used them. With a nod and a squint, she told herself, "Top shelf."

On her tiptoes, she pulled them both down, gripping tightly with her fingertips. Feeling collected, she knelt and stuffed them into the largest segment of her orange bag. It was the sort of backpack someone would use while hiking to the top of a mountain or maybe on a day of cross-country skiing. Every inch was covered with pockets, zippers, and buckles.

"Ugh," she growled when the zipper of the aging rucksack stopped sliding before sealing the opening shut. "Come on," she pleaded with it. Dylan tugged so hard her fingers slipped off, causing the nail on her thumb to bend back when it rubbed across the rough, plastic zipper.

"Owe," she exclaimed, again shaking her hand in agony. "Stupid!" she moaned under her breath. "Stupid bag!"

Deciding to just carry the sack to class with the pouch half open, she slammed the metal locker shut. When the bottom portion of the long, rectangular door didn't close, she gave it an irritated thump with her knee. The door did latch closed, but her leg took punishment that didn't seem like a fair trade. Surely, a bruise would form overnight on her delicate kneecap.

Turning to walk the long corridor, Dylan felt a harsh shove to her left shoulder. Stumbling forward, nearly losing her balance, she was barely able to stay on her feet.

Passing in front of her, she saw a flash of yellow: a wavy mane of shiny, conditioner-volumized, blonde hair. Acting like she hadn't just violently hammered her history book into Dylan's back, Carrie smiled and joked with her adoring crew of cheerleader cronies.

While sensing a red welt forming on her shoulder blade, Dylan stood and watched as the group moved like a school of brightly colored, tropical fish through the Great Barrier Reef, dodging obstacles in sync like they were a single being that had just one brain to share between them. Just before turning down the 500 Hall, Carrie snuck a peek back at the new girl, shooting a look, a glance that sent a chill down Dylan's spine.

Like it was happening in slow motion, Dylan watched the entitled little princess round the corner out of sight. Motionless, Dylan thought about the wicked, laser-like glare that had streamed from Carrie's black-lined, blue eyes to her own.

And that it very well might be the second most frightening thing she'd ever seen.

6

The torn paper menu had seen its prices edited with a red pen over the years, before being slid back inside the dingy, plastic casing. It was tri-fold: breakfast on the left page, lunch in the center, dinner to the right. Dylan's current options were limited to the dinner segment.

"How about I start you with a drink, if you're *still* not ready," said the waitress, April, visibly annoyed with Dylan.

"Yeah…" Dylan scanned the filthy menu for beverages, holding off the panic that came with making even the smallest decisions.

"Back page," April impatiently grunted out, not even looking up from the small pad of paper she used to write down orders.

Flustered, Dylan flipped to the back. After a few seconds, she saw red-painted, chipped nails on the ends of bony fingers holding a chewed-up Bic pen with remnants of cheap lipstick smudged on it pointed at a small, outlined area at the bottom of the page. Under April's pen, Dylan saw the word *Beverages.*

"Um," Dylan stuttered, "Just a… Diet. I guess… Pepsi."

April trotted her scrawny, underdressed self a few feet over to the next table, leaving Dylan unsure if she'd heard her or not. Continuing to stare at the white pages with black text, Dylan was no closer to a decision than when she first sat down.

"She's Carol's daughter," Candice told her, quietly.

Dylan raised her eyes to the consoling woman across the table from her.

"April. The waitress," Candice clarified. "She's Carol's daughter."

Looking down at the menu again, Dylan saw the name *Carol's Restaurant* in large, plain looking font spread across the top.

"Oh," the hungry teen replied, understanding.

"She could never hold a waitressing job anywhere else, being so rude," Candice assured Dylan, with her voice lowered. "It's shameful, her behavior. Just rude. Always was rude even when she was little."

Dylan momentarily imagined herself being a waitress: eye contact, smiles, speaking to people for a living. It all scared her to death.

"Are we ready?" April blurted, returning with a hand on her hip. The flannel shirt she wore was tied into a knot leaving her belly exposed. Dylan sat, eye level with the circular navel ring that pierced through the woman's skin.

"Um… just a, just a cheeseburger?" Dylan said, with

the tone of a question.

"Fries with it?"

"Sure," Dylan nodded confidently. If there was anything in her life she was sure of, it was that she never said "no" to French fries.

"How you want your burger?" the snarky waitress asked between smacks of her teeth on the bubble gum she was smugly chewing.

Forced to make yet another decision, Dylan could feel heat rushing to her face. Her mouth gaped open with an unsure expression.

April turned her scowl towards Candice when she heard the woman chime in. "She'll have it medium." Candice gave April a grin of fake gratitude before the impolite woman left the table again.

"You'll like it medium, Dear," Candice promised her granddaughter. "That's how I always made them for Father. Well, *Grandfather*."

Dylan peeked across the room through the window out at the street, seeing that the rain had finally started to ease up. Rain had poured so hard all weekend, she wouldn't have been able to hear during her experiments even if she had tried. Instead, she'd spent most of Saturday and Sunday alone in her bedroom avoiding having to make small talk with her grandma.

Against the bright window, the woman looked like a silhouette until Dylan's eyes adjusted and could see it was Ms. Castle, the teacher she had for study hall, seated at the table beside it. Alone, she held her phone over her finished meal with both hands staring into the luminescent rectangle.

"Carol has always been so nice. I'm not sure what went wrong with April," Candice informed. "I don't know Carol extremely well, but anytime I've spoken with her, she's been pleasant. I sat next to her at a spaghetti dinner, a fundraiser for a woman with cancer – poor woman died – and Carol was just a joy the whole time. An hour, we sat there and chatted." Candice's words were the infamous type of small talk Dylan so desperately wished was either eliminated from Earth or miraculously made easier for her.

Dylan viewed Ms. Castle casually alternate between gazing out the wet window and whatever she was reading on her iPhone.

"April is a rough woman. The tavern next door is where I think she spends most her nights. A favorite amongst the gentlemen." Candice quickly corrected herself, adding with a whisper, "Well... the *not-so*-gentlemen."

Dylan looked at Candice and forced a smile. She was listening but was better at studying the white, plastic vase holding a cloth red rose between them than she was at holding conversations. Dylan's eyes constantly wandered to avoid eye-contact with people; instead, she gathered detailed information of her surroundings. Inside Carol's Restaurant was ripped carpet, random nails in the fake wood paneling holding no pictures, and water stained ceiling tiles. Some tiles protruded like the belly of pregnant woman, ready to burst.

The rusty bell over the entryway clanked as the shabby wooden slab swung open. Dylan's head instinctively followed the rattle to find a drenched Mitchell Wolf standing in the entrance. He threw his soaked, black bangs from his eyes as he wiped his feet on the small welcome mat just inside of Carol's. He took both his palms, slid them from his forehead to the back of his neck, and slicked his thick hair smoothly down. He dried his rough, wet hands on his faded denim pants. For a moment, Dylan swore she was in one of those over-the-top commercials for expensive perfume and that Mitch was an overpaid, wonderful looking model.

Mitch walked slowly between tables of eating patrons until he reached the cash register near the kitchen. Dylan kept her head down. She doubted he'd notice her but didn't dare take the chance by looking up.

He pulled off his soaked jacket and hung it on the standing coat rack in the corner.

"Man, that thing is wet," the boy said with a smile, seemingly to no one. "Mr. Peterson," he said, throwing his voice across the room accompanied with a polite wave to an older man and his wife enjoying dinner. The man and woman waved back. In fact, people at three other tables exchanged greetings with Mitch, too.

"Mitchie, is that your steak sandwich they've got sizzling back there?" April asked, showing slight signs of decorum. It was the first time her face had found a genuine smile since Dylan and Candice had arrived.

"Sure is," Mitch replied, leaning one elbow on the counter.

Dylan watched, ready to hide her face at a moment's notice if need be. Mitch had a way about him. From April's reaction to him, Dylan wasn't the only one who thought so.

"Should've known," April teased. "Eight dollars, sixty-three cents, Hun. I think they're about to box it up. I'll go grab it."

As Mitch reached for his wallet, Dylan's view was suddenly obscured by a tall woman wearing skinny jeans, Ugg boots, and a messy bun: Ms. Castle.

"Hi, Mitch," she greeted with elongated syllables and

dramatic fluctuations.

"Hello, Ms. Castle," he replied. He strangely pronounced *Ms. Castle*, like it was the punchline to a joke: an inside one shared by two, very friendly individuals.

"If I'd known you were coming in I'd have waited and eaten with you."

"I'm just grabbing takeout."

Dylan could clearly hear the exchange in the small dining room. Just like she had heard about small towns, there seemed to be no secrets inside Carol's.

"Well, then let me pick up the tab for you," the much older woman warmly offered.

Mitch shifted his weight from one leg to the other. "Oh no, that's not necessary."

"But, I insist," she told him, grabbing his left arm with her manicured hand. Her tanned skin nearly matched his natural golden shade. Dylan watched as the teacher squeezed his firm bicep and noticed something sneaking out from under his t-shirt sleeve: a tattoo.

"Really, it's really no big deal. I'll just pay for it. But, thank you very much for the offer," he gently persuaded the nice-looking educator.

With her hand still lingering on the boy's muscular appendage, she backed down. "Oh, all right. But next time, I promise, whatever you want, on me."

Mitch coolly looked down at the woman's grip, causing her to finally let go of him. "Thanks again," Mitch said, his dimples holding her stare for a few extra seconds.

"Here you go, Kid," April announced, walking up and holding a brown paper bag.

"Money is on the table," Ms. Castle told April before turning away and heading towards the door.

"Have a good night, Tamara. Come again," April said to the trendy woman's back as she left. Ms. Castle couldn't see the way April stared at Mitch, as she left the restaurant into the drizzle filled air, but Dylan could.

"Here you go." Mitch handed her a ten-dollar bill. "Keep it."

"Oh, gee, thanks. I'll finally be able to go to college." April slapped Mitch's shoulder in jest.

"Right?" Mitch laughed taking the bagged sandwich from her. He put his jacket back on and said, "Until next time," to an adoring April.

With his still dripping, long hair, Mitch turned and left without seeing or noticing Dylan. Tingling nerves floated off her and were replaced by the soothing sensation of relief. Candice continued to talk about Carol and her family, telling Dylan how the restaurant owner's father had started and operated it until about fifteen years ago. Dylan tried to listen but struggled mightily.

"Here." April plopped a heavy ceramic plate down in front of Dylan. A few fries fell off onto the mangy table top from the impact. She also placed a plate of lasagna down for Candice in the same careless manner.

"April, our drinks?" Candice reminded the fleeing server.

April's head tipped forward as if the task of bringing their Iced Tea and Diet Pepsi was just too much to ask. "Right. Be right back."

Candice scowled and shook her head at the unprofessional behavior of the waitress who could obviously be cordial when she felt like it.

Dylan briefly gave a look of agreement to her grandmother but then went right back to staring at the walls, floors, and ceiling. After a moment, she sank her teeth into the flavorful, juicy cheeseburger. The bold taste, laced with black pepper and salt, was a welcomed pleasure.

As she ate, Dylan didn't speak. She just remembered the image of Ms. Castle's hand clutching Mitch's arm and wondered.

What in the world could the sixteen-year-old kid possibly have tattooed on his arm?

7

Though the persistent rain had come to an end, Dylan still found herself soaked. A half-mile of collecting drizzle from the thick haze hanging low across the cornfields and dirt roads of Black Willow Creek compiled quickly. Potent fog invaded her lungs, and Dylan coughed away the gagging tickle.

After sealing herself behind the stubborn front door, Dylan calmly unloaded her tough and reliable backpack. The three flashlights she pulled out gave her eyes relief from the darkness. She positioned them in a triangle, all facing the center of the wide living room. Yellow beams cut through the blackness with ease, allowing her to clearly see the abandoned belongings in the deserted space. Cobwebs illuminated when the rays touched them, like invisible ink under UV light, but Dylan told herself that the brilliant architects behind the intricate designs had all gone dormant for the rapidly approaching winter months. She was convinced enough to cease her worries about eight-legged monsters dropping down to visit her.

"I hope you're here tonight," Dylan warmly stated into the empty room. Her tone was pleasant and welcoming. "And if you're with me, I hope you are in the mood to communicate."

She kept a friendly grin on her brightly lit face, believing she'd appear more approachable to the *innocent* spirit. It was the opposite tactic Dylan used in her day to day encounters where she hoped her blank stares and ambiguous scowls would ward people off.

"I want to thank you again for making my Mel-meter alert the other night. That was really kind of you." The aged smell of dust boldly lingered in the still air as a constant reminder that not a soul had been around for years. At least not one inhabiting a body...

"Remember this?" she questioned while holding up the digital recorder that looked tiny even in the palm of her small hand. "This is what you spoke into. This is how I heard your voice. *Innocent.*" She paused, waiting for some dramatic response: a loud slamming door, a disembodied scream, a full-bodied apparition.

Nothing of the sort happened, of course.

Quickly curbing her expectations down a few notches so they were back in line with reality, Dylan laughed at her own foolish disappointment. Especially, with what was at stake. Building a relationship with a spirit seemed silly. But, if that's what it took to get what she needed, she was willing to do it.

Casually, she rotated herself in a stationary circle, her

eyes wandered in all directions, as if she would suddenly see the source of the voice she had captured days earlier. The three torches cast different sized shadows in multiple directions against the walls and dirty curtains.

As if speaking to a group of kindergarteners, Dylan spoke clearly with a balance of enthusiasm and authoritativeness. "I am going to be asking you some questions. And what I want you to do is try your best to answer them into this recorder." She held it high for the nonexistent class of children to see. "There is a microphone on this thing. It's very sensitive. So sensitive that it can hear things that my ears can't."

She cleared her throat. "Okay." She let a deep breath slowly exit her body, and closed her eyes for a moment before saying, "Here goes nothing."

Holding her head high, she explained her strategy. "I'm going to ask simple questions. Ones that require brief but detailed answers. I will wait for ten seconds then I will rewind the recorder and listen for your response. Make sense?" She shook her head at her own question. "I'm sure you get it."

She placed her thumb on the recorder's only red button and pressed it down. "What is your name?" Following her question, Dylan held completely still. She didn't budge, didn't even breathe.

One. Two. Three. Four. Five. Six. Seven. Eight. Nine. Ten.

Relaxing, she again hit the red button then REWIND. Putting the digital recorder against her left ear, she played it back. Sounding almost like a stranger, her own voice asked the question, *"What is your name?"*

As quietly as she waited during the recording, Dylan

listened for a response on the playback. She heard nothing.

"Okay," she uttered, and pressed the button again. "How old are you?"

One. Two. Three. Four. Five. Six. Seven. Eight. Nine. Ten. STOP. REWIND.

Straining her ears for anything that might be an answer, Dylan heard only silence.

"What town are we in?"

One. Two. Three. Four. Five. Six. Seven. Eight. Nine. Ten. STOP. REWIND. PLAY. Nothing.

"Are you male or female?"

One. Two. Three. Four. Five. Six. Seven. Eight. Nine. Ten. STOP. REWIND. PLAY. Nothing.

"What color is this house?"

One. Two. Three. Four. Five. Six. Seven. Eight. Nine. Ten. STOP. REWIND. PLAY. Nothing.

"What color is my jacket?"

One. Two. Three. Four. Five. Six. Seven. Eight. Nine. Ten. STOP. REWIND. PLAY. Nothing.

"What is *my* name?"

One. Two. Three. Four. Five. Six. Seven. Eight. Nine. Ten. STOP. REWIND. PLAY…

…*sssssss*…

"That was something!" Dylan yelped, and quickly rewound the ten seconds that now seemed like an eternity. Pacing with anticipation, she held the device close to her ear. Halting, she held still and listened.

…*sssssss*…

"What the hell?"

The excited girl's thoughts tumbled in her mind like clothes on spin dry in the oversized machines she and her mother used to use in the basement of their building back in

Evanston, before the house... before the wedding. Dylan's shoulders shivered; a tingle tiptoed from her hairline to the small of her back.

She ran the audio back again. Her body bounced up and down, prodding the recorder to move faster.

...sssssss...

Dylan clenched her teeth, struggling to make out the word, desperate to hear it. It was a murmuring sound, a mumble. It was a hard exhale – no, a gasp.

What is it saying? she pleaded with herself to figure it out.

She pressed REWIND again, walked in a circle while the device casually returned to zero seconds. Her team of shadows followed from all directions like dedicated assistants at the ready. Stopping, Dylan stood motionless, silent. If she could have temporarily willed her heart to skip a few beats, she would have: anything to make this noise, this message, discernable.

...sssssss...

Disappointed, Dylan's shoulders sank, and her sweaty palm ran through her thick curls as she pulled her knit cap off and tossed it to the once beautiful wood floor. She grumbled a frustrated moan to her own elongated shadows climbing the walls. She had shifted her weight, tiring from the stress, when she heard the noise again.

...sssssss...

The skin on her cold cheeks burned. If they weren't already pink from the cool air they'd have been red from embarrassment. This time the sound, the growl, the whisper didn't come from the digital recorder. It came from the floor. If it hadn't been so stupid, it may have even made her laugh.

"Oh my God," she whined loudly with her head tilted straight back, eyes facing the sponge-painted ceiling. The noise she had captured, the message from the other side was nothing more than her foot shuffling on the floor. EVP collecting rule number one: *stand still!*

She shook her head, scolding herself internally. She needed to be more careful, more disciplined. And not only that, she needed to be mindful of her approach to this. Her line of questioning, although sounding simple enough, was too complex. She and her infantry of shadow soldiers needed to regroup; begin again with a simpler strategy, concise and easy *yes* or *no* questions.

Dylan shrugged it off and dug in her heels. Back to business.

"Are you a child?"

One. Two. Three. Four. Five. Six. Seven. Eight. Nine. Ten. STOP. REWIND. PLAY. Nothing.

"Are you an adult?"

One. Two. Three. Four. Five. Six. Seven. Eight. Nine. Ten. STOP. REWIND. PLAY. Nothing.

"Are we in Black Willow?"

One. Two. Three. Four. Five. Six. Seven. Eight. Nine. Ten. STOP. REWIND. PLAY. Nothing.

"Are you male?"

One. Two. Three. Four. Five. Six. Seven. Eight. Nine. Ten. STOP. REWIND. PLAY. Nothing.

"Are you female?"

One. Two. Three. Four. Five. Six. Seven. Eight. Nine. Ten. STOP. REWIND. PLAY. Nothing.

"Is this house white?"

One. Two. Three. Four. Five. Six. Seven. Eight. Nine. Ten. STOP. REWIND. PLAY. Nothing.

"Is my jacket gray?"

One. Two. Three. Four. Five. Six. Seven. Eight. Nine. Ten. STOP. REWIND. PLAY. Nothing.

"Is my name Dylan?"

One. Two. Three. Four. Five. Six. Seven. Eight. Nine. Ten. STOP. REWIND. PLAY. Nothing.

Dylan's jaw stretched wide as an uncontrollable yawn escaped out like a silent scream. The cracks in her dry, frozen lips stung as they pulled at the seams. She slid her iPhone from her back pocket and yawned again when she saw the time was just after 10:00 p.m. The unfinished homework on her desk in her room was calling her name through the cornfields.

Reaching to click off one of the flashlights, it suddenly dawned on her. Like an icy bucket of water waking her from a deep sleep, an idea washed over her.

Standing high and hopeful, Dylan pressed the red button. "Are you guilty?" she boldly asked.

Her words echoed through the hollow shell of wood and Sheetrock. She waited, holding her breath, locking every joint, relaxing every muscle into gelatin until she could feel herself melt between the splintering tongue and groove boards. After ten gut wrenching seconds; one, two, three, four, five, six, seven, eight, nine, ten... STOP. REWIND. PLAY.

It came so quickly on the playback, Dylan hardly had time to prepare herself. Clear, distinct, and bold – it was there. An exhaled whisper; a declaration. A word so powerful Dylan had to grip her hand over her mouth to stop from shouting.

Even though this is what she came to the house for, this is what made her ignore her school assignments, this is

42

what she had dedicated her life to long ago, it still startled her. A response, an intelligent reply, an answer to her question.

"*No.*"

8

Both of Dylan's feet lifted off the ground, her body twisted like a cat falling from a tree only she didn't land on her feet. Instead, she laid flat on her stomach, one cheek pressed against the dirty, splintered floor. A bee stinging the right side of her butt wouldn't have surprised her more. Just after the word *"No"* had wonderfully crept into her ear, her back pocket vibrated like a taser, sending her leaping into the air and tumbling back down. Her phone had started buzzing.

Inhaling dirt particles, she reached back and grabbed it. She only had two contacts in her phone and only one of them would ever dare call her.

"Grandma?" Dylan asked as though she didn't know. Her pulse was speeding at an unsafe clip. "Okay. I was... I was about to head home."

After ending the call, she rolled to her back, took a

moment to regain her composure. With her arms and legs out in the shape of a snow angel, she let it sink in: she had recorded the voice of a spirit. And not just a random word, some residual voice floating through time and space, but an actual answer to a direct question. She had communicated with someone! A spirit! More importantly, she was a step closer to finding what she needed. Every bit of evidence brought her closer to changing the past – fixing everything.

The frazzled teen gathered her tools and carefully tucked them away in their designated pockets. In a single motion, she zipped up the backpack and scooped it off the floor. Slinging it over one shoulder, she busted the sticky door loose and slammed it closed behind her.

The outside air tasted fresh and clean after breathing the stale oxygen in the unventilated space. The fog, thicker now than when she arrived, gave the giant tree in the backyard and the miles of corn an unsettling ambience. The tree was black and erratic with bare branches tangled every which way. Growing close to the house, one long, sturdy arm reached out towards the building, nearly touching an upstairs window. Its long, narrow leaves were now laying scattered on the ground beneath it.

The scene felt unusually eerie to Dylan, yet she was overjoyed with excitement. Thinking ahead to the gravestones that decorated the cemetery, Dylan grabbed one of the flashlights from her bag, just to be safe.

As crispy leaves crunched under her skipping feet, the low visibility wasn't a deterrent from galloping like a child down the driveway. Now she knew she had been right all this time. All those moments of doubt - *Are they right about me? Am I crazy?* - were gone. Dylan had a sense of freedom different than anything she'd ever felt before.

The ray from the flashlight she held in front of her did little to help guide her. Instead of creating a visible path, the light bounced brightly off the low hanging cloud that was paying the fields of Black Willow Creek a late visit. If there had been any turns required to get to Candice's, she might have had trouble finding it. But she had walked the straight shot numerous times, dedicating the distances between landmarks to memory. This would not be a problem at all. Until...

Thump.

"I s'pose you can't move that truck by walking into it. You'll probably have to go 'round."

The deep, but gentle, voice gave Dylan as much of jolt as running directly into the front of the pickup truck had. Her right knee began to swell immediately. Rubbing it, she considered running away, but the sound of footsteps from behind trapped her against the vehicle.

Dylan's jubilant, carefree smile flew off like a spooked raven avoiding a passing car. Not breathing, she hesitantly turned to find a man standing just a few feet from her.

"That sounded like it hurt. That was quite a thud."

The dark night and the gray fog teamed up to hide his face from Dylan, but his white hair and moustache glowed through like an *OPEN* sign at a twenty-four-hour drugstore. From the shape of the groomed hair over his top lip, she knew he was smiling at her... although it did little to comfort her.

The stranger sidestepped the nervous girl, reached into the open driver side window and flipped on the headlights. Engulfed in the overwhelming glow of the high beams, Dylan again suppressed the strong urge to flee.

"You live just up here? With the Smiths?" His short

steps brought him into the light. Dylan's lack of replies didn't stop him from continuing the one-way conversation. "Well, I s'pose it's not the Smiths anymore. Just Candice, nowadays."

Both of his hands were inside the front pockets of his dirty, blue work pants held up by red suspenders that rested tightly over his plaid shirt. The oversized frames holding thick bifocals sat on his large nose and matching ears. Up close, the gravedigger looked older, more fragile, and less threatening than she previously would have guessed. From a distance, her imagination had created someone more sinister, dangerous. However, seeing him like this, hearing his kind voice, still didn't warrant lowering her alertness.

"Should I give you a lift up the road to Candice's?" he offered with a question. He had a genuineness that Dylan couldn't deny but she didn't give trust easily, especially at night in the fog at a cemetery with a stranger that spends all his days caring for rotting corpses.

Dylan heard the words *"No, thank you"* inside her mind. But somewhere on the way to her lips they had reduced to an awkward sounding, *"No."*

Her eyes only stayed on the man for seconds at a time before shifting another direction. She made note of his scuffed work boots tightly laced over his ankles. Dylan had gained a vast knowledge of footwear from years of avoiding eye contact.

Still wearing a soft smile, the cemetery groundskeeper and gravedigger told her, "So long. I'll see you again. I'm here a lot. I work the graveyard shift." He chuckled at his own play on words. "Be careful on your way."

The old man nodded his head and his tired knees carried him around to the driver's side. Dylan thought she politely returned his nod but wasn't sure if it was noticeable. In the end, she decided it didn't matter.

Briskly walking the entire way, with her arms swinging at her side, she couldn't get through the front door fast enough. Finally sitting at the kitchen table with a glass of cold water, Dylan, thirsty and weary, felt glad to be at her grandmother's.

For once.

9

With a violent burst, Dylan thrusted upright in her bed. Wheezing, she gripped the blankets with one hand and placed the other over her thumping heart. She coughed, fought ferociously to catch her breath, as it slipped away from her gasping lungs. Flipping her hair back from her face, she wiped beads of sweat from her cold forehead. The bed rocked as her body swayed back and forth.

Sniffling, she gradually began to regain control of her senses in the oppressive darkness. Dylan dropped, flat on her back. She sank into the memory foam mattress Candice had purchased when Dylan had arrived a little more than two weeks ago on a soggy, hot afternoon after a long, awkward ride from Chicago in the back of Candice's Buick. She stared at the ceiling but could see nothing except the empty blackness that surrounded her.

Dylan knew what had awakened her – nothing. Just her subconscious remembering those terrible nights back in her old bedroom in the high-rise. Those nights when all hell began to break loose in her life.

She rolled out from under the covers, still shaken from the images that woke her, still groggy from lack of sleep. Her curly hair dropped to cover her shoulders, as she concentrated to keep her balance, being hardly awake when her feet touched the carpet. Her bare legs felt the bite of the cool air having been unprotected by the thin t-shirt that hung just below her backside. Autumn had quickly fallen on Black Willow, and Dylan knew it was time to add a pair of sweatpants to her nighttime attire.

Blindly walking to the wall, hands outstretched, she felt the light switch and flipped it up. Groaning, she covered her squinting eyes until they could look without being rudely burned out.

Like she already knew, there was nothing there. It had only been a dream. *Again*. Looking down, Dylan inspected her legs anyway, turning slightly to see her calves. She pulled up her shirt, checked her belly, quickly, just to make certain. As expected, she found nothing out of the ordinary. Nothing, but smooth, unscathed skin, pale and cream colored.

The harsh light disappeared as she returned the switch to the off position. Slithering back beneath the covers, she was embraced by the warmth her body had left behind when she got out of bed. Rolling to her side, she grabbed her phone from the nightstand where it sat charging. It was 4:37 in the morning. Relieved that it wasn't time to get ready for school, Dylan snuggled in like a caterpillar in a cocoon. If only she could wake up different: not alone and unafraid.

With her thumb hovering over the contact listed as *Chicago Teen Crisis*, Dylan internally debated pressing it to send a text. As the screen on her phone timed out and went black, she considered it a sign. The decision had been made for her: it wasn't the right time.

A touch more than an hour later, Dylan's phone came to life with a pleasant melody that slowly nursed her from precious sleep. Reluctantly, she swiped her thumb across the screen and stopped the dreamy score that easily could substitute as the soundtrack for a cheesy, G-rated, cartoon film.

Like a robot obeying what it had been programmed to do, she walked to the hall, grabbed a towel from the closet, and locked herself in the bathroom. In front of the mirror, she stared at the reflection and accepted that she was still, unfortunately, just a caterpillar. Shivering, she turned on the shower and let steam build inside the cold room and collect on the glass while the bathroom warmed like a sauna.

When the hot streams of water began to blast against her body, her mind finally caught up with the fact that she was out of bed. Forgetting her dream and the uncomfortable encounter with the gravedigger, Dylan thought about the answer she received on her recorder the night before. The joy that had her skipping down a dirt road in the fog last night returned as a wide, ear to ear smile stretched across her face.

Walking the short trip from the bathroom back to her bedroom wrapped in a towel, Dylan inhaled the potent smell of bacon. Veering on a slight detour, she popped her head into the kitchen, her wet hair glued to her shoulders.

"Again?" Dylan asked rhetorically with a tinge of pink forming on her face.

Candice flipped the thin crispy slices of meat trying to avoid the unpredictable splatters of scorching grease. "I made your grandpa breakfast every day for a hundred years," she told Dylan with happy memories clearly playing in her thoughts. "Besides, if you get any thinner, I'm afraid I'd lose you between the cracks in the porch."

Dylan sauntered back down the hall to her room. Candice's practice of cranking the thermostat up on the cold fall mornings had significantly warmed the house. Dylan's wet self was quietly thankful for that.

She got herself dressed, black yoga pants, and an oversized zip-up hoodie with deep, soft pockets in front, and checked the time. Seeing she was running just slightly behind, she figured there was still plenty of time to get something into her rumbling stomach.

Returning to the kitchen, she found a warm plate of scrambled eggs, bacon, and buttered toast with silverware placed elegantly beside it.

"Here you go," Candice said, placing a steaming cup of black coffee next to her hungry granddaughter. "It's a little warm. Watch your lips."

Dylan held the hot, dark beverage with both hands until her palms could no longer take the burning. Slowly, she lifted it and slurped the liquid, making a strange noise. The food smelled and looked amazing, so Dylan didn't hesitate diving in head first.

Candice Smith washed the frying pan, wiped the grease coated counter and oven, and put things away in the refrigerator. All the while, she talked to Dylan. "This little grocery store here in Black Willow... The one by the gas station?"

Dylan nodded.

"There's just not much selection. And a lot of what they have is often expired. A great family owns the place. I wish I spent more money there, but… Oh, well." Candice pushed away the regret of opting to leave town for all that she purchased.

"It's just that the big supermarket in Greenville is so wonderful to shop at." The much larger town of Greenville is where Candice purchased the bacon and eggs they ate that morning.

"If you ever need a library, Greenville is the place to find that, too. I don't know if kids use libraries much anymore, but, Dylan, it sure is a nice one. Just a few years old. High-tech, too. They had one on State Street for a hundred years, but that one is long gone now. I think it's a physical therapist's office now. Maybe? Something medical."

In her thoughts, Dylan had questions about Greenville, places to go and see but, like always, she failed to verbalize them. Instead, she threw an occasional "yeah" or "nah", at least letting Candice know she was listening.

The talkative woman, who was now Dylan's not-exactly-legal guardian, wasn't deterred by the girl's lack of enthusiasm for conversation. And it wasn't like Dylan didn't desire to be a better communicator. She just *couldn't* be.

"Grandma!" Dylan alerted Candice with wide eyes noticing the green numbers on the oven. Lost in her appetite, she had neglected the ever-changing clock.

"Oh dear," Candice worried. "Go get your things." She dried her hands on a turquoise dish towel and hung it neatly on the handle of the stove, before grabbing her jacket from the closet.

Dylan rushed out, fingers still slimy from the fried slices of fatty pork, and barged into her room. She jammed her folders containing unfinished assignments into her backpack, deciding there wasn't time to unpack the gadgets still inside from last night's experiment. Tossing the strap over her shoulder, she jogged out.

The Buick carefully pulled onto the road with Candice behind the wheel and Dylan beside her. Through the dew-covered window, Dylan gazed down the dirt road towards the Black Willow Creek Cemetery. Sure enough, the gravedigger was already unloading something from the bed of his beat-up, rusty truck. She recalled the man's face from her memory and knew there was something familiar about him. She didn't recognize him from anywhere, but his features, his expressions were like someone from somewhere that she had seen before.

"Anytime you're ready I can take you into Greenville to take your driver's test. Be nice for you to be able drive. Get a car," Candice offered, hands at ten and two, her posture straight and tall.

"Um… I don't even have a permit yet," Dylan replied softly, trying hard to sound at ease.

"Well we can head there to get that part done. Then you can start to drive with me."

"Sure…"

Most of the crippling fog had dissolved, and the tall, tangled trees around the school appeared like the silhouettes of otherworldly-beings stalking the students and teachers inside. Candice stopped the car against the cement curb near the front entrance. It was nearly time for class to start which left the loop-shaped driveway mostly bare.

As Dylan said, "See ya later," she noticed two people

walking from the area of the blacktop lot designated for faculty. She watched them, as loose pebbles crunched under Candice's slow rolling tires behind her. On the left was a tall, fit looking young man whose fine, silky hair swayed with each step. On the right was a tall, lean, hourglass-shaped female dressed in all black except for bright red high heels that made the matching lipstick she wore pop through the mist with a loud bang.

Mid-stride, Tamara Castle nudged her elbow into Mitchell Wolf's arm. An echoing laugh escaped as carefree as the leaves being dragged around by the gentle autumn breeze. The teacher's skirt, cut just above her knees, flowed over her thighs with her exaggerated strut worthy of a New York City runway.

Before the curious girl could lower her eyes and scurry to class, Mitch looked Dylan's direction and noticed her. As the bell blared across the property, he let a sly grin sneak from the edge of his mouth before Ms. Castle's hand gripped the sleeve of his jacket. Dylan quickly broke Mitch's stare and bolted into the school wondering why a student was coming from the faculty lot and why a teacher was arriving to school after the morning bell had rung.

But mostly, Dylan wondered why they were together.

10

When the tightly-threaded carpet that stretched across the 300 Hall maliciously reached up and grabbed the toe of Dylan's sneaker, she helplessly tumbled forward. Although officially tardy, she found herself only inches from her first period class, directly in front of the wide-open door. Falling, her twisting body collided into another late-arriving teenager. Dylan's grimacing face hit hard into an unexpecting, muscular chest. Strong arms squeezed around her body, keeping her from crashing to the floor.

The scent of a musky forest savagely attacked the tiny, black hairs that coated the insides of her nostrils. Whoever caught her mid-fall either lived in the deepest part of the woods or had scrubbed himself with a strong, masculine body wash in the shower that morning.

Dylan found herself eye to eye with a thin, curvy tattoo

peeking out from under the sleeve of a one pocket, plain white t-shirt.

"Whoa!" blurted Mitch, fully embracing the quiet new girl as if they were swaying all alone on a dimly lit dance floor to an emotional ballad about lost love and heartache. Dylan quickly pushed herself away, barely looking at the boy.

"Has anyone seen Dylan Klaypool?" Mrs. Whitbeck's voice drifted out to the hall from the back corner of the classroom.

Breaking away from the light grasp Mitch still had on one of her skinny arms, Dylan charged into the classroom, leaving the tattooed boy staring at her with wonder from the corridor.

From a desk in the front row, Carrie Holland glared at Dylan with the same potency the fog had the previous night. Dylan felt the heat of the girl's gaze and quickly moved to her seat to escape it.

"You're late, Dylan," Mrs. Whitbeck notified her as though she was enlightening her with some newly discovered, valuable piece of knowledge.

Dylan began to nervously explain. "I just... We were..."

"Sit down," the gray-haired woman commanded, not in the mood for excuses.

Dylan dropped her weight down on the hard, plastic seat. Carrie's smug grin was bright enough for Dylan to see clear through the back of the popular girl's head.

Glancing up while sliding a folder from her backpack, Dylan could see Mitch still curiously standing outside the classroom, looking in. The narrow fingers on Carrie's bony hand waved at him through the open doorway. Mitch pulled his thick, dark hair behind his right ear and walked away without acknowledging Carrie's friendly gesture. The blonde girl's shoulders sank.

The rest of Dylan's morning moved on peacefully. She sat low in her seat through her classes, meandered from room to room, and avoided contact and conversation. The other students utilized those few minutes between classes to gossip, flirt, and exchange tidbits from the classes they had just finished for the ones coming up. But not Dylan.

Mid-day, on her way downstairs to the cafeteria, Dylan imagined the awkwardness that would arise once she was seated next to Mitch Wolf in French class immediately after lunch. She knew that the first time she looked his direction, he would certainly try to say something about her recklessly crashing into him that morning. She hoped and prayed that Mr. Amal wouldn't be so rude to employ his "practice your French with someone in the next row" tactic.

Approaching her locker, Dylan reached out her hand to turn the combo lock. A forceful blow shoved into her back. Powerlessly, her petite body tumbled to the floor colliding with random legs and shoes on her path downward.

Because she had been ready to stow away the items she used in her morning classes in exchange for what she would need that afternoon, the large zippered pocket on her backpack was wide open. The force from her hard fall sent its contents flying out, scattered in all directions.

Dylan's soft palms burned from the skid of breaking her fall on the rough, wiry carpet, and its sandpaper quality did little to soften the blow of the solid concrete floor underneath it. Bursts of laughter accosted Dylan, along with sneering remarks, like "Walk much, Loser?" or "Nice fall!" But the starved students soon cleared the hall and raced toward the food lines outside the cafeteria.

Dylan laid motionless, wishing away the last of the stragglers that still mingled in the hall. None of them now paid a lick of attention to the odd girl sprawled out on the floor amongst her books and papers.

Sensing she was finally alone, Dylan picked up her drooping face from the trampled rug when a subtle breeze in the form of Mitch Wolf kneeled next to her. Like a seed attached to a white fluffy parachute leaving a withered dandelion, Dylan's final shred of dignity floated away leaving her naked and exposed.

"You're having quite a morning," said the handsome boy with dangling hair. "Are you okay?"

A moment that Dylan thought was already bad enough had just gotten worse. She leaned up on one elbow, bashfully peeking up at him. A shadow gradually approached from behind him followed leisurely by a blond girl staring down at the uncomfortable heap of insecurity.

Leaning over Mitch's shoulder, Carrie's voice displayed great concern worthy of an Oscar. "Oh my God, are you okay?"

When Dylan's nervous eyes met hers, Carrie's mascara-caked lashes narrowed, and, like a spoiled child, her tongue prodded out from her scrunched mouth, taunting the fallen girl.

"This fell out of your bag," Mitch said, holding out a small black device that looked like an old AM/FM radio from the nineties. "What is this? SB7?" he asked reading the item's printed label.

Carrie glared at it from his back before adding a fake, "I hope you're okay." She turned to leave, walking proudly down the hall away from them.

A pair of bare knees, clenched together, very lady-like came squatting into view. Ms. Castle put her hand on Mitch's back, her black skirt rising on her toned and tanned thighs.

"Everything okay here? Are you hurt?" the teacher asked, her attention focused transparently more on Mitch than Dylan. Tamara Castle's perfume smelled expensive and imported, most likely not from one of those gift boxes found in department stores around the holidays. It was so potent, Dylan nearly sneezed.

"She seems okay," Mitch informed, moving his eyes to the attractive woman momentarily before again gazing down at Dylan.

Holding her stare at Mitch, without even a glance back towards the embarrassed Dylan, Ms. Castle leaned into him. "Let me know if you need anything." Standing up, her calf muscles flexed on her long, smooth legs. Her knees, level with Mitch's line of sight, fought to turn his concerned eyes from Dylan. Seeing him reach down and take the misfortunate girl's hand, Tamara Castle turned, her flowing skirt gliding around with her, and slowly walked away. Dylan saw the woman briefly sneak a look back at them as Mitch politely helped her stand. His strong arms pulled her weight up with little effort.

"Thanks," Dylan tried to say loudly with an appreciative smile, but only heard herself whisper it through an apprehensive frown.

"You're sure you're okay?" he asked, giving her a once over as if he were a trained physician looking for visible injuries.

"Yeah… I'm, I'm fine. I just…" Dylan moved her head left and right, looking up and down the empty hallway, taking an unsteady breath to calm herself.

Mitch swayed back and forth, jokingly waved his hand trying to get the flustered girl to look at him. "Hey, you sure you're okay? What are you looking for?"

Dylan shook off her bewilderment, forced herself to focus on the only person who seemed to care that she had been knocked over. "Um… I was just looking for someone." Fighting off nervousness, she squatted to gather her dispersed belongings. After sloppily scooping them up, she slid a few feet to her right to where her locker was. Dylan turned the dial on the lock, miraculously able to recall the combination amid a chaotic and stressful moment.

Following immediately behind, Mitch leaned on the locker next to hers with his bulky shoulder, pressing his hidden tattoo against the cold metal door. "Are you always this clumsy?" he inquired, sweetly smiling. His determined eyes never left hers. Dylan had to continuously look away, uneasy with how engaged he was.

"Um… I was…" Dylan struggled to get her folders and books put away on the top shelf. A few papers slid out, floated to the ground like paper airplanes, some going one direction, others going the opposite.

"Whoops," Mitch said, playfully. He jutted down attempting to catch one of the wily papers. He stabbed at it, gripping it from the air so forcefully it crinkled into a wadded ball. "Sorry," he apologized, again making solid eye contact with Dylan. "I hope you didn't need to still turn this one in."

Dylan shyly looked away, feeling her cheeks begin to blush. "No… I don't need that one." Her pulse raced, fretfully, while she shooed him away with her thoughts.

Deep dimples sank themselves into his face. His

eyebrows were low at his nose, arched over his eyes, but his long eyelashes kept his look calm and peaceful. Dylan wondered if Mitch's eyes always looked so soft and kind.

"So, you're having quite a day. Can't seem to stay on your feet."

Dylan scowled. "Excuse me?"

"This morning. I caught you. Remember?"

Nodding, Dylan remembered. "Right. Thanks... for that."

"My pleasure. Too bad I wasn't here this time when you tripped."

"Um... I, uh, I didn't trip this time."

His mouth straightened. "What happened? How did you fall?"

Looking behind her, wondering if she was about to get slammed into again, Dylan told him. "I was pushed."

"*Pushed?*"

"Yeah... someone... someone knocked me over."

"Are you kidding me? Who would do that? On *purpose?*" he demanded to know with what appeared to be genuine concern.

"Look... It's," Dylan cleared her throat. "It's not important. Aren't you, like, hungry, or something? Shouldn't you go have your lunch... or whatever?" She closed her locker and zipped up her bag planning to quickly escape.

"But, who would've shoved you?" Mitch wasn't letting it go.

Dylan shook her head, raised her eyes up at the ceiling tiles, avoided answering.

Mitch lightly rested his hand on her tense shoulder. She looked at his rough, calloused hand from the corner of her eye. A hand that, by the looks of it, wasn't a stranger to working with tools.

"If someone is bullying you, you really need to tell someone. I can go get Ms. Castle right now." Mitch's offer was sincere, but ratting Carrie out would only bring more attention to herself, so Dylan ignored his pitch.

She exhaled deeply, spun the numbered dial on her locker, sealing it shut. Her silence, she hoped, was enough to let Mitch know she wasn't interested in discussing it.

"Oh, don't forget this," Mitch remembered the small plastic unit with the name *SB7* printed on it still in his hand.

"Oh," Dylan mumbled. "Right. Thanks." She quickly nabbed the instrument that works in conjunction with radio frequencies to bolster voices that go otherwise unheard from his sturdy fingers.

"What is it?" Mitch blurted out before she could jam it deep into her bag out of sight.

Again, Dylan didn't respond. It was her favorite method of avoiding conversation. She would just ignore a question, act as though it had never been asked, and just hope the person asking would also forget. Surprisingly, it often worked. But not this time.

"Is it a radio? I think I've seen my grandpa use one like that. Where did you get it? A thrift shop?"

"Yeah, it's a radio," Dylan said, eager to just shut the inquiring boy up.

"Can I see it again for a minute?" Mitch requested, with his empty hand open.

Dylan put her backpack on. "I need to grab some lunch. So... maybe another time."

"I'll walk with you," Mitch said following next to her as she began her getaway.

"Um… I need to use the bathroom," she lied. "Go on without me."

"I can wait for you," he suggested, happily.

"It's okay."

"It's no problem."

"Really. There's no need."

"That's silly. We're the only two kids not already in the cafeteria. I'll walk with you."

"It's fine."

"It's really no -"

"No! *Okay?!*" Dylan blurted. "Just, please… Just… just go without me."

Mitch stopped, held his hands up, surrendering. "Sorry. I just thought…" The strong-looking boy's voice suddenly lost confidence.

Dylan turned around to see the big high school junior feeling about a foot tall. "I'm sorry…" She paused and put both hands over her face. "I didn't mean to… I, I didn't mean to snap, yell… whatever."

"Yeah, um… I'll see you in Mr. Amal's class after lunch." Mitch placed his hands in his front pockets and hung his head. He turned and headed down the stairs, leaving Dylan the way she preferred: alone.

11

The gravedigger raised his wrinkled hand, and held it motionless, high above his sweaty brow on his outstretched arm. Dylan saw the man leaning on his shovel at the back corner of the cemetery on the other side of the dozens of headstones that separated them. High walls of tan and brown cornstalks surrounded three sides of the graveyard. The rough gravel road Dylan walked on with bashful feet ran the length of the fourth side. When Dylan noticed him waving, she promptly put her head down and studied the dirt.

Nearing the house, her heart warmed, and her steps quickened. She jogged across the overgrown lawn and up the creaky, rotted steps. The giant, black tree along the back of the house peeked over and watched her force the front door open, as the vacant building swallowed her up into its dark belly.

Speeding through the kitchen, she paused only to give the light switch a couple rapid flicks, before proceeding through to the living room. Within minutes, Dylan had three flashlights positioned, brightly lighting the room. Sitting down on the coffee table, she crossed her right leg over her left knee, cleared her mind, settled her accelerated pulse, and caught her breath.

Each day, the air outside seemed to be slightly cooler than the day before. The colder it got, the more energy Dylan exerted during the half-mile trek from Candice's to the abandoned property. She sniffled to stop her nose from running and inhaled a few long breaths, her chest shaking slightly with each exhale.

Dylan looked at her hands, holding the strange device that Mitch had picked up off the floor when she was knocked over. Her thumbs traced the buttons, the blank screen, the knob that pulled out forming a long chrome antenna; the gray print - *SB7*. She remembered the many times she attempted using it: the many failures. The day it had arrived in the mailbox back at the Evanston house, she had excitedly imagined how it would change her life. So far, it hadn't. Not even a little.

Into the silence, the determined investigator spoke.

"It's me, Dylan." Walking in the cold air had made Dylan's eyes watery. She rubbed them dry with her sleeve and tucked her curly hair back from her face. "This thing," she held the plastic rectangle up for display. It was roughly three inches wide, five inches long, and a half inch thick. The bottom portion had a tight pattern of tiny holes so that sound could be heard coming from the speaker under the plastic casing. The top portion had a series of buttons and a digital readout screen.

"This piece of equipment is pretty special. It scans radio frequencies at the rate of ten per second. So, it goes very quickly." Dylan moved it around like she was doing a demonstration on an infomercial in front of an overly eager, live studio audience.

"Like the digital recorder, it will allow me to hear you. Only this time... if it works," she raised her eyebrows. "If it works, I'll hear you immediately. Right as you speak." She pressed the power button, causing static fuzz to blare from it. She set it to FM and FORWARD SWEEP. When the sweeping activated, the static turned choppy, like the noise a helicopter makes when hovering overhead. The digital readout showed numbers with a decimal place changing the way a car radio does when an annoying passenger continuously scans through without stopping long enough to even hear what is on the stations.

Dylan's foot anxiously bounced as it dangled over the floor. The white laces on her sneaker were flapping wings keeping it afloat. Loudly, she talked over the pulsating static.

"Let's start with what we already know works. I know you're innocent. Who is claiming that you're not innocent?"

Waiting, she listened to the SB7 scan digit after digit of FM frequencies. The quiet living room amplified the tiny speaker's brazen sound. Staring at the device, Dylan envisioned words floating out from it: answers, clear and obvious.

After a minute had passed, she asked again. "Who is claiming you aren't innocent? You can tell me. Who is saying that?"

Again, she waited. A few random, short stuttering

voices came from the speaker. Half words, just syllables. Nothing greater than the length of a tenth of one second. Nothing complete. Dylan knew these were just words of a radio DJ, or fragments of commercials or songs being picked up from the signals of nearby radio broadcasts. These weren't what she was looking for. If this experiment worked, she would hear something much different. It would be a distinct sound not like the cut off, chopped up, incoherent babbling that was erratically happening every five or ten seconds.

Remaining determined, Dylan asked the question again. "Who is claiming that you aren't innocent? What – *who* are you?"

The static echoed across the house, reverberating from wall to wall, swirling about the living room, circling Dylan's body. Closing her eyes, she sat still on the coffee table, legs crossed. She listened, intently, focusing deeply. Her mind felt blank. No thoughts about her mother, her father, her new school, her new home. Not about Black Willow, not about anything other than what was happening right then and there. About who was innocent and who was saying otherwise. The rhythm of the static was hypnotic. Her empty thoughts began to drift away with the static until she was no longer even paying attention to the sweeping frequencies.

"Girl."

Dylan's frantic heart skipped a beat. A voice had spoken through the speaker – a whisper like the words she hear on the digital recorder. Yet, it was vocalized fully, clearly. Loudly, but softly: *"Girl."*

Dylan had committed a cardinal sin of paranormal investigation: she'd asked two questions without allowing time for the first to be answered. *"Who is claiming that you aren't innocent?"* and *"Who are you?"* Before the excited investigator could ask for clarification, the genderless voice spoke again.

"Father."

Shocked, Dylan almost dropped the SB7. Quickly, she stood up. "I heard that! I heard you!" Her stomach turned. Nervous energy fluttered through her insides, her legs became weak and tired, as the room seemed to spin circles around her.

"Holy crap, I heard you," she whispered with welcomed surprise, feeling the reality of what had occurred sinking in.

Sitting down and crossing her legs, she spoke into the SB7 like it was a walkie talkie or a phone set on speaker with a direct line to the spirit world. "You said 'girl' and 'father'. I heard you, clearly. Is it a girl's father? Some girl's father? Are you the girl or the father?"

"House."

The monotone voice had calmly spoken again.

"House?" Dylan repeated the spirit's word attempting to confirm what she thought she may have heard.

"Window."

"Window?" Dylan stood again, unable to keep her excitement contained. "House? Window? Girl? Father? Tell me more. Whose father?" The voice now seemed to be speaking random words unassociated with her questions.

The chorus of static carried on at a torrid pace. Eager to keep communicating, Dylan began to feel hurried, rushed, like she was battling against time itself. Afraid this window of opportunity might suddenly slam shut, her speech became rapid, distressed. "Tell me more. I need more. I'm hearing you. Are you still here? Are you still with me?!"

Three voiceless minutes that passed like three hours turned her eagerness into desperation. She moved from corner to corner pleading with the soul whose voice she had heard.

"Please, don't stop talking. Just tell me something, *anything!* Please!" Sitting once again, she put her head into her hands. Laying on the table next to her, the SB7 carried on a meaningless racket.

"I'm sorry," she said calming her emotions. "I'm sorry. I don't mean to be a total wreck. I've just… I've had a long day. Did you ever have a day like that? A day that just got off to a poor start and never seemed to get on the right course?" She pulled her legs up, spun, and laid flat on her back, arms over her head. The coffee table was just long enough for her outstretched body.

"I was late this morning," she said with the static from the device hammering directly into one ear. "I was tardy. The teacher made a spectacle in front of the whole class, which happened to include my… my bully." She rolled her eyes, disgusted at how pathetic it sounded when she said it out loud.

"Yeah, that's right. I have a bully. She pushed me down today. From behind, like a coward. I don't think she would dare do something like that to my face. Maybe she would. Truthfully, I don't even know her. I don't even know why she is doing this to me: picking on me.

"Then there's this kid, this boy. I can't figure this kid out. He's nice. *Overly* nice. It's strange, actually. I've never seen a teenage boy just be so unnecessarily nice. There's something weird about him, too. It sounds stupid, but I think there could be something going on between him and one of my teachers. That sounds gross, right? I don't know… They just have some sort of chemistry between them. I've never seen a student and a teacher so comfortable around each other the way they are."

Dylan put one hand over her eyes, slid it down her entire face, stretching her eyes, cheeks, and lips. "I don't even know why I'm telling you this. Why *am* I telling you this anyway? Whatever."

Shaking her head, she sat up and pulled a notebook from her backpack. With a yellow No. 2 pencil, she turned to a specific page and wrote *GIRL, FATHER, HOUSE,* and *WINDOW.* Above, already written, was the word *INNOCENT.* She pondered over the words, the loud sounds from the SB7 still flooded the room like the beat of speedy techno music too fast to dance to.

Running her fingers through her hair, she contemplated the mysterious words on the paper. Deciding it was getting too cold to continue, and considering that the line of communication had gone totally silent for a lengthy period, she reached for her jacket.

"Well, I guess that's it for tonigh -"

"Room."

With one arm halfway sleeved, the other still not even started, Dylan scrambled for the box.

"Did I just hear you? Did you say something to me? Was it - was it *room*?"

She waited, hands trembling, silently praying for more.

"Bed."

"Whoa!" she squealed with a jolt. "Bed!" she yelled out. "Room. Bed. Room. Bed. Bedroom!" Dylan's head jerked to her right towards the open staircase. "Oh my God, *bedroom!"*

Quickly up, Dylan sprinted to the stairs with her scattered brain running faster than her feet. On the fourth step she tripped and slammed her knee into the wood. On the ninth step she slipped again, landing on her elbow as she tumbled. The thud her bones made breaking her fall was loud, the impact painful, but she didn't slow down! She was up and moving, instantly, after both clumsy missteps.

Dylan knew from a brief exploration of the upstairs when she first set foot in the house that there were three bedrooms on the second floor. The one on the right had apparently been used as an office by the family that last lived there. It had a desk, some rusty filing cabinets, no computer, but an awkward looking printer. White paper, sheet after sheet held together with a perforated line fed in through the back of the plastic machine. The trail of paper led to a stack, folded accordion style, that filled a box on the floor.

Dylan shined her flashlight at it, seeing the pages had holes that ran the entire length of the long, pleated pile. The holes were used to spool the sheets through the mechanism on little posts when it was printing.

She spun left, shining her flashlight at the bedroom across the hall from the office. The door was shut but the tarnished, brass-colored handle wasn't latched. Dylan pushed on the squeaky door, ready to leap away from it if a ghoul were to jump out screaming. The spider webs bridging the narrow gap between the edge of the door and the jamb easily broke apart as it opened. Half of the insect snares drifted lazily off the swinging door, the other half hung limply from the stationary frame.

Her light beam snuck inside and searched the

unoccupied room. A large bed, king size, was perfectly made with a burgundy comforter and matching throw pillows with abstract patterns. The room had the appearance that it was patiently awaiting the return of its inhabitants from a long day at work. But, Dylan knew better.

The dresser, tall and expensive, stood with half full bottles of cologne and perfume. Thick layers of powdered dust unapologetically coated everything. Dylan slowly moved inside, erasing the blackness with her flashlight like a misspelled word on a book report.

She flicked off the SB7, finally stopping its pulsating fuzz. The silence it left behind was daunting, leaving her feeling isolated and alone. Billows of warm air from her lungs hauntingly filled the visible path created by the sticklike lantern she held.

An eerie wave of emotion began building inside of Dylan, looming heavily. A moving sadness hit forcefully against her chest, then retreated when she came close to tears. Again, and again, it brushed across her senses with no discernable pattern. One moment she was focused on the slight tinge of fear that came with being alone in a dark, abandoned house with obvious paranormal activity. In the next, she could only think about crying. She'd fight the urge to weep until it would fade, leaving her slightly weaker each time. The pressure magnified in strength every time it arrived. During one of the respites, Dylan backed out of the room into the hallway where she once again felt she had control of her emotions.

Passing a bathroom with nothing more than a short glance inside, Dylan moved to the end of the second-floor hallway where a closed, six-panel door begged her to come open it. The third and final bedroom surely expected her.

Certain that the isolated room sitting alone at the end of the hall was where she'd been instructed to go, Dylan moved steadfastly. The white door turned yellow as she walked closer and closer with her light glaring off it. Moving slowly, she carefully placed each foot down before raising the other. Her throat was dry, dust filled. The water bottle down in the side pouch of her bag would quench her thirst soon enough. No way she was turning back to fetch it now.

Shivering from the cold she wiped her nose, and cautiously approached. Holding the flashlight at the end of her extended arm like a weapon, Dylan stopped.

Her imagination raged like wildfire engulfing all her reason and logic, like dry underbrush and evacuated homes. What could be on the other side? What would be waiting for her once she opened it? Would something jump out to grab her? Would it slam her defenseless body against the wall? Would it release a scream so vile and putrid that she'd forever be different just because she'd heard it?

Gingerly, her shaking hand touched the freezing metal handle and slowly twisted it.

12

A hollow thud echoed down the dark hallway when Dylan forcefully stomped her heel down on the floor with frustration. Letting out a deep sigh, she rapidly wiggled her wrist, rattling the knob to no avail. The old door was tightly locked.

Kicking, she rammed her foot into the solid oak piece, not realizing how little the cloth at the end of her sneaker would protect her toes.

"Ouch," she yelled, letting her flashlight fall with a shining crash, before dropping to a sitting position and squeezing her throbbing toes. With malice, she balled her hand and swung it mightily at the door in retaliation. The darkness caused her to misjudge the distance to the slab of nearly petrified wood, so instead of landing a punishing blow with the side of her fist, the small knuckle on her pinky grazed the door at the perfect angle to send a sting through her entire hand.

"Ugh!" she howled with raw angst. Dylan pushed her cold, scraped pinky between her dry, cracked lips, attempting to soothe away the pulsing pain. Removing it, she studied the glistening, red nick where the skin had been stripped away. She shook it at her side before grabbing her flashlight off the splintered floorboards.

Dejected, Dylan lumbered down the stairs with her bruised knees, dragging her swollen toes, sucking on her skinned knuckle, while wading across a sea of self-pity. She clipped her way, step by step like a slinky flirting with the bottom stair dangerously close to stopping on each step.

With lazy movements, she placed her belongings into their respective pockets of the unfailing backpack and buckled it onto her weakening body. She was ready to go.

Still reeling from the dramatic ups and downs of the evening's festivities, Dylan shuffled her feet and kicked stones down the bumpy driveway, listening to how far each would go while they disappeared into the dark.

The night was clear, stars twinkled brightly across the black sky like pin holes in a dark piece of paper with a light behind them. The vast cornfields rolled nonchalantly into the distance, and Dylan gave little thought to any of these wonderful things as she slowly walked towards Candice's house.

The cold air stood still and silent, without even the slightest current of a breeze touching Dylan's curly hair. There was no movement around her at all. Not a rustle in the corn, not a wandering leaf – nothing.

With her mind clouded with thoughts of the house, the tranquil night carried on almost unnoticed by Dylan. That was until the serenity surrendered the unmistakable sound of footsteps on the gravel behind her.

Dylan stopped, asking herself if what she had just heard was real or if that it was even possible. She had passed no one while walking to the house that night and saw no one. And the gravedigger's dirty, rust-infested truck was nowhere to be seen, leaving her certain that he wasn't around.

Blaming her imagination, Dylan began walking, and ignored the tinge of fear that began to creep into her inventive mind. When she undoubtedly heard the steps again, she quickly turned to look behind her – no one was there. Just the long dirt highway fading into the nighttime of Black Willow Creek greeted her.

Scanning the dark road from left to right, the paranoid girl watched for movement along the edges of the shifty cornfields. When she first moved to Black Willow, Candice had pointed out herds of deer wandering through the hayfields on the route to school. Knowing the graceful, hooved animals abundantly populated all the surrounding forests, Dylan figured that she had overheard the sound of one of them crossing the road from one cornfield to the next, filling up on the nutritious yellow maze.

Dismissively, she shrugged off the thought of someone following her and spun herself back in the direction that would lead her home. Taking long, determined strides that swiftly carried her light frame, causing her curly hair to bob on her shoulders, Dylan walked. She kept her ears open, suspicious of her own flippant conclusion that a deer had been on her trail.

From her left, a few rows of corn deep, she heard the long, drooping leaves of the stalks brush against each other.

She stopped and unclasped the latch on her sternum that held her bag in place. Quickly, she slid it around front of her and pulled a flashlight from inside.

She shined it at the corn, but the stalks had gone silent. Not a single husk in the ocean of crops moved; no sounds could be heard.

"Hello?" Dylan questioned. Her voice sounded the way it did when she answered a blocked number on her phone. *"Hello?"* She called again; a crackle of fear snapped the word at its midpoint. She knew what she had heard; something had been walking in the corn alongside her.

"Is someone..." Dylan swallowed a dry lump. "Is... someone there?" The few seconds she waited for a response seemed an eternity.

"I heard you!" she called out, boldly. "I know you're there, so you might as well... You should just..." When she'd planned her words, they were menacing, intimidating: a pitbull barking a threat. Leaving her mouth, though, the words were the unsure squeal of a scared puppy.

With hesitation, Dylan slowly moved her eyes from the dense cornstalks to the sandy dirt road at her feet. Something, or someone, could easily be just a few rows deep and remain completely concealed from her vision. Nervously, she looked down at her black Nikes and followed her own footsteps with the beam. The impressions in the dirt weren't deep, but the Swoosh marks from the bottom of her feet were easy to recognize as her own.

Dylan exhaled loudly. "Stupid," she mumbled and shook her head. She then teased her own flighty behavior. "Sometimes, I swear..."

Retracing her steps with the light, walking gingerly over them, she kept a close ear to the cornfield in case the noise started again. She counted her footprints, one by one, closely examining the area surrounding each one when, suddenly, her pointy chin dropped. Her free hand raised to quickly cover her gaping mouth. Spinning, she shined the light over to the masking stalks that teamed to easily secrete anything that may be lurking off the edge of the road.

"Oh, my God," she whispered. "Oh, no."

Pointing the torch back to the ground, Dylan studied wide boot tracks on top of her much smaller prints. They veered off to the side, undoubtedly into the camouflaging rows of dry, sturdy corn. Someone else had been on the road that night.

Whether she really had heard it or not, she didn't know, nor did it matter. When what sounded like movement came again from a few rows deep into the corn, Dylan sprinted fully. Without thinking, she burst down the dusty road, like a track star after hearing the loud bang of the starting shot.

She may have never moved as fast in all her life. A streak of fear, blazing through the night: a blur of fright leaving a clouded trail of dust and dirt billowing behind her.

Dylan never looked back.

13

"Hi, Dylan."

The two, seemingly harmless words crept over Dylan's shoulder and jumped into her unexpecting ear. The words arrived with such surprise the startled girl dropped the overfilled math folder she was stashing on her locker's highest shelf. Old assignments and worksheets dropped to the floor in tragic disarray. Students, putting away their things ready to head for home, stood shoulder to shoulder on both sides of her and crowded the already narrow hallway.

Dylan squatted to collect the disorganized mess and caught a glimpse of Mitch Wolf with a split-second glance. Beside her, he kneeled to lend a helpful hand.

"Sorry about that. I didn't mean to sneak up on you," he told her with regret. "You drop stuff all the time, huh?"

She gave him a brief glower before accepting his apology with a forced half-smile and nod. Rushing, she gathered all the loose sheets before the mysterious looking boy could provide much assistance. After him handing her only one paper, Dylan stood to shove them all back into the folder. Mitch raised invasively next to her.

"Are you okay?" he asked, concerned.

She stopped rustling papers and gave him an inquisitive look.

"I mean," he started, "It's just that you've been really quiet today."

Dylan raised her thin eyebrows, awkwardly.

"Well, you're always quiet, you know? Just today I've tried to get your attention a few times and you've, kind of, well… you, kind of, seem to be ignoring me." Mitch's voice trailed off lacking the usual confidence a teen with his looks and stature normally carried.

Without notice, Dylan's social avoidance defenses kicked in. Her mind was a hail storm of excuses battering her tongue. But, with the heat of the situation, the words melted away before they could be verbalized. What she ended up with was silence. Dylan looked away and closed her locker.

With her back to him, Mitch misinterpreted Dylan's awkwardness for a rude, symbolic slap in the face. Embarrassed, Mitch's broad shoulders sagged.

Sliding his hands into the front pockets of his jeans, he hung his head, and stared down at his brown, leather boots. "Sorry to be a bother," he told her while turning away to leave. His slow, dejected walk appeared immobile amongst the other speedy students racing down the hall, excited the school day was officially over.

Dylan blew away the curl that dangled over her face and tangled with her long eyelashes. As if forcing a square peg into a round hole, she pushed the words out.

"Hey, wait." The barely audible words left her lips timidly, hardly loud enough for even her own ears to hear. She watched his long, black hair flicker against his red and white flannel shirt as he walked between the last few straggling kids. Her heart thumped; a rush to her head caused a dizzy sensation and blurred vision. Then Dylan surprised herself...

With enough gusto to lift her to her toes, she hollered, "Mitch!"

Mitch.

It sounded so strange. She'd heard people say it. She'd even thought his name, in her mind. But never had she ever actually *said* it.

Mitch.

As it formed in her mouth, the *M*, the *I,* the *T*, the *CH*, it felt like a complete sentence. Her lips, tongue, and teeth worked together to complete the name without so much as even asking her brain for permission. They had gone rogue; they had betrayed her.

As his name floated from her mouth, she thought that maybe he wouldn't hear her. Maybe it hadn't been as loud as it sounded to her. Maybe she'd be safe.

Any hope of being able to just put her head down and pretend the absurd outburst hadn't actually happened was quickly vanquished. Just as her heels touched back down to the carpet, Dylan saw Mitch turn in response to her call. With an unsure swipe, he pulled his shiny hair behind his ear and, with his head forward, lifted his eyes to hers.

Watching him slowly approach, Dylan wanted to run.

She shut her eyes for a moment, hoping he'd be gone when she opened them. He wasn't. She looked left, right, up, down – but every time she looked forward, he was still there, still getting closer, still staring directly into her eyes. Rolling her ankles so she was on the sides of her feet, Dylan fidgeted. She bit her bottom lip, squinted her eyes, and twitched her nose, having no idea what to do or how to act.

Normally, if she was being stared at, she would leave or totally ignore the person. Neither was an acceptable option now. Not after her foolish call of his name. *Mitch.*

"Hey," Mitch greeted, looking almost as uncomfortable as Dylan was feeling.

The bashful girl stuttered. "I didn't mean to… I didn't mean, I mean… I wasn't trying to be rude. I just -"

"Don't know how to act when someone you don't really know is talking to you?"

Surprised to hear Mitch pinpoint what she had felt so accurately, Dylan couldn't respond and just nodded.

"I know exactly how you feel. I get that way too, sometimes," his dimples confessed.

"You do?"

"Yeah. Well, I *used* to. A lot." he explained, "When I was somewhere new, a place where I didn't know anyone, I would get sorta' tongue tied."

Dylan furled her eyebrows. "Sorry, but you seem so confident." Quickly, she looked away.

"Well, I've lived here my entire life. I mean there is virtually no one in this school that I haven't known since before I could walk." He laughed. "Well, you know what I mean. And, with new people, it was just something I shook off over time. I guess, I just got over the fear of it."

Dylan nodded. She pulled her phone from her back

pocket after feeling it buzz. Before looking, she already knew it was from Candice. The only other contact in her phone never sent unsolicited messages.

I'm running late, Dear. Got held up at the doctor's office in Greenville.

Having read the disappointment on Dylan's face, Mitch leaned in. "Everything okay?"

Dylan put on her best, fake smile. "Yeah, no biggie. My grandma is going to be late getting me."

"Well, I can take you." Mitch eagerly blurted, catching her off guard.

"Excuse me?"

"I can take you. Home."

She touched her hair, scratched a pretend itch on her cheek, checked the time on her phone. She was exposed and unable to shield her vulnerability. She needed an excuse. Pronto.

"Don't you have football or something? Practice? Or... *something?*" Her eyes begged him to say "yes", to suddenly remember something he needed to do. Something important that couldn't be delayed for even a second.

"I don't play football."

Feeling even smaller than standing beside the tall, broad boy already made her feel, Dylan cowered. "I just thought..." She made a gesture with her arms silently describing Mitch's dominating physical stature.

"I get that a lot. Last year, the coaches, amongst some other people, really pressured me to play." He looked down at his feet. Dylan suspected he might be blushing.

Dylan swayed, nervously. Her busy hands found a place to hide in the front pouch of her fleece hoodie. "Why *don't* you?" She watched his unusually shy face until he raised his eyes. In a flash, she looked away, dodging eye contact.

"Well, I've just never really wanted to hit someone. At least, I've never found it necessary to hit someone. Ya know?"

Remaining stoic, Dylan hardly responded. Just a short smirk and shoulder shrug.

"So... How about that ride?" he asked with gently raised, welcoming eyebrows. His voice was warm, inviting. Still, she wished he'd just leave.

Dylan hesitated until her silence became uncomfortable even by *her* standards. Looking at his chest, she cleared her throat and lifted her eyes to meet his.

"Sure." The word slipped out of her lungs, sounding like a cough.

A panicked rush of energy burst through her skin cells from head to toe. The sourness of immediate regret filled her stomach and threatened to climb to her mouth. Unusually, she was unable to open her Swiss Army knife of excuses and cut her way out of the terrifying situation.

"Should you text?"

Dylan, clueless, looked up again wondering what Mitch was talking about.

"Your grandma? Should you text her and tell her you don't need her to hurry?"

"Right," Dylan nodded, her cheeks pink. *I must look like an idiot to this kid*, she thought.

Strangely, it was the first time she could remember giving the slightest care what anyone thought of her.

***

A deafening crack of thunder resembling a shotgun blast boomed overhead as Dylan and Mitch ran across the soaked blacktop through the pouring rain. Like Dylan accepting Mitch's offer of a ride, the thunderstorm had sprung from nowhere, launching a full assault over the school and town.

"The blue one!" Mitch shouted, pointing at the small blue pickup sitting under a lamppost. The gesture seemed unnecessary considering his was the only automobile still parked in the student lot.

Yanking the door open, Dylan stepped up onto the passenger side floor, thrusting herself inside. Drenched, the fabric of her denim pants wrapped snuggly over her shivering thighs. Gasping for air, she used both hands to slick her hair back, as raindrops pelted the roof of the tiny, mid 1990s, Chevy S10 truck. The cab filled with echoing sounds like they sat inside a hollow tin can.

A thick mop of dripping hair dangled in front of Mitch's grinning face. He tossed it back with a quick movement of his neck. "Wow," he said, smiling. "We timed that perfectly."

Dylan smiled strangely at him while he turned the key forward waking up the old, rebuilt engine. Sputtering at first, gasoline infused the motor stubbornly as it settled to a mild hum. Mitch forced the long, stick lever beside the steering wheel into DRIVE and flipped on the windshield wipers. Dylan watched as they battled the harsh sheets of rain. The wipers were no match for the downpour, but Mitch took his foot off the brake and began towards the street, nonetheless.

Leaning up to the glass, Dylan intensely squinted her eyes. "Can you see the road?" she questioned, worriedly. Her voice barely eclipsed the pounding raindrops.

"Uh, kinda," Mitch replied, jostling in his seat as if he might find an area of the windshield that wasn't blocked by water. "I think as long as people have their headlights on, I'll be able to see them. Speaking of which," he paused to turn the truck's lights on. "There we go." He smiled casually at her as though he had just resolved the entire situation. "So, Dylan Klaypool, where did you move here from?"

"You need to go left here."

"Oops," Mitch said, flipping his blinker from right to left. "I guess I'm just used to going *right* here. I live that direction." Dylan sat quietly until he repeated himself. "Where did you live before here?"

She took a deep breath to prepare herself for the chore of conversation. If she concentrated, she thought she might be able to defy the odds and pull it off long enough to make it home.

"Evanston. Illinois."

"I'm not familiar with that town."

"It's pretty much Chicago."

Mitch's face went straight. "Oh, wow. Was it dangerous?"

"Dangerous?"

"Yeah, I've heard that a lot of people get shot there. Like, all the time."

Dylan squirmed a little, adjusted her wet jeans and pulled at her sweatshirt. "I don't know anyone who's ever been shot."

"Oh," Mitch uttered, almost sounding disappointed. "I've heard people say it's basically a war zone there."

Dylan shrugged her sopping wet shoulders. "I don't... I mean, I... Where I lived wasn't unsafe."

"Well, I guess people tend to exaggerate."

"Don't get me wrong," she clarified, wiggling in her wet pants. "If you spent time in the wrong... areas, it's probably worse, I guess... I'm sure you can *find* danger. Turn right here." Dylan cleared her throat. "If you went looking for it."

Mitch slowly turned right after stopping at the red and white octagon. "How far from Lake Michigan were you?"

"Not far. Walking distance."

"Weird."

"Huh?"

"Well, you know, here we are, like, an hour drive or so from Lake Michigan."

"Yeah, we are completely on the other side of it though. In another state. Another world." Her eyes drifted to the window beside her. Her blankly staring reflection looked back at her, equally uncomfortable with what it saw.

"What do you miss?"

Dylan clenched her jaw, wondering if Mitch would talk the entire drive. She remembered walking the shores of Lake Michigan, finding random items and wondering who had lost them and where they were now. The mystery that came with finding such things as an earring, for instance. Who lost it? Did she search her apartment for days looking for it? Had it been a gift from someone who loved her? Had she been walking hand and hand with that special someone near the water after a romantic dinner? Did a passionate, overzealous kiss knock it from her ear?

She then remembered the fishermen on the pier and how nice they were. They were some of her favorite people. She could sit near them and watch them all day sometimes and they never found her silence to be strange. They would let her sit for hours and never feel the need to pry or to ask countless questions just to fill time. Unlike Mitch.

She missed those things; however, she truly longed for one thing from Chicago. Maybe it was because of the memories linked with it.

"Pizza," she told him. "I really miss the pizza."

Mitch laughed. "Really? It's that good? The crust is thick, right?"

Dylan put her icy hands under her legs. "It's not thick. Well… the crust isn't thick, like doughy. It's… It's deep."

"Deep dish, right?"

"Not thick bread crust. Cheesy, gooey, deep." Dylan's lips held a pizza fixated grin. "Left here. And the house right -"

Mitch took the left turn and swooped into Candice's driveway before Dylan could even finish her instructions.

"How'd you know to pull into this house?" she wondered, with confusion.

Shifting into Park, Mitch slightly turned down the blasting heat that blew from the vents. "Well, the only other house down Cemetery is that boarded up abandoned one. I was pretty sure you didn't live there."

Dylan waited for a moment before pulling the handle to open her door. Until that moment, it hadn't dawned on her that anyone else even knew about the house. Of course, she understood it wasn't a secret, but to her it had seemed like her own private refuge, a place for her and only her. Maybe the boot prints that followed her the previous night wasn't someone specifically following *her*. Maybe it had something to do with the *house* instead… or maybe it was Mitch.

"Thanks for the ride," she said, hopping out into the

rain. From the porch she watched him pull away, tires splashing in the brown water that filled sporadic holes in the muddy driveway, and racked her memory… *Boots.*

Mitch wore boots.

14

As quickly as the pop-up thunderstorm had arrived, it vanished. Moisture evaporating off Dylan's wet skin pulled her body heat away. With a shiver, goosebumps rippled across every inch of her. She hung her soggy jeans and shirt over the shower on the curtain rack and rung her hair out into the tub.

She slipped into the warmest sweatpants and sweatshirt she owned and pulled thick, wool socks over her cold feet. Standing on top of the register in the bathroom floor, the warm air snuck between her toes and climbed up her legs, settling her chilled bones.

"Dylan?" Candice's voice was muffled by the walls that divided the house into separate rooms. The bathroom where Dylan warmed herself was a fair distance from the front door where her grandmother had entered the house into the kitchen.

"Dylan, Dear, are you home? I stopped and picked up dinner for us."

Not wanting to remove herself from the blasting flow of air engulfing her, Dylan hesitated. Demanding attention, her rumbling stomach loudly protested the decision to stay on the register. For whatever reason, she had not eaten much lunch and her empty belly won the battle of desperation with her cold skin.

By the time Dylan reached the kitchen and inhaled the smell of a fully cooked dinner waiting for her, the memory of being cold had faded.

"I didn't know if you like original or extra crispy, so I got a few of both," Candice explained while setting two plates on the table.

Dylan, wanting to help, pulled open the drawer left of the sink and removed two knives and two forks.

"Thank you, Dear," Candice told her, kindly. "Those plastic ones they give you are never strong enough."

Unable to resist the tease of Colonel Sanders' smiling face sketched on the side daring her to dig in, Dylan could hardly wait for her grandma to sit down before she was reaching into the cardboard bucket of Kentucky Fried Chicken.

"I'm sorry I couldn't be there when school let out," Candice apologized. "I was held up at the pharmacy waiting on a prescription. I don't want to go without my pills, or I would've just left."

Dylan gave a look of "no worries" to Candice as she dumped a blob of fluffy mashed potatoes onto her plate. She picked up the small, foam container that overflowed with light brown, creamy gravy and poured some over the white mound. Running down the sides, the thick fluid pooled on the plate around the fried drumsticks like piping hot lava rushing against the mud huts of a small, hidden village on an island in the middle of the ocean.

"We used to have a nice little pharmacy right here in Black Willow, which was very convenient. That one is long gone now, though. We had it when your mother was little." Candice talked while picking small bits of chicken breast from the bone with her fork.

Dylan ignored the reference to her mother, as the salty explosion of flavor dancing on her taste buds made thoughts of Jill Klaypool much more tolerable than usual. She took one of the buttery biscuits and dipped it into the whipped potatoes and gravy. Her fully stuffed mouth became the perfect excuse to not participate in the pointless conversation.

"We had a video store back then. I guess they don't even have one of those in Greenville now either, though. People just watch videos on the Netflix." Candice's ability to carry on a chat with herself suited Dylan perfectly. "Did it rain here?" she asked the chicken scarfing girl. "There was quite a storm in Greenville."

"Yeah," Dylan told her, "It poured," she paused to swallow. "It rained a lot."

"So, who was it that gave you a ride?"

"Um… Just a… kid from school."

"A new girlfriend?"

"*Excuse* me?"

"Girlfriend?"

"Oh," Dylan tore off a chunk of dark meat coated in the colonel's eleven secret herbs and spices, and spoke while chewing, too hungry to worry about talking with her mouth full. "People don't really say that anymore."

"What's that, Dear?"

"Girlfriend… Unless, you know, you're a lesbian."

"Oh," Candice exhaled. "I see."

"It's just that you can confuse people if you say that."

"Are you a, um…" clearing her throat, Candice touched her sternum.

"Lesbian?"

"Yes, Dear. A, um…" The word Candice was trying to repeat was one rarely used in the tiny community of Black Willow Creek.

"No."

"Very well. I mean, not that I… not that I… Dylan, I…" Candice looked directly at Dylan and spoke with clear confidence. "Dear, if you are, I love you exactly the same."

"Grandma, it's fine," Dylan assured the stuttering, gray-haired woman.

Candice continued her rambling. "I just want you to know that if you were one of the… One of those…"

"I get it. *Okay?*" Dylan begged Candice to get past it with wide eyes and raised eyebrows.

"Very well. Was it a friend that is a girl?"

"No. It wasn't a friend. Just a person."

"A girl?"

"A boy. A very nosy, annoying boy."

"I see." Candice began to inquire but stopped when she saw Dylan standing up with a cleared plate headed for the sink. "You're finished?"

"It was really good. Thank you." Dylan rinsed her plate, sat it down, gently, into the sink.

"You ate that so quickly."

"Yup," said Dylan, exiting the kitchen, leaving

Candice seated at the table surrounded by half full red and white Styrofoam and cardboard containers.

***

Warmly bundled in layers of heavy apparel, and energized by a full stomach, Dylan bent at her waist and studied the ground. She walked slowly, slumped with her hands deep inside her coat pockets, her hair contained under a bright red knit cap, and her warm breath visibly floating around her. She paced forward and back, left to right, from one edge of the road to the other with disappointment quickly waging a war on the small glimmer of hope that had brought her out to search for what would most likely not be there. Boot prints.

As logic had predicted, the heavy rain had wiped away any trace of the tracks left by both herself and whoever had been carefully following her the previous night.

From the corner of her eye, Dylan picked a slight movement at the end of the road. Slowly, a rusty, red pickup truck turned onto the gravel lane. Shiny and refreshed from the bath the clambering rain storm had so graciously given it, the truck lazily approached her. Rolling to a soft halt, it parked in front of the cemetery about fifty feet from where Dylan was scouring the dirt for footprints.

Discreetly, she meandered towards the edge of the field, kicking rocks and acting casual. With her back turned, she heard the engine stop and the door clang open then closed. Not turning to look, she hoped that she would appear occupied and too busy to be bothered. Instead, the short, slow steps that crunched the stones by the vehicle moved to her with an irresistible attraction. As he neared,

Dylan knew she would be forced to interact with him.

"Did you lose something?" asked a low, scratchy voice. The person cleared his throat and fought off a rippling cough that sounded like it had originated deep inside his chest.

Dylan peeked up at the gravedigger, shook her head, and gave a polite but obviously forced grin from one side of her mouth.

Finally reaching her, the old man huffed, noticeably out of breath from the short distance. "Quite a shower we had there," he remembered, hands inside his pockets. He quickly pulled one to cover his moustache roofed mouth, as he coughed again. "You weren't out here during that, were you?" he worried.

There was something sweet about the old man, something gentle. That night in the fog, she didn't notice the softness of his wrinkled face, the constant welcoming smile that permeated from it, or the sparkle that glowed from behind his eyes. It was the kind of twinkle she always imagined Saint Nicolas would have while enjoying cookies and milk after stuffing the hanging stockings of dreaming children. It was a charm, a wit. One Dylan was sure once cast spells on any young woman that crossed his path. Dylan found herself with an honest smile that she failed to hide from him.

"No... No, I wasn't out here," she told him, softly.

"I guess you'd have been swimming," he speculated through a low chuckle that quickly shifted itself seamlessly into a fit of coughing.

Dylan found his humor appealing, gave a giggle that left her body with a flutter. By force of habit, she gazed at the ground and eventually at the man's feet. His brown leather boots caught her eye.

Boots.

The cloth cuff of his army green work pants drooped over the uppers that were snuggly strapped to his ankles with laces looped through hole after hole. The leather over the steel toes had scuffs and tears. Dylan concluded that money in his house either needed to be stretched sparingly or this man cherished getting his money's worth for the things he paid for. His boots and truck both were far beyond a standard upgrade.

It couldn't have been him last night, she thought. Whoever had been trailing her was agile, quick, fleet of foot. Yes, this man was strong, obviously, but he was certainly not agile or quick. He was panting and wheezing from just walking to her from his truck. Moving as quickly as the person had last night would surely put this old fellow into such a desperate condition that hiding from her would've been impossible. His coughing would have given him away immediately.

Feeling unusually natural, Dylan felt the curtain hiding her well-guarded insecurities slip to the floor. It still created a barrier at her feet between herself and the gravedigger, but she was exposed, nonetheless.

As he looked to his right, she saw his attention was noticeably grabbed by the old abandoned house up the road. He held his stare on it, as Dylan waited for him to look back to her. When he finally did, the gravedigger's smile had been wiped away. With a solemn expression, he blankly contemplated her. After a moment, he spoke. "So long, now."

Slowly turning from her, he covered his mouth, hacking and wheezing, and leisurely walked to his truck.

Dylan watched as the old man, an obvious shadow of what he once was, pick a shovel off the truck bed. Staring, she observed him head into the cemetery and begin his chores without even a glance back her direction.

15

With her camcorder in one hand, Dylan twisted the long, folded legs of the tripod until the silver, threaded post spiraled the depth of the mating hole on the bottom of the camera. With one last, forceful turn, she nodded knowing it was as tight as it would get.

She popped the clasps on the three rods, so the plastic segments could release and grow the legs to their full length. Standing the tripod at the start of the second-floor hallway, near the edge of the first step of the staircase, she flipped open the flap on the side of the camcorder. The two-and-a-half-inch LCD screen came to life as the camera powered on.

Pressing a small, round button, she watched the black screen reveal the locked bedroom door at the far end of the quiet hall. Through her eyes the upstairs was pitch black;

her shoes below were unable to be seen. But to the full-spectrum, night-vision camcorder, it looked like all the lights in the lonely house had been restored and turned on.

She dragged two legs of the chair that she had carried up from the dining room along the uneven wooden floor, causing an echo in the otherwise empty corridor. After placing it against the locked door, she sat herself down facing the recording camera. She yanked one of her stretchy, yarn gloves off, slid her cold hand through her frizzy, hard to manage mane, and let out a sigh. Laying her palms flat on her thighs, Dylan closed her eyes and soothed her fluctuating emotions into a placid, crystal lake.

"I know you want to tell me about this bedroom, about something that happened in there," she announced into the blackness. "And I want to hear what you have to say, too."

Opening her eyes, she saw only a tiny red dot shining from the camera confirming that it was saving whatever it saw, currently a shy teenager sitting alone, onto the thirty-two gig SD card.

"But I realized I'm not being fair. I'm asking a lot from you but not giving much of myself in return. So…" she paused, rethinking what she was doing, "I want to… tell you about… me." She cleared her throat with a nervous cough.

"My name is Dylan Klaypool, I'm sixteen years old, and I'm from Evanston, Illinois. You may be more familiar with Chicago. I'm pretty much from Chicago. Well, what we like to call the Chicagoland area. I *did* live in Chicago until I was seven. A high-rise… fancy."

Waiting just a few seconds, she shrugged her shoulders at her own words wondering if whoever she had been getting whispered messages from cared even a little about her past.

"I just moved here, to Black Willow Creek, into my grandmother's house. Candice Smith is her name. Her husband, my grandfather, passed away several years ago. She's my mother's mother. Why did I just move in with her, you ask? Well… it's, um… It's, uh, complicated."

Flinching at a small sound, a tick, coming from the door behind her, Dylan's nerves squirmed under her skin. Quickly, she convinced herself it was only a natural sound coming from either the wooden door frame or the tongue and groove wooden floor settling into the foundation.

Dylan knew that assuming every sound she heard during a paranormal investigation was a signal or message from the dead is not only silly, but also detrimental to her own work. Being critical was as important as being alert. Otherwise, she could pollute her own research with misguided and erroneous information. And there was simply too much at stake for inaccuracy.

Her heels raised slightly from the dust coated floor, as she slid her fingers in between the chair and the backs of her thighs. Ironically, the darkness that was swallowing her whole body felt protective, like a mask or a veil. In the dark, she felt as though she had pulled the covers over her head, like she did when she was a small girl back in Chicago hiding from the terror standing at the end of her bed. Some nights, hiding under the covers worked. Other nights, it didn't.

"It started a long time ago… when I was little." She thought, silently, for a moment about those nights, those nights that she dreaded. The nights it didn't happen were sometimes worse than the nights it did. Just waiting in fear for it to happen could keep her awake for hours with frightening anticipation.

"I've changed my mind," she explained to the empty hall. "I don't want... I don't..." Dylan remembered Dr. Belmonte and how the educated head-shrinker made it so easy to talk to her. Too easy...

By no surprise, she felt a lump begin to build in her throat. It pressed against her thin neck from the inside, hard and firm, relentless. Choking it down, she swallowed, forcefully.

Lost in her past, Dylan nibbled on her thumb nail, nervously, then tore away dry skin from her bottom lip with her two front teeth. Pulling off a hunk still firmly attached, she felt a surging sting where the soft flesh was exposed. Spitting the slice of skin to the ground, her tongue picked up the taste of blood from the fresh gouge in her chapped bottom lip. The bleeding gash wasn't the only wound being opened that night.

"This is so stupid," she mumbled, second guessing not only her reasons for bringing up such a sensitive topic, but also her ability to do so while remaining composed.

Out of her control, the throat lump was back, this time with more aggression and determination than before. Dylan clenched her jaw, pressed her top and bottom teeth together with all her might, but her feelings magnified, boiled ferociously in her belly until they climbed their way to her eyes. Liquid filled them until the dam created by her lower lid could no longer retain its potent charge. A single tear seeped out, filtering through her lashes, descending her chalky cheek.

Gasping for air, Dylan froze solid from the startling surprise. The lonely, sad moment had instantly transformed into one of absolute terror; utter amazement.

A touch, soft and comforting, a hand reaching through the black, through time and space, gently wiped away the solitary tear from Dylan's unexpecting face.

A ghost had *touched* her.

16

Avoiding drawing attention, Dylan scooted onto the bench attached to the long, shiny lunchroom table. From her bag she pulled a crumpled and tattered brown paper sack and sat it next to an ice-cold Diet Pepsi she had purchased from the vending machine outside of Mrs. Whitbeck's room. Condensation dripped around the prints left on the cold aluminum from her warm fingertips.

Unlocking a clear, Ziploc baggie, she removed a beaten-up peanut butter and strawberry jelly sandwich. A stressful morning of jamming books into her backpack had taken a major toll on the two pieces of soft, white bread stuck together with the gooey substances. Luckily, she thought, the classic, timeless flavor would not be compromised.

Sinking her teeth into the crisp, deep crimson apple she

brought along as the perfect complement to her favorite sandwich, the ripe fruit melted in her mouth, as if she had somehow taken a bite from a bottle of apple juice. A sticky stream of clear fluid dripped down her chin from the sweet explosion.

Dylan's wishful antics of staying slouched, quiet, and letting her hair cover most of her face was normally a foolproof method of going unnoticed. Today, however, those trusty tactics couldn't prevent lunchtime from taking an unwelcomed and strange turn for the worse.

An overwhelming scent of tropical, salon-bought shampoo and conditioner rudely invaded Dylan's personal space. Swallowing a swig of Diet Pepsi, she sat the can down with a thud and gave a half-hearted glance to her left, feeling the warmth of another body sitting dangerously close to her. The person she found there was the one and only Carrie Holland. Right next to Dylan. Too close for comfort.

"You know, you're the only teenager in the entire world that drinks diet soda, right?"

Dylan couldn't help but notice, even envy, how precisely the blond cheerleader's makeup had been applied to her flawless eyes and lips. Dylan opened her mouth, trying to respond, but couldn't form even a syllable. With her jaw gaping open, Dylan watched Carrie's gang of popular female-tyrants swoop in around her. One sat across from her, another on both her left and right, and the surrounded Dylan could feel one hovering behind where she sat. Whatever was happening, wasn't good.

Making a split decision, Dylan decided to escape, make a run for it. Immediately standing up and pushing her way out of the intimidating ring they'd formed around her would be her best option. Carrie alone, she felt she could handle. Enclosed inside a circle created by the entire clique, vastly outnumbered, was another story.

Carrie quickly snatched Dylan's backpack off the table before the over-matched girl could get her anxious hands on it.

"Hey! Give me -," Dylan cried out, reaching for her precious bag.

Carrie slid several feet down the empty bench while two of her sheep gripped Dylan's sweatshirt and arms. The frightened girl struggled at first, but soon found her noodle arms stood no chance against the clutches of the gang members.

With a wickedly arrogant flare, Carrie unzipped the main pouch of Dylan's backpack. Her golden hair swayed playfully as her head tipped side to side with exaggerated curiosity.

"Can you just -," Dylan began to plead.

"I wonder what sort of things the creepy new girl keeps in her bag. What secrets does a freak like her hide in here?"

Childish giggles came from all around Dylan. She spoke up again. "There's nothing -"

"Quiet!" Carrie snapped at Dylan, her demeanor changing from insultingly mocking to harsh anger. "I'm looking for something." She held her sinister glare on Dylan momentarily before slowly returning to her unauthorized search of Dylan's private items. Digging deep, the popular girl poked her head inside knowing exactly what she was looking for.

Dylan jerked suddenly, thinking she might pop loose from the grasp of her captors, but their hold was firm and steady.

"Ah ha," Carrie blurted, her evil grin returning. "Here it is."

Dylan's stomach sank when she saw Carrie pull the SB7 from the bottom of the bag. Dreadfully, her limp shoulders sagged.

"Sherri, do you know what this is?" Carrie asked the girl sitting across from Dylan. The red-haired, loyal follower shook her head and raised her thin, plucked eyebrows.

"How about you, Jen?"

One of the girls holding on to Dylan answered, "Well, I'm just not sure, Care."

The tone in their voices gave Dylan reason to believe that this entire conversation may have been rehearsed on a prior occasion. Probably while in the girls bathroom in front of a mirror with puckered lips.

"See, girls, I saw this klutz with this thing the other day when she fell down. I went home and searched it. The SB on it stands for *Spirit Box*."

Dylan sighed, cursing herself. She knew that keeping her equipment in her bag while at school was risky.

"It's used to communicate with ghosts. Dead people." The leader of the pack stood up on the bench, raised the Spirit Box high over her head. "Hey, everyone! Come look at what the new girl has. She has a phone that talks to ghosts!" Carrie and her brood laughed hysterically with malice. "I guess she's friends with dead people since no one alive would ever talk to her!"

Thrusting upwards, Dylan's anger created enough strength to bust free from the four gripping hands that held her down. With one foot on the bench, ready to go toe to toe with her obnoxious adversary, Dylan was blinded by a whoosh of black, flowing hair. Looking up, she saw the long legs of Mitch Wolf standing on the table top.

"Give it," he commanded, with his palm out. His deep voice reverberated like the hum of an engine.

Carrie stared, defiantly, at the boy, her face straight. A large group of students had gathered around the scene, gawking and quietly chatting with hands covering their mouths. Clearly, it was the most interesting thing happening in the cafeteria at that moment.

"What's going on here, Mitch?" Ms. Castle called out, slinking her way between members of the impromptu audience.

"Are you okay like this, Mitch? Or should we wait for the rest of your fan club to show up?" snarled Carrie.

"Excuse me?" Ms. Castle hissed at the snotty teenager.

"Tamara -," Mitch started.

Carrie loudly cut him off. "God! *Really*, Mitch?"

"Ms. Castle," Mitch noticeably corrected himself, "Carrie was just giving Dylan back her things."

The lunchroom stared in silence at the boy and girl standing on the table. Dylan sat herself back down, unsure of what all was unfolding. What started as a bully taking something from someone now looked like a personal showdown between two students and a teacher. Tamara Castle stood firmly with her hands on her hips eyeing Carrie with malevolence.

Carrie glanced around the room at the crowd, then locked eyes with Mitch. With her voice low, she said, "One day you'll break the wrong girl's heart, Wolf." She tossed the Spirit Box into the air, carelessly. Mitch casually caught it in one hand with little effort. "If you haven't already," the salty girl added with fire burning from her lips.

Mitch reached down and handed Dylan the device.

Carrie climbed down, nearly bumped her body into the teacher's. Nose to nose, she looked the woman up and down. "I hear people say you used to be pretty. That must have been a long time ago, because I just don't see it."

Carrie smugly walked past Ms. Castle, grazing her shoulder against the woman as she went by. In a conceited mass, the group of elitists rudely pushed their way through the rubberneckers to join their leader.

Interested only in climbing under a rock, Dylan dove for her backpack and escaped quickly before Mitch or Ms. Castle could stop her.

17

One of the longest afternoons of Dylan's young, yet eventful life was finally over. After sitting on her bed and removing any ghost related items from her backpack, she was on pins and needles in front of the thin, fifteen-inch monitor of her laptop. All day, she had awaited this moment.

The infrared night-vision, black and white video of her sitting against the locked bedroom door down the road played while she leaned forward and closely studied each frame.

Her skin, pale and bright, glowed; her eyes, white and reflective, gleamed. The dark that impaired her vision that night was illuminated, radiantly. She watched herself fidget in the chair, listened to her quaking voice speak into the emptiness. Dylan was obsessing over one specific moment, but forced herself to sit through the video in its entirety.

Her voice sounded odd entering her own ears. No matter how many times she had heard it playing back like this, it still had a different tone than what she could hear in her head when she was speaking. Weird, is was it was. She couldn't imagine being a singer or an actress, having to hear and watch herself all the time. Gross.

Strangely, seeing the Dylan on screen start to become emotional had no effect on the Dylan intently watching for visual evidence of ghosts with her elbows resting firmly on the desk. The Dylan viewing the video was focused, determined, and had no time to feel sorry for the girl on screen. That sad girl in the chair against the wall began to stir, and Dylan knew it was almost time. The moment she was waiting for had arrived.

Almost completely blurring out the frame, a slow-moving ball, a bubble, clear and weightless, floated before the lens. It hovered, freely, away from the camera, down the dark hallway heading for the locked bedroom door. The on-screen Dylan was completely unaware of what was about to happen to her. Spectator Dylan held her breath in disbelief.

Inching closer, the glowing orb of energy pushed onward, until it finally stopped what looked like a foot or so in front of where the distressed teen was about to fail at containing her tear.

Just as the salty drop began to slide down Dylan's porcelain cheek, the orb glided to her, pressed against her face, and quickly - like it was running away from something - vanished to the right, off screen.

"No way," Dylan whispered with her hand touching her lips. "I don't believe it."

Sliding her index finger along the sensitive mouse pad,

she moved the tiny arrow cursor to the controls under the video. REWIND.

Again, she watched the orb hauntingly approach her and graze her left cheek. Noise from the rain outside filled her room, as her heart thumped incisively.

"This is crazy," she mumbled under her breath while rewinding the clip for another look.

Estimating, she figured the ball of light was roughly three to five inches in diameter. The way it moved was strange, creeping gently, hesitantly, almost afraid to approach her at first, then somehow finding the courage to comfort her.

Looking down at her arm, she pulled back the long, cotton sleeve that covered it. Every hair stood on end, hotly responding to the ball of light she was viewing. Never had she seen something like that. Never had she felt anything like the sensation of touch that night when this thing, this ghost, thoughtfully wiped away her tear.

A knock on her bedroom door nearly sent her falling from her chair.

"Geez," Dylan quietly complained, huffing to catch her breath.

"Dylan, Dear," Candice called from the hallway.

"Yeah?"

"There's someone here to see you."

Dylan wasn't even sure how to respond to those words. She couldn't remember the last time she'd even *heard* those words. *There's someone here to see you.*

Dylan could hear her grandmother's feet shuffle closer to the door. With her voice low, Candice whispered three dreadful words that gave Dylan instant heartburn. Words that held their own against any of the horrific things Dylan had heard in her life.

"It's a boy."

18

Knock. Knock. Knock.

"Dylan? Dear?" Candice slowly opened the door just wide enough to peek inside and witness Dylan closing her laptop.

"Yeah?" Dylan spun in her chair, crossed her legs hoping to look less frightened than she felt.

"There's a boy here. On the porch." Candice hardly verbalized her words. Instead just moved her lips.

Dylan gripped her forehead with her hand, massaged one temple with her fingers, the other with her thumb. "God, okay. I... um... I just... Okay." Dylan stood up and blankly stared at Candice. She tossed her hair to one side, then sat back down. "So, what – I mean, what does he *want?*"

Candice looked over her shoulder as if the boy were

sneaking up behind her to eavesdrop. "He wants to talk to you. To *see* you."

Dylan exhaled a long breath through puckered lips, and closed her eyes. She held both palms forward like a mime trapped inside an invisible box. This is no big deal, she told herself.

"Dylan," Candice said. "He's outside on the porch." The old widow signaled her granddaughter to follow her with her hands.

Dylan rapidly nodded, silently, stood up and grabbed her jacket off the bed. She heard Candice's voice echo through the house. "She'll be right with you, Dear," she hollered through the kitchen to the boy standing opposite the screen door.

Dizzy, Dylan sucked in a long drag of air, held it inside so the oxygen could absorb into her blood and provide some rationale. "It's no big deal," she promised herself. "It's just not a big deal."

After slipping her jacket on, Dylan scratched the back of her neck then reached across her front and nervously rubbed her left elbow with her right hand. Slowly, she made her way to the kitchen.

"Hey," she said to Mitch. The ultra-tight pattern of black netting on the screen door separated them. Candice curiously observed from the sink, pretending to be too occupied by the dishes in the soapy water to care what was going on behind her.

"Dylan," Mitch's breath formed in the chilly air with the sound of her name. "How's it going?"

Wearing an expression of discomfort, Dylan felt like she was forcing herself to speak. "Um… fine. You?"

"It's cold," he complained, coolly, hiding his plea to

enter.

"Let the poor boy in," Candice chimed in from behind Dylan. The aging woman peeked her eyes around her granddaughter's shoulder.

Dylan didn't acknowledge Candice's suggestion. As she opened the door, Mitch took a step forward to enter, but instead of letting him inside, Dylan exited to join him on the porch, closing both the screen and the solid, insulated front doors. Mitch exhaled, casually, like he knew she wasn't inviting him in all along.

"I just wanted to see how you were doing. You, um, you know, avoided me all afternoon," he told her, waiting for her to make eye contact. She stubbornly refused to.

With a shrug, she shook her head. "I'm fine. What are you... Why are you here?"

"Just with what happened. You know, Carrie thinks she can do whatever she wants. She never used to be that way. I don't know why she's like that."

Dylan bounced, slowly, on her toes still looking anywhere but at Mitch.

"Ms. Castle spoke to her after school," he added.

"*Tamara?*" Dylan quickly interjected.

Mitch cleared his throat with a gruff cough. "I don't think you'll have to worry about Carrie doing that again."

Dylan took a long breath, finally turned to face her visitor. "Thanks for... Well, thanks."

Mitch's face opened with a wide smile. "No problem. Hey, you wanna go to a Halloween party Saturday night?"

"Excuse me?" Dylan blurted out through an uncontrollable, shy chuckle.

"Yeah," Mitch said, tapping one of the pumpkins on the porch with the toe of his boot.

Boots, Dylan thought. *Large boots*.

"It's Halloween on Saturday. Couple days away, is all," Mitch reminded her.

"I don't, um - I don't do - I'll pass." Dylan tried to graciously decline the invite, but instead sounded awkward and unsure – rude.

"You don't do Halloween? You wouldn't have to wear a costume."

"I don't do parties."

"Not everyone will be partying. I don't drink either, so… It's really like a gathering."

"I don't… *gather*," she said, rolling her eyes, recognizing how stupid it must have sounded.

With her eyes at the height of his shoulder, she gingerly looked up at him, but he was facing the driveway, with cold, red cheeks.

"Look, I'm just not -," Dylan began explaining, but Mitch cut her off.

"Hey, it's okay. I get it."

"Actually, you probably don't."

"It's not like a date. I'm not, like, asking you out. Just a party, a get together. I thought it'd be fun."

Mitch, with his hands inside the pockets of his jacket, stood still, silent. Dylan saw him floating away into the sea, desperate for her to throw him a lifeline. But instead she matched his silence with her own, leaving him with no choice but to say goodbye and drift away on the waves of hopelessness.

"Okay, well, you know maybe some other time," he offered, unsuccessfully attempting to mask his obvious disappointment.

As he stepped down the warped stairs, Dylan could

feel the entire porch droop under his strong legs. Her cold dismissal of Mitch's friendly gesture hadn't been intentional. In fact, remorse of how awful her rejection sounded quickly flooded her, leaving her already pink cheeks blushing from embarrassment.

Dylan threw her voice at Mitch's back like a poison dart. "Thanks again for earlier." What was meant to be a sentence of kind parting words had a reverberating sting, adding salt to the dejected boy's already throbbing wound.

Before Mitch was even sitting in the driver's seat of the small pickup he'd worked all summer with his grandfather, and legal guardian, to save up and buy, Dylan was safely inside the kitchen with the door closed. Her nervousness manifested as strength and the door forcefully slammed shut.

Candice, choosing to ignore the loud bang, turned with a grin. "Seems like a nice boy."

Dylan huffed a sigh, gritted her teeth, and swiftly moved across the kitchen. She sucked up the sharp pain from smashing her hip into the corner of the kitchen table as she passed by it, hurrying to her room. Without stopping, she blurted out a single, determined sentence dripping with so much resolution Candice dared not challenge it.

"I'm skipping tomorrow."

The harsh slamming of her bedroom door was a noticeable punctuation mark: a period ending the brief, one-sided discussion.

19

Using the long sleeve of her flannel pajama top, Dylan wiped cold beads of sweat from her brow. Sniffling, somewhere between too hot and too cold, she struggled to pull herself awake and away from the dream that had disturbed her rest. Hazy tiredness distorted her vision, but she could see well enough in the darkness to view that there was no one standing at the foot of her bed. Unlike when she was seven years old, it had only been a nightmare.

Would they ever stop? Would she be forced to endure these dreams, these night terrors her entire life?

Pulling the covers up to her chin, the tired, frightened teen stretched her legs under the covers and fought to eradicate the negative emotions that always accompanied the haunting visions of *him*. The one piece of useful advice that she took from countless hours of therapy with Dr.

Belmonte was that positive thoughts have the power to push out negative energy. And Dylan was convinced if she let the negativity invade her spirit, grab hold of her, he might one day return, find her again, and this time refuse to let go.

It was early Friday morning. Earlier than Dylan would normally wake up for school, but her mind had crept to a point where sleep was a distant mountain range on the horizon. Reaching it seemed an impossible journey.

Lying awake, waiting patiently until she heard the Buick crunching on the gravel, Dylan finally got out of bed. Candice's Friday morning book club and coffee with the ladies at Carol's paired with the hasty decision to skip school would be the respite from the world Dylan knew she needed.

Home alone. It felt wonderful.

A hand-written note on a yellow legal pad informed Dylan that the ever-caring, always thoughtful Candice had a plate of eggs and bacon in the refrigerator waiting for her. Having never in her life had someone give her such attention, such care, Dylan appreciated her grandmother's consistent kindness. But in Dylan's confusing, hard-to-process world, gratitude was a foreign concept. And the barbed-wire, electric fence constructed around the girl's fragile heart made it as difficult to get out as it was to get in.

Kill today, she thought. That was the plan. Stab October 30th in the heart and sit by to watch it slowly bleed to death. After microwaving a cup of cold coffee from the long switched off pot on the counter, Dylan planted herself in the soft cushion of the sectional couch in the living room.

Clicking on the TV, she found a disheveled Peter Falk smoking a cigar and playing dumb with a suspected killer. Asking questions that made the interrogator appear clueless until, when his suspect was sure he was leaving, Lieutenant Columbo would turn with his cigar raised in the air and say, *"Just one more thing..."* The homicide detective's final observation would always give his suspect something to think about, a reason to lose sleep at night.

Of course, Dylan was reminded of another detective – one from her real life – Detective Miguel Rodriguez, Chicago P.D.

Rodriguez would kneel, look her straight in the eye, and pretend that her answers to his leading questions mattered. Still, now at age sixteen, Dylan wondered how differently, if at all, things would have gone had she just been able to find the courage to speak up, to tell him directly what had happened. If only the lovable Peter Falk had been on that case, then maybe…

Strangely, the bad memories of those intimidating interrogations in Chicago didn't spoil the entertainment value of the mystery program. The marathon of 1970's episodes of Columbo was precisely the sort of temporary escape Dylan needed.

After seeing the short, messy-haired gumshoe discover the truth about two well-planned murders, Dylan felt inspired, motivated to jump on the case that she herself had begun to gather clues: the stirring presence in the abandoned house on Cemetery.

Following a scalding shower, Dylan set up camp in front of her laptop. On the desk in front of her was her notepad and each of her pieces of investigation equipment. The digital recorder sat to the right: it had captured the initial message of *"innocent"* and also the response of *"no"* to one of her questions. On the left was the Mel-meter that had signaled a flash and beep indicating that something -

someone - had made physical contact with it. In the center was the Spirit Box that gave her the words *father, girl, window, house,* and *bedroom* that had led Dylan to the locked room upstairs. Above was the full-spectrum, night-vision camcorder that captured an apparent show of empathy when a tear was touchingly wiped from her eye.

She read the words on the pad, searching between the lines. A story, although only bits of it, was there. Minutes fell from the clock like orange and yellow leaves from the trees outside and drifted away in the unnoticeable passing breeze called *time.* Over and over, she played the recordings, watched the clip from upstairs, searched for something, anything she may have missed.

Hearing Candice return and stir throughout the house, slowly broke Dylan's dedicated concentration. Needing a break, she left her work behind and headed to the kitchen.

The bewilderment plastered across Dylan's droopy face was twofold. Not only did the time of 1:03 p.m. displayed by the green numbers on the oven surprise her, but also the fact that Candice had the kitchen door wide open, letting the outside air in through the screen.

"It's absolutely gorgeous out, Dylan. Sixty-four degrees. Might be the last day like this until spring. It's a shame you're cooped up inside," Candice said, entering the kitchen behind the awestruck girl. Dressed in jeans and a short-sleeved shirt, Candice wrapped her arms around her granddaughter. Dylan fought off the instinct to pull away for as long as she could, but eventually gave in to it, awkwardly.

"Maybe I'll head out. Get some air," Dylan said, stepping away. She moved quickly towards the mild breeze that was sifting through the screen. Maybe Candice wouldn't notice that she had prematurely pulled away from her embrace.

"Yeah," Candice calmly agreed, only allowing a slight bit of disappointment to escape through her tone. "You should get out there and enjoy the warmth while it's here."

Dylan formed a half smile and glanced at her grandmother. "I'm just gonna' head out. Take a walk."

Inhaling the fresh, mild air, Dylan let the screen door close with a squeak and a thud behind her. Off to the abandoned house on Cemetery, she went.

20

With amazement, Dylan looked around the room. She couldn't believe how much light on a sunny, early afternoon could creep in through the boarded-up windows. The house looked differently in the daytime, foreign. Unlike at dusk and after sunset, it felt unusual to be there: inside someone's house without permission.

Dylan flipped the kitchen light switch, like always, and proceeded into the living room where she had spent most of her time conducting her tests. She knew it was absurd, but still she treaded lightly, avoiding making too much noise as if someone were asleep upstairs.

A large, square television with a glass, convex screen displayed her reflection in the style of a carnival funhouse. Leaving lines in the dust, Dylan let her fingers graze the edge of a long, wooden shelf as she moved along the wall.

Picture frames and knick-knacks sat undisturbed, unaware that architecturally-savvy spiders had built detailed infrastructures connecting them together.

A girl, seated on a dock that protruded into a lake, wore a flannel shirt and jeans and smiled brightly at Dylan. *Class of '94* printed in gold letters on the bottom corner of the photograph looked dull under the years of dust that had settled over it. Dylan ran her small fingertips lightly across the girl's pleasant face. The photogenic teen's knees were casually captured under her arms that connected with locked fingers. Her hair, brown and curly, was familiar, and, though pictures can be deceiving, Dylan couldn't help but notice that the girl was comparable to her own height and weight. The only difference was the stranger's carefree, beaming grin – an expression Dylan wondered if her own face would ever learn to make.

Nearby was another framed photograph. The girl from the Class of '94 photo was standing behind two sitting adults with an arm over each of their shoulders. A family. Mother, father, and daughter. A meticulously decorated Christmas tree filled most of the background. Their matching, red and white sweaters gave a sweet touch of unity to the professionally posed image.

Dylan, picked the frame from the shelf, blew off the webs and dust with a firm, hearty exhale. Turning it over, she unclasped a series of tabs, then pulled the cardboard backing off. Out of the frame, the family photo felt and looked as crisp and dynamic as the day it was printed.

The family. One that had celebrated holidays and birthdays here. The family that lived here. This was their home. But where did they go?

Quickly, Dylan cranked her neck towards the staircase.

A noise from the second floor stole her attention. Holding her breath, she waited for it to happen again, but nothing came.

With an accelerated heart rate, Dylan placed the happy family back into the frame, firmly latching the clips on the back. Surveying the room, she heard the sound from upstairs again: a thump. Standing motionless, Dylan watched for movement while taming her vibrant breathing.

"Hello?" Her voice cracked, the word spoken so low she barely heard it herself.

There's no one up there, she thought. *No way.*

She gasped, still frozen, at the sound of something shuffling on the upstairs floor - feet shuffling! Dylan leaned her body, trying to get a look upwards without having to change her position.

All those night and evening hours she'd spent in the old abandoned house on Cemetery and never once did she hear something like that. Never did she get the sense that another person - *another living person* - was in the house with her.

Dylan grimaced, held her forehead in her fingertips, and rolled her large, brown eyes at her pathetic paranoia. Shaking her head, she bravely walked towards the stairs, placed her still trembling hand on the banister, ridding her mind of the ridiculous notion that someone was stalking her.

"Racoons," she told herself, convincingly. She let out a sigh and a small laugh, mocking her own foolishness. The idea that the old abandoned, haunted no-less, house in the middle of a cornfield, down a lonely dirt road was more frightening on a warm, sunny day than during a cold, rainy night was impossible. Nonetheless, Dylan found herself promptly leaving the property.

For the first time in over a month, Dylan's eyes squinted from the brightly shining sun. In fact, it had been so long, the pessimistic girl wondered if the star that pulled the rotating planets around it would ever be seen again. Now that it was back, she wished it away with burning eyeballs.

With a stiff, flat hand Dylan shielded the scalding, yellow rays from her face. Carousing down the road, it didn't take long before she spied the gravedigger's familiar, red truck parked on the shoulder in front of the cemetery. Although, this time, something was slightly out of the ordinary. Dylan had to double-take from disbelief.

Either the torturous sunlight had altered her vision or there was a small, blue pickup parked on the road next to the gravedigger's. Unless her eyes were deceiving her, she recognized that second truck. She'd ridden in it earlier in the week.

It was Mitch Wolf's truck.

Wishing she could pull the hood of her black, zippered sweatshirt up and magically disappear, Dylan tried to speed past the out-of-place burial ground, unnoticed. But, good luck was not a companion that often traveled with Dylan Klaypool.

"Hey!" called an excited voice from somewhere within the headstones. "Dylan!"

Hesitantly, Dylan stopped her attempt at invisibility, and turned towards the loud yell. Sprinting, with hair flowing like a cape behind him, Mitch sported a smile as wide as his muscular shoulders. Enjoying the sunny afternoon, he wore a t-shirt, sleeves extra short. Finally, when he reached her, Dylan could see the teenager's peculiar tattoo. Two animal tracks – paw prints. Presumably, wolf tracks.

"What's up? Dyl?" he asked, gleefully.

"Just... walking. Taking a walk," Dylan answered, repeating the abbreviated name – *Dyl* – that Mitch had used to address her in her mind.

"Why weren't you in school?"

"Um... Didn't feel well. Sick day."

"Well, you look good," he observed. "I mean, you look great. *Well.* You look *well.* Not sick."

Dylan now had two uses for the make-shift visor she'd made with her palm: blocking the sun and hiding embarrassment.

"Why aren't *you* in school?" she queried, instinctively changing the topic from her appearance, sounding unnecessarily confrontational. Any topic other than herself would have been more comfortable.

"It's three o'clock. School's out."

Dylan nodded. "Right." She looked off into the cemetery and saw the gravedigger raise his deceptively strong arm and wave. Timidly, she returned it with much less enthusiasm than he had shown.

From under her flat hand, Dylan peeked at Mitch. "What are you doing here?"

"Oh," he glanced back at the old man, "this is my grandfather. He works here."

Dylan suddenly understood why the man that mows the grass and digs the graves seemed so familiar to her. Although carrying an extremely lighter complexion than his grandson, the gravedigger shared some similar facial features. Mostly, Mitch's warm, welcoming eyes. "I see," she responded, putting two and two together.

"Once and awhile I stop by here, kinda' help out. Do you walk this road a lot? I'm surprised I haven't seen you strolling by before." Dylan didn't answer. Nor did Mitch give her time to before starting his next sentence. "So, I had an idea. I know you don't do Halloween. Or parties." He paused, lowered his voice like he was prying for personal, intimate information. "But, how do you feel about payback?"

"Excuse me? I don't…"

"Revenge."

Dylan stared, confused, at Mitch with her barely opened eyes, keeping her pupils safe from the bright sun.

"How do you feel about revenge?" he asked again.

Shaking her head, wondering if this kid could get any stranger, Dylan stayed silent.

Mitch kept pressing. "Tomorrow is Halloween, right?"

"Right… And?"

Closing the already small gap between them, Mitch moved in with a single, invasive step. "Around here we call the night before Halloween *Devil's Night*." His height cast a shadow that blocked the sun, as Dylan slowly lowered her hand from her forehead, embracing the relief his stature provided. Mitch's eyes sparked. "It's the one night that I can pretty much promise you we can get some revenge without having to worry about someone calling the cops."

"Whoa, wait a minute. What are you suggesting?" Dylan pulled back, restored the personal space that he was rudely stealing and felt the sun slam into her face again.

"Look, I'm not talking about hurting anyone."

"Okay… What then?"

Slyly, looking each direction, as if spies were all around hoping to overhear his plot, the handsome boy's face was veiled in mischief. "How about this? I'll be parked in front of your house at nine tonight. If you wanna come, meet me out front. If I don't see you... Well, then I'll leave. And we don't ever have to discuss it."

Dylan hid her intrigue from the unapologetically shadowy, tattooed teenager. The dark eyes she stared into suddenly seemed as endless as the cornfields that surrounded them.

"Just think about it," he told her with a final smile. "Oh, dress warm... And wear black."

Turning away he ran, full speed back to his grandfather and never looked back, leaving Dylan confused and uncontrollably curious.

21

"What's up, Dyl?"

The dull, yellow dome light on the ceiling of the high-mileage, blue truck barely shined enough to reveal Mitch's welcoming face.

To Dylan's own surprise, it took almost no self-prodding to get herself out the door that evening. The wild intrigue of a mysterious jaunt to incite revenge couldn't be tamed. Not even the layers of shyness built over years of avoiding such things was able to keep her at bay. Dylan needed to see what this strange, overly friendly kid had up his sleeve next to those wolf track shapes permanently traced onto his skin.

"Hey," she greeted him, wondering if he would notice how she needed to force a warm, friendly tone. Thankfully the light turned off with the closing of her door, leaving her hidden from him. In a matter of seconds, they were cruising down the dark, country road together, headed for God-knows-what.

The lightly sprinkled raindrops on the windshield twinkled from the headlights of a passing car in the opposite lane like stars in a far-off galaxy. As far as Dylan was concerned, they may as well have been just that. She had entered uncharted territory, going where no Dylan had gone before.

"Looks like rain," she told him, tilting her head in a futile attempt to see clouds in the night sky.

"Just drizzle," he comforted. "I looked at the radar, and I'm pretty sure the heavy stuff will miss us." Just like her, he wore all black from head to toe.

Dylan felt Mitch's eyes moving along the length of her body from her sneakers, up her black jeans, to her jacket, stopping at her black, knit cap. "You feel warm? Are you warm enough?" he asked.

"Um... yeah. Sure."

Dylan wasn't sure what to make of another obvious gaze from Mitch, focusing strictly on her thighs, until he reiterated his concern. "If you get cold, or think you will, I have a pair of sweats in my bag that you can slip on over your pants."

Relieved that the stare towards her body from a practical stranger wasn't wrought with inappropriate intentions, Dylan replied, "Oh... Right. Thanks."

"Let me crank the heat until we get there." Mitch reached for the dial, twisted it all the way to the red side. A blast of hot air gushed from the floor vents through the breathable material Dylan's shoes were constructed with.

"I knew you'd come," Mitch said, grinning,

delightfully.

Dylan felt her cheeks grow warm, as she returned a nearly unnoticeable smile, raised her eyebrows and shrugged. She convinced herself that it was the heat from the car and not a blush from being flattered that the attractive boy was so happy she had joined him for a night of promiscuous havoc.

A few moments of silence passed before Dylan felt her face return to its naturally pale, nearly glow-in-the-dark hue.

"What exactly are we doing?" she wondered, attempting to sound at ease.

"It's gonna be great."

"Okay…" She urged him to share the details with her through her impatient tone.

"I'll explain it all to you in a few minutes."

"You're not driving me off into the woods to chop me into little pieces… Are you?"

Mitch giggled. "Nope. I would never do that. I would tie a weight to your body and toss you into a pond."

Dylan, not fooled for a second, took a verbal jab back at him. "Right. The guy who won't play football because it's too violent is going to murder me."

"You don't think I'd murder you, Dyl?"

"I wouldn't be riding alone with you at night in the dark on an isolated country road if I did. So, no."

Dylan could feel a burning sensation building in her chest cavity. Different than the heartburn the acidic sauces some pizzas gave her, it was sour and seemed to escalate with each sentence she spoke. Sentences that, somehow, didn't contain broken, mumbled words, or stuttering.

For some reason, with the excitement of the unknown or just Mitch's unusual charm, talking with him didn't seem stressful tonight. Dylan, dare she think it, almost felt comfortable riding into the night with the gravedigger's grandson.

Mitch slowly turned left down a narrow road that looked to lead nowhere in the gloomy, rural darkness. While still driving, he flipped off the headlights. Without a street light for miles, Dylan wondered how Mitch could see anything at all.

"Hold tight," he instructed, leaning forward, putting his nose close to the glass. After about one hundred feet, he turned sharply into an overgrown two-track in the middle of a forest just off the road. When the truck rolled to a stop, Mitch turned the key, killing the engine.

The thick mass of tall trees surrounding them gave the scene an eerie ambience. Hauntingly, they towered over Dylan and Mitch on the bench seat inside the cab, where she could hardly see his face just a few short feet away. Watching while he had driven to this desolate, isolated spot, Dylan noticed there were no visible houses around, just trees and cornfields. If Mitch did want to kill her, he'd located the perfect place to do it. No one would see, and no one would hear her panicked screams for help.

Blinding her, the dome light came to life as Mitch opened his door. "You ready?"

Dylan silently nodded, excited, but hesitant, unsure of what she had gotten herself into by joining Mitch on Devil's Night. A girl not unfamiliar with taking risks, she normally at least was aware of what she was doing. This night, she had blindly trusted someone she hardly knew, and now part of her had started to second guess her judgement. Still, she willingly opened her door and stepped out into the forest.

Standing at the rear of the automobile, Mitch slowly

swung the tailgate down, trying to keep the squeaky hinge from making much noise. Reaching, he wrangled a blue, plastic tarp off from a bumpy white mound that rested on the truck bed. Pointing a thin, long flashlight like a magic wand at the stack of packaged toilet paper, Mitch let out an enthusiastic whisper. "Tada!"

The normally stoic Dylan cracked an uncontrolled smile. Devil's Night had just taken a comical turn and finally was beginning to make sense. She couldn't help but laugh at the outlandish antics of her partner in crime. "Oh my God, Mitch," she teased, her reluctance fading. "Okay. I'm listening."

Mitch peeked out at the barren, vacant roadway. Opposite the two-track entrance stood a cornfield, just like the one on Cemetery Road. Mitch stepped closer to Dylan, dimmed the flashlight, and spoke quietly and intensely. "Just over the hill, about a quarter mile from here, is Carrie Holland's house."

Dylan felt her eyes light up at the thought of what Mitch was about to propose. Emerging adrenaline worked diligently to diminish the potent bite of cold, night air. Mitch pulled two black garbage bags from his backpack.

"Have you ever done this before?" he asked, sure what Dylan's answer would be.

"I can honestly say I haven't."

He ripped open the first package of extra fluffy, triple-ply toilet paper. "After tonight, you'll be a real country gal."

Dylan smiled as Mitch filled one of the over-sized plastic bags with the soft, white rolls. "See, using this thick stuff makes it easier to throw."

"How's that?"

"Well, the cheap, super thin paper tends to break when

you throw the rolls. It's hard to get good coverage that way." Tearing open the second package, he continued explaining. "And, let's say we get blessed with some rain showers tonight. The thin one-ply rolls practically dissolve. These thick ones just get extra nasty, more difficult to clean up when they get wet. They stick to everything. It can last days, weeks sometimes."

After filling both thirteen-gallon, drawstring garbage bags with rolls of extra-soft, guaranteed-to-get-you-clean toilet paper, Mitch slung one over his shoulder and reached the other towards Dylan with his long arm.

Putting on an act, she gave a look of second guessing, but only briefly. Truthfully, she couldn't wait to grab it from him, march up that road, and give Carrie Holland a taste of her own medicine.

It was time to even the score.

22

Laying their stomachs against the cold ground, propped on elbows, shoulder to shoulder, Mitch and Dylan peered over the short stack of chopped wood in the Holland's backyard. A comforting scent of timber rushed across Dylan's nose. The pile of short logs protected them from the surveillance of white beams spying from the light attached to the side of the house. Warm breath rolled from Mitch's mouth in the near freezing air.

"That," he pointed with a finger inside his black leather glove, "is the sliding door that enters into the family room in the basement."

Dylan studied the large glass doorway at the bottom of the huge, beautiful home. Other than there were no neighbors, it made her remember the house in Evanston. The one she last shared with her mother and stepfather.

Nearly all the windows of the Holland house were black, save one lonely window upstairs that was bright yellow showing that someone was still awake.

"They keep their blinds drawn at all times. There's virtually no chance that someone walking past a window or door will see us out here."

"What if someone comes out?" Dylan worried.

"They won't." He reached for his phone and showed her the time - 10:08 p.m. "Her parents crash early every night. That's their bedroom window there." Mitch pointed to the window below the lit one. All the glass squares were sandwiched between fancy, wooden shutters.

"The light upstairs. Is that Carrie's room? She's awake." Dylan saw faint shadows moving through the curtains.

"Yes, that's her bedroom. She won't leave it until morning. She has all she needs in there. En suite bathroom, TV, computer. In fact, I guarantee you right now she's so focused on posting selfies and Snapchatting that I could break in the house, cook a three-course meal, and she wouldn't notice."

Dylan turned to look at her scheming companion. "How do you know so much about them?"

Mitch raised his eyebrows before quickly wiping his wet nose. After a deep breath, he told her, "Let's just say I've spent a lot of time in that house with those people."

"You mean with *her*. Carrie."

Other than a noticeable pause, Mitch ignored Dylan's comment. He rustled with the trash bag, pulled out four rolls of the bright white, cushy towels.

"Right here, behind these logs, is where we'll keep our stash. Take these." He handed Dylan two of the rolls. "This will also serve as our base. If you're in any trouble, if you get spotted or if you see someone, this is where you should come."

"How will you know if I'm in trouble?" Dylan asked.

"Well, for the most part, let's stay together."

She nodded.

"But," he told her, "if we split up and you need me, text me."

"But, I don't have your number."

"Give me your phone. I'll punch it into your contacts." Mitch held out his leather glove-covered palm, waiting for her to give him her iPhone. He glanced at the house until he realized she wasn't handing him the device.

"Dyl," he said, looking at her, "this could be important."

Dylan didn't give her number out to people. No one had it, and that was how she liked it. She hardly knew Mitch, which made being there in the dark crouched in someone else's yard, trespassing, about to vandalize their property even weirder.

Suddenly, she was asking herself why she had gotten in his truck at all that night. Her senses, her defensive instinct rushed back from the rock it had been hiding under. Dylan just stared blankly at the boy.

"Dyl, this wasn't some grand plan to get your number," he explained in a whisper. He sat up to take another short look over the top of the wood pile at the house. "Besides, I'm just going to put my number into your phone. If you don't ever text me, I'll never get yours."

Sniffling from the cold, Dylan kept her eyes on his empty hand, avoiding looking at his face. She could feel that the brisk air had turned her cheeks and nose pink.

Slowly, she reached behind and removed her phone from her back pocket. Feeling helpless, with no other option, she put it into his hand.

"Thanks," he said, holding a stare at her, waiting for her to meet his eyes. She didn't. Instead, she just waited as he pulled his glove off with his teeth and added himself as a contact.

"Here you go."

Dylan quietly watched as Mitch propped himself on one elbow, turned on his side to face her.

"Okay, Dyl, here's how you do it. You let about a foot and a half of paper hang loosely. Like this." He gripped a roll with a tail of paper dropping off. "Then, you just launch it as high as you can into a tree."

Dylan could feel her body begin to relax as she focused intensely on keeping herself poised. Mitch's number in her phone was no big deal. It was nothing. She was staring at a sixteen-year-old kid, hiding in someone's backyard, explain to her how to throw toilet paper rolls. It was funny, and if there was ever a time to let herself enjoy something, it was now.

Out of nowhere, came something that Dylan had almost forgotten could happen - laughter. She burst into a fit of jovial, thunderous laughter from deep in her gut.

"Shhh!" Mitch begged. "Quiet!" he whispered, loudly.

"Sorry!" Dylan blurted, followed by another outburst. She slammed her palm over her mouth, as her body rocked in silent convulsions. Mitch nervously popped his head over the wood pile to confirm the coast was still clear. "It's just so…" Dylan covered her mouth again, desperate to muffle the sound of her uncontrollable giggling.

Mitch held still, while Dylan slowly gained control

over her outburst at the situation's hilarity. She could see he was beginning to lose patience with her, as she finally reigned herself in.

"Okay, Mitch, I get it. We throw the toilet paper as high as we can and make as big a mess as possible."

"Right," he said, again sneaking a peek over the wood pile. He turned to Dylan with a look of determination. "Are you ready?"

Watching the moonlight shine off Mitch's glassy, dark brown eyes, Dylan could almost see her own face reflecting off them. With certainty, she clenched her jaw and spoke assuredly through gritted teeth.

"I'm ready."

23

"...innocent..."
"...innocent..."
"...innocent..."

Wiping sleep away from her dry eyes, Dylan played the isolated, two second clip of audio repeatedly. She turned the volume up, pushed her earbuds in deeper, and firmly held them, canceling any sounds that might hinder her ability to hear the wonderful word.

"...innocent..."

Surely taking great force to verbalize, the word sounded painful. It wasn't a casual whisper; a statement. It was a plea; a desperate calling. A cry for help. The tired girl held her breath, let the softly spoken word seep into her body. Goosebumps covered her skin under the sweatpants and hoodie she had slept in.

Pausing the looped recording, she nibbled the salty, crispy bacon from the plate that Candice made that morning and delivered to Dylan's room. A cup of hot, black coffee steamed next to the strips of thin, fatty meat.

Her body still longed for sleep, but Dylan's thoughts drifted to images of her and Mitch prancing and running through Carrie Holland's yard under the luminescent yard light. She shook her head at the strange act of social spontaneity that she had uncharacteristically jumped into last night. She pictured Mitch standing under the giant willow tree in the Holland's backyard with streams of white toilet paper surrounding him. The flowing paper glowed with an eerie beauty. A destructive scene that somehow had the peaceful presence of a jellyfish swimming deep in the ocean.

Mitch's smile topped off the scene as the sea creature wrapped its tentacles around the boy dressed in all black, his long, silky hair teasing her from under his cap. She hadn't laughed that hard in a long time. Maybe ever.

Coming out of the daydream, Dylan caught herself staring at her phone still plugged into the charger on her nightstand. What would happen if she texted him? Her pulse raced from the mere thought of it. She shook off the frightening notion with a chilled shiver.

"Don't be stupid," she said out loud to herself, like hearing it would be the secret to warding off the foolish idea.

"Ugh!" she growled, frustrated. She clenched her fists and flexed her muscles. "Don't be stupid," she repeated.

Swinging her knees back under the rustic, wooden desk, she clicked play.

"...innocent..."

Although disembodied and distant sounding, there was someone in there. A real person was reaching out to her, longing to be heard, waiting for the chance to defend themselves. The haunting whisper crawled over her senses. And, no matter how many times it played, the voice created a feeling inside of her that, if it wasn't so glorious, would have scared her to death.

"...innocent..."

The bitter taste of the bold java screamed, *"Wake up,"* as she slurped it under her perched upper lip. The hot liquid danced over her tongue with glee; the caffeine raced to her blood, surely to charge her cells with energy.

She pressed STOP, yanked the miniature speakers from her ear sockets, and minimized the sound editing software window with a determined click of the mouse. A large gulp of the bean drink went down like a slap across the face and jolted through her. Dylan sat up straight, ran her fingers through her curly, brown hair, and placed both hands on the keyboard, index fingers on F and J. Into the search engine, she typed *Black Willow Creek crime*.

A long list of pages instantly appeared on the screen. *Sperling's Best Places*, *Neighborhood Scout*, and *City-Data* were among them. They and several others that Dylan quickly identified provided the same information - that Black Willow Creek had a remarkably low crime rate compared to the national average. And, when it came to violent crimes, it had almost none.

Dylan jammed her fork, forcefully, into one of the pieces of bacon, then pushed the entire slice into her mouth at once. It was an unorthodox way to eat the breakfast classic, but it kept her laptop free from grease. Chewing it about two dozen times, Dylan finally slid it down her throat and chased it with more of the mood-altering brew.

She crossed her left leg over her right knee and let her foot bounce carelessly up and down. Returning to the keyboard, she typed in *Black Willow Creek history*. The plastic, lettered keys pitter-pattered rapidly under her fast fingers.

The first page she clicked on led her to an interesting story that quickly made her think of home. It detailed the tragic events of October 1871 in her birth city of Chicago, Illinois. Initially, the curious teen struggled to find the connection to her search until the second half of the story explained that forests from Black Willow and the rest of the county were harvested as lumber, sent across Lake Michigan, and used to rebuild the city after The Great Chicago Fire destroyed nearly all of it.

"Hmm. Go figure," Dylan mumbled to herself, before sipping again from her warm mug.

Dylan found the facts provocative, but they clearly had nothing to do with the boarded-up house on Cemetery Road. Hitting the back arrow on her browser's toolbar, she again scrolled down the list of search results.

She gulped the now slightly cooled coffee, each swallow strengthening her growing alertness. Pausing for a moment, she wondered if Carrie Holland had dragged her royal-self out of bed yet and looked outside of her palace. Forty-eight rolls of extra-thick, soft-for-your-comfort Charmin toilet paper twisted, looped, and knotted their way through every branch and bush on the castle grounds.

When the soft sound of dripping drops of rain began landing on the roof overhead, Dylan's chest fluttered and a numb tingle crawled over her skin under her cozy fleece attire. She downed the last bit of coffee, like it was a dose of liquid courage that made what she was about to do easy, comfortable, and… okay.

The rain rapidly picked up and was soon a full-blown downpour blasting the house, relentlessly. Spinning in her chair, Dylan studied her phone sitting on the small table next to her pillow. The opened clouds in the sky would turn the giant mess Mitch and she had created in Carrie's yard into an outright disaster. She smiled, fought off the hint of guilt and remorse that naturally tried to creep in to her thoughts, and clung to the other emotion she was feeling: joy. It flooded her, unexpectedly. Pretending she hadn't been looking for one, Dylan gladly accepted the gift the clouds had delivered.

Rolling in her chair, she glided across the room to the nightstand, confidently picked up her phone, and let her one-of-a-kind thumbprint unlock it. She couldn't imagine anyone having less contacts in their phone than she, but that never bothered her anyway. And today, there was a brand new one on the list: Mitch Wolf.

Her thumbs pecked away at the shatter-proof screen protector-covered touch screen, typing just two words that she knew he would understand.

Extra nasty.

Before she allowed herself to come to her senses and erase the message, she firmly pressed the icon that would send it to the phone most likely still lying next to a sleeping high school boy with long, black hair and a tattoo on his arm.

Like it was a stick of dynamite with a sparking fuse, Dylan tossed her phone onto her bed and pushed away from it, slamming the back of her chair against the desk.

"It's not a big deal. It's not," she consoled herself with

a calm whisper and a deep breath.

Scarfing down the final slice of bacon, Dylan wiped her greasy hand off on her thigh and stuck her nose back into her laptop. She shoved the idea of Mitch waking up to see her text as far from her thoughts as possible. The dusty corners of Dylan's mind were already crowded, packed to the ceiling with things she wanted to forget. But, this needed to get buried. Deep and fast. To expedite it, she clicked on the first link she saw.

Native American History in Black Willow Creek.

Stabilizing, her heart rate slowly tapered to its usual, healthy pattern. Words about the tribes that once flourished on the land now named Black Willow Creek jumped out at her. The images were downright fascinating. Beautiful people with dark eyes, jet black, flowing hair, and handsome, jagged facial features left her stunned. Masterfully decorated in feathers and beads, some had bright colors painted across their faces and bodies. The men appeared strong and mighty, the women meticulous, caring, and gorgeous. An image of a woman, holding a baby to her breast with one hand, and dragging a skinned deer with the other captivated Dylan. The page described a way of life involving community, family, and spirituality. The native cultures revolved around a connection to an ethereal world, filled with spirits that would protect and guide, but also ones that brought harm to those they visited.

Reaching the bottom of the page, Dylan moved the small, arrow cursor ready to click to the next one when something reached from the screen and pulled her attention. At the bottom right of the page, she noticed something she almost couldn't believe. Matching the design she had seen standing in the cemetery with absolute perfection, was an image of a drawing, a sketch. Thin black lines, curving to form a distinct shape. Wolf tracks.

Sending her into an instant frenzy, Dylan heard a terrifying sound from behind her. Startled from surprise, she nearly jumped out of her skin.

Laying on the wadded-up comforter in the middle of her mattress, her phone had buzzed. Candice would never text her while in the house with her. The contact labeled *Chicago Teen Crisis* would never in a million years send an uninvited text.

That left one other possibility – Mitch had responded.

24

The oversized, decade old Buick rolled to a gentle stop parallel to the street across from Carol's. "I don't want to pull into a spot and have to back out with all this commotion," Candice told Dylan, as she shifted the lever into Park.

Elementary school kids wandered up and down the sidewalk next to the restaurant and tavern. Other than a tiny, yet convenient grocery store that carried slightly more than milk, eggs, and a few other essentials, Carol's and the tavern were the only two businesses that still operated on the nearly deserted Main Street of Black Willow. The children all carried pumpkin-shaped buckets, pillowcases, or brown paper bags, excited to have them filled to the top with their favorite Halloween treats. Surely dressed as their favorite characters, most of the costumes they wore were covered with heavy, insulated coats due to the cold air that night. The rain had come to an end, but the wind and chill that accompanied it still laid claim to the small town.

"Do you mind just running in while I keep the car running? In case I need to move." Candice held a crisp twenty-dollar bill that she pulled from a white, rectangular envelope with *Bank of Greenville* printed boldly in royal blue on it out for Dylan to take.

"Dylan? Dear?" Candice said, vying for the girl's attention.

Dylan looked up from her phone where she studied the seven text exchanges she'd had with Mitch throughout day. "Sorry… Grandma. Sure, I'll go in."

Taking the money, Dylan popped open the passenger side door. After looking left and right, she jogged with short steps across the blacktop to the other side of the street and into Carol's, dodging a few tiny ghosts and goblins along the way.

The fact that the restaurant was nearly empty added to Dylan's level of discomfort gained from seeing April wearing a bright red wig and a teal bikini top. Her ensemble finished with a light turquoise skirt that went to the floor. The large pearls and clam shell on her necklace tried valiantly to distract from her cleavage and bare belly, but Dylan still had to fight not to stare at the half-naked, grumpy waitress.

"Welcome under the sea," April mumbled, smacking bubble gum behind her red-painted lips.

"Hey," Dylan replied, trying to smile. She noticed the thin, light hairs on April's arms standing on end. Dylan thought the woman must be freezing with such little clothing covering her.

"Lemme guess," April said with her hands on her hip bones, "you ordered the lasagna, bacon cheese burger, fries, and a large Diet?"

"Yeah," Dylan nodded, acknowledging that the mermaid was correct in her assumption.

"You know, you're the only person under forty that drinks that crap, right? Eighteen, twenty-seven." April pressed some buttons on the cash register before it made a ding and sprung open.

Handing the twenty to her, Dylan stood silent. April's question was the kind that neither required nor expected an answer.

"It's not quite ready. Have a seat, I'll holler when it's done." April handed Dylan her change and folded her arms, no doubt trying to warm herself.

"Boo," said a voice from behind Dylan, taking her by surprise. She turned to see none other than Carrie Holland lurching over her shoulder, inches from her.

"What's the matter? You look like you've seen a… *ghost,*" Carrie teased. Dylan quickly wiped away the look of fright that finding her aggressive adversary standing next to her caused.

Without responding, Dylan looked away then took a seat at a table against the wall. Close enough to the register to hear, she listened.

"What's up, Tramp? You're looking hot," Carrie told April.

The older girl opened her arms and posed, showing her scantily clad body off. "Thanks, Gorgeous. What about you? Where's your costume?"

"I'll change into it later before the party. I was waiting for all the brats to quit ringing my doorbell."

"What are you going to be?"

"A mime."

"Really? That's kinda' lame."

"I rock the black, skin-tight bodysuit."

April smiled. "Send me a pic."

"I'll post something later."

"Cool. Hey, I see you decorated for Halloween." April burst into a frenzy of laughter.

"Don't laugh. My dad is pissed."

Dylan's heart stopped for a moment when she swore that Carrie glanced back at her. She nonchalantly carried on fiddling with her phone and avoided any behavior that might make her look guilty.

"Whoever did that, did a great job. Dang, it was everywhere this morning," April recounted seeing the mess when she drove past the Holland's house that morning.

"Yeah, well it still *is* everywhere. And the rain fricking soaked it. That stuff'll still be there next spring."

"Ma'am," an older gentleman sitting with his wife called from across the dining area; his hand raised high to get April's attention.

"Yeah, hold on," the waitress snarled back causing him to grimace.

Dylan peeked at Carrie and April, inconspicuously, without raising her head from her phone. She saw Carrie hand the older April a wad of cash. Guessing, Dylan thought it totaled around one-hundred dollars. Close to it, at least.

"Did you get it?" Carrie asked.

"Yeah, it's all in the back. Go ahead and get it." April tipped her head back, motioning to the storage room behind the kitchen.

"Is it all beer?"

"No, I got your wine coolers, too."

"You coming to the party?" Carrie asked, walking past April.

"Maybe," April told her. "I'll see what next door looks like first." April tipped her head in the direction of the tavern.

Carrie dashed out of sight behind the red-wigged woman under a sign that read *Employees Only*. A middle-aged man wearing a hair net approached April and handed her a large, brown paper bag with a piece of white paper taped to it. The small, green sheet had *Candice* scribbled on it with a black Sharpie.

"Here," April called to Dylan without looking up at her.

Dylan took the bag from the dismissive woman in the bikini top and offered a soft, yet polite, "Thanks."

"Oh, don't forget this," mumbled April, annoyed that someone would dare order a to-go beverage. "I almost forgot."

Turning to find April holding a paper cup with a plastic lid out towards her, Dylan fabricated a grin of gratitude. Dark drops of diet soda covered all sides of the cold cup. Ice rattled inside of it as Dylan sat it down to grab a napkin. April held her hand away from her like it was covered in toxic waste or a terrible poison that would kill her if she didn't get it off quickly. Dylan wiped the cup clean, pretended she didn't see April's dramatic act of exaggerated displeasure.

When Dylan spun to leave, she nearly collided with a witch wearing a tall, pointy hat, a black gown, and carrying a long, straw broom.

"Oh, I'm sorry, Dylan!" the witch apologized. Behind the dark sorceress were two little trick-or-treaters. A short princess in a pink dress and tiny ninja whose identity was hidden except for a small slit just wide enough for his little eyes to peer through.

"Oh... I... excuse me," Dylan uttered, concentrating on the overfilled container of zero calorie, aspartame free, lab-created drink that was marketed as crisp and refreshing. Dylan could already taste the sweet beverage just from holding the cup in her hand. She would've been unreasonably devastated had it crashed to the ground and spilled before she could get her mouth on it.

"No costume for you, Dylan?" the wiccan priestess asked with a perfect row of bright white teeth emanating from a dimple infested smile traced with goth-looking black lipstick.

Unsure why the festive woman was talking to her or why she knew her name, Dylan paused long enough to get a decent look at her. It was none other than Ms. Castle.

"Nice get up, Tamara," April commented in a harsh tone that made it curious whether the compliment was genuine or backhanded. She reached and grabbed a dish towel from a few feet away and wiped her hands clean.

"I'm going to drive around back to load up," Carrie decided, walking up from the back room behind April.

Tamara took her eyes off Dylan and let her cheerful grin slide off her stone face to the grimy restaurant floor. "Carrie," she said, blandly.

"Well, well, well," Carrie taunted, stepping forward. Dylan turned, slightly, facing both the teen bully and the sexy teacher. Somehow, inexplicably, Dylan found herself between the two of them on both a literal and figurative

154

level.

"So, neither the creepy new girl or the old hag teacher decided to wear costumes this year for Halloween," snarked the blond, over-enabled and privileged girl, clearly implying that Ms. Castle truly was a witch.

Choosing to ignore Carrie, Tamara remained composed and shifted her eyes to April. "Look, kids," she gleefully remarked, "The Little Mermaid is going to get us a table, so we can have dinner."

As if there weren't a thick layer of obvious tension holding Tamara and Carrie apart like two magnets that couldn't touch, April casually pulled two paper kids' menus and one of the crummy tri-fold, plastic ones from the stand and pushed herself between them. "Right this way, Tamara. Hi, kids. You get a lot of candy?"

Both the princess and ninja gave her an excited, "Yeah!"

"How much of it can I have? Will you leave me some as a tip? I mean along with the tip your mother leaves me?"

As she watched the mermaid lead the witch, princess, and ninja to their table, Dylan could feel Carrie staring, relentlessly, at her. She knew Carrie wanted her to turn and give her the opportunity to say something nasty, something spiteful. But, instead, Dylan just pictured Carrie's house with every tree covered in sloppy, disgusting, soaked toilet paper clinging to every limb and confidently walked out of Carol's Restaurant without so much as a glance.

25

Everything Dylan had ever read about ghosts, whether fact or blatantly fiction, said the same thing: the veil that separated the living from the dead was at its most vulnerable on All Hallows' Eve. Halloween night. Tonight, she was banking on it.

With a single flashlight beam guiding her, Dylan carried the framed family photo from the shelf on the wall to the coffee table in the center of the living room. She placed it and the solo image of the teenage girl from the group portrait upright, facing her.

Standing in the dark, she lit their smiling faces with her torch. A breeze outside howled eerily through the slats between the boards that covered the windows, sounding alive, desperate. It gave the already menacing scene an intimidating aura that called out as a warning, a threat. A foreboding moment that Dylan quickly vanquished with deep, calming breaths. She reassured herself that her presence in the house was wanted by the spirit she'd found. The ghost trapped inside those walls had been reaching to her with purpose. It had welcomed her. It needed to be heard.

Activating it, she sat her digital recorder down next to the frames. The tiny, red dot lighting up confirmed it was working. Dylan clicked off the flashlight, placed it next to the other items, and stood in total darkness.

"I'm hoping to hear you, tonight." She spoke loudly and determinedly. "I think this is a great opportunity for you share your story with me. Do you feel closer to me tonight? If you try, you might find I'm closer than ever."

She waited an entire minute before continuing. "Is the person that has been communicating with me in these pictures?" Again, she stood silent to give the spirit time to speak through the white noise and, hopefully, imprint its voice on the recording.

"I want to know what happened here. I want to hear your story. Come close to me, like you did upstairs. I know you wiped my tear away. Thank you for that. Please, come close to me again."

Dylan slid the rubbery hair-tie from her wrist, wound it around her long curls, fastening it into a knotted ponytail.

"Can you touch me?" She unzipped her jacket, tossed it to the sofa. Pulling up her sweater sleeve, she held her arm out, exposing her bare skin. "Can you touch my skin?"

Sensing a slight change in the room, unsure what it was, Dylan pulled her Mel-meter from her back pocket and flipped the switch. Immediately, the REM feature began flashing and beeping, uncontrollably. The screen indicated an EMF reading of 3.5 milligauss. Other than a random spike when too close to a source of electricity, she'd never seen it that high.

"Are you here? Are you near me?" Her heart thumped, mightily, banging against her sternum. "Can you do something?" Her voice cracked from excitement, as she didn't want to miss out on a chance to make contact. Dylan knew she sounded desperate but didn't care. It could be now or never, for all she knew.

"Do something! Please, touch me! Move something! Find the energy! Suck it out of me, if you must! Please!"

Inhaling, trying to hold off screaming, Dylan's body quaked, as a cold sensation gripped her forearm. It was like ice touching her skin. The entire surface of her arm exploded with goosebumps and the Mel-meter jumped to an EMF of 6.2.

"I feel you! I feel you touching me!" Dylan's attempt at composure was out the window. It didn't matter. This spirit, this person's spirit, was showing her that it, too, desired contact.

"Are you the dad in this photo? The mom? The *girl*?"

When the word *girl* left Dylan's lips, everything changed again. The touching ceased, the EMF reading returned to a disappointing zero, and the REM sensor turned deafeningly silent.

"No... No... Wait... Come back. Please! Come back here!"

Like she was made of stone, Dylan didn't move. One minute passed, then another. Nothing happened. Feeling dizzy, tired, drained of energy and emotion, Dylan sat down on a chair, shivering. Her hands shook, profusely, while she closed her eyes, breathed into her nose and out through her mouth, like Dr. Belmonte had taught her to do whenever she felt overwhelmed and without control.

She had never had a sensation like the one the touch to her arm had created. She assumed that consuming too much alcohol would produce the same effects. What had happened? Did the spirit listen to her and take energy, life out of her? But for what? Nothing visual had occurred – no manifestations, no poltergeist activity: nothing. She didn't hear any footsteps, banging, clanging around, no disembodied voices, no whispers.

Wait!

During the elation, having such exhilaration from being touched, Dylan had forgotten about her digital recorder! Pulling herself upright from a lazy, weary slouch, the ghost hunter reached for the device.

Weakly, she held it to her ear and listened as she began to speak. Just hearing the audio of the moment gave her a new set of chills. Her body slowly began to feel normal again. Blood returned to her appendages to reduce the tingling, static feeling she had been saddled with from having the spirit grab hold of her.

Girl.

When she heard herself say it on the recording followed by total calm, she gasped. "What the hell?" she whispered.

Feeling one-hundred percent healthy, she stood at attention and rewound the clip a handful of seconds.

There it was! A voice.

"...ss...ssss...ss...ss...sss...ss..."

It was faint, soft, spoken like a secret between two people frantic to keep it safe.

"...he...ssss...me...ss...sss...it..."

Mesmerized, Dylan replayed it over and over, holding the unit against her straining ear.

"...he...ssss...me...he...sss...it..."

REWIND. PLAY.

"...he...ssss...me...he...did...it..."

REWIND. PLAY.

"...he...ssss...me...he...did...it..."

What is that second word?! The words were spoken through breaths, just puffs of air being forced out of someone's lungs.

"...he...ssss...me...he...did...it..."

That time she heard it. She knew what it said. *Hurt.*

REWIND. PLAY.

"...he...hurt...me...he...did...it..."

"Who hurt you?" Dylan begged the ghost to speak again. "Frick," she groaned, mad at her lack of equanimity. Quickly, she pressed RECORD, having foolishly begun to ask questions without it rolling. "Who hurt you? Tell me."

She waited.

"Is the person that hurt you in these pictures?"

Dylan heard a bang on the floor next to her, as her chest tightened around her heart. She had opened her hand, letting the recorder fall to her feet. Her question *Is the person that hurt you in these pictures?* had instantly been answered. Precisely when she finished asking, the flashlight resting on the coffee table lit up. Its yellow beam shined brightly, directly on the photograph of the family. With her jaw dropping, Dylan now knew that she was truly uncovering something important. A sinister tale was slowly unfolding each time she visited the house.

The whispers in Black Willow were telling the creepy new girl about a crime that had occurred. Dylan knew it was time to take this thing up a notch.

26

Can you meet me by the side door? Early?

Dylan read the text again. Dangling precariously beneath it was her one-word response.

Sure.

About twenty minutes prior to her usual arrival time, Dylan stepped out of the idling Buick and tossed a quick "Bye," that narrowly made it through the closing door over her shoulder to Candice.

Cloaked in a blanket of diffidence, Dylan placed each step gingerly in front of the last, confused at how conscious she felt about them. Never had she given a second thought to how her walk looked or her posture. Today, however, it seemed to matter. Keeping her head down, she peeked up just long enough to spy Mitch broadly standing with a large paper cup on each of his hands. She could tell by the color of the writing on them that they were from Carol's.

Dylan could feel his eyes on her, noticing her movements, her clothes. Something inside nudged her to stop and run away. But in bold defiance, Dylan fought against her panic and kept walking. Each step inched her closer to the boy with the wolf tracks tattoo.

A shell of faintheartedness was still there, surrounding her, protecting her infantile state of social exploration. But, it was cracking. Still not enough to let in anything dangerous, though. Yet, it allowed Dylan to look out and see the world, its inhabitants, and let the feelings it stirred swarm around her. Dylan could sense that she was slowly out growing this protective casing on which she'd always relied. And that one day, she'd bust through it.

"Good morning, Dyl," Mitch warmly greeted the girl who wore cold, pink cheeks.

"Hi, Mitch," she replied, giving him a short glimpse of her curious, brown eyes.

The sun had only just begun to rise, the sky remained dark. The light bulb attached to the brick exterior of Black Willow High produced awkward shadows on their faces as it collided with their hair, noses, and lips.

"I got it black. You seem kinda like a no sugar, no cream girl." Mitch reached out, offering her one of the to-go cups from Carol's.

"Good guess," Dylan softly congratulated him. The steaming liquid warmed her hands through the thin, biodegradable paper cup.

"It's a little hot. Don't burn your lips," he warned.

Taking a sip through the slit in the plastic lid, Dylan nodded, agreeing with his opinion of the temperature of the drink. "What about me tells you I take my coffee black?"

Mitch squinted his eyes, giving her a good once-over. She couldn't hide the smile that his cute, crinkled face gave her. "Well," he started to explain, "you're kind of under the radar. You don't do fluff; you don't do fake. You come off as the sort of person that takes things for what they are. The coffee is black, so you drink it black. Cream, sugar, those change the coffee into something other than what it is. And that's not you."

For a moment, Dylan digested Mitch's surprising and insightful observation. Without giving in, she challenged his take. "You hardly know me. How could you make such an assertion? I mean, look at me. I wear makeup. Isn't cream and sugar just makeup for coffee?"

Willingly accepting Dylan's dispute, Mitch's eyes smiled at her. "The way you wear makeup isn't changing you, Dyl. It isn't like the cream and sugar. It's more like, um, sun dried coffee beans versus beans dried in some machine somewhere. It doesn't change what they are. It just puts an emphasis on what is already beautiful."

There had been moments over the past week or so where Dylan had wondered if Mitch was coming on to her. Now, she knew he was. Exchanging texts over the weekend, vandalizing private property together had caused a shift in the chemistry between them. At least, from her perspective.

"I'm not sure that analogy even makes sense, Mitch."

"What? Sun dried coffee beans?"

"Yeah, sun dried coffee beans."

"Well... either way," he said before taking a gulp. He pulled on the door handle, held it wide open. "Come on. I'll walk you to your locker."

Dylan ducked under his long, extended arm, into the school. The warm air from inside the building blasted her with almost as much force as Mitch's unabashed flirting.

The halls were nearly empty, save a couple straggler kids in the school before the crowds to speak privately to a teacher or to utilize the library. Dylan felt an unfamiliar boldness brewing throughout her insides. Side by side with Mitch, she walked with her shoulders high, and her courage reaching a sudden boiling point, spilling out, surprising herself more than her tall, handsome friend.

"What's with the tattoo?"

"Excuse me?"

Dylan poked the boy's shoulder, playfully, with a single finger. "This thing. The tattoo hiding under your coat."

Mitch glanced at her from the corner of his eye, before quickly looking away. For the first time since she'd known him, Dylan saw Mitch harboring a tinge of embarrassment.

"Oh, come on," she teased. "A kid your age with a tattoo can't possibly be ashamed of it. What's the story?" For once, Dylan seemed to hold the upper hand in the awkward game the two of them had been coyly playing for days now.

Mitch bit his bottom lip, appeared to ponder whether to share what he was thinking with Dylan. "Well… It's sort of a strange story. I haven't really told too many people about."

Stopping at her locker, Dylan shrugged. "Hey, if you don't want to tell me…"

"It's not that I don't *want* to. It's just…weird. It's a… it's a weird story."

"I can handle weird, Mitch," Dylan assured him. "Were you not there the day Carrie showed the entire school my Spirit Box?"

165

He grinned, reminded of the day. He knew then how silly his hesitation was. "Yeah, I was there."

"I thought I remembered you being there." Dylan joked and opened her locker to trade one set of folders for another.

"You *thought?* I stood on a table, and you *thought?*"

Dylan laughed. "I'm kidding. You were very kind that day."

"Just that day?"

"Cool it," she ordered, sternly. "What's with the tattoo?"

Letting out a long exhale, Mitch stared at Dylan, and she, for once, allowed him to without quickly looking away. "I guess I can tell the girl with the Spirit Box."

"Bring it on, Mitch."

"So, it's for protection."

"I'm listening."

"My mother and father were both descendants of the Potawatomi nation."

"I knew it," Dylan whispered.

"Excuse me?"

"Nothing. Go on."

Mitch shook his head, ignored her proclamation. "I didn't choose to get this tattoo. My father gave it to me when I was eight. That's why it looks a little misshaped. It stretched when I grew."

Dylan closed the metal door, gave the dial on the lock a spin. "Why would your father do that?"

Mitch looked around, again hesitating to share. Dylan touched his arm, looked directly into his black, shadowy eyes. "Hey, you okay?" she worried.

He gave her a reassuring nod. "Natives believe, I've heard anyway, that there are two worlds. A world for Earth

People and one for Holy People."

"A spirit realm?"

"Yeah, I guess. That sounds right."

"Go on."

"My father's ancestry can be traced back to the tribes that lived here in Black Willow Creek. Um, since, like, the beginning of time. Beginning of record keeping anyway."

Leaning a shoulder on the long wall of lockers, Dylan raised her eyebrows, impressed by Mitch's account thus far. "That's pretty cool. I don't even know what country my ancestors came to America from. Let alone, which town they were from."

"Well, there wasn't a town here back then. Until, you know, the Europeans came and kinda'... well."

"Right." Dylan scrunched her face. "Yeah, not the proudest moments in American history."

"Anyway, my dad had something happen to him when I was little." Mitch joined Dylan by letting his weight fall against the locker next to hers. Both took sips from Carol's coffee before he continued. Their faces were close, the distance between their bodies narrow. Dylan sensed something electric happening in the small gap that separated them. She guessed it was chemistry.

"There is an old legend about some of the Holy People. They are there primarily to cause both good and bad things to happen to the Earth People." Mitch now pressed his eyes firmly against Dylan. Again, she didn't look away. "Some of the Holy People are called Skin Walkers."

"Sounds frightening."

"Yeah, they are almost like we would consider a witch, or a, you know, like a demon."

Dylan shivered. "Yikes."

"They're bad, right? So, my dad had something happen. Everyone thought he was crazy."

"What was it?" Dylan leaned in even closer. An unexplainable experience that made someone seem crazy hit close to home for her. She knew all too well what it was like to be sent to therapy to find out what was wrong with her just because her story wasn't believed.

Mitch took a long swig from his cup. Dylan could see he was grasping for courage to continue. She waited patiently for him to find it, not forcing, not trying to pull information from his clutching hands.

"He saw a Skin Walker," he blurted out before he could stop himself. "She was at the cemetery, actually."

"What? The one by my house?" Mesmerized, Dylan's eyes doubled in size.

"Yeah. She, *it* was supposedly able to change into a wolf or a coyote. Or, I don't know, a dog."

"Your dad *saw* this happen? A *werewolf?*"

"I – I don't know, Dyl. I've only heard this story second hand. Third hand, really." Mitch ran his hand through his silky hair. "And she wasn't a werewolf; she was a Skin Walker. It's different."

"Okay. Well, what happened?"

"Well, my dad freaked out – obviously. He was never the same. He was so upset about it, and no one would listen. No one believed him. It got to the point where," Mitch lowered his voice to a whisper, "people literally ran him out of town."

"Where did he go?"

"I don't know. No one knows."

"Your grandfather?"

"That's my mother's father. He married a woman who

was native, so my mother was half Potawatomi. My dad was full."

"But your grandfather doesn't know where he is? What about your mom?"

"She went with him. And, no, my grandfather doesn't know where they went. Hasn't heard from them since they bolted."

They shared a moment of silence before Dylan remembered why the topic had come up. "The tattoo?"

"Right. So, before they left, my dad gave me this tattoo of wolf tracks and legally changed my last name to Wolf. Apparently, it's some form of protection."

"From the Skin Walker?"

Mitch nodded, raised his eyebrows, as if her guess was as good as his.

"That's an incredible story, Mitch."

"Yeah," he exhaled, relieved. His natural bronze shade quickly returned to his blushing cheeks. Dylan could see his sudden change back to the cool and collected Mitch Wolf that she was accustomed to seeing. "It's wild, but I…"

"What is it, Mitch?" Quicker than before, Dylan saw him revert to a shy, vulnerable boy lacking self-confidence. "You what? You *believe* it? Your dad's story?"

He nodded, quietly, looking up from a bowed head.

Changing her voice to a casual, light-hearted tone, Dylan smiled. "What are you doing after school today?"

"Nothing."

"Can you come over? I have something to show you?"

Relaxing again, Mitch grinned, widely. "Sure. Yeah, definitely."

"Great."

Time had passed quicker than it seemed their

conversation took. Kids were filling the long hallway, causing a racket by slamming lockers and repeating backstabbing gossip.

"Um, I gotta' get to my own locker and grab some things," Mitch told her, standing upright and confident.

As he turned away to leave, Dylan called out his name, prompting him to turn around and look. His eyes seemed to smolder with an underlying fire of joy that he was trying hard to keep hidden.

"I believe it, too," she said, loudly.

Mitch smirked at her, gratefully. "See you in Mr. Amal's class," he told her.

Watching him walk away, Dylan saw Mitch in a way she had never seen anyone – as someone she could trust.

A comforting warmth grew in her chest, and she knew, finally, she had found someone that might understand her.

27

"Go ahead, have a seat on the bed." Dylan pushed the door of her bedroom closed until she was sure she had heard the latch securely click. For a split second, she stood facing the door wondering if this was a good idea. Dylan also replayed the look of shock she had seen on Candice's face when she and Mitch walked through the front door together.

"Why, hello again." Candice had said in that tone that people use when seeing a baby or a puppy.

"Hello, ma'am," the visitor said with his kind, inviting voice and smile.

When Candice had reached for his offered hand, Dylan could see the woman's wrinkled face turn a rosy red from flattery. It seemed women of all ages found the strapping Mitch Wolf easy on the eyes.

"C'mon," Dylan coarsely demanded, breaking up the

meeting before the useless small talk could build any momentum. There was work to be done. She clenched his sleeve in her fingers and pulled him away from the inappropriate admiration shown by her grandmother, leaving Candice flushed and battling heart palpitations.

Dylan turned, and without looking at Mitch sitting on her bed, tossed her jacket down next to him.

"What's this about, Dyl?" he wondered, while watching her fiddle with her laptop.

"Sit tight," she responded without answering the boy. Her fingers flowed over the lettered keys, punching in her password, granting herself access to the files she was about to share with Mitch. "There we go."

"Okay," she said, turning. "You might have to come closer. Here. Sit in my chair." Dylan signaled with her hand, rapidly, like a traffic cop grown impatient with a driver looking at their phone.

"Owe," he groaned, banging his knee on the desk with his long legs.

"Sorry," Dylan apologized. "I'm smaller than you."

Mitch laughed. "Yes, quite."

"Put these in." She handed him her earbuds. "Wait, let me clean them." She blurted, pulling them back just before he could take them in his hand.

"Dyl, it's fine. Just give them."

Dylan paused, looking at his eyes. He reached up and glided his hand through his drooping hair, retracting it from hanging over one side of his face.

"Okay… If… if you don't mind."

"I don't mind. It's not like you're dirty. Or diseased, or something. Geez." Placing the small, plastic speakers into his ears, Mitch turned and forced his thighs under the wooden table. "There. I'm in. Wait. Can I take my jacket off first?"

Dylan nodded, then used her hands to help the scrunched teen pull his jacket off his shoulders. His t-shirt sleeve slid upwards exposing the wolf tracks, fully. She stared at their fine lines. Clearly, the tattoo was not inked by a professional tattoo artist. But, the design was beautiful, drawn perfectly.

"What do you think?" he asked her, feeling her cold hand caress the ink.

Pulling her fingers away, Dylan gasped. "I'm sorry." She hadn't even realized she was touching his shoulder until his words broke her trance. "I'm sorry, Mitch."

"See how it's kinda warped now? I was a lot smaller when he did it." Mitch leaned his head over, trying to get a look at it for himself, completely ignoring Dylan's embarrassment. "See how it, like, sticks out right here?" He put his finger over one of the toes on the upper paw print. "Feel it."

Dylan hesitated before finally placing her palm against his dark skin. Lightly, she moved her finger across the spot he was pointing out to her.

"No. Right here." He put his hand over hers and moved it to the exact location.

Dylan felt an explosion in her chest. Her hand, sandwiched between the smooth skin on his shoulder and the rough, calloused skin on his palm, felt dainty and fragile. Mitch was strong, mighty. Dylan felt small next to him, but Mitch wasn't intimidating. In fact, next to him, she felt safer than almost any time she could remember.

"Feel it?" he asked. "My dad was no expert at tattoos." His shoulder bounced with a short laugh.

"Yeah," Dylan whispered, wondering if Mitch had the same tingling sensation running through his body that she did.

"So, what am I listening to?" He took his hand off hers, and Dylan watched the white hand print her palm had left on his shoulder slowly fade back into bronze.

Wiping her eyes, Dylan shook off the enchantment she was feeling. "I just want you to listen. Tell me what you hear."

"Okay." Mitch closed his eyes, waited for the audio to fill his head.

Dylan pressed the play button, stood leaning over Mitch's shoulder, her face just inches from him. Hoping he'd hear it, she held her breath and didn't move a muscle.

She could see him straining to pick it out.

"Play it again," he insisted, keeping his eyes closed, tightly.

Again, she pressed PLAY, having to brush against his body with her arm to reach it.

"Do it again. I can hear something. Just – just play it again."

Quietly, they hovered over the keyboard, as he listened to the few seconds of audio.

"Dylan, I hear a voice. Like, a word. Right? It's saying something. Do it again."

A fourth time, she silently waited while he listened to the recording.

"What… What *is* that?"

This time when Dylan reached over him to restart the clip, she found herself with a hand on each of his shoulders. She stood behind him, cheek next to his ear, his long, midnight-black hair mingling with her own brown curls. His scent overpowered her senses. *Boy*. The smell of boy danced through her.

"Innocent." Mitch's eyes popped open, as he declared what he had heard.

Dylan's heart leaped. Unconsciously, she squeezed both his shoulders, pressed her head against his. "You heard it!"

Pulling herself away, she stood up. Mitch yanked the buds from his ears, letting them fall to the keyboard. Rubbing his thighs on the desk, he struggled to face her. Twisting his torso, he finally turned enough to see Dylan standing with a hand on each side of her face, trying to keep her excitement to a level that wouldn't seem too weird.

"What is this? Where is it from?"

Taking a deep inhale, Dylan pressed it out through pursed lips, as relief trickled down her appendages. "I recorded that."

"You whispered it? Why?"

"No." She shook her head, sat down on the mattress. "That's not my voice," she explained. "It's a spirit – a ghost."

The girth left by Mitch's open mouth was matched only by his wide eyes. He sat back in the chair, raised his eyebrows. For a moment, Dylan thought she saw the symbols of disbelief trace across her friend. But, when he raised his eyebrows, leaned forward, and placed his trembling hand on her right knee – the one that pushed through the rip in her jeans – Dylan knew better. Mitch believed her.

"Where did this come from, Dyl?"

Relieved, she slowly found a way to control her joy. "The house up the road. Past the cemetery. I think it's a girl

– a teenager. I found her picture there. It seems someone hurt her."

"The abandoned house?"

Dylan nodded.

"How do you know it's the girl? How do you know someone hurt her?" Mitch's words spat out like rapid-fire. "What else did you hear?"

A tapping against the outside of the door caused both Dylan and Mitch to flinch.

"Dylan, Dear, will Mitchell be staying for dinner?" Candice called from the other side of it.

The two high-schoolers gazed at each other, saying nothing, until Mitch broke the silence. "Yes, Mrs. Smith. I would love to stay for dinner."

"That will be splendid," Candice quickly commented. "I will prepare enough for three."

"Better make it four," Mitch called out, all the while keeping his eyes firmly on Dylan's. "I eat a lot."

Dylan could feel the warmth of Candice's gigantic grin beaming from the hallway. "I will make some extra then. A boy needs his strength."

Candice's perky steps trailed off down the hall, Mitch took Dylan's hand into his own. She wondered if she'd ever shared a gaze this lengthy, this meaningful with anyone, ever. His voice was deep, serious, clearly displaying his interest.

"Show me more, Dylan Klaypool. Tell me *everything*."

28

"Let me get those," Mitch said, taking the plate and silverware away from Candice. "The chicken was wonderful, Mrs. Smith."

Candice sat back down in her chair at the head of the table. "Well, thank you, Mitchell. It was something I just threw together last minute, really."

"Well, I would've sworn you'd planned it for days."

Dylan watched Mitch rinse the plates in the sink from where she sat. She noticed Candice's obvious sense of achievement.

"We're going to take a walk," Dylan told her grandmother, then stood to collect the remaining items on the table. "Just for a bit."

"I'll grab our coats," offered Mitch, wiping his hands with the towel he'd found slung over the handle of the stove.

"Sure," Dylan said, smiling.

As Mitch exited the kitchen to retrieve both coats from Dylan's room, Candice spoke in hushed tones. "Well, Dylan, that is quite a nice young man."

"Yeah... He... He's cool."

"And if I know anything at all – *anything* at all, he's quite smitten by you."

Dylan laughed as she sat the three glasses they had used into the sink. "Grandma, someone in this room is clearly smitten with someone."

"Well, can you blame me? He's so handsome and polite. I'm not sure I've ever met such a gentleman. Especially, a boy that age. My, Dylan, he sure is odd."

Smirking, Dylan verbalized her thoughts without realizing it. "In a good way."

"Right. In a very good way."

"Ready?" Mitch said, sweeping into the room like a summer breeze. Wearing his jacket, he reached Dylan's out to her.

"Thanks," she said, taking it. Quickly, they stepped out into the cold and closed the front door of the house behind them.

Having walked at a healthy pace, Dylan and Mitch reached the abandoned house in no time. The only words they exchanged that didn't pertain to the events Dylan had documented at the old home were about the cemetery and the fact that the gravedigger was absent that night.

"That's quite a tree," Mitch observed, as they walked down the dirt driveway, and Dylan's flashlight exposed it in the dark night. "You can't really notice it from the road. I mean, I guess you can see the top of it, but not like this."

The black tree had several large branches stemming from only a few feet above the ground. They grew out, up, in all directions. Its mighty grandeur rose up and over the house like it had sensed the building's presence and skewed its branches to miss it as it grew.

Dylan's breath visibly left her mouth as she spoke. "Is that a -"

"Black Willow?" Mitch finished her inquiry before she was able to.

"Yeah. Is that what it is?"

"Yup. The famous tree that our little town got its name from."

"It's scary," Dylan confided. "It kinda freaks me out."

"I agree. They look a little weird," Mitch said, watching Dylan step up onto the porch.

"It almost looks like it could come to life, reach out and grab you. You ready?" Dylan took a long breath before thrusting her shoulder into the weathered front door while Mitch watched from the uneven porch steps.

"Dang. You okay?" Mitch expressed through a hand held up to his mouth.

"Yeah, I'm okay. It must have really stuck when I left last time." Dylan shook off the sting that raced through her skeleton from the jolt. With her hands, she brushed bits of splintered wood that had rained down on her from the rotting door frame. As Mitch cringed, Dylan slammed herself into the door again. This time it popped open from her weight and swung inwards. Like a chair being pulled from under her, the force of Dylan throwing herself at the door put her off balance when the support was no longer there. Down to the kitchen floor she went with a booming thud.

As a gritty cloud of dust settled over her, Dylan spit particles from her mouth in disgust. When she opened her eyes, she saw Mitch hunched over, his long hair dangling down towards her.

Brushing debris off her jacket, he asked, "Are you okay? God, you went flying."

From her back, Mitch pulled Dylan to her feet with both hands engaged with hers. His strength easily rocketed her light body upright, until it was pressed firmly against his own. Looking up at him, she studied his lips just inches from her. Only a moment passed before they both moved away, behaving as though they hadn't just shared a thought, a feeling.

"So, this is the kitchen," Dylan casually pointed out, wiping dust from her butt and thighs. "I haven't spent a lot of time in here, but you can see," she shined her flashlight on the open cupboards, "there is still food on the shelves. The cabinets are full of dishes and glasses."

Mitch took a thin, short flashlight that Dylan had given him from his back pocket and banged it against his palm.

"Turn the end a bit," Dylan suggested. "That red one can be finicky."

"There we go," Mitch said once it lit up after he followed her instructions. Joining hers, his yellow ray surveyed the forgotten items in the once state-of-the-art kitchen.

Hearing something, Mitch turned his attention towards it. "What are you doing that for?"

Taking her hand away from the light switch, Dylan raised her eyebrows and shrugged. "You know, I don't know. I just do it. Habit, I guess. Come on." Not waiting for him, she stepped through the archway into the living room.

"This is where the majority of the activity has happened," Dylan said, with Mitch tailing her closely after taking a few long, fast steps to catch up. "Watch here," she warned, grabbing his hand to lead him from danger. "That coffee table will bruise your shins for days. I still have a soft, brown spot from last week." Before Mitch could lock his fingers between hers, Dylan let go.

"Did you hear that?" Mitch spun on his heel, shined his light into the far corner of the room.

"It's nothing," Dylan assured him. "The wind, any small breeze pulls at the siding outside on that end of the house. Just wind." The darkness hid Dylan's wide grin but couldn't disguise the chuckle that came from her belly. She put her light on the startled boy's face.

"I guess that was funny," Mitch acknowledged, timidly.

Dylan continued the tour. "See the photos? In the frames?" She picked the one of the girl off the coffee table where she had left it. "Wait a minute…"

Watching Dylan stand quietly, Mitch approached her. "What's the problem? Dyl?"

She moaned, frustrated. "I'm certain I left both pictures on this table." She stood with her weight on one leg, hand on her hip.

"You mean this one?" Mitch slowly, trying to avoid any unseen obstacles, walked to the shelf. He picked up the frame with the family photo in it.

Dylan joined Mitch by the shelf, the top of her head level with his shoulder. Taking the frame from his hand, she studied it. "I'm sure I left this over there."

"On Halloween? The night she turned your flashlight on?"

"Yeah."

"You said you were pretty rattled that night. Maybe you put it back over here without even realizing it." Mitch tried to rationalize the picture being other than where Dylan remembered leaving it.

"Maybe... I guess. I was scared, so... yeah, maybe I did." Dylan turned to look at the coffee table, searched her memory, looking for an image of her carrying the frame back to the shelf. Nothing seemed to match with her recollection. "It was a hectic moment. I must have... I must have put it back here."

"Anyway," Dylan once again returned to her previous thought, "the evidence I've collected here in the living room eventually led me upstairs."

"To the locked bedroom?"

"Right."

"She's trying to tell -" Mitch stopped. He and Dylan quickly locked eyes. "Does the wind cause noises upstairs?"

Dylan pressed her forefinger against her lips, quickly moved her head from side to side. Both held their flashlights towards the staircase.

They had heard something. It was faint, but it was something.

Lowering her finger from the *shush* position, Dylan took a stark gasp before she could start the sentence, *"It was probably nothing."*

It *wasn't* nothing. It was clear, pronounced footsteps.

"C'mon!" she whispered, loudly. "Get your phone out!" Mitch followed behind a wildly walking Dylan, fumbling to unlock his phone using his quivering thumbprint. "Hurry!" she hollered, chasing the creaking boards up the stairway.

"Dyl, that sounded like someone is up there. Like a person is actually up there!" a nervous Mitch cautioned the unwary girl.

"It's her! I know it's her!"

"What am I doing with the phone?"

Stopping at the landing above the top step, Dylan calmed her breathing, and went back to whispering. "Is your flash on?"

"Is my *what*? My camera? Flash? Yeah, it's auto."

"Take photos, down the hallway. Take three consecutive shots, before moving positions. Try different angles."

"Alright," Mitch agreed, huffing from the excitement, standing at Dylan's side.

The hallway lit up like lightning with the flicker of the camera's flash. Once, twice, three times the blaring light fired.

"Is that you? The girl that touched my face the other night? Is that you?" Dylan called down the empty hall.

She could feel Mitch's eyes glower at her. She was sure he thought she was crazy, talking to a spirit, a ghost that couldn't respond. Dylan's guard was down, but she didn't care. "Keep going!" she barked at him, quickly getting back on task.

Three more bright flashes sparkled off the walls, as Mitch pressed the round circle on his touch screen. He rotated his shoulders, slightly, clicked three more pictures.

Click. Click. Click.

The synthetic shutter noise of a professional SLR camera mockingly sounded out of the Samsung phone's miniature speaker.

"Follow me," Dylan ordered. "Keep snapping shots."

Slowly, the transformed girl with out-of-the-blue leadership skills, led the rapid-fire photographer towards the locked door at the end of the dark hall. Dylan's narrow shoulders seemed wide slamming against the tight walls at awkward angles in front of the flashing light.

In front of the door, she stopped. Mitch stood behind her, his breath beating down against her hair. Dylan knew the door was locked, but something drew her hand to the knob.

Squeezing the cold, brass handle, she closed her eyes and whispered. "Come on. Let me inside."

But, before she could twist the doorknob, a loud, terrifying bang rang out from behind them, causing both to scream out from fear. They didn't need to look, both knew what had made the booming slam. The door to the bedroom on the right side of the hallway was open when they had passed by but was now firmly closed.

It had slammed shut!

Mitch grabbed Dylan from behind by both shoulders. With his lips touching her ear, he grunted a single word.

"Run."

29

With elbows spread to the armrests of a fancily designed chair far too large for a seven-year-old, Dylan intently watched Dr. Margaret Belmonte stare through her oversized eyewear frames. Even from the sixteenth floor, honking cars could be heard through the open window fighting through the traffic on Michigan Avenue a block away.

"Would you like another donut hole? There is a cherry one left." Dr. Belmonte held the small plate towards the child with a warm smile. It was one of the only times Dylan had seen the doctor with a joyful expression - as forced as it was.

"No, thank you," Dylan replied with her tiny voice, barely loud enough to reach across the small gap that separated her from her therapist.

"Very well." The woman crossed her legs, opened her notepad, and stuck the end of her pen between her bright, white teeth. The smile was gone, replaced comfortably with a prying squint.

"Dylan, for the rest of today's session, I'm going to go over some of what you've told me in the last month."

The young girl watched the doctor's lips form words in an odd fashion. Her pronunciation of letters, syllables was strange, different than how most of the people Dylan had met in her young life spoke. At their first session, Dylan giggled whenever Dr. Belmonte said anything. But, now she was more amused than humored by the odd speech pattern.

"I'm going to ask you some questions about things we've already covered. So, your answers might be things you've already told me. But, I'd like you to pretend that I don't know any of it and tell me like we've just met. Can you do that, Dylan?"

"Okay," Dylan mumbled with a slight nod of her head.

"And may I say that you're doing a wonderful job, Dylan. Soon, you'll be brave enough to talk to other people, too. Your mother and father miss hearing your voice. I'm sure your teacher at school does, as well."

Dylan shifted in the chair. The fabric it was covered with was beautifully decorated with bright pink and red flowers, but the seat was firm and the back was too straight. Dylan almost felt as though she was leaning forward.

"What has been happening at night? In your room when you're in your bed. Who comes to see you?"

Dylan sniffled, traced the flowers on the chair with her small fingers. *"A man."*

"Do you recognize the man?"

"No."

"What does the man look like, Dylan?"

"He... He... doesn't have a face."

Dr. Belmonte scribbled something onto her pad of paper, narrowed her eyes, peeked at Dylan from under her eye lashes. *"Is he wearing a mask?"*

Dylan shook her head.

"Tell me, Dylan. Use words."

"No... He's blank."

"His face is blank?"

"He's all blank."

Silently, the doctor jotted a lengthy set of notes, while Dylan watched. After finishing, the educated woman looked up with gentle eyes. *"Why does he visit you, Dylan?"*

"He tells me things."

"What things, Sweetheart?"

"I can't hear him. He whispers. It's too soft for me to hear."

"And then what?"

"I ask him to say it louder." Dylan held up her hands like she was peeking over a fence. *"Then he crouches, like this, at the end of my bed to hide from me, but I can still see him."*

"Does the man ever touch you?" Dr. Belmonte leaned forward, eager to reconfirm what the little girl who had stopped talking eight weeks ago told her during previous sessions.

"He pulls on my feet. I can feel him sometimes when he's crouched down."

"Does he ever hurt you?"

Dylan nodded.

"Words, Dylan."

"He scratches my legs and sometimes my tummy."

Again, the doctor wrote on the pad. "How long does he stay, Dylan?"

"When I sit up to look at him, he's always gone." Dylan paused while the woman circled something on the paper she was holding. *"Dr. Belmonte?"*

"Yes, Dylan."

"Can I have the donut hole now? The cherry one?"

"Sure." Dr. Belmonte handed the round cake ball with pink speckles on it to her. *"Dylan, how would you describe your father to me?"*

Chewing the dry, cherry flavored donut, Dylan murmured. *"He's nice. Can I have one of your cans of pop?"*

"It's diet. Do you like diet?"

"Yes, I do."

"He's nice to Mommy?"

"Yeah."

"He's nice to you?"

"Yeah."

"Okay, Dylan, that's enough for today."

30

Dylan sat up, stared at the foot of her bed with the lights still off, and told herself there was nothing to worry about, that she was alone, that it was only a dream. While she had slept, however, he was as real as her, as real as he was when she was little - as real as the problems he had brought into her life. During slumber, she could feel him watching her, touching her legs. She could hear his haunting whispers, too low to decipher, but too intriguing to ignore. Like he did in Chicago, his memory tortured her in Black Willow.

Freely, she dropped her upper body back to the mattress, her head nestled into the indentation in the pillow it had formed overnight. Her chest moved up and down, as thoughts of her father pushed to the front of her mind, screaming to be viewed, remembered.

Rolling to her side, she saw a small light blinking

through the tousled hair that covered her face. With a gust of morning breath, she blew the ruffled curls away and reached for her phone. The red, block numbers of her alarm clock blared 6:06 a.m. directly into her weary eyes. She was nearly blinded when she touched the screen, lighting up her phone. She had a text waiting to be read from 3:28 that morning.

Give Grandma a break. Let me pick you up for school.

Holding the device in her right hand, she typed with one thumb.

Okay.

Within seconds, Mitch replied.

I might be running behind schedule. But I'll be there.

Dylan pushed the blankets off until they piled up on the floor. Stretching the elastic ankles, she forced each leg of her sweats up over her calves. With just the light from her phone, she inspected the skin on her legs. Her heart still beat a clip just above what it should, as she ran her fingers over them, just to be certain. Dropping the phone, she put both hands under her shirt, touched her stomach and sides before rolling her eyes and sighing.

"Dream, Dummy. It was a dream."

An hour later, Dylan was climbing into Mitch Wolf's blue pickup. "Hey," she told him, purposely making eye contact.

"Look," Mitch blurted, skipping morning pleasantries, and shoving his phone into her lap.

"It's locked," she pointed out, staring at the request for a passcode.

"Here." Mitch reached over, pressed his thumb on the pad. "Scroll."

Dylan flipped through the photos Mitch had taken in

the house the previous night. "What? Did you get something?" Back and forth she slid the pictures, nothing jumping out at her.

"The very first set of three. Right when we reached the top."

Rapidly, she pushed the pictures to the left until she arrived at the first set. Carefully, she looked them over, flipping between them. "What am I looking at?" she asked, perplexed at how excited Mitch's voice sounded.

"What do you see in the first one?" Mitch tried to keep his eyes on the road but found himself alternating his concentration between it and his passenger.

"Um… I see the hall, my shadow."

"Next one?"

"Again, just the hall and my shadow." Dylan zoomed in, studied each pixel for anomalies, orbs, anything that might be evidence of a paranormal presence.

"Go to the third. What is different?"

For a moment, Dylan was quiet, looking intently at the photo. "Well, I see an empty hallway, my shadow again. And, of course, your shadow is now in this one, too. But, I'm not seeing what the big deal is."

"Dyl, I was standing to your left, slightly *behind* you, which is why your body casts a shadow in the pictures."

"I get that, but - Wait!"

Mitch happily pounded his palm on the steering wheel, knowing that Dylan was finally seeing it.

Dylan gulped a large breath. "You were obviously *behind* the camera, *behind* the flash! This cannot be your shadow in the third picture!"

"We got her, Dyl! We got a picture of her!"

Her jaw hung open, as Dylan stared at the image with

her heart pounding. Emotion stirred inside; her eyes welled with liquid, but her lower lids held it back. The picture was incredible. The shadow was distorted; it could have been anyone, but she knew it could not have been Mitch. It really was her, the girl. The ghost who needed help.

She unclicked her seat belt, slid across the bench seat, pressing against her chauffeur, holding the phone so they both could see.

"Whoa," Mitch said, steering the vehicle back straight after Dylan's unexpected crowding of him caused a swerve into the opposite lane of Main Street.

"This - is amazing," Dylan said, continuously swiping from picture three to picture two and back again. The mysterious shadow came and went with each swipe. "I'm sending these to myself."

"Yeah, you should. I was going to send them, but I wanted to be with you when you saw it."

Dylan pressed the message icon on the Android software. She touched the string of messages that were between herself and Mitch, attached the images, and watched them send. Immediately, she felt her phone buzz in her jeans. When the phone returned to the text page, Dylan noticed something. A string of texts, a conversation between Mitch and a contact called Tamara. It had to be none other than Ms. Castle. It seemed a little off; a student texting with his teacher. But, the explosion of joy from the shadow figure captured in Mitch's pictures was too powerful to be diminished by something so trivial.

"When did you notice it?" Dylan asked with anticipation and handed Mitch his phone.

"Right when I texted you in the middle of the night. That door slam," Mitch sighed, "freaked us out so much.

We didn't even think to check the photos after we sprinted out of there. I woke up around three, couldn't sleep, and then remembered we never even looked at them."

"Wow, this is such a big deal. She was with us last night. She's there. She must be trapped or stuck - something." Dylan now sifted through the same images on her own phone.

"So, what's next?"

Dylan raised her eyes to Mitch, while he pulled into the student lot and stopped the truck.

"Whatever you're planning, I'd like to help," he offered her. When she stayed quiet, he made a reassuring promise. "Look, Dyl, this is *your* thing; *you're* the boss. Whatever *you* say goes. But, I'd really love to be a part of this. I'd love to help if you'll let me."

She didn't even need to process what he'd said. "Sure, Mitch. I would really like that."

***

Like a helium filled balloon, Dylan floated to her locker, the coiled string grazing the floor below her. She hardly noticed Ms. Castle say, "Good morning," in her hot pink skirt-suit, as she passed.

So much had happened since she discovered the message *"innocent"* in the form of electronic voice phenomena on her digital recorder. That abandoned house in the Black Willow Creek cornfields had witnessed something tragic. Dylan had a firm grasp of what tragedy could do to a family, how it can rip it to pieces without leaving even a shred of anything recognizable. The tragedy expunged on her own family, terrible circumstances that derailed a family destined for generations of happiness, was something Dylan had long focused on correcting.

Yet, the girl in the house down the road had quickly become an obsession, one that walked hand and hand with her life's goal: proving the existence of spirits with irrefutable evidence. That was the only way she believed she could rest easy. The only way peace would ever return to her life.

She spied the folded, white sheet of paper from the far end of the hall. But, until she was closer, she didn't realize it was her locker that it hung from. Slowly, Dylan pulled it from the slot created by the tall, narrow door.

The hallway was clearing out as kids were rushing off to first period. Too curious to wait until her locker was open, Dylan unfolded the lonely sheet. Black, typed letters, not from a computer, but what looked like a typewriter greeted her curious eyes. As she read, an icy breeze seemed to swallow her whole.

I've been watching. I see how close you're getting. Keep your hands off my property. This is your only warning. STAY AWAY.

Dylan folded the paper in half, then in half again before cramming it into her back pocket. Knowing she'd be lucky to get to her seat on time, she hadn't a second to waste. She filled her backpack with the items her morning schedule required and slammed her locker shut.

Turning, she noticed someone standing, arms folded against the wall. The shiny blond hair was hard to ignore. Carrie Holland wore an expression cocktail: an intoxicating mixture of joy and rage. Dylan was unsure of which of the ingredients to be more afraid. The cheerleader's piercing stare penetrated Dylan's skull, instantly causing a pulsing headache.

If looks could've killed, this one would've been a mass murderer.

31

"Wow. Another set of hands is just what the doctor ordered," Dylan cheerfully pointed out while handing the Mel-meter to Mitch.

"Whoa," he said, surprised by the high-pitched squeal it bolstered when he touched the antenna. "What *is* this thing?"

"This is a Mel-meter. It's a device specifically engineered for paranormal research. It does a few things all at once." Dylan stood close, showed Mitch the features. "Here, it reports the temperature. This way, if the device signals, or if it has EMF spikes, you can also see if the temperature where you're standing is being altered."

"Temperature matters?"

"Of course. Cold spots combined with EMF spikes are a definite indication of a spirit being present."

"What's EM…"

"EMF?" Dylan smiled when she finished his question for him.

"Yeah."

"Watch this." Removing her phone from her pocket, she held it against the device. "See the numbers, the big ones? They're changing. They were zero, now they're point seven, point eight. Now zero, again." Mitch watched Dylan and listened intently. She continued to explain, "Everything with an electric current emits electromagnetic energy. Ghosts are also believed to produce traceable levels of electromagnetic energy."

"Wow. Okay, so if I see these numbers change and I'm not near a source of electricity then -"

"Then you might be near a ghost."

"And there's no electricity in this house at all."

"Right. And if the temp is changing, or you hear this…" She grabbed the silver antenna, setting off the obnoxious alarm and flashing lights. "Then you *know* you are near something paranormal."

"What's the antenna actually sensing?"

"Touch. The energy from a touch."

"This is great," Mitch looked amused. "What else do you have?"

"Well you saw this, the Spirit Box." She removed it from a small zippered pocket on her backpack. Four flashlights were positioned around the room, lighting it brightly for them to see. "It scans radio frequencies. It has AM, FM, different sweep rates. It's how I received the words *girl*, *window*, and the others."

"And the digital recorder picks up EMF?"

"No, EVP. The Mel-meter does EMF."

"Oh, duh. EVP is voices."

"Correct. Electronic Voice Phenomenon. Voices spoken inside the white noise. Vocal imprints that we can't hear with our ears."

Watching Dylan spin the camcorder onto the tripod, Mitch stated the obvious. "And that's for visual evidence."

"This has night-vision and full-spectrum. It sees more light spectrums than other cameras or eyes can see."

"This is wild, Dyl. Where did you get all this?"

"Online. There are online stores that specialize in this sort of thing. Or Amazon."

Mitch laughed. "I guess Amazon has everything. So… what got you into this? What made you become a ghost hunter?" pried Mitch, staring at the Mel-meter readouts.

Dylan froze; her mind jumped to the place she feared most.

"Dyl?" Mitch asked, wondering if she had heard him. "What got you interested in all this?"

"I just…" she shrugged, nervously looked around the room. "You know, those shows. All that stuff on TV. Just watching those." Dylan blew it off. Why wouldn't he believe the made-up, superficial reason? He had no reason not to.

Looking down at the camcorder, fiddling with the buttons, Dylan felt Mitch's stare against her back. Surely, he wanted more: the truth. But, the seven-year-old eating donut holes and drinking Diet Pepsi with Dr. Belmonte still took up residence inside of Dylan. Mitch would have to be satisfied with the cheap lie about television shows. For now.

Pushing away her recently conquered insecurities, Dylan ignored the urge to curl up into a ball and hide. "We'll start upstairs. We got her attention last night up there. Come on."

Marching with a flashlight shining from her mouth like Columbo's cigar, Dylan climbed the steps, determined to re-establish contact with the spirit: the *innocent* girl upstairs. She carried the tripod and camera in one hand, while her fingers on the other gripped the SB7 Spirit Box and the digital recorder. Mitch followed behind holding the Mel-meter, antenna extended, in his right hand, flashlight in his left pointed forward, casting a long, wobbly shadow with Dylan's body. At the top, Dylan kneeled to setup the camera. Mitch continued down the hall.

"Anything?" Dylan called to him.

Mitch studied the readouts, wandering slowly forward, rotating his waist right and left so the device could cover the width of the hall. "Not yet," he said, entering the bedroom on the left. "Wow, bed and everything is still here, huh?"

With the camera shooting the length of the hall, Dylan walked to the end, to the locked door. "I'm going to roll the digital for a bit. Let's just keep quiet for a few minutes, see if she reaches out to us."

"Can I walk around?" Mitch hollered from the first bedroom.

"Sure, go ahead." Dylan turned off her flashlight, leaned her back against the locked door at the hall's end. She listened to the footsteps under Mitch's feet, as she watched him cross the hall behind his beam of light. Dust particles floated nonchalantly through the light like the snow flurries that crept closer to Black Willow with each passing day. From the next room, Dylan heard Mitch moving things around.

"You okay in there?" she asked, hoping he'd tell her that he hadn't touched anything and that the ghost was moving objects inside the room, going full poltergeist.

With his smile evident through the sound of his voice, Mitch replied, "I thought we were having a moment of silence or something. Quiet time."

"Right... Okay, but what are you doing?"

"Investigating. The old-fashioned way."

"What are you finding?" Dylan rocked on the sides of her shoes.

"Stuff. Papers. Things."

"Gettin' any readings? Feeling anything weird?"

"Nope."

It sounded like Mitch was rifling through one of the filing cabinets. The drawers rubbed on the rusty slides as he yanked them out and shoved them back in.

"No chills?" Dylan wondered. "How's the temp look?"

"Holding steady at forty-four degrees." He stepped out of the room, pointed his light at Dylan. "Hi," he joked. "You come here often?"

Smiling at his playfulness, Dylan looked down at the recording device. "Okay, Mitch, now let's actually stay quiet for minute. Stand still."

A few feet apart, they waited, quietly. With both flashlights off, darkness covered them completely. Standing still, each breath the other took perked their own ears, as they strained to hear what might be a whisper, a clue. Minutes passed before Mitch took a step towards Dylan. He was close, directly in front of her, but she still couldn't see his face in the darkness.

"Tell me about the Skin Walker." Like the past few days, Dylan again caught herself off-guard with the confidence her voice carried. She heard Mitch's shoulders raise with a deep inhale.

"Well, like I said, it's, um… a legend. Folklore. An old Native American legend." His voice held a level of comfort that had been lacking in the hallway at school when he first mentioned the Skin Walker to her. She figured that he either was finding it as easy to trust her has she was finding it to trust him or the darkness was providing a sense of security that eased his apprehensions. "Think about it like you said before: a werewolf. You know, what people normally think of as a werewolf."

"Creepy."

"Except there are some differences. Major ones. Like, they can become different animals, and not like a giant wolfman, but a real wolf, a real raven, a bear. Actual wildlife. And they control it. They change when they want, for specific reasons. They desire to cause harm, Dyl."

"They sound awful, Mitch. Terrifying."

"Yeah, I was little, so I don't remember the fallout too well. Other than it was bad. Once my father left town, Grandpa did a great job of separating me from him in people's minds. I just…"

"What is it, Mitch?"

"I was never allowed to talk about it, you know? It was forbidden. So, it just goes unsaid. We don't talk about, so other people don't either. Do you have any idea what it's like not to be able to talk about the thing that most defines who you are? Simply because no one would believe you?"

Dylan knew exactly what that felt like. Feeling dust, or a cobweb, fall against her cheek, she lifted her hand to wipe it away. How unbelievable was it that Mitch, of all people, battled many of the same demons she herself did? Dylan was speechless.

Lowering her hand back to her side, she felt her

knuckles graze against Mitch's. Lacking words, she grabbed hold of his hand, stood silently, facing him.

"Dyl?"

"Yeah?"

"I'm feeling something, now."

"Me, too," she whispered, softly.

Something powerful raced through Dylan's veins, carrying courage to every inch of her body. She placed the digital recorder into her jacket pocket, slowly held out both of her palms until they finally cradled each side of Mitch's stubbled face. After tucking his silky hair behind his ears, she raised to her tiptoes. Even now slightly taller, she needed to pull his lips down onto her own.

Gently, he pressed his mouth against hers. Doused in adrenaline, Dylan's legs were weak; her heart ached with pleasure. The contact she had made with the spirit in the house, the touch to her cheek, the goosebumps held not a torch to the sensation generated by kissing Mitch.

Feeling his left hand touch her side, just above her hip, her body instinctively tried pulling away, but taking control, she held steady, allowing his arm to tug her into him. When their chests met, flashing lights and a God-awful screech simultaneously blinded and deafened them both. When the Mel-meter in Mitch's right hand touched Dylan, it went crazy. Switching it off with his thumb to deaden the commotion, Mitch kept their smiles firmly linked.

Thoughts, emotions that Dylan didn't recognize filled her every pore, covered her with a comfort, a safe feeling Dylan was sure she'd never experienced prior to that moment.

32

Mitch's soft lips tasted like life-saving, exotic fruit from a tree that Dylan had just discovered in the middle of a deserted isle. She'd been alone and starving. The ripe, nutritious fruit brought with it salvation: deliverance from an unwanted fate. It felt endless, until…

"What?" Mitch whispered, pulling his mouth away from the entranced girl.

Pushing forward, Dylan's wet lips again found his. Mitch kissed her, deeply, before stopping again.

"What did you say?" he wondered with his forehead resting against Dylan's.

Frustrated, Dylan struggled to grasp what Mitch was referring to. Wanting nothing more than to continue the tender, physical exchange, Dylan allowed herself to come down from the brilliant euphoria.

"Mitch… What? What are you asking me?"

"What did you whisper to me?"

"I…" Dylan pulled her head back, took her flashlight from her pants pocket, lit up the space between them. "I… was kissing you. I… couldn't, I didn't whisper anything."

"But, I heard you. Right into my ear. I…"

Dylan gasped.

As if their lips were still connected, in unison, they spoke. "The recorder!"

REWIND.

With raised eyebrows and slightly reddened expressions, Dylan and Mitch listened to the sound of moist, smacking lips fervently rubbing together. Relieved that Mitch couldn't see her embarrassment at the passionate sounds, they stood cheek to cheek with the recorder tightly between their ears. Both held their breaths, listened for the words that Mitch had heard faintly spoken there in the murky hallway.

"What?" they heard Mitch say on the playback.

"Go back. It's got to be right before I say that," he told her. She knew he was right and had begun feeling for the reverse button with her thumb.

"Here it is," she said. "Ready?"

"Yeah."

"Oh my God!" they exclaimed, in loud harmony.

"Did you hear that?" Mitch yelled, knowing that Dylan must have heard it.

They faced each other, eyes wide, jaws on the floor. Dylan ran her fingers through her hair, pulling it back, holding it there with her hand on top of her head. She nodded, as her heart thumped ferociously behind her sternum.

"Broke my heart," Dylan whispered. "Broke my heart."

"Broke my heart," Mitch repeated, confirming they had heard the same sentence.

REWIND. PLAY.

"...broke... my-heart."

The whisper was spoken irregularly, different than a normal speech pattern sounded. The words "my heart" had the rhythm of a single, two-syllable word instead of separate, individual ones.

"Go behind the camera! Watch me through it."

Hastily, Mitch followed Dylan's orders, stormed over to the tripod to view her through the night-vision camera's LCD screen.

Rushing, Dylan activated the loud, annoying frequency sweeps of the Spirit Box. The patterned, choppy static filled the upstairs, ringing off the lonely walls of the barren corridor.

"We heard you!" Dylan called out over the noise. "Who broke your heart?" She waited for a response to come through the box, while Mitch carefully watched her and her surroundings through the screen.

"We know you're here! Talk to us. We only want to help you!"

The droning sound pulsated against their ears, but, for minutes, they tolerated it and waited. Dylan held still, while no voices emitted from the device. "Did your father hurt you? Is that why you shined the flashlight on his picture?"

"Say 'Sarah'!" Mitch yelled.

"What?"

"Sarah! I think her name was Sarah!"

Dylan nodded, didn't waste a second. "Sarah, did your

father hurt you? Sarah… are you here?"

Five, ten, fifteen minutes passed: nothing.

"Keep going," Mitch encouraged. "She has to be here!"

Dylan turned in a circle as she pleaded again for the spirit to speak to her. "Sarah, it's me, Dylan. You *know* me. You've touched me, I've heard your voice. Talk to me, please!"

The EVP, *"…broke…my-heart…"*, would be all the evidence that night would provide. The house went silent as Dylan switched off the Spirit Box. Mitch flipped his light onto Dylan; she did the same towards him. Together, draped in battery powered, yellow light they stood, watching their shadows crawl up the walls behind them.

"You're good at this, Dyl," Mitch said, nodding. His eye sockets looked deep, sinking under the shadows of his square face.

"I couldn't get her to speak. I shouldn't have pushed so hard. I think I frightened her off."

"*You* frightened *her?*" Mitch chuckled. "*She* scared the hell out of *me* when that voice came through the recorder."

Dylan smiled. Mitch seemed like a giant to her sometimes. It was funny to imagine him fearing anything. But, then again, she knew all too well that fear can find anyone, anywhere. Even under your covers, in your bedroom, in a secured apartment, in a safe neighborhood.

"How'd you know her name?" she asked, feeling around her pockets, looking for her digital recorder. She found it, safe in the rear one of her Levi's.

"I saw it in the filing cabinet. There's tons of papers in there. Everything. Like the people that were in this house just disappeared, leaving even important documents."

"Creepy, right?"

"Very. I've never heard of anything like this before. We should be digging through those filing cabinets. I'm sure there's a lot of useful info about this girl in there. Maybe it can help you… I don't know, channel her."

Dylan laughed. "*Channel* her? I'm not clairvoyant. Besides, it seems shady rummaging through someone's things."

Mitch stood silent for a moment, processing her thinking. "Well, I hate to break it to you, Dyl, but you're *in* their house."

"I know. I get it, I get it. It just feels less slimy than going through their belongings."

"You're the boss. This is your gig. I'm just there to help."

She could feel his light on her face. "And I really appreciate it, Mitch."

"No problem," he told her with a wittiness like only someone of Mitch's stature could muster.

After gathering up the camera, they headed down the stairs and packed everything up into Dylan's backpack.

"What an experience!" Dylan commented, tugging on the stuck zipper of her bag. Shyly, she peeked up at Mitch. "The *voice*, I mean."

"Yeah, the *voice*," he modestly agreed.

"But, you know," she went on, "the other… thing was… That was good, too."

"Yeah… the other thing."

Feeling a rush of heat to her face, Dylan strapped on her pack. "You ready?"

"Lead the way."

Stepping out to the porch, the boards creaked beneath

them. When Mitch pulled the sticky door closed, the entire house shook from his might. Dylan wondered if she'd even be able to open it by herself after such a strong slam or if she'd need Mitch to do it. And that thought didn't exactly bother her. She watched his wide shoulders walk around the truck before he leaned his back against the hood, folded his arms.

"That really is *some* tree. That's got to be one of the largest Black Willows I know of. And it's just so out of place. Cornfield, house, and then… this." He held out his palms. "Voila."

Dylan tossed her backpack into the cab of the pickup, let the door hang open, with the dome light shining, and walked to join her friend in front of the automobile.

With the clear, cloudless night, the moonlight bleached the dark sky to a shade of gray that played as a perfect backdrop to highlight the tree's bizarre, black shapes created by the branches' twists and turns. Silent admiration of the natural spectacle by both soured quickly when one of the branches seemed to move.

Watching as the black shape slightly changed position, Dylan squinted and wondered, "Did you… Mitch?" Seconds passed before Dylan finally pried her eyes from the twitching branch to find a distant looking Mitch holding his gaze.

Quickly turning her face back towards the tree, Dylan felt relief when she heard the unmistakable caw of a raven call across the yard, and her eyes realized the suspect twig was its flapping wings.

"Let's go," Mitch said, coldly, suddenly appearing on edge and jittery.

Once in the truck, Dylan could see the uneasiness

draped across Mitch, as he watched the large, feathered bird leap off the tree and glide off into the distance, as if it had a secret to share with someone.

33

"...broke...my-heart..."

The words played continuously, all day in Dylan's thoughts, as she felt herself beginning to feel restlessly obsessed with the girl's spirit. She had spent most of Wednesday in a daze, snapping from it only long enough to converse with Mitch and to answer one of Mr. Amal's French questions.

Twisting a curl between her fingers, her occupied mind didn't comprehend Ms. Castle's calling out to her until the third and loudest time the teacher said her name.

"Dylan!"

Climbing from her faraway and isolated cavern of thought, Dylan finally turned to look. Kids passed by between them, as Dylan raised her eyes to the spectacular looking woman dressed in a form fitting skirt and a shirt that seemed too low-cut to be worn amongst the swarm of immature, sex-obsessed teen boys that attended Black Willow High.

"Do you have a moment?" Tamara Castle asked, leaning her head towards the open door of her classroom. "You *are* headed to lunch now, right?"

Dylan nodded, confused as to what reason the woman who only sees her during study hall would want with her.

"Just for a minute, Dylan," Ms. Castle urged.

Following her inside, Dylan caught a whiff of wonderfully scented perfume trailing off the teacher's neck. Surely, Ms. Castle spent some time in front of the mirror each morning. Dylan took the woman's hair and wardrobe as a reliable testament.

"Have a seat," Ms. Castle said, sliding into one of the desks in the front row of the room. Her voice was stern, almost worrisome.

Dylan awkwardly tipped into the seat next to Ms. Castle's, bending her leg under to sit on her foot. She barely took her eyes off the desktop. "What's…" Dylan cleared her throat, "What's up?"

"How are things going? Are you adjusting to Black Willow?"

"Um… sure. It's, it's okay."

"I see you've made a friend."

"Excuse me?"

"Mitchell Wolf. I see you're spending time with Mitch."

"I… I…"

Ms. Castle didn't wait for Dylan's stutters to evolve into something coherent. "Dylan, Mitch is… Mitch is different than most boys his age." Dylan noticed that

211

Tamara's eyes carried sadness, uncertainty, like she was on the verge of tears. "He's a good kid. An interesting kid."

Dylan raised her eyes, meeting the teacher's but instead of conversing, she waited for Ms. Castle to continue. The woman, with artfully done lipstick and eyeshadow, turned sideways in the school desk so her bare knees faced Dylan. "What is it you and Mitch have been doing together?"

Dylan gripped the front of the desk with white knuckles, fending off the urge to bail on the teacher. Sprinting to the classroom door seemed like the right thing to do, but, instead, Dylan swallowed a nervous lump, wiggled slightly in her chair, and forced out an awkward, crackled response.

"Nothing… really. Just kinda', you know…"

Not only did the statement not give an answer, but her delivery accomplished only one thing: raised a huge red flag. Dylan knew that Ms. Castle suspected she was hiding something.

"I've seen that Mitch has given you a ride to school, taken you home more than once. I heard he's been over a few times, as well."

What was with this woman? Did she have spies tailing them? Dylan could see a look of strong concern on Tamara's face, like she had something important to say. Like a warning of some sort sat dangerously close to the tip of her tongue anxious to leap off and find Dylan's ears.

With squinted eyes, Ms. Castle was clearly thinking something and debating whether to share it with the new girl sitting next to her. Dylan joggled her eyes from the teacher to her own hands holding tightly to the wooden desk. The moment carried on far longer than comfort would allow.

Ms. Castle sighed, touched her fingers, adorned with filed, painted nails, to the side of her nose. No doubt, a nervous habit she had probably started as a child and never outgrew. Realizing the odd silence between them had put Dylan on edge, Ms. Castle flashed her perfect smile, crossed her legs so that one of her designer high-heels hung loosely on her bouncing toes, and reached across the aisle, putting her palm flat on Dylan's back.

Stretching herself to reach, Ms. Castle spoke cheerfully. A stark contrast to the demeanor she displayed just seconds prior. "I'm sure you're enjoying his company. I'm glad the two of you are hitting it off so well. Go ahead and run along to lunch now, Dylan. I'm sure you need your energy."

Tamara stood up, straightened her skirt with a turn and a tug using both hands. She again put her hand on Dylan's back, this time allowing her fingers to run through a few of Dylan's long curls. Dylan held her breath, silently begging the teacher to go away.

"Thanks for stopping in," Ms. Castle said, before gracefully walking to her own desk at the front of the room.

As Dylan watched, still in a state of shock, the teacher elegantly sat herself into her leather chair, picked up her phone and began scrolling with her thumb. Dylan assumed she was browsing her social media newsfeeds, but the stone-faced expression Ms. Castle had made it clear she was only fidgeting with the phone to keep from having to look up at Dylan.

Nervously, Dylan carefully got up, and stood by the desk for a moment trying to make sense of what had just happened between herself and the highly attractive, highly unusual educator. After collecting her bearings, Dylan sped to the door and almost made it out before Ms. Castle called for her.

"Dylan?"

Nervously, Dylan turned herself around in what felt like slow motion to find Ms. Castle sitting up proper with her shoulders high and straight. The teacher's facial features looked scrunched. And the calm lines of her face that normally curved to create beauty now seemed precarious - even dangerous. Somehow, Dylan knew that the anxious words Ms. Castle had been holding back were about to springboard from her tongue.

"Jealousy is powerful, Dylan," the teacher explained, her voice low but firm. "You need to watch yourself."

Dylan's heart clogged her throat. Her stomach turned sour and acidic. Ms. Castle lowered her eyes back to her phone, like Dylan wasn't even there. Rather than inquire for clarification, Dylan turned into the empty hallway, decided to ignore Ms. Castle's unclear motives, and pretended that the odd conversation had never happened.

34

"Where are we going?" Dylan asked as Mitch drove beyond their regular turn towards Candice's house. He steered with only one hand and had the other tightly locked with Dylan's laying on the seat between them.

"Well," he started with a glance in her direction, "I did some work last night."

"Work?" Dylan smiled. It was nice holding hands with him. He held her tiny palm and fingers tightly enough to feel secure, yet loosely enough that it felt gentle and sweet. Mitch seemed to possess an odd balance of strength and kindness that Dylan wasn't sure she'd seen in anyone before.

"Yeah. So, you've been to Greenville, right?"

"With Grandma. A couple times. Groceries."

"That's where we are headed."

"And what for?"

"Last night when I was in the room, digging in the filing cabinet – *before* you asked me not to."

"It's okay, Mitch. You don't need to clarify when. What are you getting at?" Dylan's interest spiked. She knew he was up to something and couldn't wait to hear the details.

"Well, I found something in there that I thought might be useful. So... I took it."

"What? What is it?"

He let go of her hand, reached into the hidden pocket inside of his jacket, and pulled out a folded piece of paper. "I stuck this into my pocket last night."

Curiously, Dylan unfolded the paper once, then again until the full sheet was visible. It was a document from a bank, a statement dated *12/18/93*. She saw an address at the top, obviously the one belonging to the abandoned house. Under it, she saw a name.

Dean Michael Hodge.

She unclasped her seat belt, slid over next to the driver. While she fastened the middle belt around her waist, she pressed her side against Mitch's. She was getting to the point where any time she was near him, she wished to be making physical contact in some way. Instead of fighting or trying to understand the compulsion, she just did it.

"Okay, Columbo, fill me in," she demanded.

"Columbo?"

"It's a show... An old show, about a detective named Columbo. I've caught it a few times."

"So, you're not mad I took it?"

"No, I'm not," she assured him. "This *is* a supernatural investigation. However, a little *natural* detective work can only help."

Relieved, he smiled. "Awesome."

"So, tell me how you think this will help." She read and reread the information on the page, quickly scanning over the figures.

Mitch began explaining, "Dean Michael Hodge appears to have been the owner of the house. He's the father, I presume, in the family photo."

"Okay."

"He was wealthy. I mean, look at the money in his bank accounts. The guy was loaded."

Dylan nodded, understanding. "Sure, the house is great. The kitchen looks expensive. The furniture is all upscale, I think. For the nineties, anyway. This is interesting, for sure, Mitch. But, where are we headed? This bank?" She held the document up, confused.

"No, Dyl. We aren't going to the bank. We are going to pay Dean Michael Hodge a visit."

Dylan's eyes launched from their sockets. Strangely, the idea that the girl's father and mother were still alive – actual living people – somehow had never dawned on her. Suddenly, the situation became bigger, more dangerous than it felt before. It was one thing chasing a ghost through a haunted house but adding live humans into the equation could change everything.

"Are... are you sure this is wise? I mean, is this... dangerous?" Dylan's mind was winning the race with her mouth. She sputtered her words at lightning speed.

Mitch put his hand on Dylan's left thigh, calming her instantly, as voltage seemingly climbed the length of her body. "It's okay. We aren't going to approach him. We're not going to talk to him. I just want to get a look at him."

"Spy?"

"More like a stakeout."

Dylan nodded. Mitch still had his hand resting on her leg. She took her right hand and placed it over his, wrapped her fingers around his wide knuckles. "Okay… I'm in."

Entering the Greenville city limits, Dylan watched the buildings as they passed. There were fast food joints, gas stations, a few random small businesses, and car dealerships, too. Thinking back to Evanston and to Chicago, Dylan thought Greenville didn't look much like a city at all. But, when compared to Black Willow Creek, Greenville was a booming metropolis with endless places to eat and shop. The Super Wal-Mart on the other end of town was the only place she had been with Candice. Seeing the rest of the town made her wish that she *did* have her driver's license. She could see herself spending time in Greenville.

Mitch flicked his blinker on and turned into the Greenville Estates. Unpleasant on the eyes, the trailer park was not well kept. Some of the manufactured homes could have been fifty years old, for all Dylan could tell. They were rundown and beat up, and it was certainly not the sort of place that someone with Dean Hodge's apparent wealth would choose to reside.

As they drove deeper into the park, the homes became increasingly decrepit and less inviting. Random items – tires, washing machines, parts of cars – sat in the yards and driveways, as if that's where they belonged. Weeds had grown around some of the objects so high they were hidden from view. It was anyone's guess what hid in the tall grass.

A few people wandered the cracked streets, but hardly any. For reasons Dylan couldn't pinpoint, Greenville Estates didn't have the appearance of a community down on its luck. Instead of nice families dealing with misfortunate happenings, like job loss or unavoidable medical expenses that their insurances wouldn't cover, the entire trailer park screamed *danger*.

Dylan read the numbers on the homes and quickly looked down at Mitch's scribbled handwriting on the bank statement. "Sixty-three. Right here," she whispered, afraid that whoever was inside the trailer with number *63* on the outside would somehow hear her.

"Yup, there it is." Mitch also spoke in hushed tones.

"How did you find him?"

"Believe it or not, he's listed. Google," Mitch told her. "Dean Hodge, Greenville Estates, number sixty-three."

Mitch's small, blue truck inconspicuously crept past number sixty-three, made a left at the next intersection, then a quick U-turn. He parked far enough away that number sixty-three would pay no attention to his truck. But, close enough for he and Dylan to clearly see the trailer that supposedly belonged to the man in the portrait at the house on Cemetery. The man that they believed hurt, maybe even killed, Sarah Hodge.

***

An hour had passed, and the warm air that once filled the small cab of the truck during the drive to Greenville Estates had been replaced by cool outside air that snuck through worn seams of the aged vehicle. Dylan couldn't get her body any closer to Mitch's without jumping right inside of his skin.

Nearing five o'clock, they'd seen little action, including absolutely none at number sixty-three. The sky was dark and had it not been for the dim porch light attached to the side of Hodge's rusty trailer by the front door, they'd had no view of his place at all. Seeing their warm breaths forming in the chilled air, Mitch put his arm over Dylan's shoulder, cuddling her narrow frame tightly. She sniffled, wiped her running nose with a napkin from Carol's she had found inside the glove box earlier in their secretive mission.

"Mitch, I think we should…"

Before Dylan could finish, headlights shined from down the street towards number sixty-three. Both the undercover agents sat upright with sudden disregard for the cold.

When a small, compact, sedan came to a halt in sixty-three's driveway, Dylan pulled out her phone, struggling to unlock it with frozen, hard to feel digits. Just in time to see a tired man with dragging feet step out of the tiny, baby-blue Hyundai, Dylan gained control of the device and switched to the camera function. Spreading the screen with her thumb and finger, she zoomed up on the bearded man with shaggy, disheveled hair.

He wore a brown, oversized winter coat, faded blue jeans, and heavy, work-style boots. From his coat pocket, he pulled a bright orange, stocking cap, and stretched it over his head until it covered his ears. After opening the rear driver side door, the gruff man removed two grocery bags, and limped his way to the trailer. All the while, Dylan continuously snapped pictures on her phone.

It wasn't easy to tell but looking closely it was surely him: the man from the framed picture in the abandoned house. He was much heavier now, somewhere around fifty or even sixty pounds heftier than the image taken all those years ago. Straggly looking. Nothing resembling the well-groomed, nicely dressed man that smiled with his family next to a fancily decorated Christmas tree with twinkling lights.

Clearly, though, it was the same man. Yet, visually, he was a shell of his former self.

Stepping on the two-by-four constructed, three-step porch, Dean Hodge paused before opening the door. He turned, looked inquisitively in every direction – even towards Dylan and Mitch. Dylan held her breath as the man's eyes passed over where they sat, surveying the area for reasons they didn't know.

Seemingly satisfied with his surroundings, Hodge unlocked his trailer, staggered sluggishly inside, leaving the investigative duo with more questions than they had arrived with.

35

Leaving the street lights of Greenville, Mitch drove to the dark, country roads that led back to Black Willow. They enthusiastically chatted, traded personal views about the exciting events inside the Estates, debating whether it was more or less exhilarating than hearing the voice of a ghost. They joked and laughed at how the high it provided was similar to the one gained by sneaking through Carrie Holland's yard, tossing rolls of toilet paper into the trees.

Turning off the main, paved route that connected Greenville with another medium sized town north of it, Mitch pulled to the shoulder and put the truck into Park. Leaving the engine running, Mitch opened his door and hopped out.

"What are you doing?" Dylan inquired, truly confused by what was happening.

Standing with the door open, Mitch patted the driver's seat with his palms. "Scoot over, Dyl. You're driving us home."

Instantly frozen with fear, Dylan sat quietly in awe at the idea. "Are you crazy?" she asked. "I mean… I don't even… I don't have -"

"Come on," Mitch insisted. "You're never gonna learn if you don't do it. Come on."

With her heart racing, Dylan reluctantly scooted eighteen inches to her left, behind the wheel. "Mitch, I've never really… This is, like…"

"I gotcha'. Buckle up," he told her, closing the door. With a playful skip, Mitch walked around the front of the truck, and jumped into the passenger side. Reaching over his shoulder for the seat belt, Dylan made a demand.

"Sit close to me."

Without an argument, Mitch moved to the center of the long seat, crammed his knees in front of the radio. Dylan's knuckles firmly gripped the wheel, as she tried to keep her arms from nervously shaking. "I'm not sure I can…"

"Calm down. I'm right here," Mitch coolly comforted her.

Taking three deep breaths with her eyes closed, Dylan gave relaxation her best effort.

"Dyl?"

"Yes?"

"You're probably going to want to open your eyes."

Shaking her head, warding off the last bit of fear, she agreed. "Right. You're right."

"Ready?" he asked her, now with a sudden, but well-disguised, hint of worry.

"I am. How do I… make it go? Or whatever."

"Okay. Start by putting your foot on the brake. It's the pedal on the left. No, use your right leg," Mitch said after seeing Dylan's left knee rise so she could place her foot on the brake.

"My *right?* Then how will I push the other pedal?"

"You're going to use your right foot for both the brake and the gas."

Dylan nodded, understanding. "Right. Because I won't push them at the same time... Right?"

"Right. Now press the brake and then take this long lever and move it to the *D*. You'll have to pull it slightly towards you first."

"Can't I get into trouble for this? Can't *you?*"

"We're in the absolute middle of nowhere. There's no chance of seeing a cop. And if we did, and he stopped us, this is Black Willow, Dyl. He's not going to bat an eye at a teenage girl getting familiar behind the wheel. This isn't Chicago."

"Okay, if you're sure."

"The only way you'll get into any trouble is if you hit someone."

"*Hit* someone? That's it! I'm not doing this!" she yelled, reaching for her seatbelt.

"Dylan!" Mitch cried, trying to sound soothing and kind. Softly, he took her by the wrist. "Look at me," he said, and waited for her to turn and stare into his eyes. "You can do this."

She exhaled long and forceful. "Okay. I can do this," Dylan coached herself, hoping it would provide the confidence and strength she desperately needed. Remaining poised, Dylan pulled the lever into the DRIVE position.

"Now," Mitch delicately imparted the instructions with

care, "the truck will start to move when you take your foot off the brake. So, do it slowly."

"Slowly. Right."

"Hey," Mitch said, "this is nothing. No big deal."

"Right. No big deal."

The truck crawled forward when Dylan lifted her sneaker off the footbrake. Dylan held her breath, feeling like she was slowly rising to the top of a roller coaster about to plunge downhill at top speed. The steering wheel felt loose, easy to operate, not like she'd always imagined it would.

"Good job. Now you need to slowly merge off the shoulder and onto the road. Carefully. Just slide over, nice and easy." Mitch cranked his neck over his shoulder to see through the back window. No cars were coming, so Dylan was safe to join the right lane. Dylan tried to look in her side mirror but decided to take Mitch's word for it that it was safe to move over.

"Nice job!" Mitch commended the rookie driver on her smooth transition from the gravel shoulder to the narrow blacktopped, back road. The road was rough, patched about a thousand times because of holes caused by extreme cold in the winter and blazing heat in the summer months. Not to mention gouges caused by scraping snowplow blades.

"Just keep it steady, Dyl."

Dylan did her best to maintain control, yet silently worried she was going too slow. The speedometer never breached thirty-five miles per hour, but Mitch displayed incredible patience with her. Several cars sped past her on the left, a few even honked as they flew by, leaving her in their literal dust.

Her stopping improved with each stop sign along the

way. At first, she stopped several feet early, then had to creep up to the intersection, inch by inch. By the fourth stop sign, however, she was getting the knack of stopping *almost perfectly*, as Mitch put it.

"You can relax," Mitch assured her.

Dylan started to question what he'd meant by it, but quite suddenly realized how tight she was gripping the wheel. "My white knuckles?" she asked.

"And your face," he teased. "You look like a ghost."

"Ha, ha," she mocked through a clenched jaw.

"You're doing fine."

Dylan inhaled. The air whistled between her gritting front teeth. Tightly hugging the shoulder, Dylan attempted what seemed an impossible task: turning the car while still moving. The winding curves on that section of road made the vehicle feel shaky and disobedient.

"What was that?" Mitch blurted in response to a high-pitch squeal coming from the skittish driver.

"Wow," Dylan exclaimed, "I made it through those things."

"You mean, those *curves*?"

"Right," she nodded. "Curves."

As Dylan entered a straightaway, Mitch coached, gingerly. "Slide just a touch to the left, Dyl."

"To the middle? To the line?"

"Just a smidge." Mitch used his hand to describe by leaving a small space between the tip of his finger and his thumb.

"*What?*" Dylan breathed out. "Are you not seeing this?"

"What, Dyl?"

"There is a car, no a truck, coming at me and you want

me to move towards the *center*?"

"It's not coming *at* you, Dylan."

"I am *not* moving closer." A long sigh left her lungs as the truck passed in the opposite lane, somehow not colliding with them.

Calmly, Mitch reached with his left hand, placed it on top of Dylan's, and gently pushed the steering wheel to move his small, blue truck out of the tall weeds that lined the side of the roadway. Dylan winced, snuck a short glance at Mitch from the corner of her eye.

"You're okay," he promised.

"I feel like I'm right on the yellow line."

"You're nowhere near it."

Leaning, Dylan made a futile attempt to view the painted line through her side window. "Okay… If you're sure."

"I'm sure."

Dylan's stiff shoulders finally sagged, having grown tired and sore from her taut posture. She'd gained a reasonable level of comfort, to her own surprise. Sharing laughs and moments of fear with her instructor, Dylan coursed her way, with Mitch's careful direction, back to Black Willow Creek.

She was far from having the skill to obtain a license, but, finally, she felt like it wasn't an unattainable goal. It just might be something she could accomplish… one day.

Staring at the front edge of the hood and the way it seemed to hang freely over the road, the yellow paint stripes passed by the corner of her eye like one continuous line. The headlights spread out wide in the pitch-dark night, lighting cornfields, trees, and the occasional mailbox.

"Where are the houses?" she asked, eyes still trained

straight forward.

"Excuse me?"

"The houses that these random mailboxes belong to. I don't see any houses."

"Back in the woods."

"Houses *in* the woods. Why?"

"See there's a driveway." Mitch pointed into the darkness as they passed too quickly for Dylan to get a glimpse. "People like their privacy. That's all."

"Huh," Dylan murmured, "Isolation. I can appreciate that." Her mind wandered to the many instances she'd wished for the safety isolation could've provided. And, also the times that it wouldn't have mattered, either way. There were some things she couldn't have hidden from. Even with a quarter-mile long driveway deep into a forest.

Before she knew it, Dylan found herself in a familiar place: Main Street of Black Willow Creek.

"Hold on just a second," Mitch told Dylan when she stopped at the intersection where Main Street crossed Third Street, a block from Carol's Restaurant.

"Oh, okay," Dylan agreed, while Mitch opened his door.

"Put it into Park!" he shouted through the windshield, running through the headlight beams.

"Um…" Dylan toyed with the shifter before finally shoving it into PARK.

"Scooch," Mitch said, opening the driver side door. He pushed his way in, as Dylan moved over to the center. "You were great," he whispered, smiling at her expression of accomplishment. Before clicking the buckle of his over-the-shoulder strap, he leaned over and kissed her on the lips. She rested into his body, prepared to savor the final remaining minutes before she knew they would reach her house.

A moment later, Dylan was sitting up, perplexed why Mitch was pulling into Carol's instead of continuing down Main Street like she had expected him to.

"What's going on? Why are you stopping?" she questioned with narrow eyes.

"Let's go. I've got a surprise."

"Wow, you're just full of surprises today."

Holding his hand, she followed him to the entrance into Carol's. Dinging the bell atop it, he pulled the door open, ushered her in, again dazzling her with his unusual charm.

Dylan looked around the restaurant, a bit nervous, wondering what Mitch had in store for her. Only a few tables had customers sitting at them, a variety of Carol's classic dishes sat, half eaten, on unmatched plates in front of them. Dylan saw lasagna, cheeseburgers, baskets of chicken fingers and French fries. Starving, her stomach rumbled.

In the far-left corner of the room, she saw a table for three set with silverware, plates, and glasses. In the center sat a beautiful bouquet of flowers – real flowers. Not like the cloth roses that graced each of the other tables.

"Is it ready?" Mitch called across to April, who was placing a steaming order of vegetable beef stew down for a hungry client.

"Sure is, Mitchie. Just like you wanted," she merrily responded. "Hey, Dylan," she added before turning and heading into the kitchen. Shockingly, April had delivered an actual smile to Dylan, leaving her more bewildered than the situation already had.

"Let's go sit." Mitch steered Dylan over to the table

with the flowers, pulled a chair out for her to sit down. "I hope you like this." Mitch quickly waved to an older gentleman sitting across the restaurant wearing a flannel shirt with suspenders. The woman with the man also waved and added a "Hi there, Mitch," to go along with it.

Facing the wall, Dylan saw Mitch's eyes grow wide with glee. "Here it is," he announced, standing up to help April place the round, deep, cast iron pan on the table between them. "April, it's amazing looking," he congratulated the waitress.

"Well, I didn't make it, so…" April admitted between smacks of bubble gum. "Anyway, bon appetit."

Dylan couldn't believe it. April had brought them a real, authentic, wonderfully crafted Chicago-style deep dish pizza. It looked exactly like the ones back home.

"How did you?" she barely verbalized through a magnificent gasp. "*Mitch?*"

"Well, turns out the internet is good for more than just ghost hunting equipment and tracking down old guys who lived in now abandoned houses." He winked. "I looked up a recipe, had April give it to Joey in the kitchen. Man, it really looks good. Is this how it's supposed to look? I mean, it looks like the picture."

"It's amazing, Mitch. God, it's awesome. I can't even wait to try it."

"Excuse me, Sweetheart," April groaned, obviously keeping her smile on just to please Mitch. Dylan could tell that, like everyone in town, April liked Mitch. At least, enough to be civilized. Dylan was, even if it was clearly forced, benefitting from it tonight. April filled Dylan's glass with icy Diet Pepsi. "There you go."

"Let me get you a slice," Dylan offered, scooping a

thick, cheesy hunk of the pizza pie with a triangle-shaped spatula. She placed it on Mitch's plate, cut away the strings of cheese that were still connected to the main dish. "Try it."

"Okay, I will. Get a piece for yourself. I'm dying to see if it lives up to the legend."

Dylan served herself the biggest piece that April's imperfect slicing had created. "I'm taking the big one," Dylan announced, happily. Fiercely, it steamed, like smoke from a campfire, but it didn't deter her from digging in. Hot or not, she wasn't waiting to taste the pizza that looked like it had been sent Fed-Ex directly from Giordano's in Chicago along the Magnificent Mile. "So good," Dylan said, sounding muffled, as the piping-hot sauce burned away the roof of her mouth.

"This... this is amazing," Mitch agreed. "I can't believe you guys made this, April," he called across the room.

"Well," April bragged, giving a short bow. "Ya know."

The crust was crunchy, slightly burned on the bottom, like it should be. The cheese, a half-inch thick, was a gooey mess that stretched like a bungee cord with a thrill seeking crazy person tied to the end, until it snapped sending the diver to their death. The sauce, sweet and full of tomato chunks, had a touch of heat on the back end that could sneak up on you if you weren't careful. Under it was a layer of spicy pepperoni, and it was topped with sausage and bacon.

It was perfection.

Dylan remembered being little – before her life had begun its most unpleasant detour – and her father taking her to Giordano's. Seated by the window, the father and daughter watched dozens of people stand on the sidewalk waiting to get into the restaurant, and hundreds more pass by with large shopping bags in each hand. Her dad explained to her how most of the people were tourists visiting Chicago for the shopping and the experience of deep dish pizza. And how lucky she was to live in the most wonderful city on Earth.

For a moment, there inside Carol's, it was as if her life hadn't become a mess, like everything had always been as okay and perfect as that day at Giordano's. Dylan had drifted so far from her haunted reality that she didn't hear the bell above the door ring.

"Now this looks just about perfect," a familiar voice said, tableside.

Dylan looked up to see Candice, standing there, holding her purse, unbuttoning her winter jacket. Mitch stood up, took the old woman's coat and hung it on the back of her chair. "Hi, Dear," Candice greeted the beaming girl.

"Hi, Grandma."

"Well, Mitch told me this was going to be fun, but I had no idea he was doing *this*."

"Let me get you a slice," Mitch said, plopping a heavy, sauce-covered chunk of pizza onto her plate.

Dylan could not remember any day in her life – other than the memory of her father taking her out for deep dish – as nice as this one. She watched, as Mitch and Candice chatted about weather, old times in Black Willow, and gladly stuffed her face with the world's best pizza until she couldn't take another bite.

36

There was just enough space between the back of the couch and the wall for Dylan's miniature body to fit. If she stayed crouched, she'd remain unnoticed. She needed to stay hidden; she needed to be able to listen to what was being said.

"Jill," the man who rang the doorbell said to Dylan's mother, with a whisper. "I mean, Mrs. Klaypool. Is your husband home?"

"Sure, Miguel. I'll go and get him. Have a seat, if you'd like," Jill Klaypool, Dylan's mother, told the man at the door of their high-rise, downtown Chicago apartment. He wore a long coat over a blue suit and tie with shiny black shoes that clicked on the wood floor when he walked.

Dylan felt the couch press closer to her when the man sat down. He wasn't fat, but stocky, short, and round. She

233

knew because she had seen him before on previous visits - she'd even shared some awkward moments with him. The conversations he'd had with Dylan worried her. Well, they weren't exactly conversations. Conversations are two-way. That would've required Dylan saying something back to him. She never had.

"What do you want now?" Dylan's father said, storming into the living room with heavy steps.

"Have a seat, Nathan," the detective on the couch suggested. "Just want to go over a few more things."

"A few more things? A few more things?! We've been over everything a million times already, Rodriguez," Nathan Klaypool argued. Dylan could tell her dad was upset, a side of him she'd rarely witnessed. Throughout the previous week, she had heard her father complain several times about the inspector, Miguel Rodriguez. Young Dylan had sensed her usually gentle father was nearing a breaking point.

"Now just settle down. You know where this is headed, Nathan. It's time you start cooperating with me."

"Cooperating? I am cooperating with you! I have been since the start!"

The detective remained calm, despite Nathan's raised voice and flailing arms. He'd dealt with suspects like him countless times and knew when to escalate and when to diffuse. Dylan could hear the calmness in the gray-haired man's voice.

"I have almost all I need, Klaypool. Between Dr. Belmonte's testimony and the physical evidence, there's virtually no way you can win this. The District Attorney is chomping at the bit to press charges and is only doing me a personal favor by waiting."

"I suppose you expect me to be grateful for that?"

"Hey, I just thought you might want to peacefully walk into the police station. But, if you'd prefer I bring the boys here and drag you through the halls of this beautiful apartment building, I can do that." The detective pulled a crinkled pack of cigarettes from his trench coat, held it out towards Nathan. *"Smoke?"*

Breathing heavily, Dylan peeked enough to see her father take one from the pack. He grabbed a lighter off the mantle, lit the tobacco stick with the small, orange flame, and returned it to the shelf where he'd found it.

"Hey," complained the detective with a white and brown Marlboro hanging off his bottom lip.

Nathan ignored the man's request for a light, so Detective Rodriguez used the lighter in his pocket. Smoke quickly filled the room, and Dylan worried she'd be unable to refrain from coughing and be discovered hiding behind the furniture, where she certainly should not be.

"And might I add that this truly is a wonderful building. How long did you have to wait to get into this place? Just out of curiosity."

Nathan abruptly ceased his worried pacing and stomped fiercely on the floor. *"Stop the small talk, Miguel. I'm not interested in pretending that this, this, this BS isn't happening!"*

Dylan felt the couch shift and knew that Detective Miguel Rodriguez had stood up. His steps clicked across the floor. Laying down, she looked under the couch and saw his and her father's feet standing side by side. Ashes fell to the floor next to them, as Dylan attentively listened.

"The game is over, Klaypool. You lost," Rodriguez stated with confidence.

"You seriously think I'm responsible for this? You really believe that? Or you have no other explanation and it's just easier for you put it on me?"

The detective's feet turned, while Dylan saw her father's shuffle backwards, like he'd been shoved.

"Get your hands off me!" she heard her dad say.

"Now you listen," Rodriguez sternly ordered. *"I'll tell you exactly what I believe is going on here. I think you're a sick bastard who gets off by playing a twisted, sadistic game. It's* you *sneaking into her room at night. It's* you *leaving those horrible marks on her body. And the worst part, Nate, is that you've got that poor girl's head filled with the same ridiculous illusion that you've conjured up in your own disgusting mind. You've made her believe that a ghost is entering her room and putting his hands on her. But do you really, I mean do you really think I'm stupid enough to fall for that? You are a parasite. If something goes wrong and I can't lock you up for this, I pray that the God in heaven will let you rot in hell for all of eternity."*

"Are you finished?" Nathan asked, defiantly. Dylan saw their feet separate slightly when the detective took a step back. She was covering her mouth to contain a cough that the cigarette smoke was eager to produce.

"I'll give you forty-eight hours, Klaypool. If I don't have you booked under your own surrender, I'm sending the boys out. And you won't like it, I promise you."

37

"Go! I'll see you in French. You don't need another tardy." Dylan insisted that Mitch head to his own locker instead of accompanying her to get her books.

"Okay. See ya, Dyl." They kept their hands locked until the last second, extending their arms as they separated.

That morning, the two of them were running behind schedule. Mitch had arrived at Dylan's early enough to make it to first period in plenty of time. Then, when Candice raced outside to greet him demanding that he come in and have eggs and bacon, their chance at a punctual arrival was doomed.

"Well, it's the least I can do after last night," Candice had humbly admitted. "And he's saving me a trip to school, too. This boy, I tell ya, this boy."

Trotting down the hall, Dylan was still feeling buzzed

from the surprise deep dish pizza the night before. Candice was right: *this boy*. Somehow, some way, Mitch had made Dylan feel like she might be able to fit into society. More surprisingly still, she was even enjoying the idea.

When Dylan pried open her locker door, it abruptly slammed back closed, just missing the end of her nose. Her curly hair swayed from the violent movement the door made swinging on its hinges. Looking to her right, Dylan saw the culprit leaning with her shoulder against the next locker. The rude cheerleader's blond hair glowed magically under the bright hallway lights. Carrie Holland glared at Dylan, just a few threatening inches away.

Clenching her jaw firmly, Dylan looked at the carpet, dismayed. She didn't wish it, but Carrie made her feel small, cowardly; even less significant than she already began most mornings. It was an uncontrollable reaction: instinctively intimidated. Suddenly, she was again just a small child afraid to speak, afraid to defend herself. She was dwarfed by the drama of confrontation.

"Hey," Carrie taunted, "What's the matter? Afraid to look me in the eye?"

Slowly, Dylan peeked, just high enough to catch a glimpse of Carrie's frightening face. The cheerleader had a scowl that made a mockery of her carefully applied makeup. The space between her finely plucked eyebrows folded into deep wrinkles, her forehead scrunched over them.

Bam!

The entire wall of lockers quaked when Carrie's palm slammed into it with a quick, stunning jab. Dylan shivered, after a reactive flinch, and decided she would be better off attending first period without her textbook than standing there taking guff from an obviously deranged Carrie

Holland.

Feeling absolute, Dylan turned and started to walk away. But, then, from an act Dylan found surprising coming even from Carrie, she found herself suddenly falling backwards, landing smack on her rear end. Dylan's bully had gripped her backpack with both hands and pulled her down, catching her completely off guard. Her boney elbow landed hard, and Dylan could sense it begin to swell immediately.

A murmur of voices swiftly began to crescendo around the fallen girl. Dylan knew how these things worked from witnessing it a few times at her high school in Evanston. Fights were guaranteed to prompt two things: cheers and the use of smartphones. She didn't even have to look up to know that several kids already had their phones out with video rolling.

Dejected, Dylan pushed herself off the floor, but to a serenade of gasps and laughs felt Carrie's forceful hands shove her back down to the trampled rug: a wasteland of lost paperclips, chewed pen caps, and discarded bubble gum wrappers.

"What's the matter? None of your ghosts are here to scare me away? Or is Casper off flirting with someone's girlfriend?"

Again, Dylan made it to her feet, but before she had her balance, Carrie slammed her, forcibly, back to her butt again. A large, vibrant crowd had quickly gathered, all too busy enjoying the conflict to lend a hand at resolving it. Instead, they were, no doubt, Tweeting, live streaming, and recording the humiliating abuse Carrie was inflicting on Dylan.

A step faster this time, Dylan launched to her feet

before Carrie could knock her back down a fourth time. Obeying her nature to flee, the mortified victim pushed through the layered ring of spectators, shoving back the uncompassionate, paparazzi amateurs.

Vehemently, Carrie raced to reach the escaping Dylan and pushed her, violently, against the lockers with a hand on each of her shoulders. Dylan felt her vertebrae crack the length of her back, rippling one after the other, like a wooden mallet playing the xylophone. The sound of it, however, was much less pleasant than the uniquely cheerful percussion instrument.

Involuntarily, Dylan let out a groan, "Ugh!"

"I'm sorry. Did that hurt?" Carrie mocked.

The crowd of rowdy onlookers had them surrounded once again, caging them against the wall of lockers. Dylan peered over her attacker's shoulder at the dozen, or so, phones pointed directly at her defenseless position.

With such force that an acrylic nail snapped off and rocketed into the air, Carrie stabbed at Dylan's chest with her finger. Dylan turned her face away from Carrie's fiery words and felt the aggressor's hot breath bang against her cheek.

"I tried to be subtle when I saw him start to notice you," Carrie hissed, through gritted teeth. "But, you just didn't get the message. Maybe I should've spoken to you through that stupid ghost box. Would you be able to hear me then? You freak."

Carrie thrusted her sharp finger repeatedly against Dylan's breastplate. Badly, Dylan wanted to retaliate, fight back, teach her assailant a lesson not to be soon forgotten. But, instead, a meek stutter tumbled clumsily from her shaking lips.

"I - I - got your note. But... I'm - I'm -"

"What note? I didn't write you a note."

Dylan swallowed, dug deep into her gut for something she was always able to find in the old abandoned house on Cemetery - confidence, perseverance, courage.

A few seconds passed as Dylan stood, shamefully, with her eyes closed, in what appeared like total surrender, total compliance, complete submission. An arrogant, pompous Carrie Holland held her shoulders high and her cleft chin up, knowing that the weak, ghost chasing, jerk of a girl couldn't even protect herself, couldn't defend her cheap, love du jour fling with Mitch.

That was until... Dylan Klaypool exploded.

Raging with anger, Dylan grabbed the front of Carrie's shirt with both fists and ran full speed ahead. Clearing out, like the Red Sea at Moses' raised staff, the uninvited audience parted wide as Dylan forced Carrie the width of the hall and crashed her into the opposite wall of lockers. Enough was enough.

Dylan spied her own fierce reflection in Carrie's wide, panicked eyes. "Hey!" the snobby girl cried, disliking being on the receiving end of it. Dylan, with a sudden realization of what she was doing - behaving erratically, becoming what she despised: abusive - didn't care much for the changing of roles either. But wasn't about to stop herself.

"Is Mitch your boyfriend?" Dylan asked, in an eerily calm tone.

"We went out for a year."

Dylan leaned in, crushing Carrie's body into the blue, metal lockers. "Is he your boyfriend *now*?"

Carrie shook her dizzy head. Her heavy breaths blew Dylan's curly hair away with each exaggerated huff.

"Then leave me alone. Quit following me, bumping into me, and quit leaving me nasty notes on my locker."

"What the hell are you talking about?"

Dylan pressed more firmly on Carrie, until their bodies were laying flatly against each other's. The rage in Dylan's eyes crushed mightily against Carrie's will to fight back.

"I'm not messing around, Carrie. I'm *not,*" Dylan hissed.

"I don't know what note you're talking about. Okay?"

Dylan bit down on her bottom lip, again starting to seethe with fury. She reigned the angst in just in time to stop herself from punching Carrie's pointed, cover girl nose.

"The anonymous note! On my locker, yesterday."

Dylan kept Carrie pinned down and watched her sputter a handful of incoherent syllables, as she squirmed and wiggled with a half-hearted attempt to free herself. Finally, Carrie found the words she had been searching for.

"Do-do-do I come off as an *anonymous note* person to you? *Really?*"

In a split second, Dylan knew Carrie was right. The confrontational, loud-mouthed, Homecoming Queen seemed like the *last* person that would leave a note – let alone an anonymous one! But, if it wasn't Carrie that had left it, who *had*?

Dylan eased the pressure she'd been applying on Carrie's body. Surprisingly, the snotty blond was a timid pushover once Dylan had asserted herself with such confidence. Dylan wondered if she was the first person to fight back when Carrie had declared her dominance over them. Carrie's bark was that of a pit bull, but her bite seemingly belonged to a mosquito. One that required only a single smack to completely obliterate.

Dylan cleared her throat, unsure what to say next. Although not comfortable with the unfamiliar sense of control, Dylan utilized her current status as top dog to add an exclamation point to the moment. She grimaced and moved her face close to Carrie's. With a haunting whisper, Dylan delivered a stern warning.

"If you keep bothering me, I'll summon enough evil spirits to keep you screaming day and night for the rest of your pathetic life." She struggled to finish the hollow threat with a straight face. Dylan could easily see that Carrie believed her just enough not to test her. At least not there, not then.

When Dylan let go, Carrie didn't mutter a word. She shuffled sideways until she could get around Dylan and scurried away down the hall. Seeing that the excitement was over, the gawking kids put away their phones and scattered in all directions.

Alone, Dylan exhaled. *What a rush!* Wow. Who knew the pale, cagey girl who cowers silently with slouched shoulders and a hanging head could tame the wildest beast in the jungle? *Who knew?*

Returning to her locker to fetch the items she had left behind during her failed escape from the initial confrontation, Dylan stopped short and pondered for a moment as something popped into her mind.

If Carrie didn't write that note, there was only one other person who might have: Tamara Castle.

38

During lunch, Dylan bit her tongue to keep from questioning Mitch about the flirtatious, promiscuous Ms. Castle and why she would leave a warning about getting close to Mitch. What was the woman claiming? That Mitch *belonged* to her? Just what was *really* going on?

Dylan had grown to trust Mitch. Truly, she did. There was something about him that made her feel at ease, happy... normal. She wasn't ready to accuse Mitch of an inappropriate relationship with a teacher or to accuse him of being dishonest with her. The two unusual teens had grown close, but it wasn't like they were committed to each other, either. Although Dylan was guilty of imagining it, she and Mitch were by no means a couple. If he had a history that included the poor choice of a romantic relationship with Tamara Castle, Dylan wanted to know about it. However, she decided she'd rather find out from someone other than Mitch...

Sending Mitch home without her, claiming that Candice was picking her up because they had after school plans together, Dylan slinked her way towards Ms. Castle's classroom, dreading each torturous step. Channeling the Dylan that had heroically put Carrie Holland in her place that morning, the naturally passive girl sailed through the open door determined not to let her inhibition get the best of her. This was something she *needed* to do. She *needed* to know the truth about Mitch and Ms. Castle before she ended up getting hurt.

The pieces began to form a disgusting image. The casual touches that she'd often seen Ms. Castle softly apply to Mitch's arms and back. The two of them showing up together at school, laughing and carrying on, carefree. Mitch's constant slips when referring to his teach by her first name. Carrie's hatred of Tamara – that particular one might be the clincher. But, the strangest thing was the private meeting yesterday there in Ms. Castle's room at lunchtime. *Jealousy? Watch yourself?* Dylan should've known then what was going on. If it all wasn't so absurd, a woman in her thirties involved romantically with student, it might not have been able to sneak under Dylan's nose.

"Um... Ms. – *uh, hum* – Ms. Castle?" Dylan did not exactly get off to the most intrepid beginning.

Tamara looked up from the stack of papers she was reviewing, placed the cap on her red Bic pen, and slowly pulled the black-rimmed frames down her nose, letting them fall to hang at her chest on the beaded string around her neck.

"Dylan? What brings you in?"

Tense and uncertain, Dylan reached into her back pocket, removed the folded paper. Picking at the bent corner, she hesitated, held it, still creased, in between fingers on both hands, and pulled down, one by one, the words floating in her mind.

"I, uh, just… wanted to -"

"You look worrisome. Is everything okay?"

"Yeah, uh, I, uh, just…" Suddenly, like those trying days seated in Dr. Belmonte's office, Dylan couldn't seem to get the words out properly. "Um, I…"

Ms. Castle pushed herself away from the desk, got up from her chair, and scooted around the corner of the desk to where Dylan awkwardly stood, sputtering nonsense. The teacher reached out, placed a comforting hand on Dylan's left shoulder, and tilted her head, slightly, with soft, concerned eyes. When Tamara sat on the corner of the desk, they became nearly the same height. Dylan kept her eyes just low enough to avoid direct contact.

"Dylan, you look upset," Tamara Castle observed, massaging the front of the girl's shoulder by moving her thumb in a circular pattern.

"Well," Dylan paused to exhale, "I just have a question for you."

Ms. Castle's mouth opened, her eyebrows raised up the way Dylan imagined they would if the woman was about to stroke a furry, little puppy. With the voice she most likely used on her young twins, Ms. Castle spoke. "Anything at all, Dylan. Anythi -"

"Look, this whole thing is, um, this whole…" Dylan gazed at the ceiling with her head back.

"Hey, I knew this was coming," Ms. Castle confessed. Dylan again faced the teacher. "I knew that, eventually, you would need to discuss this with me."

So, it was true, after all, Dylan thought. Her heart began to pound, mightily. It seemed as though her entire body shook with each pulsating thud. Dylan could feel her face changing from chalky white to blood red. Not only was she desperately uncomfortable with the conversation about to ensue, she also felt anger at Mitch beginning to rise from the pit of her stomach. It felt sour, hot. It creeped up her insides, slowly picking up strength with each passing moment.

Ms. Castle's eyes moved to something over Dylan's shoulder. When Dylan heard two elfish voices accompanied by the sound of four running, kid-sized sneakers, she knew they had been interrupted. "Mommy!" the high, nasally voices screamed, delightfully.

"Hey, Guys!" Tamara kneeled to embrace her children. Dylan glanced down, saw Ms. Castle's skirt ride up her tanned and shiny, perfect thighs. *No wonder,* Dylan said to herself, holding in emotions that were pounding against her eyes from inside. She wasn't going to give this pervert the satisfaction of seeing her cry.

Another set of steps came from behind. These were heavier, slower, with a slight shuffle between each one. The voice, although female, was deep, raspy. This woman was either battling a cold or had smoked too many cigarettes over the course of her life.

Standing up, smile beaming, Ms. Castle spun Dylan around with her arms. "Dylan, I'd like you to meet my mother, Rebecca. Mom, this is our newest student at Black Willow High, Dylan Klaypool."

"Hello there, Dylan," the older, less fit, but equally beautiful woman greeted, kindly.

"Hi… Mrs. Castle," Dylan mumbled through timorous lips. She'd only ever seen a woman this age wear so much makeup on television. But, Dylan couldn't deny the fifty-something lady pulled it off easily. Just like her daughter, this woman knew how to present herself in a way that undoubtedly brought men – even students – to their knees.

"Oh, it's Moore."

"I'm sorry?" Dylan whispered.

"Rebecca Moore," the teacher's mother corrected.

"Castle is Tamara's married name. *Was* her married name. Well, still is, but she's not…"

"Mom," Ms. Castle interrupted. "It's fine. Dylan understands."

"Well, I know it's kind of a *thing*," Rebecca made a flippant motion with her hand, during a passive-aggressive attempt at defending herself. Dylan could see that maiden names, married names, and divorce must have been an often discussed, even argued about, topic between the woman and her grown daughter.

"Dylan, give me just a second?" Ms. Castle said, ushering the three visitors back towards the door, corralling the herd with her widespread arms.

"Mother, can you please take them outside? Just in the hall? For a minute or two?" Ms. Castle was making an obvious effort to keep her voice low enough that the children wouldn't hear her.

Listening to Ms. Castle ask her mother to watch the kids just a bit longer, Dylan stepped backwards towards the teacher's desk, wishing she could crawl under it, and disappear from the room. Dreading Ms. Castle's forthcoming explanation, Dylan closed her eyes.

Rebecca Moore, not quite the doting grandmother that

Candice was, huffed with annoyance. "Come on, Kids. Mommy isn't ready for you yet."

Defiantly, the two rug rats yanked their arms away from Rebecca's half-hearted grip.

"Mommy, come *on!*"

"I don't want to go out there!"

The twin's protesting whines echoed, wanting to stay in their mother's classroom while she finished up her duties, but Tamara's voice was stern. "Hey," she scolded. "Is this how we act? You don't want my friend Dylan to think you two aren't as sweet as I've been telling her. Do you?"

A child hugged each of her legs, resisting the tugs of their grandmother that would lead them back into the empty hall.

Realizing this break of after-school routine wasn't going over well, Ms. Castle took her son and daughter by the hand. "I'll be just one second," she turned and said to Dylan.

Walking her family through the door, Ms. Castle left Dylan alone, next to her desk. Flinching, Dylan looked down at the desktop covered with Ms. Castle's belongings. Pencils, pens, laptop, framed photos – her phone. It was the vibration of her supersized, leather case-enclosed iPhone Plus reverberating on the desk that had startled Dylan. The screen was lit up; Ms. Castle had received a text.

"Who is texting you, *Tamara?*" Dylan whispered, while allowing her snooping eyes to drift to the screen. An image, Ms. Castle's two kids dressed in their Halloween costumes holding overflowing sacks of candy stretched from corner to corner on the device. The picture, however, wasn't what bothered Dylan. Instead, it was the words that had popped up across the top of the screen.

Tonight works. Come over at 7?

An invitation; a plan for tonight. Dylan chewed on her bottom lip, shoved the note from her locker safely back inside her pocket.

"Are you kidding me?" she mumbled over a quivering bottom lip. "I can't even…" Dylan wasn't staying for this. She didn't need to see or hear more from Ms. Castle. It was all right there before her watery eyes.

Confirmation. Proof.

Above the text, in larger, bolder letters, was the name of the contact who had sent the message. The person who had a 7:00 p.m. rendezvous with the sexy, single mother was exactly whom Dylan had suspected it might be – Mitch Wolf.

Causing Dylan to jump, Ms. Castle clicked her heels back into the room. "Sorry about that, Dylan. Now let's get back to what we were talking about."

"Actually… um… I need to head out."

"But, I thought you needed to talk about this. I think we *should* talk about this."

"No, no really. I'm late. My grandmother is outside waiting for me. I really need to run."

"But -" Ms. Castle didn't finish her sentence, as Dylan breezed past her.

In the hall, Dylan could hear Ms. Castle's boy and girl gleefully playing with the locks on the lockers, while their grandmother harshly pleaded with them to stop. But, the sounds all faded, everything muted when Dylan turned the first corner and leaned her shoulder against the cold, brick wall, giving up her fight with the tears that now streamed freely down her face.

The flood gates had opened.

39

A steady, cold breeze carried the lightly falling snowflakes though the hole left in Dylan's heart as she passed the cemetery. Her tears were gone, emptied out while balled up on her bed after getting home, but the lump in her throat still was fresh and invasive. She felt like an idiot.

Ignoring the extended wave from the gravedigger she could barely make out from the corner of her eye, she kicked a stone in disgust. Cringing, she fought off the urge to swear from the stinging pain the stone caused when the toenail on her big toe clipped it, unprotected by the soft, cloth sneaker that covered it.

The trickling snow was pretty, but Dylan wasn't up for appreciating it. In fact, she didn't even know why she was making the walk to the old abandoned house that evening. Without her backpack full of equipment, she wouldn't be doing any investigating.

Perhaps, it was just the house itself she longed for, the presence of a spirit that needed her, *wanted* her near.

A raspy growl rattled in Dylan's throat. "*God,* Mitch!" All her muscles twitched, causing an exaggerated squirm from her eyebrows to her toes. Shaking her appendages, Dylan cast off her disgust.

"I get it," she moaned to no one, "Ms. Castle is hot. And sexy. She's… uh… uh." Abhorrence clung to her like sand after a day at the beach. Her repulse had turned into a rhythmless dance that tried to shake off the stubborn grains in vain. "Ugh! Eee-ah!" Words couldn't express her horror the way groans could.

Mitch not turning out to be what she thought and hoped was just another in a long series of disappointments for her. Dylan understood disappointment and didn't fool herself with thoughts that life should be fair.

She had never, not since the age of seven anyway, been so naïve to believe that life was easy, that people were kind, or that anyone gave a damn about her.

White snowflakes tried to cling to the stalks of corn with limited success. The wind carried most of the tiny crystals far away, and the ones landing on the road immediately vanished. The days had been chilly, but few nights had reached freezing, leaving the ground warm enough to swallow any of the billions of unique flakes that touched it.

Dylan puffed out a long breath that flowed from her mouth like she'd exhaled a long drag from a soggy, chewed-up cigar. "Mrs. Columbo once had an admirer that was much younger," Dylan said aloud, imitating the gruff voice of the glass-eyed Lieutenant Columbo, wittingly cozying up to a murder suspect without them realizing he was actually interrogating them. "Ms. Castle, would you say you're, uh, *fond* of Mitchell? Uh, more so than, a, other students?" Dylan scrunched her eyes, lowered her head, and imagined wearing the TV character's long, brown raincoat. "Is this dress, this low-cut top, which is beautiful by the way... Mrs. Columbo loves this color. Just loves it. The pillow cases on our bed are this color. And I don't know about colors. But *this* color, *this* dress... I mean, look at it. Is this a dress you'd wear in class? In front of the students?"

Dylan quickly changed her voice to a flirty much higher tone. "Oh, this old thing? Let me turn around and show you how nicely it flows."

"Would you mind? Just one spin? That would be wonderful. You're too kind." Dylan pretended to squeeze a nearly-spent cigar between her fingers and scratched her forehead, avoided getting imaginary ashes in her messy hair.

"Oh... just one more thing," she said, hardly able to keep from laughing at her own poor acting. "Do you find it odd that one of your students, Mitchell Wolf, has your number, your private cell phone number stored in his phone?"

Feeling satisfied with her make-believe, double-role, satire scene, Dylan peacefully accepted her return to loneliness, and took long strides with her head down, catching falling snow on her eyelashes.

Suddenly, though, she stopped when something out of place caught her attention and pulled it violently from her loathing self-pity. Where the driveway met the gravel road was a large, clear imprint of a boot sole.

Dylan crouched to get a closer look. Squatting over it,

she studied the lines it made, some straight, some squiggled, some jagged. The compressed, sandy earth had preserved it wonderfully.

"*Cat*," she said, reading the word molded in all capitals – *CAT* – spelled out in the center. With the sun setting behind her, Dylan didn't even have to ponder it.

"Mitch wears *Wolverine*," she said out loud to the rows of corn. "These aren't his." Mitch didn't leave these tracks while they were investigating the house.

Searching her memory, she looked down the quiet road at the gravedigger's rusty, red pickup, and tried to remember if she had noticed the brand name on his boots that day he approached her on the road. She then closed her eyes, hunted for the image in her mind of the footprint she found that night walking home, the night she was certain someone was following her. Frustrated she couldn't remember the details, Dylan grunted, "What brand does he wear?"

Dylan removed her phone, and with shivering, red hands snapped a photo of the print. Even with daylight fading, she was glad to see the image had been captured nicely with each line visible. "Gotcha', Cat," she whispered and clicked her phone screen off.

Popping from her bent knees, Dylan trotted, briskly, towards the gravedigger's truck. Light was quickly leaving Black Willow, and the gravedigger was still loading up fallen leaves in the back corner of the cemetery, so she needed to work quickly.

Breathing heavily, she slowed to a walk, peeked off in the distance between headstones, taking note of the man's location. As she had hoped, he was occupied with his work, not facing the road. She carefully, keeping her motions to a minimum, moved around the truck, looking in the soft gravel. When she reached the tailgate, where the man had unloaded some equipment, she found what she was looking for: a clear boot print.

Peering over her shoulder, she made sure the gravedigger still hadn't noticed her, then clicked a photo of the print. *Wolverine*. The same as Mitch's and different from the one near the house.

Dylan could taste clear fluid running from her nose down to her lips as she sprinted back to the old, boarded up house. Wiping it away with her bare hands, she never broke stride until she reached the driveway. Straining her eyes in the dark, she again found the track that had initially caught her attention. She scoured the area, looking for others, but the dirt on country roads was inconsistent. Some spots were soft enough to capture a boot print, others could be walked on without leaving a trace.

Not having her flashlight with her, Dylan used the one built into her phone, and shined it, hunched over, up and down the end of the driveway. It was then that her heart stopped.

Frozen from fear, Dylan stood like a sculpture in a museum and jammed her still shining phone into her front pants pocket, hiding the light. She couldn't be certain, but thought that when the cornstalks had suddenly shaken, sending the loud rustling leaves to her ears, that she had spotted something - *someone* - dash into the field. A person.

The outline of a figure, bipedal, had raced through her peripheral vision into the dried, brittle stalks of corn. Fleet of foot, the person she saw had moved quickly across the wide dirt road, disappearing into the corn. Whomever it had been, clearly didn't wish to be seen, and that frightened

Dylan even more. Without thinking, Dylan reacted to one of her body's strongest, most convincing instincts – *run.*

Speeding, full tilt, Dylan sprinted, kicking up loose gravel under every step. It wasn't the first time Dylan had run home from the house, but this time she felt like she was in real danger. She had *seen* someone. Though she'd only seen the person take their final steps into the rows of corn, she was sure they must have run across the entire road at a high clip. So, now, she knew she needed to move.

"Hey!" called a voice from behind, as she passed the cemetery, launching her striding legs into another gear. No way was she stopping.

"Hey!" the voice called again. This time, the gruff, frail voice sounded familiar. She knew who was hollering out to her. It was the gravedigger.

Instantly second guessing herself, Dylan allowed her clopping feet to slow, until she finally came to a stop. She squinted her eyes when the old, friendly man who had been collecting leaves from the graveyard switched on his headlights, shining the beams directly on her. The nearly blinded girl could see his shape standing next to the truck, reaching through the driver's side window. Putting a flat palm to her forehead to block the light, Dylan walked to where the man waited.

Snowflakes fell in the moonlight between them, as the sun had tucked itself in for the night. "What's got you running?" he asked, standing still with a hand in each pocket. He wore a thick, brown colored Carhartt coat and an orange, baseball-style cap with furry flaps that folded down over his ears.

Dylan caught her breath, swallowed the dry, cold air and swiped her hand across her dripping nose then cleaned it off on her pants. Surprised that seeing the gravedigger brought a semblance of relief to her mind, Dylan spoke directly, confident. "I saw someone. In the corn."

The gravedigger looked back to where Dylan had come from at high speed, then spun his head back to her, finding her almost standing straight in front of him. He grinned the same nonchalant grin she had seen him with during their prior meetings. It tried to hide under his untrimmed mustache, but the glow his face emitted shined brightly, giving it away.

"You saw someone in the corn?"

"Yeah," Dylan huffed and puffed, her breath flaring in the headlights. "Someone… over there." She pointed at the haunted house.

"Hasn't been anyone in that house for years. Twenty, probably. At least."

"Not *in* the house. Outside. They ran across the road and jumped into the field."

"I had a big coyote run through the cemetery just about two, three minutes ago. He must've cut through this side of the corn, broke out, crossed the road, and jumped in the other side. I bet that's what you saw."

"I *didn't*. It *wasn't*. It was a person. I saw him or her… on two feet."

"Well, he was a big one."

"I saw a *person*."

The gravedigger reached into the window again, turned the key, igniting the engine. After a series of sputters, it finally roared to life. "Ain't no people running these roads. 'Cept you, of course. There's no homes down that way at all. Just the one there where no one lives. There's no people wandering around here."

With the cold air embracing her tightly, Dylan processed the events, silently. In a single motion, she reached over her head, slid the hair-tie off her wrist around her curly hair, holding it up into a ponytail.

"You best be gettin' home," suggested the gravedigger, opening his truck door.

Dylan nodded in quiet agreement. She stuck her ice-cold hands into her jacket pockets, turned on one heel, and made her way back to Candice's.

***

Finding Candice in the living room comfortably watching a TV chef sauté a seasoned chicken breast in a pan next to chopped green and red peppers, Dylan cruised on by to her room with a softly spoken, "Hey."

Candice barely took her eyes off the sizzling stovetop that the HD screen portrayed with such detail. Dylan knew that Candice took those shows seriously. Often, the meals that Candice made for she and Dylan were from recipes Candice had discovered by watching them.

Sinking into her bed, Dylan pulled the blankets over her body, hoping to defrost her aching legs and arms. Without noticing, she must have dozed off, because she felt herself jerk awake. Dylan's eyes flung open to find the white, bumpy ceiling hovering over her. It was then, she began putting what had happened together.

Coyote.

Corn.

Person.

Corn.

Coyote in. Person out.

No way.

With nothing in her mind except what she thought she might have seen, she grabbed her phone and pressed Mitch's name. Dylan waited while it rang. Three times, four times, five times it rang, until, after the sixth, the automated message instructing her to leave a message blared into her ear.

Pressing end, she looked down at the screen. *Of course,* she thought, disappointed. The phone read 7:07 p.m.

She shook her weary head and remembered that Mitch had plans that evening: a scheduled meetup, a date with an attractive, long-legged, downright dirty, high school science teacher.

40

Mitch Wolf whispered for a third time. "Hey."

Finally, Dylan noticed his low volume calls during Mr. Amal's slideshow of images from previous years' class trips to Paris. The lights were low and Mr. Amal's monotone voice describing the images on the large screen in the front of the room had boomed loud enough to cover Mitch's soft words. Lacking enthusiasm, Dylan looked in Mitch's direction. Her eyes asked, *What?*

"I need to talk to you," he mouthed to her, irritated. Dylan knew he was upset by now with her avoiding his phone calls, not responding to his texts, and hiding from him in the halls.

Carrie's blond hair shook and a theatrical sigh floated to the ceiling from her disgruntled mouth, sitting in front of Dylan. Pretending she hadn't noticed, Dylan signaled with her hands and shoulders to Mitch. *What is it?* her motions asked.

First checking to see if the teacher was looking, Mitch handed a small, torn off strip of paper back across the aisle to her. She looked at it sitting on her desk with his scribbles strewn across it. Annoyed, Dylan inspected the ripped piece of blue-lined, white paper.

I don't think it's her.

Dylan pinched the bridge of her nose, tightly closed her eyes, then looked at Mitch, who appeared both eager to share, but also frustrated with his friend. Mitch tore another strip of paper from the partial page in his notepad, fervently jotted a sentence onto it. He again made the reach and placed it on Dylan's desk.

She wanted nothing more than to wad it up and toss it at his deceitful face. What kind of a kid, a sixteen-year-old kid, becomes romantically involved with his high school teacher? The whole thing was total insanity.

"Hey!" Mitch whispered loudly, prompting another spiteful whip of blond hair from the girl in front of Dylan. "Hey!" he whispered again, literally begging a despondent Dylan to read his latest note.

Making her disinterest in what the boy was eager to show her clear, Dylan unenthusiastically rolled her eyes with an annoyed huff. Mitch's face was red, covered with confusion at Dylan's odd behavior towards him.

For several seconds, Dylan's mind didn't grasp what her eyes were seeing. Mitch's scribbles were messy, but the words were decidedly legible. Her heart sank. What could it mean?

I found Sarah.

When Dylan looked up, Mitch was staring, waiting for

her to react. He nodded, pulled another chunk of scrap paper from his pad. His eyes pleaded with her to respond.

In Dylan's heart, she wanted to turn away and never look at him again, but in her mind, she knew that the information he'd just handed her was bigger, more important than her wounded heart. There was no sense in hiding her shock.

Seeing Dylan's eyes light up, Mitch fumbled his phone from his pocket, quickly touched the icons that would navigate to the page he needed. Reaching over, he pushed his phone across Dylan's desk.

There she was: Sarah Hodge. The woman Dylan saw on the screen was much older now, but it surely looked like the girl by the water in the framed photo at the house on Cemetery. On Mitch's screen was a Facebook profile. *Sarah Doan, Reed City, age 43.*

Under her nose, another slip of frayed paper appeared on her desk.

We're going there after school.

As badly as Dylan wanted never to speak to Mitch again, *never* would have to start tomorrow. Today, she was riding with him to Reed City after school.

41

A cold breeze was sneaking through a broken seal on the passenger door of Mitch's truck as it sped along a bumpy, patched roadway. Still, Dylan stayed as close to the armrest as she could, creating the largest possible gap between herself and an increasingly concerned Mitch.

"You okay, Dyl?" he wondered, treading lightly with his tone.

"I'm fine," she told him, keeping her eyes firmly locked on the passing trees through the windshield.

She heard Mitch exhale through his nostrils: a sign of worry, a lack of understanding. Dylan wasn't about to bring up Ms. Castle to him because, frankly, she decided it was none of her business. After all, she'd only known Mitch a short while, and their brief exchange of affection was surely nothing compared to the relationship he had with Tamara.

The entire thing was so ridiculous; Dylan planned to stay as far from it as she could. Just as she was doing with Mitch in the cab of his truck.

Obviously avoiding Dylan's mood, Mitch stuck to the topic at hand. "It looks like her. Right?"

"It does."

"I mean, older, a bit heavier. But, it's her. I think."

"How did... How'd you find her... with her name being different?" Dylan wished she could slide over, rest herself against the boy she'd grown so fond of, but knew she couldn't. She'd never be able to think of Mitch the same as she had before.

"Well, I started doing searches for Sarah Hodge with no luck. Then I..."

"Wait," Dylan blurted, "What made you so certain she was alive in the first place?"

"The evidence, your recordings. Dylan, they don't sound female to me."

"But, you can't tell. I mean, those voices on the recorder are nothing more than breaths made into words."

"I just had a feeling," he explained.

"And on the SB7, you weren't even there for those. Those didn't sound male *or* female. Just voices. Neutral sounding voices."

"I had a feeling, okay? And it seems I might be right."

Still without looking in his direction, she played into Mitch's loosely ascertained theory. "But, if it is a male spirit, then *who* is it? There appears to be no other males in the family other than Dean. And he's alive."

"What if this person was a visitor? A friend? Someone who just happened to be in the wrong place, wrong time?"

"All the evidence, the words, all of it points to that

bedroom upstairs. Someone, someone innocent, was hurt by Dean. At least… I think." Dylan paused. "If it isn't the girl, Sarah, I don't know who it could be."

"Sarah's alive, Dyl." Mitch's way of abbreviating Dylan's name had turned from annoying to flattering and now back to annoying. Dylan was so put off, it felt like Mitch was now being rude by saying it.

Mitch went on, "Well, we'll see, I guess. If we get there and are completely sure it's her, that is."

"Back to your search," Dylan said, remembering her initial question. "How did you find her?"

"I saw a group on Facebook for Black Willow High graduates. I checked out Class of 1994. There are only about thirty members. Her profile pic stood out like a sore thumb."

It was nice work by Mitch. Dylan couldn't deny it but refused to verbally commend the two-timing liar.

"Maybe it's an old ghost from the past. Like, way in the past," Mitch suggested.

"Maybe," Dylan said, giving just an ounce of credence to his thought. "But, I think Dean Hodge played a role in this whole thing. It's too weird for it to not involve him. Just the fact that the house was left to rot like that. With all their belongings still there, no less. There might be more to it, sure. But, we're on the right track with Hodge… I just know it."

The remainder of the fifty-minute drive north to the small, although slightly larger than Black Willow Creek, town known as Reed City was without conversation. Dylan, enamored with the new information regarding Sarah and the house, wished she was checking out this new lead alone.

She didn't speak again, ignoring random concerns

from Mitch about directions to the address they were looking for, until the truck came to a stop on a side street in the heart of what looked like a well-maintained, middle-class community.

"I think that's it," Mitch said without pointing. His eyes led Dylan to the house he was speaking of.

"The one with the car out front?" she asked, for clarity.

"Yeah."

"What's the plan, Columbo?" Dylan's voice dripped with ire that she figured Mitch certainly heard. "You just going to knock on the door and ask if her father is Dean Hodge?"

"No," Mitch remarked, defensively. The tension between them seemed to now be a two-way street. "I'm not going to do that."

"*What* then?"

"I'm thinking."

"We drove all the way up here, and you have no plan?"

"Hey, I'm just the helper. Remember? You're the boss."

"God, Mitch it's -"

"I've got it!" he yelled, cutting off the upset girl. "The car in the yard." He pointed. "It has a *for sale* sign on it. I'll go up and act like I'm interested in it."

It's a good idea, thought Dylan. Without giving a shred of praise to the notion, Dylan just nodded her head. The way she did whenever April asked if she'd like *fries with that*. Just a nod, nothing special. "Okay. Fine."

"You'll wait here?" asked Mitch, unbuckling his safety belt.

"I will *not* wait here," snapped Dylan. "Shut the truck off. I'm coming, too."

Mitch sighed, killed the engine. When Dylan pulled the handle on her door, Mitch began to speak. "Look, Dylan, if I've done something to upset you, I'm sorry. I don't know what it might be, but -"

Stopping the defensive boy mid-sentence, Dylan jumped out of the truck and slammed the door on him. "God!" she yelled, marching with bent elbows across the blacktop towards the yard of the house that presumably was where Sarah Hodge now resided.

Hearing Mitch's steps close in on her, Dylan picked up her pace. With no hesitation, she climbed the front steps of the house and racked her knuckles forcefully against the door three times.

"Dylan, what is wrong with you? Can't you just talk to me about whatever is bothering you?" Mitch's voice was desperate. His whisper warmed her ear in the frigid afternoon air.

She didn't acknowledge his plea for an explanation. Instead, she wrapped on the door again, impatiently.

Before Mitch could start insisting she talk to him, they could hear the lock on the other side of the door rattle. With a gust, the door opened. Standing before them was a woman with brown hair, shoulder length. She wore a sweater, black slacks, and dress shoes. Around her neck was a white, pearl necklace that matched the two in her ears. On her left hand ring finger was a gold band with a noticeably large diamond.

With a hearty, welcoming smile, the lady greeted the two combative teens. "Hi there. What can I help you with?"

Dylan poked Mitch with a quick nudge of her elbow. Instantly, his hand extended out to the homeowner. "Hi. I'm, uh, Michael… And this is, uh, Darla."

Dylan rolled her eyes. *Darla?*

"We're interested in your car," Mitch lied.

"Oh, you kids have good timing. I just got home a few minutes ago. Gary isn't here, but I can come out and show it to you. I'm Sarah," she said, shaking Mitch's hand. "Let me grab my jacket," she told them before closing the door, leaving them alone on the porch.

Sarah. With certainty, Dylan knew it was Sarah Hodge.

"What's with the fake names?" Dylan mocked, egregiously.

"It just seemed like the right thing to do. I don't know."

Sarah opened the door and stepped out to join what she thought were prospective buyers of her one-owner, never-seen-snow, lightly used automobile. She held the black, smart key fob in her right hand. Approaching the vehicle with Dylan and Mitch following behind, she pressed the remote start button, and, like magic, the engine fired up.

"Well, you can see it has remote start. Has everything, pretty much. Low mileage, only a few years old. Say," Sarah turned to them, "which of you is interested? I assume, you kids are not married."

"Uh, I am," voiced Mitch. "*Interested*, that is."

Sarah pulled open the door of the sleek-looking, slate gray, coup. "Hop in," she offered with a gesture.

Mitch climbed into the leather, bucket seat, gripped his palms around the contoured steering wheel. The entire dash was lit up with hi-tech features, from miles per gallon to tire pressure.

"Just how many lawns does a kid your age have to mow to save up enough down payment on a three-year-old

Cadillac?" Sarah passively asked.

Standing behind the woman who was leaning on the open door, Dylan quickly chimed in. "Oh, he's not paying for it. His dad is loaded. Spoils Mike every chance he gets."

Sarah stepped away, so she could see both of her visitors. "Well, I guess I can relate to that."

For a second, Dylan made eye contact with Mitch. If Sarah was willing to reminisce, they should try to keep her talking.

"Sounds like you have experience with that. Does your husband spoil your kids?" pried Dylan, casually.

"No. No kids for us. But, my dad was a spoiler. Bought me anything I wanted, whenever I wanted," the older woman explained with a voice absent of feeling. "He was… He was something else."

Mitch filled the awkward silence by throwing a baited hook, looking for an informative bite. "Sounds like a great father. I imagine you're still close with him."

They watched for a reaction, anything that might help them sort out had what happened at the haunted house in Black Willow. Sarah touched her face, rubbed her fingers along her jaw, like she was thinking deeply.

"My father passed away a long time ago… A long, long time ago."

Dylan froze. *Something isn't right*, she said to herself. *Something definitely isn't right.*

"What do you say, Kid? Take it for a spin?" Sarah said to Mitch, unaware the snooping pair knew with certainty that her father was alive and well.

Looking for one more piece of confirmation, one more tidbit to solidify what they were sure they already knew, Mitch cast his line again. "No, that's okay. We need to get back to Black Willow. Darla's mom is expecting her."

"Black Willow?"

"Yeah," said Dylan, picking up where Mitch left off. "You familiar with it?"

"Yeah… I grew up there."

"Really? I live by the old cemetery." Dylan held her breath, waited for Sarah's response.

"No kidding? *I* grew up near the old cemetery."

Just like that, any leftover doubt was wiped away. Sarah Doan from Reed City was none other than Sarah Hodge from Black Willow Creek.

The spirit that lingered in the old abandoned house by the cemetery was someone else.

42

Dylan's cold feet rattled on the floor of Mitch's truck from the uneven, pot-holed, two-lane highway. Let down from the news that Sarah Hodge was not the ghost she'd been communing with for the past weeks, Dylan hadn't the energy to be rude to Mitch – even though he deserved it. And Dylan wished no harm to Sarah either, glad to see her still alive. She just wished she knew who had been speaking to her through whispers in Black Willow.

Shortly after leaving Sarah Doan standing alone in her yard next to a sharp, shiny Cadillac, Dylan broke the silence that Mitch was too afraid to venture into. "You were great, back there," Dylan confessed.

She felt him look her direction but kept her gaze on her own faint reflection in the passenger window. "Thanks," he replied. "You were great, too. You're always great."

"I guess it's someone else... In the house."

"We'll figure it out, Dyl." Mitch reached for her hand, but quickly saw that, although her tone had warmed, the ice had not yet thawed. Dylan pulled her hand away, hid it under her leg.

Still early in the evening, the sky was already dark, and light snow began to drift down from it. The wet, frozen flakes swooped around the moving truck, passing the windshield like stars from another universe. Dylan wished she could travel there. Maybe good prevailed there; maybe hearts didn't break.

"Sure," she softly agreed. "We'll sort it all out."

She had told herself that just because she couldn't see herself having a long, intimate conversation with Mitch after learning about he and Ms. Castle, Mitch still needed to know. No matter what he'd done; kissed her, made her fall for him with his aloof, distant, yet engaging, charm while carrying on a secret, even illegal, relationship - he still *deserved* to know what she'd seen.

"Mitch, I saw something last night... at the house."

Unable to mask the rejection he was feeling, Mitch's words lacked the usual care that Dylan had sometimes taken for granted. "Another shadow? Orb?"

"No. Nothing like that."

This time when Mitch turned towards her, Dylan's eyes were there waiting. "What was it?" he asked.

As Mitch looked back to the now snow-covered road, Dylan, hesitant, tiptoed around the details. "It was something outside. On the road."

"Can - can you tell me more? Dylan what is wrong with you today?"

"Never mind what is wrong with me. Okay? Look, last

week, I don't remember exactly which day or anything, someone followed me home from the house."

"Who?"

"I didn't see, but I heard them, and I saw boot prints on the road."

"You just said you saw something last night. This person again?"

Shifting in her seat, Dylan turned her knees to the center of the truck. "I found a boot print, and while I was hunched over looking at it, I saw a figure dash past me and crash into the cornstalks."

"What? Are you - who do you - what did you do?"

"I ran, of course. I was totally freaked out."

"Who would be out there?"

"Mitch, that's not what is really bothering me about this. I mean, it does bother me that someone is hanging around the house, but there's more."

"Dyl, what is it? Come on, spill it."

Dylan let out a long sigh. "The gravedigg-" She paused again to correct herself. "Your grandfather told me he saw a large coyote pass through the cemetery into the corn. He figures it moved through the corn, then crossed the road near me."

"But you saw a *person*. Right? Not a coyote."

"I'm sure I saw a person, Mitch. On two legs, running into the field."

Void of expression, Mitch's face went colorless.

"Mitch, are you okay?"

Clearing his throat, Mitch physically shook off the nervousness. "Yeah… Yeah, I'm okay."

"Have you ever - Throughout your life, do you think you've ever -"

"Seen it? The Skin Walker?"

Dylan's silence served as a *yes*.

"Only every time I see a wild animal. At least, it feels like that," Mitch confessed.

Too dark to see, Dylan could hear that Mitch was verging on tears. She unlocked her seat belt, moved over just enough to reach him with her outstretched arm. Her fingers stroked his long hair, her nails gently rubbed against his scalp. She remembered all the times that a blowing curtain, a falling leaf, or a shadow from someone passing would send panic and fear through her. If Mitch only knew how similar they were... Dylan was desperate to spill her guts to him, show him what she'd been through. But, exposing her complicated, dreadful past was something she'd spent the previous nine-plus years avoiding. If anyone might understand, it was Mitch. Still, Dylan remained quiet.

"It may not be what you're thinking," said Mitch, reigning in his emotions. "It's most likely..."

"Mitch! What if it is? What if it *is*?"

Studying the profile of his face, his strong chin and soft lips, Dylan watched Mitch consider the possibility. *What if?* Seeing him concert a conscience effort to downplay the scenario, Dylan slouched in her seat.

"Dylan, it wasn't." He said it, almost like he was certain. "One thing is for sure, though. You shouldn't be there alone. Not anymore. I know you can handle yourself with ghosts. But, Dylan, if someone is hanging around there, following you, watching you..." Mitch shook his head, knowing he didn't need to speculate on the possible horrible outcomes for Dylan to understand his worry.

"Let's stop for coffee," he changed the subject with the suggestion. "Hungry? Bacon cheeseburger?"

Momentarily forgetting her pent-up aggression towards him, Dylan agreed. Truthfully, what could spending a few more hours with Mitch Wolf hurt?

43

Nibbling on a crust-free peanut butter and jelly sandwich, Dylan sat at the head of the dining room table. Not quite tall enough for them to reach, her feet dangled freely over the brown-stained, varnished hardwood floor. Cardboard boxes, some opened with random items sticking out of the tops, were stacked three, even four, layers high. Magic marker in Jill Klaypool's cursive handwriting written on each one designated which room they belonged in. Dylan, still reeling from watching her father being hauled away in handcuffs just a week earlier, couldn't help but eavesdrop on the conversation taking place around the corner in the galley kitchen.

Smoke from Detective Miguel Rodriguez's cigarette crawled along the ceiling, drifting over the young girl's head. "Are you both settling in?" the detective asked. His voice, even when attempting to be soft, carried well enough to be clearly heard from the dining table.

Jill's voice wasn't so easy to hear. But, Dylan knew her mother's speech patterns, tendencies well enough to piece her words together with little effort. "Considering the circumstances," Jill replied.

"Jill, you need to relax. Seriously, everything is fine."

"Fine, Miguel? How could you let something like this happen?"

"I didn't let it happen, Jill," Rodriguez claimed, defensively. "He was arraigned, in custody. My job was done!"

"Well, what if he comes here?"

"He won't."

"How can you be sure?"

"I've got uniforms covering the entire block. Besides, he doesn't even know where this new place is. And we have every reason to believe he's left Chicago."

"What proof do you have of that?"

"Wouldn't you? If you were a fugitive, someone that just escaped police custody prior to a child abuse trial? Wouldn't you leave town?"

Noises, dishes clanging, cupboard doors opening and closing rode on the gagging smoke, through the air. Dylan sipped milk from a short glass with the Chicago skyline etched into it. Her father used to nurse bourbon from it for hours, watching White Sox games. She wasn't sure he'd ever finished the glass even once.

"How's the kid?" Rodriguez asked, over Jill's sniffling.

"She's still not speaking."

"She will. Soon. Now that he's not able to manipulate

her, hurt her."

Dylan listened as Detective Miguel Rodriguez's fancy shoes clicked across the kitchen. "Let's just be glad she spoke to Belmonte. With the doctor's testimony, they'll put him away. And now that he's running from the law, there isn't a jury out there that won't give him the maximum."

Jill blubbered something, muffled by tears and what sounded like a shoulder.

"Hey, don't cry. He'll never look for you in Evanston; he won't look for you at all. Trust me, we'll find him sleeping in a dumpster somewhere in Wisconsin or Indiana."

With milk clinging to the depression between her nose and upper lip, the voluntarily mute girl thought about her father sleeping inside one of the big, green dumpsters she'd seen outside of apartment buildings and businesses.

She wondered if he was warm enough, if he'd had enough to eat, if he missed her the way she was missing him. Dylan wondered if she'd see her father again. Mostly, she wondered if anyone would ever believe that he hadn't been coming into her room at night, that it really was a man made of shadows who could come and go as he pleased, in the blink of an eye.

Luckily, Dylan hadn't seen the devilish spirit that had terrorized her night after night since she and her mother moved out of the high-rise and into their new place. That was the same day she watched Detective Rodriguez push her father's face into the floor with a knee in his back shouting at him. Seeing her father violently manhandled was far worse than being visited by the man made of shadows.

"Shows you how foolish he is, if you ask me,"

Rodriguez went on. "Running is a total admission of guilt. And Belmonte made it clear that she doesn't suspect any sexual abuse. Nathan was looking at eighteen months tops with this thing. Now, escaping from custody, God only knows what he might face. That doesn't even take into account any criminal activity he may have to commit while in hiding. We tell these idiots every time, 'don't run, it'll only make it worse'."

Dylan knew why her father ran; he was innocent.

Seven-year-old Dylan hopped down from the wooden chair, her empty glass in one hand and a plate with bread crust in the other to put in the sink like Mommy had always told her to. Turning the corner, Dylan dropped the Chicago skyline glass onto the beige tiles, shattering it into bits.

She watched her mother quickly pull her mouth away from Detective Rodriguez's. The man's hands were wrapped around Jill's waist, pulling her body into his own. Dylan heard Jill ramble ludicrous reasons why what the girl saw had happened, but her mother's smudged lips may as well have stayed closed because Dylan wasn't listening.

It appeared the mute girl's days of seeing horrible things were far from over.

44

"Mitchie!" April cheered, when she saw he and Dylan walk through the door at Carol's, after they'd returned to Black Willow from Sarah Doan's house. Carrying a steaming plate in each of her hands, the disgruntled waitress even managed to mutter, "Hey, Dylan," as she slipped by. Placing the plates in front of a gray-haired couple, she began her march back to the kitchen.

"Sit anywhere," she said with her back to them, voice fading as she departed.

"Hey, Mitch," a balding man said from a few tables away and waved a wrinkled hand.

"Mr. Birch," Mitch replied, nodding.

"Hi," Mr. Birch said to Dylan when their eyes inadvertently connected.

"Hello, there, Mitch," a middle-aged woman waiting

for a to-go order said from the chair by the cash register.

"Hi, Mrs. Rinaldi," Mitch said with a grin. The woman gave Dylan a pleasant courtesy smile.

Going places with Mitch was like living someone else's life to Dylan. When she was alone, she felt invisible. With Mitch, it was like being an A-list celebrity.

Sitting at a corner table, Dylan quickly pulled out her own chair before Mitch could reach for it. Dylan Klaypool had never needed to be pampered, especially by someone she planned to dismiss from her life in the very near future.

"You guys want coffee?" April asked, already pouring two cups for them. "Steak sandwich and a bacon cheeseburger?"

"Sure," Mitch and Dylan said in harmonized agreement.

During a couple uncomfortable minutes of shared silence, Dylan traced the checkered pattern of the table cloth with her fingernail, then took a turn shuffling sugar substitute packets like playing cards. Blue, pink, white. Blue, pink, white. She watched the steam rise from Mitch's coffee cup. Two streams that quickly spiraled around one another until they became one solid, united band of haze. She followed it up, until she reached Mitch's face, where she quickly retreated her eyes.

A frigid burst of air came barreling through the door when it swung into the dining area. Standing at the door, immediately greeted with kind pleasantries, was a tall, aging man with white hair, large ears and nose, with a prickly mustache growing under his nostrils. It was the gravedigger.

"Would ya look at that?" he said, unzipping his coat, taking short steps towards Dylan and his grandson.

Turning at the sound of the old man's voice, Mitch

welcomed his mother's father. "Grandpa, have a seat with us."

"I know you," the gravedigger said to Dylan with a charming wink. The man oozed kindness, like it was something he couldn't control: an occurrence as natural as breathing.

Dylan had to smile at him. "Hi."

"What is it you two are up to?" Mitch's grandfather asked. "Thank you," he said to April, while she poured coffee into the mug in front of him.

"Oh, August, you don't need to thank me," April teased. As nasty as April could be, lately, Dylan sensed that there was a halfway decent person in there. It seemed that it took certain people to coax it from hiding. But, it was there.

"We just took a drive. Up to Reed City," Mitch informed him, before sipping from his mug.

"What took you up there?"

"Nothing. Looking at a car, is all." Mitch glanced at Dylan, a clear signal letting her know there was no need to divulge the real reason they went.

"Did your friend here tell you about what she saw last night?"

"Um, yeah. The coyote?"

"Put a scare in her. Me, too. This thing was large enough to be a wolf, Mitch. Maybe one of those wolf-oyte, hybrid... You know, coywolves, they call 'em." The gravedigger turned his eyes to Dylan. "You okay?"

"I'm fine, thank you."

"What takes you to that house?" the soft-spoken man asked.

"It's, um, it's interesting. It's – I don't know." Dylan was stumbling. She wasn't about to share that she had been investigating paranormal activity with the gravedigger if Mitch hadn't already.

"Lot of history in that place," August Kendall, the Black Willow Cemetery groundskeeper, glibly mentioned. The flippant statement was like a slow, hanging curveball over the middle of the plate. Mitch didn't hesitate to take a swing at it.

"What do you mean, Grandpa?"

"Oh, just... There were some things that went on there. Seems like a hundred years ago, now." August tore open a packet of Sweet-n-Low, dumped the contents into his coffee. The spoon clinked the inside of the cup as he swirled it around, dissolving the manmade granulate.

Dylan looked at Mitch and raised her eyebrows. She wanted to hear more, Mitch did, too. "What sort of things? What happened there?" Mitch asked his grandfather.

Dylan and Mitch both rested their elbows on the table, leaned in closer to the man many years their senior.

"Happened so long ago, I can hardly remember it all. Hodge. Guy named Hodge lived there with his wife... and they had just the one daughter. Hodge was well off, real well off. He worked down... down somewhere. What did he do again?" The gravedigger leaned his head back, like he was watching memories projected on the ceiling tiles. "Oh, he was a lawyer. Down in Grand Rapids, down there. Big law firm."

"Did something happen to Hodge?" Mitch pried, with one eye on his grandfather, the other on Dylan and her stimulated expression.

"He shot an intruder."

"Really?" Dylan and Mitch expressed their interests concurrently. A maelstrom of ideas burst into Dylan's

mind.

"Yeah, a kid. Twenty-year-old kid, nineteen, maybe. African-American kid."

"Geez, what – what happened?" asked Mitch.

"Well, he climbed up that big tree in the back yard, right up to the daughter's window. I can't think of her name. What was it? Sonya. No, Shirly – *Sarah*. It was Sarah. She must have screamed out for help, I s'pose. Ole Hodge kicked in her bedroom door, found the fella' having his way with his daughter."

Mitch interrupted. "Like, how? What was he doing?"

Fighting off embarrassment, the gravedigger blushed, slightly. "Well, he was… You know, forcing himself on her."

"Raping her?" Dylan jumped in. "Did he rape her?"

"I guess that's what some people say." August took a long swig of coffee.

Innocent, Dylan thought. The whispered word *innocent.*

"So, Hodge shot him." Mitch deduced, somberly.

"Right. In the back, while he laid right on top of… um, Sarah."

"Wow," Dylan said under her breath.

"Kid died. Made it out of the window, hit the ground hard. Fall most likely would've killed him if the bullet hadn't. Hodge, uh, he, you know, protecting his family and what not. Did what most fathers would've, I s'pose."

April banged her hip against the table, leaned her weight against the edge of it. "August, what do you want to eat? We got that roast beef tonight."

"I guess I better have that," he told her, his eyes twinkling like he was casting a spell on her.

"Great. It's good, too, today. I've been picking at it all afternoon. Guys, yours will be out in a sec." April scurried off, bickering with a table about something they still hadn't received that she swore they didn't ask her for.

Dylan raised her head to the entrance when the bell over the door rang out. The door pushed open, letting the wind carry in a handful of dried, crumpled leaves from the sidewalk. Entering, looking more casual, homely than Dylan ever remembered seeing her, was Tamara Castle. In earmuffs, Ugg boots, gray sweatpants with a matching top covered with a long, faux fur-hooded coat, the teacher's eyes glanced around the room.

Dylan's stomach dropped. Of all the people that could've come through the door, it had to be *her*: a conniving, vindictive, cradle-robbing pervert.

Ms. Castle's face sparked like fireworks on the Fourth of July when she saw the three of them seated in the corner. Sliding her mittens off, she rushed right over to join them.

"April," she called over to the register.

"It's not ready, Tam. You got a few minutes left," April informed Tamara without an ounce of zeal.

"Hi, guys!" the teacher expressed with glee. "Oh. My. God. *Right?* What are you all doing having dinner without me?"

Dylan watched in awe as the flirty mother of two wiggled her way, snugly, between the gravedigger and Mitch. On her knees, she was sandwiched between them, one arm around Mitch's chairback, the other around the gravedigger's. In total disbelief, Dylan shuttered at what she saw next. Ms. Castle leaned to her left and pressed her face, lips puckered, into Mitch's cheek. Dylan felt broken.

Was this outlandish teacher-student relationship open

to the public? *Unbelievable.* Dylan was sick. To think she had actually fallen for Mitch, that she thought there might be something special between them, that their souls were somehow connected through a shared fate that went beyond what two high school kids could normally have.

Then, it happened. Tamara Castle turned to her right, moved forward and planted a wet, red lipstick-smearing smooch onto the cheek of the gravedigger.

What in the world is going on here?

"Don't you just love these two?" Ms. Castle asked Dylan with an ear to ear, deep dimpled smile. "I know *I* do."

With her bottom jaw on the table, Dylan didn't know how to answer the teacher.

Tamara motioned toward the chair next to Dylan with her chin. "Can I sit there?"

"Uh… Sure… Of course," Dylan mumbled, mind racing, trying to put together what was going on.

"You know Tami from school?" August asked a confused Dylan.

"I… yeah, I…do."

"This woman means the world to us. Me and Mitch," the gravedigger told Dylan.

"Oh, stop," Ms. Castle gushed with humility.

The gravedigger explained. "When my wife passed, Mitch was just a baby. And then his parents, well, um…"

"It's okay. I've told Dylan about my parents leaving," Mitch comforted his grandpa. "You don't have to hide it."

The gravedigger's face showed obvious relief. "Well, his mom and dad took off, leaving me alone with an eight-year-old. Tami was, what? A college sophomore?"

"Yup. Went back to school at twenty-four," Ms. Castle

confirmed.

"She was commuting an hour each way to classes, didn't have time for a job, but needed income, housing."

"It was a perfect storm," Ms. Castle chimed in.

"She moved in with us for four years. Right up until her wedding. She cooked, cleaned, helped with Mitch. Everything you can imagine, she did for us. She was an angel sent directly from heaven to our house."

Tamara playfully shoved Mitch's arm off the table. "I would've moved right back in after the divorce, but my mom insisted on moving up here to help *me* out with *my* little ones."

"You can take care of me when I get old," teased the gravedigger.

"*When* you get old?" Tamara playfully joked.

Dylan, internally embarrassed at her foolish misjudgment of Ms. Castle's and Mitch's relationship, breathed an enormous sigh of relief. A ton of bricks had been lifted off her shoulders.

"Tam, your food is ready. Can you hurry?" yelled April, standing at the cash register, impatiently holding up a brown paper bag.

August Kendall raised his arm up towards the ginger-haired server. "April, can you bag mine, too? I think I'll take it to go."

April's aggrieved countenance morphed speedily into one of willing servitude. "Of course, I will."

"Dylan," Ms. Castle said, standing up, "I'm sorry if I freaked you out the other day. I just wanted to let you know my Mitch is a sensitive boy. I don't want him to get hurt. And, girl, *you* need to watch it. That Carrie Holland is capable of anything. She's obsessed, like psycho obsessed with Mitch. You be careful with her. That girl is even jealous of *me*. And remember, jealousy can be dangerous."

"Okay, Ms. Castle. Thanks."

"No, not here. No, *Ms. Castle* here. Outside of school it's Tamara – better yet, Tami. If you're friends with these two trouble makers, then you're like family to me." She pointed at Mitch with squinted eyes. "He's like my kid, you know?"

Dylan couldn't help but smile. "Okay, Tami."

"Tam!" April called again.

"I'm coming, April. Keep your shirt on. This isn't the tavern."

"August, yours is ready too, Hun," April added with a smile.

"I'll see you two later," the gravedigger said, standing to join Tamara and April up front.

After paying for their dinners, August and Tamara walked out into the cold together. April brought Dylan and Mitch their food, even refilled their cups without having to be asked multiple times.

All of Dylan's heartache had been for nothing. The playfulness, the affection between Mitch and Tamara was completely normal interaction between two people that were like family. Dylan was amazed at how wrong her perception had been.

Dylan pushed her plate over to the place where the gravedigger had been sitting, got up and moved to the empty chair. Sitting down, she grabbed the cuff of Mitch's shirt, pulled him down to her height, and kissed him, deeply.

"You're not mad anymore?" he asked, smiling.

"I'm not. I'm sorry."

"What had you so upset?"

"Nothing. Just know that I'm not anymore."

"Okay… Hey, Dyl?"

"Yeah?"

"Whoever Hodge shot that night…"

"That's our ghost," Dylan said, finishing his thought, before kissing him again.

45

Dylan Klaypool and Mitch Wolf hung their warm winter jackets on the backs of the light tan chairs inside the Greenville Public Library. After she registered for a library card, Dylan planted herself in front of one of the computers and logged on with her brand-new ID and password.

The helpful, early-twenties man at the information desk assured them that every edition of The Daily News, Greenville's local publication and the county's largest paper, would be available, digitally, through the library's database.

"We eliminated microfiche a few years ago," the man, wearing a V-neck, form-fitting sweater over a white t-shirt, explained. "It was a grueling process, but well worth it. You'll be astonished how quickly you can find whatever you're looking for. And it's only here on our internal intranet. The files aren't accessible through the internet. Only here, inside of the library."

Dylan piloted the keyboard, while Mitch sat eagerly beside her, close enough that their legs touched under the table.

Designed for the ease of reading, the library lights were bright, almost overbearing, like the bulbs over a medicine cabinet that are sure to expose a face's darkest secrets. With the furnace blowing warm, almost hot, air throughout the building, the library in Greenville was cozy, inviting visitors to settle in and stay awhile.

Dylan's fingernails clicked the keys as she punched in a name: Dean Hodge.

Ryan, the librarian who had snapped the photo of Dylan while she stood just behind the strip of duct tape, had been correct. Instantly, several articles showed up on a list in the center of the widescreen, flat panel monitor.

When Dylan clicked the first line, dated July 11th, 1975, she and Mitch found themselves staring at a black and white photograph of a young man and woman, posed affectionately in front of a wall where a giant cross hung, decoratively. The woman held a bouquet of flowers, wore a long, lacy gown, pure white, and had a smile that portrayed absolute joy.

The man, positioned behind her, held her, gently, by the waist, and leaned in so his face was next to hers, so close their cheeks nearly touched. He had a bow tie, a tuxedo, and neatly combed hair that shined from whatever products he used to hold it in just the right place.

Dylan read the brief caption out loud. "Weddings: Black Willow Creek native and law school grad, Dean Hodge, and his high school sweetheart, Charity Schneider, were married on Saturday at the Lutheran Church on Main Street in Black Willow Creek. Both would like to thank all who attended and those that sent well wishes from afar. The two will reside in a house Hodge had built on Cemetery Road."

"Wow. Look at Hodge," Mitch commented. "He's so happy. And young. Try the next one."

"Yeah, okay," Dylan agreed, clicked the article closed, and selected the second one on the list. This one, dated September 9th, 1976, also appeared to have been in the paper's *announcements* section. Mitch took the honor of reading it aloud.

"Birth announcements: Mr. and Mrs. Dean Michael Hodge excitedly welcomed their first child, daughter Sarah Marie Hodge, to their budding family. Charity Hodge delivered her at 5:34 a.m. inside Greenville's Memorial Hospital. Sarah was 20 inches long and weighed 7 pounds, 10 ounces. Happy Birthday, Sarah!"

"Geez," Dylan said. "I feel like I've known this woman her entire life."

"We need to skip ahead. Find 1993," Mitch told her. Dylan did just that.

Clicking an article dated October 11th, 1993, she hit pay dirt.

This article, unlike the two announcements they'd read, was long and didn't have smiling faces or cheery statements. This one was much different. Dylan and Mitch read silently, side by side, slowly moving their awestruck faces closer with each dismal sentence their eyes beheld.

Late last night, prominent community figure and respected lawyer, Dean Hodge, used lethal force to stop what county police officials are labeling as a home invasion. Raymond Dalton Cole, a resident of Saginaw, was shot by Hodge when he was found breaking into an upstairs bedroom of Hodge's Black Willow Creek home. Cole died at the scene.

Hodge was not arrested but will be brought in for formal questioning, as will his daughter. Because she is a minor, her name will not be published by the paper at this time. If police comments are any indication of what to expect, Hodge will likely face no charges in the incident.

Police Captain, Troy Wilcox, longtime friend of the lawyer, made this statement at the scene. "What Mr. Hodge did tonight was heroic. He saved his daughter who was being sexually assaulted by the assailant and her life was unquestionably in danger. We feel that a homeowner, a father, has the right to defend his property and his family by any means necessary. Even with the use of deadly force."

The Daily News will fully cover this story as it continues to unfold.

Neither of the two researching teens spoke, as the weight of the events at the abandoned house on Cemetery landed on them with crushing force. Dylan moved the mouse, so her cursor was over the next and final article, dated just two days later. Together, they read.

Further questioning of Dean Michael Hodge in the death of intruder, Raymond Dalton Cole, 19, proved satisfactory to Police Captain, Troy Wilcox, and County Prosecutor, Lee Hansen. They will not be bringing charges to Hodge regarding Cole's death.

Hodge appeared exacerbated when The Daily News attempted to get his comments about the ordeal. His only words were that the entire situation has left his family "shaken and feeling extremely violated."

The community is praising Hodge and his decisive actions with comments defending him. Some are even suggesting Hodge and his wife of eighteen years should be selected as Grand Marshalls for next summer's annual Black Willow Fair.

Dylan, with her hand to her lips, listened to her heart tapping in the quiet room. Turning to Mitch, she stated what he already knew. "Raymond is our ghost."

Mitch, speechless, exhaled, stared into Dylan's eyes.

"He's innocent," she whispered.

"But, Dyl, we don't -"

"Mitch!" she broke in, stopping him from continuing. "He is innocent. That's what this whole thing has been about. He is innocent."

"What do we do?"

"We set up in the house, tonight. We try everything. We need to find out what really happened that night." She stood up, slung her coat on. "And we aren't leaving without some real answers."

46

Marching through the kitchen, Dylan hit the lifeless switch on the wall with her left hand, as she passed, holding her glowing flashlight with her right. Behind secured planks of wood, the windows rattled with her determined steps. Her shadow, cast from Mitch's light on her back, gave the appearance she was ten feet tall, strong, and a force with which to be reckoned.

"Raymond!" she yelled, stomping on each of the stairs as she ascended. "Raymond Cole! We know who you are!"

She and Mitch stood at the top step, listening. Mitch powered on the Mel-meter, held it still out in front of his body. Within seconds, the REM feature exploded with signals, lights and sounds.

"Dyl!"

"I see it," she calmly acknowledged. "What's the EMF

reading?"

"Seven-point-one!" Mitch exclaimed, loudly.

"Stay calm," she urged. "We need our wits about us. He's responding to his name; he's with us. We must keep calm. If *we* are using our energy with rampant emotions, *he* won't be able to."

Mitch nodded, took long, drawn out breaths through his nostrils. "Nine-point-four, Dyl," he reported, voice cracking.

"I've never seen it go that high. Ever." Dylan snuck her backpack off her shoulder, carefully placed it on the ground at her feet. Delicately unzipping the main pouch, the girl with the haunted past spoke with control and confidence to the ghost of an alleged criminal.

"Raymond," she said, removing her SB7 Spirit Box from her bag of goodies, "you need to talk to us. I know it isn't easy for you to do. But, Raymond, I also know that you want to. We know what you've been trying to tell us. We saw Sarah yesterday."

As the name of the girl that used to live in the house left her lips, Dylan felt a warm sensation on her arm that sent a ripple across her skin. With the Mel-meter still screaming in Mitch's hand, Dylan ordered her partner to turn it off.

"He's touching me, Mitch. Raymond, I feel you touching me."

She held the Spirit Box up, over her head. "Remember this? It's loud and obnoxious, I know, but it works. You spoke to me through it before. Remember? Window, girl, father, bedroom. Remember? Give us more, Raymond. Please, we don't know what happened, but we know what you were accused of. And we know Hodge killed you."

"Dyl," whispered Mitch.

"Yeah?"

"Don't turn it on yet."

"Why?"

"I have an idea."

"What is it?"

"Wait here. Trust me. Keep talking to him, but wait to turn it on."

Dylan turned and looked up at Mitch. Combined, their two flashlights made it easy to see one another. His dark eyes were full of passion, and she knew she could do what he asked of her: trust him.

With Dylan rising on her toes and Mitch lowering his head, the two shared a soft, tender kiss.

"Go," she told him, then watched, as he took off down the stairs.

Dylan stared at the locked door standing at the end of the hallway and continued to talk to Raymond Cole. "I know how a life can be ruined when someone is accused of something they didn't do, when the world believes they committed a crime that never happened. I've seen it first hand, Raymond, and I want to help you. I can only imagine the torture and pain are the same where you are as it is here in the flesh."

Approaching the bedroom door, Dylan's voice grew louder. "I hate to tell you this, though. No one will believe me if I tell them that Raymond's ghost told me that he is innocent. I need more. I'm going to need more from you."

Dylan stopped on a dime when she heard a thump coming from inside Sarah Hodge's locked bedroom. Staring at the door, she flinched when she heard a loud crash followed by a series of bangs and thuds so powerful that she could feel the floor beneath her feet quake.

Raymond's touch was no longer against her, she knew he had moved from where she stood. Knowing he must have entered the room, Dylan lowered her arms and tried to relax.

Concentrating on keeping her breathing steady, she focused on the brass door knob. When it rattled and jiggled, slightly, Dylan knew exactly what was happening. It turned to the left, then right, then left again! It wiggled, as the door began to push in and out, but it seemed jammed and unwilling to break free.

Suddenly, the latch detached, and the door swayed easily on its hinges. At the command of a powerful tug, it swung inward. At long last, Sarah's bedroom was open.

Proudly standing with one hand on the doorknob and the other coolly in the front pocket of his blue jeans, Mitch Wolf basked in the beam of Dylan's flashlight.

"Nice work!" Dylan clamored with excitement.

"Thanks," he said, "I had a little trouble with the boards on the windows, but other than that, it's like that tree was put there just to climb up here."

Bursting into the room to join him, Dylan blew by Mitch, and flipped on the Spirit Box, sending pulsating static resounding in the twelve feet by twelve feet room. A jet stream of cold air funneled in through the open window, sending ripples over the investigators' skin.

"Raymond!" Dylan called, loudly, "We are in here! Give us something, please. Tell us what we need to know!"

Clear and bright, not whispered, a voice bellowed through the device. Now, perhaps spurred by Dylan's precise words about what happened there in the room, the voice sounded more human.

"Corner."

"Corner!" Mitch repeated the message. "What do you mean? Where? What corner?"

With her knees bouncing from hope, Dylan grabbed one of Mitch's shoulders to balance herself. The Spirit Box's emphatic, throbbing static raged on, with no voices.

"Come on, Raymond!" Dylan demanded at the top of her lungs. "Come *on!*"

"Room."

"Room!" cried Mitch.

Dylan gripped Mitch's shoulder tightly, frustrated and eager to hear more. "We are in the room!"

"Carpet... Corner."

Dylan and Mitch locked eyes, both understanding what Raymond was telling them. Frozen from the sheer exhilaration, neither could process the thoughts to move.

"Peel, corner... carpet."

Bumping into one another, Dylan and Mitch nearly tumbled over. Moving around Mitch, Dylan leaped over the bed, her light trembling in her nervous hand. Next to the closet door, she dropped to her knees. Mitch had done the same in the corner by the doorway.

Dylan tossed the Spirit Box onto the bed, propped the flashlight up so she could use both hands. She dug her fingers into the shaggy carpet and pulled with everything she had. Mitch, behind her, did the same.

"Nothing here, Dyl!" he called out.

"Go to the other one!" Dylan pleaded, feeling the staples that held the rug down break free. She found nothing underneath.

"Window."

Hearing Raymond say 'window', Dylan crawled on her

299

hands and knees to the corner of the room nearest the window that Mitch had climbed through moments earlier.

"Dyl, nothing here!" Mitch cried out, his voice loud enough to eclipse the stuttering chaos being emitted by the Spirit Box.

"Sarah... break, heart... Don't shoot."

Dylan shrieked, as she popped free the brass tacks that held the narrow boards to the hardwood. Several inches of the carpet pulled up off the floor. The sudden release sent her plummeting backwards onto her elbows and butt. Her knuckles burned from the carpet, bled from the staples and nails that had scraped them.

She looked up at Mitch, as he bounded over the bed to land at her side. Placing his hand under her neck, he swiftly, yet carefully, lifted her off the carpet. Their flashlights exposed Sarah's belongings, which, for at least that moment, felt welcoming. Posters of rock bands on the walls, a jacket with leather sleeves and a large *B* for Black Willow High sewn on the back next to a *'94.*

There was a dirty-clothes hamper next to the wall, a dresser with perfume, dried-up flowers, and a jewelry box. A full-body mirror with snapshots of Sarah and her friends tucked into the wooden sides. A life left behind. A life, for some reason, never lived.

Dylan gathered herself, as Mitch ran his fingers through her tousled hair, and sat up on her knees. Reaching down, she lifted the large corner of the rug that she had pulled from its fastened state, to look under it.

There, untouched since Sarah Hodge hid it there in 1993, was a stuffed envelope just waiting to be found, dying to be opened.

47

"I swear to God, you guys, if I'm still waiting tables next year, I will literally die," April groaned, setting a plate of bacon, eggs, and toast in front of Dylan. "Mitch, your French Toast is gonna be another sec. Okay?"

"Sure, April," he told her. He was hungry, but could wait. He and Dylan had been up most of the night studying what they had found hidden in Sarah Hodge's bedroom. Still, every time they sifted through the envelope's contents, it felt as fresh as the first.

Dylan didn't touch her food, right away. Instead, she held onto one of the photographs they had found inside the hidden envelope. It was long, narrow, and had three different images stacked, separated by thin, white lines. It came from a photo booth. The type of quarter-operated machine found in shopping malls, arcades, and sometimes at weddings. This one had a logo along the bottom edge. Written in fancy, cartoonish lettering were the words *Zain's Pizza*. Posed romantically, side by side, surely after devouring a slice of pizza at Zain's were Sarah Hodge and Raymond Cole. The middle picture showed them with their eyes closed and their lips locked, kissing. His dark skin, her light complexion created a stunning, beautiful contrast on the black and white image.

"They were so cute together, Mitch." Dylan's words floated, as she stargazed at the two teenagers, who appeared to be happy and in love.

"Yeah," Mitch agreed, snagging a slice of thick-cut maple flavored bacon off Dylan's plate. "They really were."

Dylan removed another image from the envelope discovered underneath the carpet and flipped it between her fingers, facing it towards Mitch. "Look at this one." The Polaroid, an instantly developed photo, lacked the brilliant colors and fine lines modern day cameras captured. But expressions, emotions appeared the same as on crystal clear high-definition pictures. "They are so in love here. Look at her face."

"I agree," Mitch said before plunging another slice of Dylan's bacon into his hungry mouth. "They both look really happy. But," he spoke through chomping teeth, "it doesn't mean Raymond wasn't really breaking in the house, uninvited."

"How so?"

"Couples break up all the time, go from best friends to mortal enemies overnight sometimes. Geez, look at Carrie."

"I still can't believe you dated her."

"Well, it's a prime example. Right?"

April sat Mitch's order of French toast down on the

table. "It's good," she informed him, before quickly heading to the table next to them. Dylan observed, as Mitch noticed a mouth shaped chunk missing from one of the cinnamon flavored, egg-coated, powdered sugar sprinkled pieces of sourdough. Shaking his head, he glanced at April, who shot a wink and smile his direction. Dylan laughed.

"Here," Mitch offered, tossing a few strips of the bacon that were on his plate onto Dylan's. "Eat these. What if Sarah broke it off with Raymond, and he just wouldn't take 'no' for an answer? Let's say, he's angry, but she won't see him, won't talk to him. Suddenly, he can't take it anymore and goes to her house and breaks in."

"Does that justify shooting him?"

"I wasn't there. I don't know what he might have said or done to provoke it. Some of what we heard from Raymond, 'broke my heart'… It could make sense."

Drooping in her chair, Dylan knew Mitch could be correct although she didn't want him to be. "Yeah, there is a lot we still don't know."

Already half finished with his late arriving breakfast, Mitch recapped some of the lingering questions that remained unanswered. "Why did they leave the house the way they did? Why leave everything behind? Where is Charity Hodge? Why did Sarah tell us her father had died?"

"He killed the boy she loved."

"Maybe. That could be it. Could be more to it."

"I guess… But, I think I'm right." Dylan made sure to stake claim to her theory. Dylan's eyes left Mitch and followed April as she passed their table. "What's with April?"

"What do you mean?"

"You and your grandpa are like the only two people in

Black Willow that she doesn't treat like trash."

A sly grin stretched across Mitch's wide face, a deep dimple formed on each side of it.

"What is it?" insisted Dylan. "Do, tell."

With a mouth full of syrup-drenched French toast, Mitch mumbled an explanation. "My grandpa is going out with Carol."

"You're serious? The gravedigger has a love life?"

"Surprised?"

"Not really, I guess. I just never..." Dylan smiled. "How long?"

"Just over a year."

"Wow."

"We're all having Thanksgiving together. April, Tamara, too. You should come with Candice."

Using her fork, Dylan toyed with her eggs. Looking down at the pattern the black pepper made on the over-hard egg whites, she tried to graciously decline. "I would, but I'm going to be... I'm *hoping* to be away... Out of town."

"Really? What's going on, Dyl?"

She gave him an honest look, her eyes asked for leniency when it came to an explanation. "Once I sort it out, I'll let you know, Mitch. I promise I will."

Without saying anything, he seemed to accept what she said, taking her at her word.

Dylan snapped the silent exchange. "If I'm here... in Black Willow, I'd love to join you all."

"Great. I would really enjoy that."

Lightening the heaviness caused by the intense, still somewhat held at bay - yet, completely embraced - attraction between them, Dylan teased the boy she felt tightening his grip on her heart. "So, that's what it takes to get on April's good side, huh?"

"Believe me, before this, she used to spit in *our* food, too."

Dylan's eyes exploded.

"Well," Mitch retracted, "I don't have any proof that April spits in people's food. I don't *think* she does anyway."

Dylan packed away the photographs, placed them in the pocket of her jacket that hung on her chair back. They ate, said little, focused on what lay ahead of them that morning. They had arrived at Carol's early, before the usual Sunday morning rush had hit. There were a few fellows, wearing camouflage, drinking coffee, and trading fishing stories, scattered at tables. Their conversations crossed the room, back and forth. April, on three different occasions, suggested the men slide a couple tables together and sit closer. But, when they ignored the waitress' suggestion, April stomped off to the kitchen.

"Are they spit-worthy?" Dylan joshed, with her head lowered to match her voice.

"Oh, if anyone ever was," Mitch whispered, playing along.

Dylan wiped her hands clean on a napkin, took the final sip of her coffee, then leaned way back, arching her back, with her arms spread out.

"You tired?" Mitch wondered, seeing her yawn.

"Nope," she assured him. "My body is yawning from habit. It's early, but I'm ready to rock."

"Then let's roll," he said, dropping a ten and a five down on the table. "April, it's all set," he shouted, standing up and throwing his coat on.

"Okay, guys. I'll see ya," April cordially replied, just before letting a plate of biscuits and gravy drop in front of one of the fishermen from about five inches high. The loud bang brought all conversation to a sudden halt, as April stormed off.

Dylan raised her eyebrows at Mitch. "I'm glad I've found my way to her good side."

"Tell me about it," Mitch agreed, pulling open the door leading to the sidewalk.

After only a few steps into the cold, morning air, Dylan stopped, and felt Mitch walk into her back. "What's..." Mitch started to ask, but, tall enough to see over Dylan's head, he didn't need to finish the question.

Wearing tight jeans, a thick sweater, mittens, and a stocking cap with a yarn ball at the top was a cheerleader leaning against the grill of Mitch's blue S10 pickup. Carrie Holland was hell-bent at getting what she wanted: her ex-boyfriend.

Mitch put a hand on each of Dylan's shoulders from behind her then scooted himself in between she and Carrie Holland. "What's up, Carrie?" he warily asked.

With the sun barely risen, Dylan and Mitch relied on the street light over his truck to see the suspicious girl's face. It was clear, by her demeanor, she was up to something terrible.

After taking a long inhale, Carrie then slowly pushed it out through her nostrils, flaring them. She closed her eyes, tightly, clenched her jaw momentarily before speaking, loudly and directly.

"Mitch, this has all been a mistake. I know what you said last summer, that you felt things weren't working out. I remember, but you were wrong, Mitch."

"Look, Carrie, I don't know what you think this is going to accomplish, but I'm not interested. It's over,"

Mitch treaded lightly with his words, like he'd seen a similar situation before when things might have taken a turn for the worse. Dylan shuffled her feet sideways to get a glimpse of Carrie from around Mitch's wide frame.

"Mitch, seriously? God, I knew it. I could see how you looked at her," she lifted her open hand forward, as if Dylan was an item on display, "when she first came to our school. I thought there was no way it would become something. I mean, I was sure you'd come to your senses, but – God, Mitch, aren't you finished with her yet?"

Mitch gave a stern, but politely delivered warning, "Carrie, I think you need to leave."

"Oh, what do I need to do? Buy a Ouija board? Hold a séance? Is that what you're into now?"

Mitch turned, looked at Dylan. "I'm sorry about this. She's -" Mitch stopped speaking when Carrie's belligerence increased.

"Is she a witch?!" Carrie's voice was loud, unstable. "It's so weird, Mitch. I mean, wasn't it some sort of witch or ghoul that screwed your whole life up to begin with? Now you're running about chasing ghosts with this – this, paranormal freak?"

"Don't call her that!"

Dylan hadn't heard Mitch raise his voice before.

"Or what? Or what will happen?" Carrie's taunts became progressively nastier. She was growing visibly unhinged, irate. Her posture changed from leaning on the front of the truck to now lunging forward keeping time with her syllables and her expressive arm motions.

"What are you doing?" Mitch wondered, keeping his voice tempered, calm, when he saw Carrie walking along side of his truck. She reached in the back, lifted out a shovel that Mitch used when helping his grandfather from the truck bed. "Don't!" Mitch hollered, stepping towards her.

Aggressively, Carrie swung it, holding the wooden handle at the end, hurling the metal spade like an axe at Mitch forcing him to stop. She then turned, bashed the passenger door, denting it and scratching the paint as the shovel head slid down to the pavement.

"Stop!" Dylan cried out to no avail. Carrie smashed in the nearest headlight, shattering it. Hearing the door open behind her, Dylan turned and found April barging past she and Mitch.

"What the hell are you doing?" April screamed. "Knock it off!" The thin, lanky waitress dove forward, carelessly reached her hands out, and intercepted the flailing shovel handle just above the sharp edged, rusty scoop, mid swing.

"Hey!" yelled Mitch, as he and Dylan fretfully watched the two of them play tug of war with the long digging tool. "April, she's gonna hurt you!" Mitch took a long stride forward. "Enough, Carrie!"

"No, Mitch!" Dylan begged, tugging his wrist with both of her hands.

Running out the door of Carol's came the group of fishermen, looking like soldiers in their green and brown patterned attire. Boldly, they rushed the scene. One of the anglers stepped in between, grabbed the shovel handle with both hands, and wrestled it from Carrie. April quickly backed away, and let the man keep possession of Carrie's shovel-turned-weapon.

"Get out of here, Carrie!" April howled at the top of her lungs. "Or I'll have the police here!"

Carrie Holland growled, stomped her tan-colored boots

hard on the cement on her way to her car. After leaping inside, she squealed her tires when she backed out into the street, then peeled out, shooting loose pebbles several feet behind.

"Is everybody okay?" the man holding Mitch's shovel asked, concernedly looking them over.

"Yeah, thanks. I wasn't... I just didn't want to... Thanks," Mitch told him.

"This yours?" The brave peacekeeper held the shovel out towards Mitch and Dylan, who stood surrounded by the other fishermen.

"Yeah," Mitch answered, taking it from him.

April turned to Dylan. "You good? Everything okay?"

"Yeah, thanks. I'm okay."

April put her hands on her hips, tilted to one side. "Okay, boys, back inside. Breakfast is getting cold."

As the man who intervened stepped by April, she grabbed his bicep with her small hand. "Your breakfast is free today," she told him.

"Okay, great," he responded. "Thanks, April." Slowly, holding his stare at the waitress, he joined his buddies back inside the restaurant.

Moving her eyebrows up and down, April whispered to Dylan. "He's cute, right?"

"Yeah... Sure." Dylan forced a smile with her heart still racing from the commotion. "Go for it, April."

"Oh, I'm going," the infatuated server promised and skipped back inside.

Now alone with Dylan next to the battered vehicle, Mitch apologized. "I'm so sorry, Dylan."

"Mitch, it's okay. Seriously, this wasn't your fault."

"You're not scared to be with me now?"

"Are you *asking* me to be with you?"

"Well, you know, like, be together? Be a thing? Girlfriend, boyfriend? We're a good team. Real good."

Touching the broken headlight, Dylan grimaced. "It's bad."

"It's not terrible. Replacing it won't be too awful."

Dylan stood, looking up at him. "Sure."

"Sure?"

"Sure. I'll be your girlfriend." Dylan slapped her hand against Mitch's tattooed shoulder. "Let's get out of here, Boyfriend." She pulled open the door of his truck and slipped inside, slamming it closed behind her.

Mitch smiled, jiggled his keys in his hand, jogged to the driver's side, and hopped inside. "Ready for this?" he asked her.

Scooting over to the middle seat, Dylan took Mitch by his rough, calloused hand. "Yup. I'm ready."

Side by side, hand in hand, Dylan and Mitch, girlfriend and boyfriend, started the fifty-minute drive north to Reed City on a cool, cloudy, and already eventful Sunday morning.

48

Covered with a long, furry robe that nearly touched the floor, Gary Doan, wearing the shirt and flannel pants he had slept in, groggily opened the front door.

"Morning," he grumbled, rubbing his eyes. "Can I help you kids?"

"Is Sarah home?" Dylan promptly asked.

"She's, uh," Gary peered over his shoulder towards the kitchen, "she's here, yeah. Is she expecting you?" What hair Gary had left was pushed in all directions, his thick beard, as well.

"No, she isn't," confessed Dylan. "But, it's important."

Unsure if Gary was rude, or just tired, Dylan and Mitch watched him walk around the corner, leaving the door wide open. "Sarah!" they heard him call. A few seconds later, he returned to the doorway, now with his robe tied closed, fending off the chilly air that was creeping in.

"She'll be just a moment."

"No problem," Dylan kindly assured him.

"If you don't mind, I'm going to ask you to just step inside here, so I can close the door. Bitter cold, this morning."

"Thank you," Mitch told him, allowing Dylan to step in first with himself right behind.

The Doan house was lovely, well-kept. Able to see most of it from the entryway because of the open design, Dylan's eyes glossed the place. Hanging near the dining table, Dylan could see a large, expensive canvas print of Sarah and Gary's wedding day. Next to Gary were two well-dressed people, presumably his parents, while next to Sarah was only one person: a woman. Dylan, even from ten feet away, knew it was Charity Hodge. Notably missing was Dean.

"Hi guys," Sarah said, obviously curious why they were at her house so early in the morning. She rounded the corner from the hallway that concealed part of the house, most likely bedrooms and a bath or two. The high ceilings in the main room made Dylan feel small, until she heard her voice carry through the space with the same loud reverberation that Sarah's had.

"Hi, Sarah. Do you remember us?"

"Of course, I do. Gary, these are the kids that came and looked at your car. Did you decide you'd like to take it for a spin?"

"Not exactly," Dylan eased into it. "We... we are here for something other than the car."

"Let me see... it was Mike and?"

"It's Dylan and Mitch, actually," Dylan pointed out.

"My apologies," Sarah humbly admitted. "I've never been strong at remembering names."

"Can we come in?" asked Mitch.

"Maybe we could sit at the table?" Dylan suggested, seeing it was just a short distance from where they stood conversing.

Sarah's voice began to suspect something. "What's this about?"

"Maybe you kids should leave," Gary butted in.

Sarah held up her hand, signaling that she didn't want that, necessarily. Not quite yet, anyhow. "What is this about?" she repeated, this time firm and demanding.

"Cemetery Road," Dylan told her. "It's about the house on Cemetery Road."

"What did you do, go home and study up on me?" accused Sarah. "I never should've spoken to you two." She folded her arms, looked away.

"It's not like that," Dylan began to explain. "We weren't interested in your car. We came, even the first time, to see *you*."

"You *did* tell me your name was Mike, *didn't* you?"

"I did, Mrs. Doan. I'm sorry I lied," Mitch admitted.

Dylan decided it'd be best to cut to the chase. When she held up one of the photos of Sarah cuddled, romantically, with Raymond, the woman's hard exterior cracked.

"Oh my God, where did you find that?"

"Raymond led us to it." Dylan's words brought an unusual expression across Sarah's face. Unsure whether she was going to force them to leave or burst into tears, Dylan felt she and Mitch were walking on thin ice that would either safely guide them across the lake or swallow them up into the frigid waters never to be heard from again.

Sarah's voice trembled. "He... he did?"

"He did, Sarah." Dylan pulled another image from her pocket. Sarah gasped, held her fingers up to her gaping lips.

Gary placed a supportive hand on his wife's shoulder, stood patiently behind her. Seeing the images, he too seemed to let down his guard. "Invite them in, Honey," he said to Sarah.

The emotional woman nodded. "Yeah. Come in, please."

Sarah, Mitch, and Dylan sat at the dining room table. Gary placed fresh cups of coffee in front of all four placings, before filling the last chair himself. Looking both eager and hesitant all at once, Sarah sat tall in her seat.

"Please, tell me what you know," she said to the teenagers that, out of nowhere, had opened the door to a past she'd long left behind.

"Well," Dylan began, while Mitch willingly remained silent, "we know about the shooting that took place there. That, um, Raymond Cole was inside your house, your *room*, when your father, Dean, killed him."

"So far, you're right."

"I have – *we* have," Dylan glanced at Mitch, "reason to believe that it might not have happened exactly the way the police, or your father, said that it did."

"Go on," Sarah invited Dylan to continue.

"I have heard Raymond claim his innocence."

Gary interrupted. "Wait a minute. You've *heard*? Are you a psychic or something? Um... a, a, a medium?"

"I'm not," Dylan calmly clarified. "I have equipment... devices, things that allow paranormal contact. Um, voices, even visually sometimes."

Mitch chimed in. "We even heard him vocalize without the instruments once."

"What did he say?" Gary asked, now leaning forward the way Sarah was.

"That he was innocent," Dylan said. "That his heart was broken."

Sarah closed her eyes, rested her head in her hands, and leaned her elbows on the table. For a moment, Dylan thought for sure Sarah was going to ask them to leave. But instead she took a long breath, looked Dylan directly in the eyes, and began to tell a story she had never told anyone. Not even her husband of twelve years, Gary Doan.

"Raymond lived about an hour and a half away. Over in Saginaw. We had a mutual friend in Greenville and happened to be at the same party one night the summer before he died... Before my father killed him." She took a second to catch her breath, as three sets of itching ears waited for more.

"It was love at first sight," she smiled. "Truly, it was. He was so sweet and kind, and I'd never met anyone like him before. He was so funny. He used to," Sarah cleared her throat, "he used to make these faces and do these voices." She paused to remember, eyes lighting up from visualizing Raymond in her memory.

"He wanted to be an actor. He dreamed about going to New York City and joining the cast of Saturday Night Live. But, he would joke that since they already had a black guy on the show, they wouldn't be able to cast him."

"He sounds nice," Dylan encouraged the woman. "He sounds like a great guy."

"He was," Sarah confidently stated. "He really was."

"Did you two break up?" Dylan pried, seeing that

Sarah was feeling more comfortable sharing now that her memories were flooding back to her.

"No," she shook her head, spun her coffee mug in a slow circle with her thumb. "We didn't. We had a nice summer together, went a lot of places. We would meet in Greenville, sometimes he'd take me down to Grand Rapids. This picture here," she pointed at the middle one. Dylan had laid all the photos on the table. "This one, I remember was the day he asked me if he could meet my parents. Oh, what a day…"

Dylan carefully pressed, with kid gloves. "Did you allow him to?"

"Yes, I did. He drove me all the way home that night. I was excited; I really liked this guy… a lot. I thought I had met someone that I could be with for a long time… Forever."

"What happened?"

"We walked inside, Mom and Dad were in the kitchen by the front door… My face hurt from smiling so much; I thought they would be so happy."

"They weren't?"

"Well, they treated Raymond with dignity, I'll give them that. They were polite, enough, but I could sense what they were thinking. Dad, anyway. I think Mom could see how much I liked Raymond and was glad about it, honestly. But, Dad ruled the house."

"Sarah, what happened next?" Dylan sensed the emotional woman's story was nearing a dramatic twist.

"When Raymond left, hardly down the driveway, my father made it clear that me dating him, someone who was black, was not acceptable. I was taken by such surprise. I'd never heard my father use racial slurs, say anything negative about people based on skin color. I was shocked."

"How did your mother react?"

"She I don't think agreed with him, but she did what she was taught to do by her mother. She stood by what her husband said. She didn't challenge him, but she was sympathetic towards me about the whole thing. She comforted me, told me it would all be okay, and all that." A single tear dropped over Sarah's eyelid. The skin it streamed down had aged since that day in the house on Cemetery, but her heart hadn't. She sniffled, shook off the emerging sorrow.

"Um, my dad, he, um," she regained her composure, "told me to break if off with Raymond. You know, it was 1993. Of course you kids weren't around, but people didn't discuss racism, prejudices the way we do now. It was almost taboo to even acknowledge it still existed. Society was okay with it being there, being real, if everyone just pretended it wasn't. And I was a kid. I didn't know what to do."

"What *did* you do?"

"Well, I told my parents I had done what they'd asked me to. And I told Raymond that they were against our relationship because he was already nineteen and out of high school. I told him we'd need to keep our relationship a secret, until I was eighteen, anyway. I figured by then, maybe my parents would come around. I just couldn't bring myself to tell him that they didn't want me seeing him because he wasn't white. I was so embarrassed."

Dylan reached across the table in an act that was completely out of character for her and held Sarah's shaking hand. "You kept the relationship secret? Sarah, there's nothing to be ashamed of. You were a kid. Believe me, I know all too well what it's like to see people you love adversely affected by things you think you could've prevented."

More tears made their way onto Sarah's cheeks. Gary slid his seat over, placed a devoted arm around her, in a show of admirable support for the woman he loved.

Sarah continued. "Keeping the relationship a secret was easy back then. No social media to worry about. Only the people we wanted to let know knew anything. On the other hand, without texting, messaging, and cell phones, it was hard to maintain it. It meant a lot of lying, sneaking. A lot of feeling trapped. I felt so guilty for something I shouldn't have had to feel guilty about. It wasn't easy, but Raymond was worth it. I fell so in love with him."

Sensing that Sarah could speak all day about how wonderful her time with Raymond Cole had been, Dylan turned the conversation to what happened that fateful October night at the house near the cemetery. "Sarah, tell us... How did it happen? What led to the shooting?"

"God, it was all my fault."

"No, Sarah, it wasn't your fault. None of it was your fault."

"I missed him so much. And he wanted to see me, too. Raymond was at our friend's house in Greenville, so I called to talk to him. I asked him to come that night. Of course, he was willing to. A boy in love will do anything to see a girl. I suspect the two of you know that already." She gave a sly look to both Mitch and Dylan. "Oh, to be young again... Anyway, Raymond agreed to come. He parked his car down at the cemetery, back off the road, and cut through the cornfield behind the house. Luckily, it was dry that week, or he'd have been soaked."

Mitch, under the table, put his hand on Dylan's knee. Almost like a supernatural power had emitted from his palm, she felt his love for her.

"Around," Sarah shook her head, searching for details, "I want to say, nine-thirty? I guess? I heard a tap on my bedroom window. Raymond had climbed that old tree in the backyard – Is that tree still there?"

"Yes, it is," Mitch verified, having just recently made that same climb himself. "Still reaches right to that window."

"When he came inside, it was so exhilarating! Here was the boy I loved, sneaking through a field in the dark, climbing a tree just to see me! And then there was the whole idea of my parents being right downstairs. Wow, what a terrifying, amazing feeling!" She reached her hand up, placed it on top of Gary's still resting over her shoulder. "It didn't last long, though. As he greeted me with a long, passionate kiss... all hell, quickly broke loose."

Sarah guzzled some of her cooling beverage, quenching her dry, troubled throat. "I think my dad must have heard Raymond outside when he went up the tree. Maybe the limbs scratched the side of the house or something. Within a minute, he was trying to open my bedroom door. As a precaution, I had it locked, but he started banging on it, yelling for me to open it. Raymond dove under the bed. We – we didn't know what do to; it was so chaotic.

"I tried to be calm, let my father in, acted like nothing was going on, but it was obvious I was hiding something. I wasn't good at lying, especially to my parents. I crumbled... I didn't tell him that Raymond was there, but my shuttering voice, my nervousness was just... it was obvious."

"Your father found him?"

"No," Sarah gazed at the ceiling, still amazed at what had happened. "Raymond, being the brave, lovestruck hero-type that he was, rolled out from under the bed to declare his love for me. He started this long speech about how he was only a year and a half older than me and how silly it was to keep us apart based on that insignificant age difference. How I'd be graduating in the spring and how *nothing* would be able to keep us apart when that happened.

"I was heartbroken, seeing the look on Raymond's face, the demoralizing, pain-stricken look that he had when my father let him know that it wasn't age that was the problem. It was his skin color."

Sarah paused again, holding off a total emotional breakdown. "That was the first time I'd heard my father... He used awful words. I won't repeat them... Dad stormed out, marched down the hall. I thought it was over, that Raymond could just leave, and we could sort it out the next day. But – God, it all happened too fast – seconds later, my father had a shotgun pointed through my bedroom door, screaming at us both... I took a step forward, tried to grab his arm. Just as I did that, Raymond turned to run for the window and... next thing I knew, my ears were ringing. It was like I had gone deaf. The gun fired directly next to my head."

Sarah finally lost control of herself and began crying. Gary wrapped her in his arms, Dylan stood and walked around the table to the sobbing woman, offering any condolences she could. Gritting her teeth, Sarah pushed them away. "I can finish," she said, resolute. "I *need* to finish this."

Dylan kneeled on the floor next to Sarah's chair, holding both hands around hers.

"I turned, and all I could see was blood. He'd shot Raymond square in the back. My mother must have called 9-1-1, because next thing I knew, policemen were pulling me off Raymond's body asking me if I was okay, if *I'd* been hurt. I had his blood all over my clothes…" She stopped to breath. "I gave them my statement, you guys. I *did*. I told them he wasn't an intruder, that *I* had *invited* him! But, when they made their conclusions… I was too much of a coward to fight. I did *not* give Raymond what he deserved, what I know he'd have given me."

No one spoke, as Sarah's account of the events that night felt like a bomb going off. Dylan, speechless, made eye contact with Mitch. *Now what?* said the silence between them.

"Take me to him," Sarah whispered. "Take me to Raymond. Help me hear him. Let me speak to him."

"Yes, of course," Dylan instantly agreed. "Under one condition, Sarah."

"What is it?"

"You have to let me video you. In the house."

"Okay… That's no problem."

Dylan knew what that could mean. Having Sarah back at the scene of Raymond's murder not only could bring resolution to Raymond's spirit being stuck in that house, but it could also release years of guilt that filled Sarah and, undoubtedly, tortured her soul.

Those were important things.

But, for Dylan, there was more to it. She knew that Sarah's presence could spark an energy strong enough for Raymond to show himself, to manifest into a visible apparition. One that she could capture on video, one that might ultimately set *her,* Dylan Klaypool, free from years of existing in her own unbearable hell.

49

"I can't believe what I'm seeing."

Sarah Doan stood in the center of the living room of her childhood home, in awe. Placing her hand over her chest, she slowly spun, shining the flashlight Dylan had given her at all the walls, the furniture, the pictures on the shelves.

"You going to be okay?" Gary asked her, seeing his wife react to the burst of nostalgia.

The emotion caused by reliving the events verbally at their Reed City home had finally tapered off during the drive to Black Willow Creek. Sarah had jumped back in the pool of bad memories, head first into the deep end.

By then, it was late afternoon, the sun was still up, but clouds in the sky kept it concealed. Traces of the small bit of light that covered Black Willow Creek found its way inside through the gaps in the planks over the windows, but provided almost no visibility. All four people in the house held flashlights that collectively lit the room.

"Something is different in here, Mitch," Dylan warned him, quiet enough so that Sarah and Gary couldn't hear her. "I can't tell what it is, but something feels different."

"Is it Raymond reacting to Sarah?"

"I'm not sure. Do you feel it, too? Can you feel something?"

"I can. It's almost buzzing in here," Mitch described the feeling they were both sensing.

"When is the last time you were here, Honey?"

Sarah turned to Gary, smiled from embarrassment. "The night I graduated high school, May 22, 1994."

Dylan stepped closer, so Sarah could see her face. "You left?"

"Yeah, that night, the twenty-second. After the shooting, I stuck it out until I finished school but couldn't wait to get away from here, from him. I stayed with a friend for a while, until I headed off to college. My father, wealthy and proud, had paid my entire four years of tuition to State when I was in eleventh-grade. So, I went."

"You never visited? Not even your mother?" Dylan wondered.

"How could I?" Sarah asked, shaking her head. "Mom left him and reconnected with me. She moved closer to the university, and we started over, together. She couldn't stand knowing what had happened any more than I could. She needed to get away, move on. Funny thing is, we both had so much trauma caused by it all, went through so much, but we never really discussed it. I think it came up once, for a minute, but that was it." Sarah shined her light around. "Is he here? Can I speak to him?"

"I'm sure he is," Dylan answered with a smile. "I think we should move upstairs. Is that okay with you?"

"Honey, you'll be okay?" Gary added, again, concerned and unsure.

"Yeah, if Dylan and Mitch think that's where we should go, let's do it."

Dylan handed Mitch the night-vision camcorder. "Keep it on Sarah at all times. Whatever you do, don't take it off her."

"Got it," he said, eager to accept the responsibility.

Leading the group up, Dylan spoke direct and clear. "Everyone needs to keep their emotions in check. The less emotional energy we use the more Raymond will have access to, the more he'll be able to use from us. Understand?"

"Yes, Dylan," Sarah said, following behind the girl who had been in contact with her slain lover.

"Sure," Gary agreed. "Whatever you say, we'll do."

Halfway up the stairs, Dylan stopped the group, turned to face them, one on each of the three steps behind her. "It won't be easy, Sarah. Trust me, it won't. If you can hear him, if his voice comes through, it will overwhelm you. If you feel his touch, it might scare you."

"Raymond could never scare me, Dylan. I loved him. I trust him."

"Gary, you going to be okay?" Dylan shifted her speech to the faithful husband there to support his wife in a time that wasn't only strange, but awkward for him.

"I'll manage. I promise. If not, I'll let you know and dismiss myself," Gary told Dylan.

"Perfect. Thank you." Dylan felt relieved that this

experiment might be just what they all needed. Sarah for closure, Raymond for peace, and herself for the evidence she'd been hoping to find. Evidence that could change her life.

"Before we enter the bedroom, I want to explain what we are going to do," Dylan coached the team. "Sarah, I want you to go in and sit on the side of the bed that faces the window. Mitch, you're on the bed with her, keeping the camera on her. No matter what, on *her*."

"Sure, Dylan," Sarah said.

Mitch nodded.

"Gary, I hate to tell you this, but I think you should stay by the door. Enter the room, but stay by the door. I don't believe your presence will startle Raymond, but you need to realize, for him, he's still the nineteen-year-old that was here sneaking in to see his girlfriend. If he feels any of your concern or feelings towards Sarah, which he could, he may hide from us. Or -"

"Or what? Possess me? What can he do to me?" Gary worried, nervously.

"No," Dylan tried to calm him. "Don't be afraid. I just can't predict how he'll react."

Turning to Sarah, Dylan continued, "I'm going to come in and stand near you, but not too closely. I'm going to speak to Raymond, let him know what is going on, let him know what happened to him."

"Do you think he doesn't know?" Sarah frightfully wondered.

"It's very possible that he is still confused after all these years. He may not even fully understand that he's no longer living."

"That is terrible," Gary whispered.

"Dylan, I'm ready. Can we begin?" Sarah couldn't wait any longer. Dylan could tell that what she just said about Raymond being confused and unsure had struck a chord with the sympathetic woman. Ending Raymond's suffering clearly was important to Sarah.

"Okay, guys. Let's go." Dylan led them up the remaining steps, down the echoing hallway and into the room where Dean Hodge had heartlessly murdered Raymond Cole.

50

Dylan watched, as Sarah sat motionless on the bed. Mitch sat at the foot and faced Sarah with the camera steadily trained on her.

"Dylan, this room feels different to me than downstairs," Sarah described. "He's here. I can feel that he is here."

"I'm rolling on this digital recorder. I'm going to set it next to you." Dylan carefully placed the device next to Sarah on the bed. "We are going to do what is called an EVP session. A burst session. EVP is electronic voice phenomena. Raymond's voice can be captured, imprinted on the recording inside the white noise. I'd like you to ask him some questions, Sarah. Can you do that?"

Naturally, without reluctance, Sarah spoke, as if Raymond was standing right before her in the flesh.

"Raymond, Sweetheart. I miss you. I've missed you so much."

Dylan held the Mel-meter with the REM feature disabled. She could read the EMF levels, without the lights and sounds of the instrument activating.

"I appear to be getting some low-level interference, but I just spiked to an eight-point-zero," Dylan reported.

"Interference?" Mitch asked. "What kind of interference?"

"I don't know… Almost like I'd see in a building that had power, electricity. It's no big deal. The spike indicates that Raymond is attempting to join us. Sarah, ask questions. Pause several seconds in between."

"Are you here, Raymond?"

Dylan watched the unit in her hand again spike, this time above nine.

"Do you remember me, Raymond? Do you know who I am?" Sarah asked.

The group stayed still, silent, hoping that Raymond's answers would be heard during playback.

"Mitch, are you seeing anything?" Dylan inquired.

"No," he answered.

"Seeing anything? What will he see? What is going to happen?" Gary's troubled voice came from behind Dylan.

"Shhh," she hushed him. "Gary, please stay quiet. Stay calm."

Sarah's voice became desperate. She needed to hear Raymond. "Do you know what happened to you? Do you remember that night? Do you remember my father?"

"One question at a time, Sarah," Dylan reminded her. "You need to give him time to answer you."

Several seconds passed before Sarah broke in. "We

need to check it!" She eagerly begged, no longer able to wait.

"Calm down," Dylan commanded. "Stay calm."

"I can't! Please check it!"

Dylan grabbed the recorder from the bed, pressed STOP, REWIND. She sat on the bed, between Sarah and Mitch, and played it back. The three of them leaned their heads close to listen.

"Raymond, Sweetheart. I miss you. I've missed you so much."

"………………………"

"I appear to be getting some low-level interference, but I just spiked to an eight-point-zero."

"Interference? What kind of interference?"

"I don't know… Almost like I'd see in a building that had power, electricity. It's no big deal. The spike indicates that Raymond is attempting to join us. Sarah, ask questions. Pause several seconds in between."

"Are you here, Raymond?"

"………………………"

"Do you remember me, Raymond? Do you know who I am?"

"……………Sarahodge…………"

Dylan pressed STOP. "Did you hear that?!"

"Oh my God, I did," Sarah whispered.

Dylan rewound, played it again.

"……………Sarahodge…………"

It was whispered quickly with no break between her first and last names, but it was clearly a voice saying the name *Sarah Hodge*.

Sarah put both hands on her face, instantly began sobbing. Barreling through, Gary forced his way to his wife.

When he sat next to her, she collapsed in his lap.

"Sarah, you need to reign it in," Dylan ordered, growing impatient with Sarah's emerging use of emotion.

"She can't! Can't you see that?" Gary shouted.

"I can. I will." Sarah stated bravely, choking down tears, sitting upright. "I *will*. Play the rest, Dylan."

Dylan pressed PLAY.

"Mitch, are you seeing anything?"

"No."

"Seeing anything? What will he see? What is going to happen?"

"Shhh! Gary, please stay quiet. Stay calm."

"Do you know what happened to you? Do you remember that night? Do you remember my father?"

"One question at a time, Sarah. You need to give him time to answer you."

"…………………………broke…my-heart…………"

"Oh, Raymond!" Sarah cried out. Dylan stopped the audio playback.

"Wait!" Mitch frantically bellowed. "I just saw a ball of light, an energy thing… an orb!"

"You did?" Dylan hopped up and ran to look at the camera's screen.

"It just shot at Sarah. Flew right into her!"

Dylan grabbed the camera to rewind and watch the footage, but Sarah began breathing heavily, panting with her chest bulging up and down. "Are you okay?" Dylan asked her, poised.

"I'm freezing," Sarah told her.

"I feel it! It's so cold. The air around her is so cold!" Gary worried, holding his hand out in the space around his wife.

Dylan tried not to panic. The group was losing control of themselves, burning too much energy between them. They needed to relax, find a way to calm down.

Dylan grabbed Sarah's hand, and instantly her own arm rippled with goosebumps. Raymond was touching Sarah and his energy was passing from her to Dylan. Now, worried that she herself might lose control, Dylan took long breaths.

"Sarah, just relax. It's okay. He's here with you now. He's here for you."

"Okay, Dylan... I'll try... I'll try to relax."

"Mitch, keep rolling, but go to my bag, get the Spirit Box," Dylan instructed, using long syllables and a level tone.

Mitch clicked on the SB7, stood with his back to the window, continuing to record. The blaring static sound of the Spirit Box pounded against their ears.

Raising her voice enough to be heard above the static, Dylan explained to Raymond what had happened that fateful night. "Raymond, you were killed here in this room. We all know what happened to you. Sarah knows you're innocent."

Almost instantly, a clear, fully verbalized male voice spoke through the speaker. *"Innocent."*

"Yes!" Dylan bounced on her toes. "Yes! You are innocent!"

Sarah jumped to attention, stared at the Spirit Box.

Dylan continued talking slowly to the ghost. "If you're stuck here, if you're somehow waiting to leave, you can. You can move on, Raymond. We know you are not what the newspapers said you are. We know you would never hurt Sarah. We know that you would never come here to break into the Hodge house."

Again, the man's voice, Raymond's voice, responded. *"Love you. Love you, Sarah."*

"I love you, Raymond. I've never stopped loving you." Sarah assured him through flowing tears.

"Sarah. Love you."

Mitch spun to face the window. "Whoa!" he said, standing alert.

"What? What is it?" Dylan moved forward to stand next to Mitch, as he pointed the camera outside the open window.

"It-it-it left, Dyl. I just saw the ball fly out of Sarah. It passed right through me. I think he went out the window."

"Raymond, are you here? Are you still here?" Dylan called out, over the blaring static pulses of the Spirit Box.

"Raymond? Raymond, I'm so sorry! God, I hope you can hear me," Sarah called to the boy she once loved.

Minutes passed. Dylan and Sarah continued to reach out to Raymond, pleading with him to speak again through the SB7. Nothing but static was heard. Just loud, throbbing static. Finally, after fifteen minutes without hearing Raymond's voice, Dylan clicked off the box, letting the silence surround them.

It seemed Raymond, after decades of haunting the halls of the abandoned house on Cemetery Road, had left.

51

Expeditiously, with her head down, Dylan rushed out of the room, leaving Sarah sobbing in Gary's arms and Mitch standing and looking out of the window down at the ground.

With disappointment rapidly transforming into frustration, Dylan leaned her shoulder against the wall in the hallway, one hand gripping the top of her curly mane.

"Hey." Mitch's voice came from the doorway of Sarah's old bedroom. Dylan didn't respond. Mitch, shining his light on Dylan, stepped closer, and was able to see her unhappiness. "Hey, what's going on?"

"It's not enough, Mitch. We didn't get enough."

"I don't – Dylan, what are you talking about?"

"They just couldn't keep themselves under control. They blew it. I can't believe after all these years of searching, I had found it. And they couldn't stay calm. I *need* more. Don't you get it?"

"No! Dylan, I *don't* get it. You haven't even explained to me what this means. Not enough? Not enough *what?"*

Having yet to look his direction, Dylan refused to elaborate. "Forget it."

"I don't want to forget it." Mitch moved into Dylan's line of sight. "It's all sorted out, Dylan. We connected Sarah and Raymond. Okay? We've proven that Raymond did nothing wrong, that he was murdered in cold blood."

"Police officers, detectives don't believe ghosts, Mitch. Definitely not EVPs, or voices that come through a Spirit Box, and-and-and balls of light that fly in and out of people."

"I'm going to the police tomorrow," Sarah said, stepping into the hallway. "They'll believe me now. Things are different enough now that they will. I won't stop until they do."

"That's great," Dylan commended her, still carrying a tragic expression that she knew Mitch could easily see. The case of Raymond Cole mattered to her; she wanted to see justice served.

But, the case she was hoping to resolve didn't happen in Black Willow Creek.

"Hearing him tell me he loved me... I've never received a greater gift. Thank you, you two. Dylan, thank you." Sarah approached Dylan with extended arms and squeezed the girl between them. Turning to Mitch, she reached up and hugged the tall boy with the wolf tracks tattoo.

"When will you go to the police? Do you want any of us to go with you?" Mitch asked her.

"No, I can do this. But, the first thing I'm going to do

is make a trip to see his parents, whatever family I can find. I'm going to change the past, and it's all because of you two."

"It was all Dylan," Mitch corrected her, illuminating Dylan's pasty white face. All Dylan could think about was the part of her own past that still *hadn't* changed. She was happy for Sarah and all that had transpired, but those feelings of joy were buried under too many years of grief and pain.

"Guys," Gary's voice piped up from the dark bedroom, "If you don't mind, I'd like to get out of here. Can we go?"

Sarah met Gary in the open doorway, took each of his hands, leaned in to give him a kiss, then wrapped herself around the bearded, balding man who was still trying process all that he'd just witnessed. "I love you, Gare Bear. Thank you, so much."

"I love you, too," he assured her. "I'm with you 'til the end of this. Whatever it takes to get the truth of this matter recognized."

Dylan watched Mitch, Sarah, and Gary gingerly move down the stairs through the dark with the light of her torch. Alone, she shook her head, wondering if she had just blown her only opportunity, her chance to capture enough proof to change the minds of those in Chicago with the power to set things right.

Scuffing her feet on the dusty, splintered flooring, she descended to the living room. Hearing Mitch pop the front door open, she stopped near the coffee table to reflect a few more moments and wondered if she'd ever set foot again in the Hodge house.

With the house now empty, that strange feeling she picked up on when they first arrived that evening pricked her senses even greater. Her pulse began to race, as she listened, scratched her head, confused. Something was different, out of place: something was *wrong.*

Moving over to the wall, the one holding the shelves with the family photos, Dylan strained her ears, but couldn't figure out what she was hearing. Pulling the Mel-meter from her back pocket, she held it out close to the painted drywall. Zero-point-zero.

Squatting, Dylan's uncertainty increased when she moved the device near an electrical socket by the floor. The chord of a lamp was plugged into the top, a long cable from the TV filled the bottom socket. The EMF reading quickly jumped to two-point-eight. This didn't make sense to her. There shouldn't be any electromagnetic energy left in those outlets after twenty-something years sitting vacant.

Something was positively wrong.

"Mitch?' she called, but not loud enough for him to hear her from outside on the porch. "Mitch, I think…"

Dylan stood and moved to the other side of the room, holding down the nerves that pressed against her skin from inside. Finding another outlet near the steps with a tall floor lamp plugged into it, she held the detector close. "Three-point-one," she mumbled to herself, confused by the high reading.

With an idea exploding in her mind, Dylan moved, with fast feet, to the kitchen. She closed her eyes, "No way," she told herself. "There's no possible way."

Reaching her right hand to the light switch that she'd flipped dozens of times for no other reason than it had become a silly habit, Dylan held her breath. So excited to get Sarah in front of Raymond, she remembered walking right past the light in the kitchen without performing her ritualistic, quick up and down flicking of the switch.

Dylan knew what was going to happen, although she wished it wouldn't. "Please, let me be wrong," she prayed. Finally, like jumping into the cold water of a swimming pool, she raised her finger, and heard the dull click of the light switch.

Even through her closed eyelids, it was bright enough to prove she'd been right. The kitchen light had come on.

52

"Mitch!" Dylan screamed, nearly blinded when her eyes opened to be invaded by the bright light shining from the fixture on the ceiling.

As she yanked the front door open, she found Mitch, Sarah, and Gary standing together, side by side, on the porch. All three had their attention focused to the right, none moved a muscle when Dylan barged through.

"Guys, we gotta' get out of here!" Dylan frantically warned them, but her claim of imminent danger had come too late.

"Stop!" A gruff, tired and agitated voice slammed into her from a few feet away.

Dylan knew what was happening, and quickly obeyed the order. Calmly, she turned her body, without sudden movements, towards the unfamiliar voice. There, standing with the end of a shotgun barrel less than a foot from her chest, was the one and only Dean Michael Hodge.

"Get back inside," he growled. "Now! All of you! The Indian first. All of you, move it!"

"Dad," Sarah started, quickly stopping.

"Shut up, Sarah! You *shut up!* Into the living room," he said, walking behind the group, gun pointed and ready to fire. "Sit down. On the couch."

Dean Hodge walked backwards, all the while keeping his aim, and clicked on the first lamp that had triggered Dylan's Mel-meter moments earlier.

"You wrote the note. Didn't you? The one on my locker," Dylan said, realizing that once she ruled out Carrie and Ms. Castle, she had completely forgotten about the anonymous letter left on her locker door.

"What?" Mitch whispered, unaware that she had received it.

Dylan ignored Mitch, focused on Hodge. "The note warning me to stay away from what belongs to you."

"I did," Hodge proudly admitted. "This is *my* house! Mine!"

Mitch spoke up. "Mr. Hodge, we all know what happened that night. We know you killed Raymond out of rage, not out of defense."

"No, no, no. None of you know anything at all. You know *nothing.*"

Hodge moved the end of the barrel down the line, from one person to the next, showing no regard for their lives. Dylan watched his arms shiver and fully expected the gun to fire at any moment.

"This is what happened that night. She, Sarah," he held the gun on his daughter, "is a lying tramp. She carried on a relationship that I, her father, forbade. Right under my nose, she lived a secret, all the while turning me into a giant fool."

Hodge sidestepped his way to the wall, flicked on the living room light. Dylan peeked down at the boots on Hodge's feet. Instead of seeing the word *CAT*, like she anticipated, the patch sewn to the tongue of the boots said *Coleman*.

"I had given her everything thing she'd ever asked for. Sarah, there was nothing I wouldn't have done for you!" Each word Hodge spoke grew louder, as his instability was magnifying. "I lost everything that night. My daughter ended up cutting me out of her life. My wife eventually left me. Everything changed that night."

"You got away with murder," Sarah accused her estranged father. "You murdered my boyfriend."

"That's not what the records show," he refuted. "According to the authorities, I did nothing wrong."

"You're disgusting," Sarah muttered.

"Oh, really? I'm not the one that disowned my father!" Dean complained, thrusting the barrel of the gun at his only daughter.

"Screw you!" Sarah shrieked.

Dean Hodge rushed towards her, pinned her to the couch by jamming the barrel of the gun into her sternum. As Gary reached for Hodge to protect his wife, Dean jerked the barrel and pulled the trigger.

Inside the boarded-up house, the blast resounded like a cannon. Smoke filled the room, and Gary screamed in agony as the bullet entered his right shoulder at the ball-joint. His body slouched on the sofa, as crimson blood flowed from his gaping wound.

Hodge stepped back, nearly tripping over the coffee

table, and fired a bullet into the wall behind them. Mitch tore off his coat, jumped up and held it firmly against Gary's shredded shoulder.

"Gary!" Sarah cried, then turned to face her menacing father. "How *could* you? How *could* you?"

Even-keeled, Dean Hodge's voice was stern. "Don't tempt me, Sarah. Don't." He held the barrel of the gun inches from her red, swollen face.

The scent of gunpowder engulfed them, as they watched Hodge carelessly point the gun at them, staggering. Through a cloud of smoke, he looked like a phantom, as it drifted deviously around him, backlit from the lamp behind him.

Catching his breath, he turned and stared at Dylan with raging malice.

"When I first saw you sneaking around this house, I didn't think much of it. I figured you were just looking for a place to smoke pot or take dirty pictures of yourself to send your boyfriend. But, then, one night, I waited for you to arrive, hid upstairs, and heard you. I heard you trying to talk to him."

"You were here?" Dylan asked, feeling lucky to be alive.

"Yes, this is my house, after all."

"This house is abandoned," she told him "It's no one's house."

"It's *mine*. I own it. This place was paid off before Sarah graduated high school. All I've had to do was pay the measly property taxes each year. Sure, after eventually being disbarred for unethical practices, money wasn't the easiest thing to come by. But, I managed."

"Why didn't you just keep living here? Why leave it so

abruptly, full of all your things?" Dylan couldn't help but ask questions, thinking that as long as Hodge was talking, he wasn't shooting. Mitch pressed his weight against Gary's bleeding shoulder, while Sarah, entering a state of shock, was colorless and quiet.

Hodge let a bizarre sounding laugh creep from his throat. "My life became a living hell. You see, once Sarah moved out, it all started. The lights would flicker, items would show up in places I didn't leave them, doors would slam shut on their own. I began hearing voices, whispers in my ear... warnings, threats. That stupid boy's spirit was here; I knew it was. I even saw it! I'd catch it as I passed by a mirror or briefly when I entered a room. I couldn't get away from him. This house was *haunted!*

"I hadn't slept in weeks. I was going crazy. One night, I couldn't take it for another second, and I just left. Never set foot inside again, until you came along." Hodge forcefully spit a ball of saliva to the floor.

"Periodically, I'd drive by, make sure the damn place was still standing. I still own it, after all. One night, while it was dark, I saw a yellow light pass by the front window, through the spaces between the boards."

"My flashlight," Dylan whispered.

"Your flashlight," the gunman confirmed with a wicked grin.

Hodge stopped, spun backwards, looked in all directions, like he had heard something behind him. Turning back to Dylan, a disturbing gleam formed in his eyes. "Did you hear that? That was him... He's trying to get to me again."

"He's gone," Dylan told him. "His spirit found peace when he was able to speak to Sarah tonight. Mitch saw him leave through the camera."

"He's gone, Hodge!" Mitch loudly repeated Dylan's claim.

"No, he isn't," Hodge told them, eyes darting every which way. "He's here, all right. I can feel him."

"Why didn't you just call the police one of the nights I was here? Have them tell me to keep out?" Dylan desperately tried to keep Hodge focused on herself instead of Raymond.

"I wanted to scare you off. I couldn't risk having you say something to the police. These damn kids on the force nowadays will believe almost anything you tell them. Especially, if it concerns a privileged white guy shooting a black kid. You know how these liberals are. Guns and blacks... Geez, you'd think *I* was the one living on a reservation, sponging off the government."

"Hodge, I'll -" Mitch turned, ready to charge the bigoted and bitter killer.

"Stay right there!" Hodge's voice cracked with anger. "Stay right there or I swear there'll be two ghosts haunting this house!"

Mitch had no choice but to back off and return his attention to Gary's injury.

"It was all too perfect, really," Hodge boasted. "I went and had the power turned on here in the house. I planned on putting a real scare into you kids. Then, low and behold, my Sarah shows up with you. It's nice to see you, Sarah, but I can't let you put me in prison. I'm going to have to kill all of you. I have no choice."

Behind Hodge, Dylan saw it happen. The framed family picture, violently slammed down on the shelf, shattering the glass with a loud thud that echoed through the room.

Hodge jumped, spun to see it. "See? I told you! He's here! He wants me!" Erratic, Hodge fired off two rounds at the wall, plummeting slugs into the Sheetrock. The tall lamppost on the other side of the room suddenly tipped and fell to the ground. Hodge, indiscriminately, fired again at nothing. The bullet lodged into the floor.

"Come on! I'm not afraid of you!"

Two more shots launched from the shotgun, this time at the ceiling. Chunks of paint and drywall rained down on Dylan and her co-hostages.

"Dyl, you okay?" Mitch called out and began to lift his hands from Gary's shoulder to rush over to her.

"Mitch," Dylan replied, "stay with him. Keep pressure on him!"

The situation had quickly escalated and Dylan worried that, before they could do anything to stop him, Hodge would plant a bullet in each of their skulls and be able to walk away like nothing had happened.

"Just stay with Gary," Dylan repeated, convincingly.

Mitch nodded, pressed his weight down on the wound.

Carelessly, like a tennis racket, Hodge took two aimless swipes at nothing with his shotgun. "Stay away from me! Get back! Get back!" Flinching and dodging, he began behaving as if there were bumble bees swarming his hair and face. Dylan knew what was happening. Raymond *was* still in the house and was determined to terrorize Dean Hodge, his killer.

Dylan felt every hair on her body stand alert, as the room filled with an energy like she'd never experienced. The lights began to flicker, like flashes of lightning in a thunderstorm. Items throughout the house rattled, moved, some slammed onto the floor. There was pounding against the walls, strange, disembodied voices flew through the air, attacking Hodge with reckless abandon.

Hodge's voice had quickly grown hoarse, and crackled through his throat. "I know it's you! I know you're here!"

The gunman began to spin in circles, unable to see the source of the touches he was feeling all over his body. His screaming became inaudible, terrifying, as the poltergeist continued to torment him, relentlessly. Bending like a contortionist, Hodge suddenly arched his back, pushed his chest out towards his prisoners, and with eyes wide open stared into space.

As the lights turned on and off, Dylan watched the figure appear between the shadows. "Unbelievable," she said under her breath. In front of a frozen Dean Hodge was the only thing she'd ever hoped to see, tried to find, searched for her entire life. Unlike the shadow man, a horrible being determined to destroy her in every way, Raymond's spirit glowed, angelic, like a ray of sunshine serving justice to a cold winter day.

Fully manifested, Raymond's apparition held Hodge in a state of defenseless shock. Dylan, without even deciding to, sprung off the couch, dove straight through the transparent ghost of Raymond Cole, and slammed her shoulder into Hodge's gut. The shotgun fired another round when it hit the floor after falling from Hodge's hand.

Dylan pinned the old, motionless man to the ground, and found herself straddling his chest, uncontrollably clenching her hands around his throat. Breaking from his trance, Hodge's murderous eyes boiled with hatred towards the girl he found choking him. He gagged and wheezed, as Dylan could feel years of desperation, anxiety, and sorrow fill her body, strengthen her grip.

Empty of empathy for the pathetic criminal, Dylan knew no oxygen was making it through his esophagus to his lungs. But, she didn't care. In that moment, the fragile, shy girl whose life had been irreversibly altered at age seven when a dark, evil spirit began visiting her in her bedroom, had only one purpose: killing this terrible man.

Rage burned her insides when Dylan remembered watching her father hauled off in handcuffs while her mother did nothing to stop it. Instead, the woman who vowed to never leave his side went on record testifying against him. And she knew better! She knew her husband would *never* do what he was accused of. Never!

For Jill Klaypool, it had been a way out. A way to cleanly sever a man she no longer loved from her life so that she could appear guilt free and never need an excuse to keep Dylan from him. Her affair with the detective would seem justified, reasonable… understood by her peers.

Dylan's unapologetic hatred for her mother became hatred for Dean Hodge. And the bashful new girl wanted him *dead*.

"Dyl! Dyl! Get off him!"

Jerking her head towards Mitch's desperate call, Dylan kept her tight hold on the man's neck, keeping him from breathing. She saw Mitch, holding the shotgun, pleading with her to stop. The memories of what happened in Chicago turned into salty liquid and poured from her eyes.

"Dylan, let's get out of here."

She saw Mitch's hand extend out to her and it felt as if someone, finally, was willing to rescue her, pull her in from the life raft that somehow had kept her alive while floating in a sea of sadness most of her life.

Swallowing the pain, the anger, the hatred, Dylan eased the pressure she had against Hodge's throat, and raised her sore and bruised hand to the one person she knew would not let her down. As their fingertips touched, and they brought an end to the threat of Dean Hodge, another equally dangerous situation arose.

Boom!

An orange and red cloud surrounded by black smoke filled the room in the blink of an eye.

The kitchen had exploded.

53

Heat from the raging fire in the next room slammed against them. Dylan dropped to the floor, blinded. "Mitch!" Reaching into the black, her hand found the unmistakable feel of denim: Mitch's blue jeans.

"Dylan!" he said, gripping her hand. "We gotta' get out of here." Choking from the smoke and flames, they crawled, feeling for one another, unable to communicate without gagging.

Mitch held his shirt over his mouth, pulled on Dylan's until she realized she needed to do the same. Slowly, they moved away from the couch, but stopped when Mitch butted heads with someone - Sarah.

On the ground with Gary, she was also trying to navigate their way to Dylan and Mitch. Visibility was zero, and oxygen was quickly disappearing from the house when another loud explosion rocked them. The entire house shook from the force of it. As a train of bodies, the four of them wiggled on the floor, staying as low as possible. Mitch as the conductor, Gary as the caboose.

"Mitch, where are you going? We can't -" Dylan started, but stopped with a straining cough.

"Just keep coming! Keep moving!" Mitch coached.

The journey across the living room seemed endless, dire. They couldn't exit through the kitchen, as it burned ferociously, and heading upstairs to the open window might have proven fatal if another explosion occurred.

Coursing around furniture, Mitch had been in the house enough times with Dylan to know where he wanted to go. There was a window, next to the bottom of the stairs, that would lead them safely into the back yard, if they could just get to it.

Dylan felt Mitch stop and heard his head bang against the wall. She knew where they were and crawled to her knees to help Mitch. With the side of her hand, she broke out the glass in the window, feeling the chards cut deeply into her flesh, while Mitch pulled Sarah and Gary closer to them.

In the muted moonlight that was coming through, Dylan saw that her hand was red, entirely covered with oozing blood from the cuts. She didn't stop until all the glass was knocked out of the frame. Feeling it slicing her knees through her jeans, she wiped away as much of the broken glass from the floor as she could with her damaged hands. With her elbows and fists, she pounded against the wood planks that were nailed over the window from outside. "Come on!" she pleaded with the water-logged boards and rusty nails. Dylan plowed her shoulder against them, banging her head on the window frame. Knowing she had no choice but to continue, she pressed on.

Dylan felt the powerful grip of Mitch's hands on her shoulders. "I'm getting it! I'm almost through!" she said, fighting to free herself. She was no match for Mitch's strength, as he pulled her aside and began thumping his palms against the boards. With a crack, one of them popped loose from the exterior. Mitch twisted and turned it until the board fell to the ground outside. Seeing it break free, Dylan knew Mitch had felt a sudden burst of adrenaline, because within seconds, he had the remaining planks busted off, leaving the window wide open.

Dylan tasted safety in the cold November air.

Mitch grabbed Dylan's waist and pushed her out into the yard. She took a long gasping breath, coughed and wheezed uncontrollably as her body fought to clear out the smoke she had inhaled. Dylan's burning eyes opened just long enough to see Sarah crawl out, then Gary. Sarah and her husband fell into the weeds and unmanicured grass, chests heaving, bodies trembling.

Dylan waited, expecting to see Mitch climb through next, but he didn't.

"Mitch!" Dylan cried out. "Mitch!"

She moved up to the window, leaving bloody handprints on everything she touched. She was not able to see even an inch inside.

"Mitch!"

He wasn't there. Dylan pounded her ripped hands on the window sill, desperately calling him.

"Mitch!"

Weeping, Dylan heard sirens blaring down Cemetery Road, screeching their way towards them. Dylan knew

Candice had heard the explosion from her house and called to report the ferociously burning fire.

"Mitch!"

The smoke intake impaired Dylan's now weak, hoarse voice. Black clouds billowed from the window, like the chimneys Dylan used to see on factories when passing certain areas in Chicago. When Dylan desperately tried climbing back inside to find Mitch, Sarah tackled her down.

"No, Dylan! You're not going back inside!"

"Get off me! Get off me!" Dylan begged, kicking and punching at the woman. "Let me go!"

Sarah laid her body directly on top of Dylan's on the freezing ground, while the sobbing girl's body shook mightily and convulsed violently. Dylan slammed her bleeding fists into the ground, still begging to be let up, but without the strength to fight herself free from Sarah's protective hold.

Dylan wailed a blood-curdling howl when another massive explosion erupted from inside the building. "No!"

But, before her drawn-out scream ended, Mitch's exhausted body tumbled through the window, falling hard to the ground. Sarah and Dylan both rushed to his aid, but he flailed his arms, pushing them away.

Mitch, struggling to stand, reached inside the waist-high window, and let out a cry of suffering. The boy with the wolf tracks tattoo yanked a motionless, charred-skinned Dean Hodge through the narrow window, before falling helplessly to the ground.

Dylan threw herself on top of him, grabbed his face with both of her tattered hands. Her blood streaked across his cheeks and covered his hair as she ran her fingers through it.

"Mitch, are you okay? Open your eyes! Please, open them!"

Snorting and sniffling, Mitch fought to catch his breath and clear his throat of the fire and smoke. When his eyes finally opened, Dylan slammed her mouth onto his, tasting the burning the fire on his lips.

Blue and red lights bounced off the trees and cloudy sky, sirens serenaded the scene. Loud, helpful footsteps came running around the side of house in the form of firefighters, wearing heavy, yellow suits, helmets, and masks. Their flashlights quickly discovered the survivors.

Gary Doan laid flat on his back, bleeding from the bullet hole in his shoulder. Sarah Doan sat upright, on her knees, staring at her father, unwilling to try and revive him with CPR. Dean Hodge was motionless, under the window, not breathing. Mitch Wolf was on his back, with Dylan Klaypool draped over his tired body kissing him, like there was no one else on Earth.

54

Seated on the back of an open ambulance, wrapped together in a warm, insulated, emergency rescue blanket, Dylan and Mitch shared body heat. Neither had much to say, other than the simplest answers possible to the bombarding questions being hurled at them.

First, it was the paramedics.

"Are you in any pain?"

"What hurts?"

"Follow this light with your eyes for me."

"Are you warm enough?"

Then it was the police.

"And how do you two know each other?"

"Where do you live?"

"How old are you?"

"How many shots were fired?"

"What was happening when the house exploded?"

Luckily, for them, once Sarah Doan began detailing everything starting back in 1993, the police had little interest in Mitch and Dylan.

When the firefighters had found them, scattered around the backyard, one of the trained, highly skilled rescuers began conducting immediate, lifesaving assistance to Dean Hodge. Remarkably, once able to, Hodge denied the testimony of the group, claiming that all he had done was protect his property from intruders and that he did nothing wrong that night, or the night back in 1993 that had started it all.

"Sarah! Sarah! Sarah!" Hodge called with such force he gagged. A police officer shoved him into the back of a patrol car, pressing the top of his head clear of the vehicle. "Sarah!" he continued screaming.

Sarah refused to look at him. Not even for one second.

Lastly, questions came from people that Dylan and Mitch knew. And, even though they weren't up to holding a conversation, having them there was precisely what they needed. Candice, April, Tamara, and August - the gravedigger - surrounded the two high schoolers, attempting to comfort them in any way possible.

"Here you go, Dylan," April said, reaching an ice-cold paper cup of Diet Pepsi to her. "I made a quick run to the restaurant. Thought you'd be thirsty."

Dylan couldn't get her hands out of the snug blanket soon enough. The way it soothed her throat when she finally took a sip, Dylan thought was heavenly. "Thank you, April. It's so good."

"You're both lucky," Candice told them. "We are all lucky that you're okay." She gave Mitch a friendly hug, before fully embracing Dylan.

"Grandma," Dylan whispered.

"Oh, Dylan, Dear," Candice said, with watery eyes. "Thank God, Dylan. Thank God."

The crowd expanded, quickly, until it appeared the entire town of Black Willow Creek was standing in front of the once forgotten house on Cemetery.

"Damaged wiring, propane still in pipes of the stove," the fire chief said. She was certain that was what caused the explosions. "When Hodge, after all those years," she explained, "had the power turned back on in the house, it was a recipe for disaster."

"You think?" one of the firefighters asked, shaking his head at the cloud of smoke.

"Just a theory," she pointed out. "We'll have a full investigation done. We'll get it figured out," the chief assured her team. "We'll get to the bottom of it. For now, let's just be glad no one was killed here tonight."

The abandoned house on Cemetery had been reduced to a pile of ashy rubble, but ironically, the giant Black Willow tree that Raymond Cole had used to make his fateful climb stood tall and pronounced.

Tired and dazed, Dylan stared at the driveway, hardly able to keep her eyes open. Candice's voice drifted around Dylan's ears, never quite finding them.

"Grandfather would never believe this. You know, I thought a bomb had gone off," Candice retold the story from her perspective. "Just about knocked me from my chair. What a blast, it was."

All Dylan could think about was the moment she had been strangling Dean Hodge and how frightened she was at the certainty that she was going to kill him. She supposed, given the right circumstances, anything had been possible.

With her eyelids becoming too heavy to hold open, something in the dirt caught Dylan's attention. Working to focus her vision, she spotted something as blue and red flashes traded turns lighting the ground.

A boot print.

Staring, she read the impression in the sand: *CAT.* Sniffling, Dylan lifted her weary head from Mitch's shoulder, to get a better look, when she noticed that, standing next to it, was a boot – the boot that made the track. The tan colored boot alone wasn't what made it a curious sight. It was the fact that the leather was scorched, seared black from fire. Her eyes darted around at the rest of the feet that stood in the crowd in front of her. None had burns on them, none were charred black. She turned her eyes back to them, certain that whoever wore those boots had been in the fire with them.

She lifted her eyes, just as the person wearing them turned away from her. Dylan followed the legs up, until she could see the back pockets of the person's tightly fitted jeans – women's jeans. In the pocket, easy to spot, sticking slightly out of the top was a cigarette lighter. Walking away, the person never looked back, but Dylan didn't need to see her face to know who it was. She'd been staring at the back of this head in Mr. Amal's class every day for weeks.

That blond head of hair was unmistakable.

"Carrie," Dylan whispered. "Carrie Holland."

55

Knock. Knock. Knock.

"Come in, Grandma," Dylan said, her voice still scratchy from the night before.

It was early in the day, but Dylan, understandably so, decided to skip school. Truthfully, her body wasn't up to the challenge. Neither was her mind.

Candice opened the door, peeked inside. "Dylan, Dear. Mitch is here."

"Let him in, Grandma. I don't want to get up."

"Very well," Candice agreed, heading down the hall.

A moment later, Mitch Wolf stepped into Dylan's bedroom, sat on the bed next to her where she was buried underneath several layers of blankets.

"Still can't get warm, huh?" Mitch teased with a friendly smile.

"I'm still freezing. I swear, I'll never feel warm again."

"You will, Dyl."

"Maybe if you were holding me."

Mitch leaned down and kissed her forehead. "Dang, you *do* feel cold."

"I'm telling you, I'm, like, made of ice, or something."

"What a night, right?"

Dylan nodded. "Yeah. I-I can't believe it."

"You know, he's claiming he didn't, but the fire department believes Hodge intentionally lit the fire. They say they have evidence of arson."

Dylan sniffled, thinking of Carrie Holland's boots, "They might be onto something there."

"I'm sure they'll figure it out," Mitch said. Dylan removed one of her arms from her cocoon, held his hand with her own tightly bandaged fingers and palm.

"What made you do it, Mitch?"

"What's that, Dyl?"

"Go back for Hodge. You could've died."

Mitch exhaled, letting his cheeks puff up, as the air left his lungs. He moved his head from side to side. "I don't really know. I just... I just went back for him. I didn't really... think about it."

"I thought you had died..." Dylan felt the tears swell in her eyes again, remembering how she felt when she thought she'd lost Mitch forever.

"Wow, you must really like me."

Dylan cracked a smile. "Oh, shut up." She playfully slapped his leg. "Owe."

"Be careful with that hand, Dyl. I plan on holding it a long time."

"Oh, yeah? How long?"

"As long as you'll let me."

Dylan knew Mitch meant it. Returning to her previous thought, Dylan asked again. "Seriously, what made you save that wretched old man? I mean, I almost killed him with my bare hands."

"Have you ever heard that saying, 'An eye for an eye'?"

"Yeah."

"Have you ever heard the one that says, 'An eye for an eye leaves the whole world blind'?" Dylan nodded, quietly understanding. "I just couldn't let him die," Mitch told her.

Scooching herself upright, Dylan pulled Mitch close, kissed him. "And you wonder why I like you so much?"

"What was the note? What were you talking about?"

"Oh, well, funny story. I had a note on my locker last week that said something like, 'stay away from my property', like a warning. I thought for sure it was Carrie. I confronted her about it and realized that she didn't write it."

"What then?"

"Well, I totally assumed that Ms. Castle wrote it."

Mitch scrunched his face up. "What? Why would she – why would you assume it was her?"

Blushing, Dylan couldn't hide her embarrassment. "I thought you and she were... *you know*..."

"What?" Mitch wasn't going to let her off easily.

Dylan raised her eyebrows, letting Mitch know that she wasn't happy about having to divulge such a foolish idea to him. "I thought you guys were a thing."

"A *thing*?"

"Oh, shut up, Mitch."

Mitch's shoulders bounced from laughter. "Really? You thought that? You're as bad as Carrie!"

"I know," she confessed. "It was stupid."

"Wow, so you were jealous of Ms. Castle? You really *do* like me!"

"Mitch," Dylan's face went straight, prompting Mitch to stop his giggling.

"Yeah?"

"I love you."

Their eyes held a powerful stare, the kind that only happens a few times in a person's life. The kind of stare when someone realizes they've found another person, another soul, that belongs nowhere else than right next to their own.

"I love you, too, Dylan," he told her fearlessly.

"I never could've imagined myself being the first one to say that," she sheepishly confessed.

"Well, I've known it for a long time. I didn't want to scare you off. I know how guarded you are." He kissed her again. "Oh!" he quickly pulled away. "Duh, I have something to show you."

"Okay, what is it?" Dylan asked, curiously.

He stood up, grabbed Dylan's laptop off the desk and placed it on the bed next to her.

"Mitch, what is it?" she wondered, watching him barely contain his excitement.

He put his hand into his jeans pocket and pulled out a tiny, SD memory card. His smile said it all.

Dylan's heart leaped. "Is that from the camera? Is this the orb footage?"

With a glimmer in his eye, Mitch silently shook his head, excited dimples jumped off his face.

"Well, what is it?" she begged to know.

"Boot this thing up," he said, patiently.

Once the screen was on, he inserted the card into the narrow slot on the side of the computer. He navigated his way through the files to find the ones kept on the card and double-clicked. What Dylan saw, put her mind into a frenzy.

The footage, with the camera shaking in Mitch's wild hand, started too blurry and out of focus to see anything of value. But, after a few seconds, the picture cleaned up. In the middle of the screen was Dean Hodge, motionless, like a statue, staring straight forward, gun in his right hand, with all the lights flickering, rapidly: on, off, on, off.

Suddenly, because of the camera's night-vision functions, something incredible was revealed in the moments that the lights were off – a ghost.

Dylan bounced on the bed, nearly knocking the laptop to the floor. Mitch luckily caught it, and paused the video. "I saw it, Mitch! I saw the ghost in real time, as it was happening."

"So did I."

"When did you - how did you shoot this? I thought you were so focused on Gary's gunshot wound that -"

"Dyl, when all the commotion began, the objects flying, the lights, all of it – I turned around and, for a split second, I saw Raymond's ghost."

"Wow!"

"Yeah, so the camera was sitting on the couch next to Sarah, so I just grabbed it and pressed RECORD."

"What was the camera doing there?"

"I had it in my hand the whole time. When we left upstairs, I had it. I had it when Hodge held us at gunpoint and just carried it with me to the couch. Here! Look."

Mitch pointed to the frozen image. "It's not as detailed

as a human being, obviously, but, look," he moved his finger around the screen, "legs, arms, torso, shoulders, head, it's all there, Dyl. It's literally a full-bodied apparition."

"Play it." Her heart was threatening to leave her chest.

Mitch pressed PLAY. A couple of seconds later, they watched Dylan leap off the couch towards Hodge. Amazingly, her body passed directly through Raymond's ghost, sending Hodge to the floor.

"Could you feel that?" Mitch asked, his words desperate for information.

"I-I-I don't know! I *saw* him there. But, with my eyes, he was clear. It was clearly Raymond."

"Yeah, me too. When I first caught a glimpse of him, I actually thought it was a real person standing there. That's how detailed he was. He was even solid."

"Is there more?"

"No, I stopped recording when I saw you flying through the air, tackling a guy wielding a fricken shotgun."

Jumping out of bed, Dylan paced the floor, rubbing her forehead, thinking. That was it! That video, a clip just a handful of seconds long was what she had always needed. Mitch, not just because of his physical heroics at the house the previous night, but because of that seven seconds of footage that he was cognizant enough to capture, could truly be a life saver.

Dylan grabbed her phone off the nightstand.

"Who are you texting?" Mitch wondered, confused by Dylan's suddenly overwhelmed demeanor.

Raising only her eyes, she made direct, important eye contact with the boy she loved. "I'll explain everything to you, Mitch. You deserve to know everything."

"What don't I know?"

"A lot. There's so much you don't know."

"Please, sit here and tell me."

"I will. Just a second."

Thumbs tapping away at the screen, Dylan fired off a text to *Chicago Teen Crisis.*

I have it! I have it! I have it!

Less than a second later, not even long enough for Dylan to look away from her phone, a reply arrived.

It's enough?

Jittery, from the realization that it could all finally come to an end, Dylan typed out a couple descriptive sentences.

Full body, full ghost. Paired with my recordings, it's undeniable.

"Dylan, are you okay?" Mitch said from the bed.

She nodded, stared at the screen in her hand, awaiting another message. Seconds later, it came.

You're amazing. You really did it. Better let this line cool off. Wait a few weeks.

She smiled, bounced on her toes. Unable to hold back, she typed in a final message. It was one that she knew was dangerous and would upset the person receiving it, but she could no longer resist – she had to send it.

Disbelieving that her thumbs were typing it, after all those years, she pressed SEND.

I love you, Dad.

In a snap, responsive words appeared on the screen.

I love you, too, Dylan.

56

Dylan and Candice pushed open the door to Carol's and were hit by a wall of the incredible scent of roasted turkey.

"Hey!" hollered Carol, in her full-length apron and two oven mitts. She ran to the door and took the tray of cookies from Dylan. Carol looked like an older April, but with less grit and more charm. "Welcome, welcome! Candice, set that dish right here. I'll grab it in a moment."

Candice placed her green-bean casserole down, and removed her coat. Mitch came from the kitchen, gave Candice a warm hug before giving Dylan the squeeze of her life. The restaurant was closed on Thanksgiving, but because of its convenience, August and Carol decided to use it for their celebration.

Dylan went around the room, greeting everyone as they all moved about, lending a hand wherever they could. She gave the gravedigger a long embrace, thanking him for including she and Candice on the chilly holiday.

"S'pose, it was the only thing I could do," he clowned with an amiable smile and laugh.

April trotted over to Dylan, proudly flaunting the fact that she wasn't alone. She was holding hands with the fisherman who had broken up the dispute with Carrie the morning of the fire.

"Dylan, do you remember Todd?" The tall, muscular outdoorsman that had stopped a shovel-swinging Carrie Holland smiled and gave a polite greeting.

"I do!" Dylan said. "I'm really happy things seem to be working out."

"Oh, *you're* happy about it?" April winked and nudged Dylan with her elbow. "*I'm* ecstatic."

Tamara's mother and young children were setting out napkins, while Ms. Castle stopped pouring glasses of water and rushed to Dylan. She hugged her, affectionately.

"Dylan, I am so glad you and your grandma came. This is going to be so much fun."

It had been a couple short weeks since the fire, and Dylan still hadn't heard another word from her father. Being in hiding, he had to be careful. She understood that and had been dealing with it for as long as she could remember. Still, the weeks, sometimes months, of silence were agonizing.

She had filled Mitch in on her life's tragic tale. With his own haunted and mysterious past, he fully understood and appreciated it. Having witnessed all the paranormal events at the house on Cemetery, Mitch was ready to do whatever he could to help his girlfriend do what she needed to do.

"Can you believe it?" April asked, excitedly, looking at her phone. "They just arrested Carrie Holland for starting the fire at the Hodge house!"

Tamara gasped. "I told you, Dylan!" She shockingly held her hand over her mouth. "That girl is capable of anything!"

"Scary stuff," Mitch commented, already knowing the arrest was going to go down that day. He and Dylan had given interviews to the police that week. April had, too, being witness to the crazy scene outside the restaurant. However, the police didn't give April the insight Mitch and Dylan had been given about the ensuing arrest.

Dylan enjoyed the dinner, every bit of it. She did her best to wear a smile, engage everyone politely, and give herself a chance to have fun. She believed she deserved it, given all that she'd been through. But, that morning something had occurred that had her stomach tied in knots. Even the warm mashed potatoes and gravy, perfectly seasoned stuffing, and delicious, moist and juicy turkey punctuated with homemade cranberry sauce couldn't settle it. What she had discovered that morning put a scare in her that wouldn't leave, despite how much love was being spread around the room.

Suddenly, a jolt stole her attention. Feeling her phone buzz, she knew, that with all her friends in the room with her, it could only be one person. Keeping her phone in her lap, hidden from view, she read the text.

Getting close. End of December. Christmas Eve.

She quickly replied.

Okay. I'll be there. I'll have everything.

Back came a reply and a strict order.

I'll see you then. DO NOT contact me until we meet.

I'm tossing this phone tonight. Bye.

Nonchalantly excusing herself from the table, Dylan slipped around the corner into the ladies room. She knew why her father had to dispose of his phone. He'd been using that number longer than any of the other numbers he'd had over the years. There was no telling how close the authorities could be to Nathan Klaypool, wherever he was. And the giant task before them wouldn't be simple. Him getting caught and arrested now, before Dylan could deliver her evidence, could jeopardize the entire thing.

They didn't need to convince the entire world that ghosts existed and that one was responsible for what her father had been charged with. They only needed to convince one person – the District Attorney in charge of his case.

Dylan stared at herself in the mirror of Carol's restroom, wondering *why now?* How could today, of all the days it could've happened, be the day. The return of a nightmare. She hadn't been touched since the high-rise in Chicago when she was just a little girl. But, today, her life seemed to be taking a trip back to a time she thought she'd never see again.

She lifted her foot up onto the sink, in the cramped, single toilet washroom. Pulling up the pant leg of her jeans, Dylan ran her fingers over the three swollen scratches on her shin. Just like they used to, they'd appeared overnight, out of nowhere.

Placing her foot back on the ground, she lifted her shirt, looked at the reflection of her belly in the mirror. There, too, were scratches. She shook her head, afraid, disgusted, worried. Unlike when she was little, she didn't see the shadow man last night. But, Dylan knew he'd been there. There was simply no other explanation.

When she opened the door, she found Mitch, alone, waiting for her. "Hey," she said, warmly, pretending as if all was well.

"Are you okay?"

"Sure, I am. Let's go back and enjoy the food."

He grabbed her arm, as she tried to speed past him. "Dyl, you can't fool me. What's going on?"

She didn't want to hide anything from Mitch, but also didn't want to ruin Thanksgiving dinner. Ultimately, she had no choice. "My father texted me."

"What did he say?"

"I need to be in Chicago on Christmas Eve."

"I'll take you."

"Mitch, you don't have -"

"I said, I'll take you."

Dylan nodded, agreeing. She wanted Mitch to come but worried what troubles might come his way if he did.

"*And?*" Mitch forcibly pried.

"What do you mean?"

"Dylan, you're acting afraid. Your father texting you wouldn't cause fear. What else is going on?"

"Anything could happen. Anything could go wrong on that trip. I'm just nervous."

Mitch looked at her, demanding the truth. She knew she had no choice but to level with him. It was only fair.

Dylan exhaled, lifted her shirt for Mitch to see the scratches on her stomach. "There are more on my leg. Just like these."

"Dyl..." he whispered, studying the deep, red cuts. "Oh, man, Dyl..."

"It'll be okay," she said, forcing confidence where there was none. "It'll be okay."

"Okay," Mitch told her. "It will be."

"Four weeks, we head to the Windy City?"

"Yes. We're there, Dyl… I love you."

"I love you, too, Mitch."

***

Dear Reader,

Thank you for reading *The Haunting of Dylan Klaypool: Whispers in Black Willow*. I hope you enjoyed reading Dylan's story as much as I enjoyed writing it.

What's next in store for Dylan? Ready for a sneak peek? Beginning on the next page, you'll find Chapter 1 of *The Haunting of Dylan Klaypool: Shadow Summoner*. You will not believe what Dylan and Mitch will face in Book 2. I can't wait for you to read it.

I would love it if you would take the time to log in to either Amazon or Goodreads and give Dylan a positive review and rating. Your positive feedback makes a huge difference.

Thanks again.
James

Shadow Summoner

1

With a cream-colored, ceramic mug gripped in her knuckles, Dylan sipped steaming, black coffee and watched Mitch grind a clenched fist into his eye socket. "Need a refill?" she joked, as his mouth began to stretch open, allowing the crawling escape of a determined yawn.

Exhaling, Mitch's wide, handsome face formed a tired smile underneath squinted, barely-opened eyes. "I can't believe we are up this early."

Freshly washed and conditioned curls bounced around Dylan's soft grin, as she shook her head at the boy whose quick thinking not long ago captured a piece of paranormal evidence that carried with it the potential to change her life. A chance, though understandably still slim, to rewrite history. To set things right.

A lonely street light above the cracked and deserted

sidewalk outside the large front windows of Carol's Restaurant shined just bright enough to illuminate the gingerly falling snowflakes, making the black sky behind them appear even darker.

"Watch your arm," grumbled April, causing Mitch to jolt awake. She nearly poured the java onto his flannel sleeve. The knee on his long leg popped up and banged against the underside of the table, causing a rattle of wobbling plates and utensils. The black liquid in Dylan's cup swirled around and breached its rim, spilling a few drops onto the red and white tablecloth. Quickly, she nabbed it from the rocking table, stabilizing its contents.

"Sorry," Mitch apologized to the notoriously rude redhead who had just topped off his beverage.

Dylan couldn't help but laugh at the look April shot at Mitch while filling his cup. Turning to Dylan, April complained. "This is stupid. I mean, really stupid."

"What is?" Dylan asked, slurping from her cup.

April's shoulders dropped. "Being here. Now, so early the day after a holiday. And what made you two decide to do this? You want more?"

Dylan waved off April's offer to refill her coffee. "We decided to be normal today. It's a stab at moving forward, pursuing some normalcy after all that happened on Cemetery Road."

"Whatever. You're not normal." She peered at Mitch again. "Neither of you are."

April had been a tough person for Dylan to figure out. But now that she had, she found the disgruntled waitress' insults refreshing. April proved to Dylan that she had a soft heart underneath the rough exterior she displayed so unapologetically. And, when she dared show her caring side, April had a wonderful smile to boot. Deep down, there was someone hidden inside that Dylan really liked.

"I think I agree with April that this isn't exactly *normal*," Mitch said, leaning forward and looking directly into the eyes of the girl he loved. At times he would get lost in them. They were as deep as an ocean, and sometimes as volatile.

"Well, let's just give it a -" Dylan stopped when the bell over the door clanked. A shrill burst of air funneled in behind a tall stranger before he could push it closed with a leather-gloved hand.

Curious, Mitch turned to spy who had entered. "Oh, I thought it was Tamara," he told Dylan, turning back to face her.

"She's just a few minutes late," Dylan replied with her eyes glued to the gruff looking fellow standing at the door. Her voice sounded hollow and far away from her thoughts.

"Can you just pick a table and sit down? It's *seat yourself.*" April's voice foully bellowed from back in the kitchen through the dining area.

The tall gentleman removed his cap and rolled his eyes at April's impolite greeting. "Coffee?" the man called back to her with a deep growl that came from smoking too many cigarettes.

Annoyed, April grunted her response. "Yeah, *sit*. Okay? I'll be out in a second."

The man's boots sounded heavy on the sagging floor boards as he casually meandered to a table in the front corner of the restaurant by the window. He let out a sigh when he leaned back into the wooden chair. Dylan hadn't lived in Black Willow Creek long, but believed she had seen most residents of the tiny community at one time or another. This man, she didn't recognize. He pulled out his phone, flicked it a few times with his thumb, as the wrinkles on his worn face lit up from the screen in front of it.

"Do you recognize him?"

"What?" Mitch asked, rubbing sleep away from his eyelids.

"The man that came in. Do you know who he is?"

Mitch peeked over his shoulder to take a second look at him. "I don't think so."

"You've never seen him?"

Raising his eyebrows, Mitch reached up with his right hand and pulled his long, shiny black hair behind his ear. "No, Dyl, I don't think so. You okay?"

"Visiting family, maybe? He might just be in town for Thanksgiving."

"What are you – Why are you so interested in what he's doing here?"

Dylan looked at her iPhone lying on the table next to the plate that April had brought her bacon, eggs, and toast out on earlier. With uncertainty, she imagined texting her father, asking him how he was doing, if he was okay. She wished her relationship with him would one day be so simple.

"Hey," Mitch said, breaking her away from the daydream. "Any surprises this morning? Any new…" He let his voice fade, finished his inquiry with a look of concern.

Unconsciously touching her stomach, Dylan shook her head. Luckily, the deep scratches she had found on her abdomen and legs the previous morning hadn't multiplied. Reading the worry on her face, Mitch stretched his arm across the table and took her hand. "It's gonna be fine, Dyl. Everything will be. This will all be resolved. All of it. Your dad, too."

"Yeah," she agreed, forcing herself to think positive. "I know."

Abruptly, the door swung open with such force the bell on top hardly chimed. "What the heck are you guys doing? We gotta' move!" an erratic sounding voice erupted.

Happy to see her, Dylan smiled at Tamara Castle standing in the open doorway, hand on her hip, wrist turned towards the two teens to show her watch face to them.

"Oh, God, you're in on this, too?" April whined, making her way towards the teacher.

"What's the matter? Jealous?" Tamara taunted with a sly grin.

April clenched her jaw and held up her hand, holding the tip of her index finger and her thumb a centimeter apart – *Just a little.* "Shut the door," she mumbled. "It's cold."

"Ma'am?" the outsider at the corner table called out. "Could I get some coffee?"

"Can you, like, chill for a sec?" The corners of April's eyes were lethal.

Now timidly slouching, the man began to ask, "Can I at least see a -?"

From several feet away, April tossed the menu she was carrying onto the table in front of him. "Chill, okay? I'll get your coffee."

Dylan and Mitch stood up and began zipping their coats, putting on gloves and stocking caps. "We're ready," Dylan assured Tamara.

"April, we'll be back around lunch time. And we'll be hungry." Tamara stood to the side, allowing Dylan and Mitch to pass through the door.

"Gee, I can't wait," April sneered, sarcastically.

"Anyway, good luck. Buy one of everything."

Tamara Castle seemed surprisingly energetic for such an early hour. Her voice was high, loud, and rapid. "Chop, chop, Guys! Move!" Her hands smacked together two times, rapidly. "I've got this all figured out. I've studied the layout of each store, assigned items for each of us to grab. And they're all ranked. The first item by your names listed for each store is your top priority. If you don't see one left on the shelf, you bail, immediately. No messing around, you're on to the next item on the list."

She assured them, if they did as she instructed, Black Friday would be giant success. But only if they listened to her. "I'm telling you two, there is a reason my mother isn't here. She's slow. She doesn't have what it takes. Too passive."

"You're scaring us, Tamara," Mitch teased. Dylan smiled at him, agreeing.

"Well, hey, this isn't a game. This is, like, war."

"War?" Dylan asked, laughing.

"Okay not *war*, exactly. Closest I've ever been to it. Besides my divorce, anyway." Tamara rolled her eyes. "Forget about that. But, there have been too many times I've missed out on the doorbusters, the best Christmas gifts because of slow, unfocused people dragging me down."

Dylan listened to the woman who had become a trusted friend and took her words seriously. If Dylan hadn't planned to execute the single mother's holiday shopping plans, she would've still been home in bed, warm and cozy. She wouldn't have dragged herself out just to let Tamara down.

One final time, Tamara asked, "Ready, Dyl?"

Dylan grinned. "Ready, Tam."

Sitting shotgun, with Mitch already sprawled out and half asleep in the back seat, Dylan glanced through the still frosted windshield at the soon to be packed and crowded restaurant.

The unfamiliar man at the corner table sat, finally sipping a cup of coffee, and stared out the window, eyes on her. She told herself that from inside, that close to the glass, he'd see only his own reflection and that he couldn't possibly be watching her.

But, somehow, it didn't feel that way. Instead, it seemed his stare was fiercely locked on her, and, for reasons she couldn't figure out, she returned it, daringly.

Until they pulled away in Tamara's car, Dylan's eyes never left the stranger.

"You."

Dylan swore he had mouthed the word through the glass to her.

You.

***

ACKNOWLEDGMENTS

I would like to give a special thank-you to my family and friends for their never-ending support. Maka, Jade, Sidney, Mom, Dad, Jeana, Matt, Emma, Joe G., and Jerry F., you all play larger parts in this creative journey than you realize. I love all of you.

Leslie Bauman, thank you for all that you do. And thank you for showing Dylan so much love and care during this process. You are incredible, and I'm not sure what I'd do without you in my corner.

A special thank-you goes out to all of you who follow me on social media and come to see me at events, and to those who are members of my Black Willow Paranormal Group on Facebook. You guys make being an author so much fun. Thank you!

Made in the USA
Middletown, DE
17 January 2020

83182136R00231